BY THE SAME AUTHOR

THE GALACTIC COLD WAR
The Bayern Agenda

The Caledonian Gambit

PRAISE FOR DAN MOREN

"The perfect blend of humor, empathy, and gritty action, Dan Moren is one of the most exciting voices to enter the literary world in a long time."

Myke Cole, author of 'The Sacred Throne' trilogy

"Moren's latest entry in the Galactic Cold War series, The Aleph Extraction, ratchets up the action, tension, and wit... the interstellar heist caper you didn't know you needed, but not to be missed."

Eric Scott Fischl, author of *Dr. Potter's Medicine Show*

"Moren ably plays with trope and archetype to bring new life and new dimensions to the tried-and-true Heist Plot, but the best action is found around the kitchen table and other quiet places where the characters come together. Major Simon Kovalic and his covert-ops team of misfits come together at their broken places, and their bond is stronger and more realistic for it."

RWW Greene, author of *The Light Years*

"Immersive, intergalactic spy-fi. Moren gives us a Cold War thriller with wormholes and anti-grav fields."

John August, screenwriter of *Titan AE* and *Big Fish*

"A wisecracking caper that nevertheless doesn't skimp on the details and human cost of interstellar war, like John Le Carré meets The Stainless Steel Rat. Moren is one to watch."

Antony Johnston, creator of
Atomic Blonde and *The Coldest Winter*

Dan Moren

THE ALEPH EXTRACTION

THE GALACTIC COLD WAR
BOOK TWO

**ANGRY
ROBOT**

ANGRY ROBOT
An imprint of Watkins Media Ltd

Unit 11, Shepperton House
89 Shepperton Road
London N1 3DF
UK

angryrobotbooks.com
twitter.com/angryrobotbooks
Iced Heist

An Angry Robot paperback original 2020

Cover by Georgina Hewitt
Edited by Simon Spanton-Walker and Paul Simpson
Set in Meridien

Distributed in the United States by Penguin Random House, Inc., New York.

ISBN 978 0 85766 841 7
Ebook ISBN 978 0 85766 848 6

Printed in the United Kingdom by TJ International Ltd.

9 8 7 6 5 4 3 2 1

In memory of Dick Yasi: legendary teacher, font of wisdom and encouragement, and patron saint to a pack of nerdy kids.

CHAPTER 1

Simon Kovalic slid the disc-shaped microdrone beneath the door and into the apartment, then watched through its eyes.

"Room looks clear," he murmured. "Check in."

"Overwatch in position – no sign of movement, Paladin," said Nat.

The gravelly tones of Sergeant Tapper came next. "Shotgun here. Everything quiet outside, boss."

"Well, the *car* is just peachy." Eli Brody, around the corner in the vehicle they'd acquired. And none too happy about it. Kovalic rubbed his temples. The kid had been moodier than usual since the job on Bayern three months ago, and it was starting to eat at Kovalic's usually even-keeled demeanor. He'd have to sit down and have a talk with him. Maybe after this mission. For now…

"Give it a rest, Flyboy," said Nat.

"Also, that is a *terrible* codename. Can I pick my own next time?"

"*No*," said Tapper and Nat in unison. Oh well, good: something both of them could agree on for once. Kovalic would take the common ground where he could get it.

He shook his head: he had more pressing things to worry about. There had been a meet scheduled with Takashi on

Kolyana Bridge yesterday, but the man had been a no-show. Nor had the signal site at the bakery on Laviero Street been used. Had the Illyricans found him? They hadn't had much of a presence on Haran after the Commonwealth Intelligence Directorate had cleaned up its local intelligence network a couple years back, but they wouldn't stay gone forever.

More likely, Tak had finally run afoul of one of the many gangs that he owed money. Which was the whole reason Kovalic had hired him – and paid him generously from the Special Projects Team's slush fund: the man knew people in low places, and keeping plugged into the criminal element had its advantages.

Kovalic double-checked the smart fabric display embedded in the sleeve of his coat, but there was still no movement in the room. He touched a control and the disc's top and bottom expanded into spheres, letting him gently roll the microdrone forward into the apartment's main – well, *only* – room.

The floor-level wide-angle view through the microdrone made everything look enormous, as though Kovalic were an ant. He rolled by a towering chair whose metal legs gleamed like skyscrapers, and then around a giant's shoe.

Empty.

Kovalic rubbed at his mouth. So Takashi wasn't at home; he hadn't been at any of the half dozen haunts, dive bars, and underground betting parlors that they'd checked over the last several hours. It was like he'd just… disappeared.

The sphere clunked to a stop. With a frown, Kovalic checked the screen for obstacles, panning through the cameras around the drone's circumference. The feed was grainy and low-res, but there was no obvious obstruction. He rolled the drone back and then forward again.

Clunk.

It was like it was running right into empty air. He cycled through the various cameras: infrared, heat sensitive, low-light. All confirmed there was absolutely nothing in front of the drone and no reason for Kovalic to look any further.

"Eyes up, everybody," he said quietly. "I'm going in."

He hated using the autopick – there was no art or elegance to it – but it was undeniably the fastest option. Two seconds later, the door swung open and he stepped into the room.

Takashi clearly hadn't blown all the Commonwealth's money on new furniture. The ripe odor of unwashed laundry and sweat suggested the man hadn't spent it on a cleaning service either.

Closing the door behind him, Kovalic crossed the plasticrete floor to the drone, sitting by its lonesome in the middle of the floor, nothing for a foot in any direction. In fact, in a room that was almost uniformly messy, the area between the drone and the apartment's row of windows looked surprisingly clean.

Kovalic leaned over to pick up the drone. A soft, pliant surface bumped into his forehead and he felt his skin tingle. He looked up; a moment ago there had been nothing but an empty room, but now there was a shimmer in front of him, like a heat mirage. He put out his hand and watched a ripple of colors bloom in mid-air.

"Son of a *bitch*," said a voice.

Kovalic stepped back and lashed out with a kick. A thin film running from floor-to-ceiling collapsed in a heap of fabric, leaving him face-to-face with a young man whose black hair was streaked with deep, dark purple. He froze in the midst of hefting a backpack.

"Really, Tak?" said Kovalic. "An active camo screen? This can't have been cheap."

Tak stared at him, then shrugged. Too late, Kovalic's eyes darted to the open window, but even as he stepped forward, Tak was diving out of it.

"Shit," he said. "He's running!" Feet tangled in the heap of the camo screen, Kovalic stumbled toward the window in time to see Tak hop to the next building over, glance over his shoulder, and then take off.

"Why the hell is he running?" Tapper asked over the channel.

"I don't know!" said Kovalic. "Overwatch, tell me you've got eyes on."

"Got him," Nat's voice came back almost immediately, "heading west across the block."

"On the move," said Tapper, his breath coming in short puffs.

"I can come around the 300 block," said Brody.

"No, stay in the car."

"But I–"

"Stay. In. The. Car," said Kovalic through gritted teeth as he ducked through the window. There was a thin ledge right outside, hardly wide enough to stand on, but the next building was only a large stride away. Even so, he still didn't look down – the last time he'd jumped roof-to-roof, it hadn't gone so well.

The second his feet were firmly on the next building, he was off and sprinting, his shadow stark against the white reflective pigment of the roof.

Up ahead, Tak had changed course, veering south. Launching over a gap to the next building, he hit the red tiles with a clatter and rolled out of view.

"Lost visual," Nat said, frustration creeping into her voice. "The building's in the way."

Some days Kovalic hated this job. "Heading due south, towards Akingbade Plaza."

"Gah," said Tapper, and Kovalic could almost hear him sliding to a stop and reversing course. "Wrong way. Gonna be a minute, boss." Damn it.

Kovalic pushed off the edge, his legs kicking as he sailed across the chasm, catching a brief glimpse of people milling below. Then he hit the tiled roof in a roll, pain rippling up his arm and side. He climbed to his feet.

"Paladin, there's a gravtrain station on the other side of the plaza," said Nat. "He makes it there, we're going to lose him."

Shit. Shit shit shit. They should have had somebody posted there. Or maybe two people outside the building instead of just Tapper. Maybe if they had more bodies. Or maybe if Kovalic had been a little more cautious on the initial recon. There were a lot of maybes to go around.

Ahead of him, Tak reached the roof's peak and disappeared down the other side. Kovalic's blood pumped overtime as he followed, his boots slipping and sliding on the tiles, threatening to send him sprawling at any moment.

Cresting the rise, he was just in time to see Tak sliding down the solar panels that coated the south side of the building's roof. Kovalic windmilled his arms to keep his balance, then swung over and slid down on his side, gritting his teeth in pain, despite the adrenaline rush.

"Moving to intercept," called Nat and, out of the corner of his eye, Kovalic saw her airborne drone, big brother to the micro model he'd used in Tak's apartment, blur past, making a beeline for his quarry.

But before the drone could reach him, Takashi disappeared over the edge of the roof – hopefully not in freefall. Kovalic would find out soon enough: the lip was coming up fast and he was only gaining speed. He rolled to his back, dug his heels in and put his hands down, the panels searing his palms.

Ahead, the edge loomed. Beyond it, the open plaza, forty feet below.

This really wasn't how he'd expected to go out.

He cast about for something, anything to slow his fall – what the hell had Tak done? – when he heard something whir overhead, and looked up in time to see Nat's drone boomeranging back around towards him.

"Simon!" said Nat sharply over the comm.

The bad ideas just kept on coming.

As he slid off the building's eave, he somehow got his legs under himself and leapt forward. For a moment he hung suspended over the plaza and time slowed; gaping faces stared up at him.

His hands caught the drone's landing skids. The machine sagged as it took his weight and Kovalic could hear the repulsors sputter and whine as the whole thing started drifting towards the ground. That was just fine by him, as long as it did so slowly.

There was a pop and a smell of smoke as one of the repulsors overheated and the whole drone listed to the left. The other three repulsors strained to compensate but he was still dipping towards the west side of the plaza, skimming dangerously close to the neighboring building.

"Overwatch, how much weight can this thing take?"

"Not this much!"

"I knew I shouldn't have had that croissant for breakfast…"
As the drone sank, he scanned the plaza and caught sight of
somebody pushing their way through the crowds, making for
the far side and the stylized "G" logo of the gravtrain station.
The drone dipped further to one side and his boots rasped
against the building as he strode along its face.

Another pop as a second repulsor went, and the drone
wobbled precipitously and sank another few feet with a jolt.
Only about twenty feet off the ground now. He might be
able to make that, but he'd really prefer to keep his ankles
unbroken.

"Shotgun, tell me you're almost here."

Tapper's voice came back in between huffs. "Two blocks
out, Paladin."

Two blocks was too far. They'd lose Takashi in the transit
system. He may not have been the smartest guy Kovalic had
ever met, but if there was one thing the man was clearly good
at, it was laying low when people were looking for him.

Kovalic looked down as the drone sank over one of the
green bazaar awnings, then back up at the last two repulsors.
The drone was swinging erratically back and forth and tipping
further downwards. Time for an exit.

"Thanks for the lift, Overwatch." And with that, he let go
of the skids and fell the ten feet to the awning below. The
impact still hurt; the taut plastic sheeting slapped at his face
and he half-sank, half-rolled off it, just managing to grab the
support struts and swing beneath, to the wide-eyed surprise
of the woman selling handmade spice racks below.

Kovalic hit the ground running. Behind him, he dimly
registered the sound of the drone limping slowly back into
the air.

"Overwatch is out of commission," said Nat, frustration creeping into her voice. "You're on your own, Paladin."

Without the advantage of altitude, finding Tak was more challenging, but he followed the susurrations of the crowd that rippled in the man's wake.

Approaching the center of the plaza, Kovalic caught sight of the distinctive purple streaks of Tak's hair reaching the far side. The station lay just across the street, the stairs descending out of sight. Above the entrance a sign flashed a notice: "Southbound gravtrain, now arriving."

Kovalic poured on the speed, darting in between commuters and shoppers, each yelling at him in a seemingly different language. He stumbled as an uneven paving stone turned his ankle and he limped to the edge of the plaza just in time to see Tak crossing the street. The other man glanced over his shoulder and met Kovalic's eyes with a grin, tipping a two-fingered salute as he took his last steps to safety.

And then a hovercar ran a red light and hit him head on, sending him sprawling to the pavement in a heap.

Kovalic blinked and looked up at the car's windshield, through which he could see Eli Brody raising his hands in defense, his voice coming over the comm. "*Technically* I'm still in the car."

They brought Tak around about half hour later, having dragged him back to his apartment. Kovalic had sat him down in a chair in the middle of the room, right in front of the crumpled camo screen, and taken up another chair opposite him. Tapper had examined their quarry, proclaiming him bruised and unconscious from the hovercar impact, with possibly a mild concussion, but not in any life-threatening danger. Then Kovalic had had the sergeant take Brody outside and give him a talking-to about procedure and safe driving.

Running a hand through his hair – the temples seemed to gray more by the day – Kovalic gave Nat a nod. She pressed a hypo to Tak's neck and the man started to come to.

"Jesus," Tak groaned. "I feel like I've been hit by a truck." He blinked and rubbed at his face with his hands. One, anyway. The other had been strapped to the chair with a plasticuff. Kovalic wasn't making the same mistake twice.

"Late model sedan, actually."

Tak looked up. "Oh, hey, Conrad…" He blinked in confusion. "Wait… weren't you here before?"

Kovalic exchanged a glance with Nat. Concussion, for sure. "Yeah, we had a merry little chase."

Recognition flooded into the other man's eyes. "Right, right…" A smile crossed his face. "Almost made it, too." Tak rubbed his head, wincing as he found the tender spot where it had hit the pavement.

"Almost only counts in horseshoes and thermonuclear weapons," said Kovalic. "That was a neat trick with the auto-winch harness, by the way." They'd found it under Tak's jacket when they'd loaded him into the car. That was how he'd made it down to the plaza; clipped to the edge as he'd fallen, it had let him make a controlled descent. Preferable to relying on the kindness of drone operators.

"Hey, you never know when you might need to make a quick escape."

"We had a meet yesterday, Tak. When you didn't show up, I took it kind of personal."

"Did we?" said Tak, trying to look both innocent and puzzled, and not really nailing either.

"Then, when I came to check on you – out of the goodness of my heart! – you did a runner."

"Needed the exercise."

Kovalic raised his sleeve and flicked up a holoscreen, pointed at Takashi. "So I started wondering: what's he got to be afraid of? My partner," he nodded to Nat, "ran a facial recognition scan on the local security grid, and imagine *my* surprise when we found this. Why… that's *you*, isn't it? Talking to that woman?"

Color drained from Tak's face and even the purple in his hair seemed to lose some of its luster. "That's, uh, my sister."

"Uh huh. Well, bad news for you, Tak: your 'sister' happens to be on a list of known Illyrican assets on Haran."

"I can explain! You, uh, hired me to dig up dirt on the Illyricans, right? Well, who better to pump for information on them than themselves?"

Kovalic glanced at Nat. "You know, it's such a dumb idea that it's *almost* smart."

She made a face. "I think you're giving him too much credit."

"I usually do." He turned back to Tak. "*Alternatively*, and this is my personal theory: you're working both sides of the fence."

Takashi squeezed out a hoarse laugh. "C'mon, Conrad. Would I do that? Do I look like an idiot?"

"You're cuffed to a chair, so, yes, you kind of do." Kovalic leaned back. "We paid you a lot of money, Tak, and we're going to need to recoup our investment."

"Uhhhhhh…" Tak's eyes darted around the room, and this time it wasn't all from the concussion. But with Nat between him and the window and Kovalic in front of him, well, his options were limited. "I'm not really *liquid* right now, but if you come back next week, I'm sure we can work something out."

"I get it. You've got debts. Working us and the Illyricans against each other seemed like it was all upside. But your next mistake was that you didn't use that money to pay off those debts. Seems there are more than a few folks who were willing to pay handsomely for your location. Really, it's a win-win. For us, anyway." Looking at his sleeve, Kovalic nodded. "They should be here any minute now."

Tak's throat bobbed. "What? You can't do this!"

"It's done. Really, it's just a question of who gets here first. There's going to be quite a line."

"Come on, man! This isn't cool!"

"No, what's not cool is taking our money and running. Literally *running*."

From the hall came the sound of raised voices. Even muffled by the door, it wasn't hard to make out an irate one bellowing "Where is he?"

The color had drained from Tak's face. "Look, you can't turn me over to them. You know what they'll do?"

"They won't be buying you lunch, that's for sure."

Tak's eyes jumped between the door and Kovalic, who maintained an air of studied indifference. "You gotta get me out of here."

"And why would I do that?"

"I... I know stuff! That's why you hired me, right?"

"You betrayed that trust when you started talking to the Illyricans."

Scrambling backwards, Tak jerked against the plasticuff that attached his wrist to the chair. He rattled it and gave

Kovalic a plaintive look. "I've got valuable intel, man!"

"Oh?" said Kovalic, looking up from an inspection of his fingernails.

Somebody pounded on the door. "Open up! We know he's in there!"

"Get rid of them!" said Tak. "And I'll tell you everything the crims wanted to know."

Kovalic tried not to roll his eyes at the slang. Illyrican intelligence officers didn't even wear crimson uniforms while they were in the field. "That's one option. But you're operating from a deficit here. Tell me first, and you have my word that whoever is on the other side of that door won't hurt you."

A bead of sweat dripped down Tak's forehead. He glanced at Nat, standing behind him with all the interest of someone watching a particularly dry chemistry lecture, then back to Kovalic.

"OK! OK!" Tak looked around, as though someone might be listening in. "So there was this black market auction. Priceless antiquities, works of art, that kind of thing."

"Art theft is kind of outside our jurisdiction," said Nat. "Why should we care?"

"I'm getting there!" said Tak. "Look, this is a little bit stressful what with the pounding on the door and the fearing for my life."

Kovalic gave an "ah" then nodded. "Fair enough. One sec." He went to the door and, over a squeak from Tak, opened it. "Sergeant, would you mind keeping it down? We're trying to have a conversation in here."

Tapper peered over Kovalic's shoulder, a faux contrite expression on his face. "Oh, sure thing, boss. Sorry about that. Didn't realize you were in the middle of something."

With that, Kovalic closed the door and sat back down opposite a confused-looking Takashi. "Now, where were we?"

Tak looked at the door, then back at Kovalic, then at the door again as his slightly addled brain processed everything. "You... fucking asshole."

Kovalic snapped his fingers in the other man's face. "Focus. Why do we care about the auction?"

But Tak's expression had turned stubborn. "Why should I tell you anything?"

Kovalic glanced at Nat. "Should we tell him? I think we should tell him."

"Oh, allow me," she said with a too-wide smile. Raising her sleeve, she touched a few controls and a holoscreen popped open in front of Tak, perfectly framing him in his conversation with Kovalic. "If you *don't* tell us, I'm going to send an anonymous tip to the Imperial Intelligence Service that one of their assets is feeding information back to the Commonwealth. Something tells me they're not going to be as forgiving about it as we are."

"OK, OK! Look, all I know is the Illyricans wanted info on where the auction was taking place, and on one specific lot. Number 2187."

"What is it?"

Tak's shoulders went up to his ears. "No idea! I told them what I knew, which was that the auction's at the Citadel Hotel on Tseng-Tao's Divide, two days from now. Oh, and I overheard them using a name..." His eyes flicked back and forth as he searched his memory. "Arcade? No, Arkady. I think. I don't know who that is."

An auction? On a third-rate moon? Running a hand

through his hair, Kovalic shook his head. "We came all the way here for this?" He pushed himself up out of the chair. Fatigue swept over him and he was starting to feel all the aches and bruises he'd racked up during the chase.

Kovalic nodded at Nat to join him in the hallway and sent Tapper in to keep an eye on Tak. Just in case he tried to make a break for it, chair and all.

"What a clusterfuck," sighed Kovalic, prodding his side again. "We should have had someone at the station."

"We've only got so many bodies," said Nat. "There was no way to know he'd run."

Maybe not. But Kovalic should have expected it anyway. That was his job: to foresee all the possibilities and plan accordingly. As with everything else on the team, the buck stopped with him.

"This job should have been a cakewalk. But everybody's wearing thin. They have been since Bayern." Kovalic swallowed the lump that rose in his throat. That was on him. His decision. "Brody's temperamental. Tapper's head isn't in the game. Even I feel like I've lost a step. We're barely firing on *one* cylinder, much less all of them."

"Maybe we just need a break. We've been going flat out for the last three months. We're not the only unit in the Commonwealth – somebody else can carry the load for a little while." She shrugged. "Just a recommendation from your XO."

A break. So he could go home to his empty apartment and twiddle his thumbs while the Illyricans got on with whatever they were doing? "You heard Tak's intel. Does this sound like a good time to take a vacation?"

"Yeah, I heard it. I just don't get it. The Imperium's buying up art all of a sudden? Three months ago, they were teetering on the edge of financial ruin."

"We both know the Illyricans don't make a cup of coffee without an upside. If they're spending time and resources, they have a reason." The idea of leaving a job unfinished rankled like an ill-fitting suit.

"What about that name?" said Nat. "Arkady. You ever heard it before?"

"Doesn't ring any bells," said Kovalic. "But I know who to ask."

CHAPTER 2

"Ducks? Really?"

Leaning on his cane, General Hasan al-Adaj looked up at Kovalic from beneath the brim of a gray herringbone flat cap. The skin around his eyes wrinkled in the approximation of a kindly grandfather. "Ducks, Simon. Don't look so surprised."

A pond stretched out before them, bordered with thin reeds. Sure enough, a few ducks were gliding about, trading conversational quacks. The general pulled a handful of breadcrumbs out of a bag and tossed them into the water.

"There were swans, you know," he said. "At the Imperial Palace on Illyrica. White *and* black. Nasty, vile, ill-tempered creatures, swans. As if the world needed another reminder that beauty is ever an illusion."

Kovalic shifted uncomfortably. The general's past, as the former director of the Imperial Intelligence Service and close confidant and advisor to Emperor Alaric himself, had always been a source of discomfort, and that had only gotten more awkward in the last three months. Ever since Bayern, when Kovalic's team member, Aaron Page, had suggested the general was still pursuing an ulterior agenda – something codenamed LOOKING GLASS. But Page had also been funneling intel back to Aidan Kester, a deputy director of the Commonwealth Intelligence Directorate, which kind of undercut any accusation of treachery.

Kovalic hadn't told anybody the whole story about Page. Not Nat, not Tapper, and definitely not the general. The way he saw it, after six years of working together, the general had more than earned his trust. But Page's allegation still stuck with him, a piece of gristle between the teeth. He just hadn't decided what to do about it.

All Kovalic had told his team was that Page wasn't coming back. It was vague and unsatisfying, he knew that, but he couldn't bear to tell them the same lie he'd put in his after-action report, that Page had been killed in a random hovercar accident at the conclusion of the Bayern mission.

Telling them the truth would, in the long run, be even worse for everybody.

He knew what his vague story would sound like to the team, the conclusions they'd draw. But it was better for them to not know all the details. Safer. Kovalic could carry the load of their scrutiny, pack it away into cold-storage somewhere deep in his mind. Making the hard choices was a commanding officer's job – so was living with them. He rubbed a knot of muscle in his neck.

"Not that I don't enjoy our little discussions on the relative merits of waterfowl..." Kovalic began.

The general chuckled, returning the crumpled bag to his jacket pocket. "I read your report on the Haran operation, and I believe Mr Takashi's intel has merit."

"Really? An auction for art and antiquities? Seems like a waste of time."

"I might have thought so too. Until I saw the name Arkady."

"You know them?"

"It's not a person: ARKADY was the codename for one of the emperor's personal projects. I'd thought it long since defunct, but it appears I was... mistaken."

Kovalic's eyebrows went up. It wasn't every day that his boss copped to an error. "Care to fill me in?"

The general waved him to a bench nearby. "In his younger days, Alaric was obsessed with a particular object that he thought might be the key to conquering Earth. He had a collection of experts, scholars, and agents all searching for it. Every time there was a report that it had surfaced, he'd dispatch a team."

"And?"

The general ground the tip of his cane into the dirt. "He never found it. The team would arrive and it would be gone, usually not to be seen again for years."

"That's a lot of time and energy to spend on a single object. Was he looking for the Ark of the Covenant or something?"

"No. The Aleph Tablet."

Kovalic rolled his eyes. "Oh, come on. Pull the other one. I thought everybody had agreed that the tablet was a hoax."

"It's never been conclusively proved one way or the other. Alaric was certainly convinced it was real. But as I said, we never found it." The general raised his hands, palms up. "It's an open question."

"I just don't buy it."

"Good. I value your skepticism."

Kovalic could hear the other shoe falling with terminal velocity. "But you're still sending us after it."

"It's a matter of strategic practicalities, Simon. There are a lot of people convinced that the tablet *is* real."

"What do you think?"

"I believe that there's something behind all the stories. Whether or not it truly is what it's purported to be, well, that's another question entirely."

"You mean the whole story about it unlocking some ancient alien race's advanced technology?" Kovalic waggled his fingers. "Death rays and instant terraforming technology?"

"No need to be snarky, Simon. Strategy is as much about perception as it is about action."

"You're saying it's important because *other* people think it has value."

"Precisely. It's a bit like the stock market."

Kovalic pinched the bridge of his nose. "If we never have to deal with another financial institution it'll be too soon."

"I know that the conclusion of the Bayern job was not entirely satisfactory to you, but from a big picture perspective, it went about as well as could be hoped."

"Not entirely satisfactory" was putting it lightly, but they'd stopped the Imperium's plan, and that was what mattered. "What do you hear from your little birdies these days?"

Any twinkle in the general's eyes faded. "Less than I'd like. We know from public reports that the deal we made with Colonel Frayn has been upheld: Crown Prince Hadrian has taken a step back, letting his siblings assume a larger role in the Imperium's administration as the emperor remains in ill health. Overall, it's been relatively quiet. Even CARDINAL hasn't had much to offer."

CARDINAL. The general's most highly-placed source, whose identity was still shrouded in secrecy, even from Kovalic. The general had been clear that he didn't want to jeopardize his source, so the fewer people who even knew of CARDINAL's existence, the better. The idea of getting intelligence from an unvetted source made Kovalic's stomach churn, but there was no disputing that CARDINAL's information had been critical to the success of the Bayern operation.

"I take it that means we're also no closer to discovering who's sitting behind your old desk at IIS?"

The general frowned. "I'm afraid not. I have continued to eliminate suspects, but whoever they are, they're doing an excellent job of shielding their identity. Everything we don't know about them only makes them a more dangerous adversary."

More good news. "Well, the good news is that worrying about it is your job."

"Indeed. As for you, I'm giving the SPT the greenlight to head to Tseng-Tao's Divide."

Kovalic hesitated, Nat's words about lightening the load still lodged in the back of his brain. "I have some... operational concerns."

"Oh?"

"We're shorthanded and it's taking a toll on the rest of the team. In other circumstances, I might advise we stand down the SPT for a couple weeks, give everybody a chance to recharge their batteries."

"Ah," said the general. "That does complicate matters. Since we've learned that Deputy Director Kester is overly interested in our activities, I would rather not turn something this sensitive over to CID. And while there are other assets I could dispatch, none would be as qualified as your team for this kind of mission."

Kovalic straightened. "Of course, sir. We'll make it work."

Gnarled knuckles gripped the cane's pommel. "I haven't thus far pushed you to replace Lieutenant Page; I realize the wound is still fresh. But if it's affecting operational efficiency, then it's time. I'm sure Colonel Benton at the School has a number of possible candidates. But make it quick. We're on the clock here."

"Yes, sir."

"As always, I trust your judgment. Major."

Kovalic's jaw tightened at the rank. He hadn't asked for his recent promotion, much less expected it in the general's little off-books unit, but the general had somehow finagled it after the Bayern job. This job wasn't about recognition; if they managed to avoid open war with the Imperium, well, that was all the success he needed.

"Sir." Kovalic turned to walk away.

"Simon…" He rarely saw the general unsure, but there was a catch in the older man's voice. "If there is even the slightest chance that the tablet *is* real…we've got to get it before the Imperium does. We can't let them have it."

"Understood, sir."

Kovalic caught a military transport from a nearby base; an hour flight took him to the equatorial Novan continent where the School was located. He spent most of the time hunched over the console at his seat, catching up on correspondence.

The general wasn't the only one with his own off-the-book sources. Over the years Kovalic had developed an extensive network of assets and agents around the known galaxy. A catalog of encrypted virtual dead drops accessible only to him kept the sources secure and compartmentalized.

He'd put out feelers about the Aleph Tablet to a handful of the most likely to be in the know. So far the only information he'd gotten back was the seller of the tablet: a Hanif shipping baron under investigation for some shady dealings was liquidating her private assets before they could be seized – hence the black market auction. Beyond that, though, Kovalic might as well have been asking about intel on Bigfoot or the Loch Ness monster for all the response he'd gotten. Still, something about the quiet felt pointed, like the eerie calm before a storm broke loose.

Circling back around, he checked the dead-drop marked NOMAD again, a feeling of tightness in his chest. But there was still nothing waiting for him there, as there hadn't been for weeks.

When the flier landed, Kovalic emerged into the thick, humid air of swampland. Crenshaw Airfield was about a half-hour's drive from the school. Escorted by a young corporal driving a treaded rambler, Kovalic arrived just as the day was wrapping up, and was ushered promptly into the commandant's office.

Colonel Jean-Paul Benton was not quite two decades Kovalic's senior, his close-cropped hair gone entirely over to white, a stark contrast against his dark brown skin. A web of laugh lines were etched finely around his mouth. He looked up as Kovalic entered and leaned back in his chair. "Well, I'll be. Our distinguished graduates *do* remember us."

"Sir," said Kovalic, coming to a parade rest.

After a moment, they both broke into smiles, and the colonel rose and embraced him. "Simon. Always good to see you."

"You too, Ben." Kovalic sank into a chair. "It's been a while."

"It has at that," said Benton. "But I'm guessing this isn't a social visit, so I'll keep the bourbon in the drawer."

"Afraid not. I'm here because I need a body."

Benton rested his elbows on his desk and exhaled. "I heard about Bayern – I don't know the details, but, well, let's just say when we lose one of our own, it gets around. I'm sorry, Simon."

Kovalic's stomach clenched. "Thanks."

"Aaron Page is going to be a hard man to replace. One of the best this program has ever seen."

Which still hadn't stopped him from making a damn fool mistake. Kovalic's shoulders tightened. It was one thing to maintain the hovercar accident story for the official paperwork, but damn it, Page had been through the School. Benton had trained the man; they both deserved better.

"But I'll do my best," said Benton, getting to his feet. "Let me get my files. I'll be right back."

After a moment alone in the office, Kovalic pushed himself out of the chair and paced over to the wall. In a place otherwise so heavy on the idea of anonymity and interchangeability, it was the rare beacon of individuality: fifteen years' worth of photographs, of each graduating class. How many of them, Kovalic wondered, were still alive out there? His eyes tracked up to one specific picture, picking out the serious young face of a newly-minted lieutenant who looked like he might try to win the war single-handedly.

"Boy, am I glad you finally lightened up a bit," said Benton, re-entering the room with a stack of flimsies under his arm. "The whole grim reaper thing gets old, especially for a kid under thirty."

"We all came in wanting to be badasses."

"And now?"

"Now? Now, I think we're just tired." Glancing back at the

wall, he studiously ignored another, more recent class picture. "Twenty years I've been at this – you and Tapper even longer – and what have I got to show for it? A list of dead men and women."

Benton pressed a hand to his shoulder. "They chose the life, Simon."

Kovalic couldn't contain a snort. "Yeah. As if there's ever really a choice when there's a war on. What are you smiling at?"

The laugh lines were getting a workout. "Just an old man thinking back on time past. Come on. Sit down and we'll go through these candidates."

Thirty minutes later, they'd been through the admittedly-not-very-tall stack of personnel jackets. Kovalic had to admit that they were all supremely qualified, with field combat experience and a wide variety of skill sets: explosives, languages, technical expertise. But every time he opened one, he saw Aaron Page's face as it had once appeared in one of these files. And then saw Page's face as it had been on Bayern, when Kovalic had pulled a weapon and pointed it at him.

Page had been perfect on paper too. But something – the stress of the job, maybe – had broken him. Could any of these soldiers really be built from sterner stuff? What was to say they wouldn't follow the same path?

He sighed as he set the flimsies down on Benton's desk, a little harder than intended. A single sheet drifted to the floor, beneath Kovalic's chair. Reaching down, he grabbed it and was about to return it to the pile when he saw the large, black stencil stamped across its front.

DISMISSED.

"What's this?"

Benton peered over the desk. "Oh, one of our washouts. Which one is... ah." His mouth twitched, the smile tinged with regret.

Kovalic pored over the page, eyes widening. "Quite the record. I'm a little surprised the School would even admit someone with this kind of history."

"I confess, there was a favor involved. You remember John Boyland?"

"From your old unit? Sure. I met him a few times at those vet events. The cop, right?"

"Yeah, in Salaam," said Benton. "He actually passed away a couple years back, but before that he'd asked me to keep a lookout. One of his pet projects; he always had a good eye for talent. But talent's not everything, especially when you insist on coloring outside the lines."

No, talent wasn't everything, but it sure didn't hurt. A little rough around the edges, maybe, but nothing that Kovalic couldn't deal with. He'd whipped plenty of soldiers into shape in his career.

"Simon." He looked up to find Benton's eyes on him, wary. "Just... be careful. You can't save everyone."

"Don't worry, Ben," said Kovalic, the smile coming easy. "I know what I'm doing. So, where can I find this Adelaide Sayers?"

CHAPTER 3

The woman slammed the glass down on the bar, the back of her hand already wiping her mouth, and nodded to the bartender for another.

Hesitation flickered in his eyes, but he pulled the tall, thin-necked bottle off the shelf and poured another dram in the glass, the excess spilling slightly over the edge. He didn't push it over to her.

"I think maybe you've had enough, soldier."

Her mouth cracked into a brittle smile. *Soldier.* "That, Jonesy, is one thing I'm not. Not anymore." She reached over and plucked the shot glass from where it sat, then tossed it back in one swift motion.

She didn't much like tequila, she remembered, as it burned a path down her throat, but any spaceport in an ion storm.

Jonesy sighed, a ratty white cloth appearing in his dark, calloused hands as he sopped up the spillage. It vanished, along with the cloth, and the bartender leaned forward, elbows on the pitted and gouged wood.

"Getting room-spinningly drunk ain't going to fix that."

She wrinkled her nose. "Nope," she agreed. *Nothing is going to fix that.* "But it sure as hell passes the time." She tapped a finger next to the empty shot glass and looked at him expectantly.

With a sigh, he shook his head, then poured another glass. "Take that one for the road, Addy."

Adelaide Sayers raised the shot glass in salute, but the big bald man didn't say anything, just turned and walked towards the other end of the bar.

So she'd failed out of their little school. Big deal. She ignored the hollow pit in her stomach. Wasn't the first time someone had told her she wasn't good enough, and probably wouldn't be the last. It was all bullshit, anyway. Rigged. They wanted to churn out little gingerbread soldiers, all perfectly alike. Sure, they claimed they were looking for initiative, wanted them to think for themselves, but the second you took a liberty – one single little slice of individuality – they were all over you like disappointed parents. Not that she'd know.

Bullshit, she thought again, sniffing as she stared at the shot glass.

So she was done with it. Maybe they'd tossed her out, but she could have quit anyway. Time to find something else to do. She could hire on as freightline security, maybe. Or see if any of the private contractors were hiring. There were a few that might even look past her permanent record, if they were looking for the right sort of pers–

The door to the bar slammed open and a crowd filed in, raucous and jeering. Addy scowled at her tequila. The day just kept getting better and better.

"Jonesy!" shouted a voice. "A round on me."

"Can you even afford that, Mathis?" called a woman's voice.

"Stuff it, Kazuo!" He sidled up to the bar, and Addy caught a whiff of sweat and a familiar revolting cologne as he blithely invaded her personal space.

Blinking, Addy glanced around without turning her head. The bar had been empty aside from her, so why he'd felt the need to plop himself right here... well, actually she could guess.

"Mind?" she growled.

"Oh, sorry, Sayers," said Mathis, affecting an air of apology. "Didn't see you lurking there."

She looked up at him. Fair-haired, square-jawed, she could see why everybody thought Mathis was a charmer, but somehow that charisma never reached his beady little piggish eyes.

"Fuck off."

Mathis spread a hand on his chest, looking aghast. "Such language from a lady." He turned towards Jonesy, who had tossed his bar rag over his shoulder and stood opposite. "A round of your finest amber for everybody in this place – even my friend Sayers here." He rested a hand on her shoulder.

Addy tensed at the touch, shrugging the hand off. "Don't want nothing from you, shitheel."

The good-natured expression slid off his face. "Here I am, just trying to be nice. But I should've known better than to feel sorry for a washout."

Her teeth ground together, and she placed the tequila shot delicately on the coaster in front of her. "Walk away, Mathis."

"Come on, leave her alone," said another voice from the crowd. Kazuo, Addy thought, but she was having trouble distinguishing it over the pounding in her ears. A figured appeared on the other side of her, at the edge of her peripheral vision.

"Nah, I want to know why this failure thinks she's too good to share a round with us. I didn't see *her* out there with us today, getting the once-over. We're the ones heading to the big leagues, so she can stop acting so fucking superior for once."

Addy looked up at him slowly, taking in the heavy crease of his brow, the flared nostrils, the slightly forward-pointing ears. *He really does look like a pig,* she thought, and in that moment, she could see nothing else.

She laughed.

Mathis's anger boiled over and his beefy arm swung for her, but Addy wasn't there anymore. A head shorter than the man, she'd ducked under his arm and dug her knuckle into his armpit. He grunted and she watched his eyes widen as his arm flopped like a fish on a dock.

"Hey, guys, break it up," another voice said, seizing Addy's arm. She didn't know who it was, and it didn't really matter. The grip on her arm was enough; she seized it with her opposite hand, wrenching it off of her and rotating it up and around. She heard a shout of pain, but she was already in motion, lashing out backwards with a mule kick that took one of Mathis's knees out from under him. Still massaging his dead arm, the man's head thunked hard into the bar.

Her vision had narrowed into a tunnel, her ears filled with a roaring of a ship's engine on full blast. Someone grabbed her from the side, attempting to put her in a headlock; it was a woman with a milk-and-honey scent familiar from hours of sparring practice. Yadao. She had a shoulder injury that hadn't quite healed yet, which meant that all Addy had to do was lean heavily towards her weaker right arm. She dropped into a dead weight, felt the grip give out, and hit the ground in a roll.

Somewhere, Addy vaguely registered shouting – Jonesy, maybe? – but it was virtually inaudible over the sound of her own breathing whooshing in her ears. She popped up from the ground, putting all that momentum into an uppercut that glanced hard off a chin, sending another aggressor reeling away.

From opposite sides, two separate people grabbed each of her arms in iron grips, trying to lock them at the elbows. She struggled against them, growling and trying to wrench her way free.

A face filled her vision, not the blunt-nosed Mathis, but another familiar visage. This one looked more concerned than angry, and its lips were moving, forming words that Addy couldn't quite make out.

The ocean roaring in her ears started to ebb and her vision widened once again, enough to see that it was Kazuo and Reza who had her arms locked. The green eyes in front of her belonged to the deceptively soft features of Song, her bunkmate. And the words she was saying...

"Calm the *fuck* down, Addy."

A breath huffed out of her mouth, and she felt her balance waver slightly. All at once she was reminded that she had a stomach and that it was largely full of tequila, now sloshing against her insides.

"Lemme go," she muttered, wrenching her arms against the people who held her.

"Not until we're sure that you're not going to lose your shit again," said Song, arms crossed over her chest. "Jesus. You almost broke Reza's jaw." She nodded to the man holding Addy's right arm, his teeth gritted and eyes glassy.

"Shouldn't have touched me," said Addy.

"Probably not," Song agreed. "But that doesn't mean you should beat the shit out of him either."

Anger flared in Addy's chest. *Don't tell me what to do!* She pushed it down, hard, trying to put it away, push it someplace else. "Yeah," she managed, unable to keep the sullen tone from her voice. "Probably not."

"Right. OK. They're going to let you go now, and you're going to go back to the bunk. Take it easy." Song raised a hand. "I'll settle up with Jonesy for you."

Aw, crap. Jonesy. She risked a glance over her shoulder at the bald barkeep, who was staring back at her with something more akin to fear than pity. Rule one of Jonesy's was "no fighting" – the only thing you'd ever get a ban for, the old man had said on their first week at the School.

What does it matter? You flunked out. You're not coming back here anyway.

The anger spiked, sweeping over her like engine wash, but she fought it back once again. Her arms were released and she yanked them away, scowling at the ones who had held them, her former classmates. Emphasis on "former." They were supposed to have her back, but they'd let her down, just like everybody else, all the way back to the parents that had died and left her on her own, barely more than a toddler.

Without another look, she stalked to the exit and kicked open the plywood screen door, stepping out into the warm summer evening of Terra Nova's southern continent.

A cloud of gnats divebombed her, and she shooed them away with an angry snap of the wrist, but they persisted, drawn to the faint sheen of sweat now drying on her face and arms. She took a deep breath and was about to walk down the steps when something pinged her danger sense – she wasn't alone.

Everything redlined.

"Those were some nice mov–" The voice didn't even get to finish before Addy was already lashing out in its direction with an elbow.

And then she was lying on her back on the ground, staring up at the stars twinkling overhead. Her breath returned in a *whoosh* as she sucked it in like she'd just broken the surface of the ocean, and she tried not to groan.

"–but, as I was about to say, your discipline needs a little work."

She rolled back onto her spine, hands up by her head, and did a kick up, springing from the ground and landing on her feet.

The man standing a few feet away from her had brown hair streaked with gray and a couple days' worth of stubble. He raised an eyebrow in her direction.

Cocky bastard, she thought, as she drove at him, feinting with her left fist before following with a strike from her right. *Just like the rest of them.*

He weaved away from the feint and blocked the other strike with his palms, but Addy could tell that he was holding back. There was a faint patronizing smile on his face, like a parent play-fighting with a child.

His mistake. She spun around with the momentum of her blocked right strike, aiming her left elbow at his temple. But the elbow once again whiffed, meeting only air as he ducked under it.

A blow caught her in the sternum as she finished spinning, knocking the air out of her once again, and putting her ass back on the ground, where she lay for a moment to catch her breath.

The man stood above her, his palms up and towards her. "Take it easy, soldier."

Easy. Take it easy. A surge of fire licked at her muscles and she nodded as if in understanding before she lashed out with a scissor kick at his ankles.

Once again, he seemed ready for it, taking a slight leap in the air to avoid being knocked off his feet. But Addy had expected that, and she turned her scissor kick into another kick up – but when she landed on her feet, she launched herself directly into the man's torso, knocking him off his feet, and taking the fight to the ground.

Weren't ready for that, were you? She grinned to herself as they grappled, each trying to find purchase on the other and pin them to the ground. Knees and elbows struck out in both directions, glancing off shins and arms, like a writhing mass of octopi trying to untangle themselves.

"OK, OK," said the man. "I give!"

Addy's blows paused, wary of some sort of gambit or trick, but the man had put his hands up.

"I suppose this'll teach me not to come up on someone unaware," he said. "Duly noted." He cleared his throat. "Can I get up now?"

Disengaging, Addy rocked back on her heels, letting the man dust himself off and slowly rise to his feet. He brushed off his gray military-style coat and his trousers, sending the brown dirt off in great clouds. Raising a fist he coughed into it. "Sorry about that."

Addy blinked, standing up and crossing her arms. The fire in her belly was still there, but it had been banked to embers. Then again, that was about as low as it ever got. "What do you want?"

"Well, Specialist Sayers, I came to have a chat with you. It was, uh, supposed to be less physical, admittedly."

Her eyes flicked up and down a second time. No rank insignia. No unit patch. Nothing identifying at all, for that matter. But his bearing and his skills, well, those were military, no question.

"Who the hell are you?"

"Ah," he said, looking uncomfortable for a moment – an odd expression for someone who a minute ago had been holding his own in combat. "You put me in a bit of an awkward position with that question, so I'm afraid I'm going to be rude and answer it with another question: How would you like a job?"

It would have been frankly *less* surprising if the man had taken another swing at her. Her jaw dropped slightly.

How much tequila had she had?

"A job?" she echoed. "Doing *what*?"

"Oh, this and that. Something that makes use of those skills that you so ably demonstrated a moment ago."

Covert ops. This guy's covert ops. The skills, the lack of insignia, the fact that he even had any idea who she was, it all added up. But the Commonwealth had a number of intelligence agencies and secret special operations divisions.

"What are you, CID?"

He laughed. "I probably shouldn't confirm or deny – that's the company line. But no, I'm not CID. Or NICOM. Or MIG either. Whew. We do love our acronyms, don't we?"

Naval Intelligence Command and the Marine Intelligence Group, the other two major Commonwealth military intelligence outfits and, if Addy was being honest, the only other ones that she knew. That made this seriously off-the-books stuff. She swallowed. "OK, so I know who you're *not*. How about you give me something to work with?"

"Well, I *did* offer you a job."

She snorted. "Beware of Greeks bearing gifts."

"I'm Slavic, actually, but close enough."

The temperature had dropped slightly as they talked, especially as the sweat of her second fight of the evening started to cool on her skin, and she rubbed her arms against the pimpled gooseflesh. "Why me?"

"The usual reasons. Your qualifications are impressive: graduated top of your class from sniper school, trained in stealth and infiltration, and all of your instructors have remarked that you're quick to pick up new skills – and master them."

"When you put it that way, yeah, *I'm* a hell of a catch. So why should I go work for you?"

"Well, there's the matter of your temper. Your general insubordination. The *seventeen* reprimands in your official file."

Heat rose in Addy's cheeks at each additional bullet point, and her teeth ground against each other. *This is some stupid joke. Mathis and the others, they brought this guy along to humiliate me. I'm not going to stand here and take–*

"And, of course," the man concluded, his gray eyes meeting hers, "the fact that you just washed out of the Commonwealth military's most prestigious special operations program. But I've read your jacket, specialist. All of it. And I still think you're the right person for this job."

Addy bared her teeth in a parody of a smile. "Even with all those black marks?"

"*Because* of them. If I'm being honest, what I need is someone who can think like a criminal."

"And I *was* a criminal." Addy's chest tightened. She'd had the word hurled at her plenty of times, a convenient excuse to bounce her from orphanage to foster home and back again.

"Dabbling in shoplifting and petty theft I can understand. But moving up to fraud and larceny before you turned seventeen shows ambition. Most kids that age are playing soccer or binging vids."

"It's an easy label to slap on someone from a position of privilege. I was just trying to survive."

"Well, survive you did. And that says something about your grit and your determination, both of which happen to be qualities that I value."

"I don't get it," said Addy, shaking her head. "You could have any soldier in that bar. Why me?"

The man let out a long breath, his eyes going up to the sky, fading into night. "I knew John Boyland. A little. Not well."

Addy's breath caught in her chest. *Boyland. Of course.* "I don't need any pity job."

"This isn't about pity. He was convinced you had potential – the last thing he would have wanted was to see it squandered." He smiled. "But ultimately, it's up to you. We raise ship tomorrow at 0800. Crenshaw Airfield, Hangar 3. I hope you'll be there."

With that, the man tipped her an informal salute, then turned and walked away into the night, leaving Addy alone with the summer breeze ruffling through her hair.

Boyland. Still trying to help her from beyond the grave. The one person who'd never given up on her, no matter how many times she'd let him down. He'd always believed she could do better, could make it on the straight and narrow. "Too trusting" wasn't how Addy would have described most of the cops she'd known, but Boyland, well, he had been a special case.

A burst of laughter escaped the bar's screen door, rippling out through the night, and she heard her classmates – *former* classmates – carrying on and the sound of glasses clinking together. Warmth and camaraderie emanated from the bar, but it faded out mere feet from the door. There was nothing inviting about it; just another group of people who wouldn't ask her in.

Her hands clenched again. That was just fine by her. She'd made it this far on her own, and she sure as hell didn't need any of them. She turned on her heel and stalked away from the bar, heading back towards the School's campus and her room.

Besides, she had to pack.

CHAPTER 4

Hangar 3 was an unremarkable building: a big, white, squat box that looked like it needed a fresh coat of paint.

The guards had waved Addy in after she'd presented her military ID – she might have washed out of the School, but she hadn't been officially decommissioned yet. Nobody else seemed to give her a second glance, even though she was wandering around in her civvies. She carried her olive green duffle over one shoulder, packed with all of her belongings. It wasn't particularly heavy.

She'd left Song a note, thanking her for everything, along with her remaining scrip to settle last night's bar tab. And the weekend before that. Honestly, she probably owed Song for more than that, but she wasn't going to be able to cover it all.

The rest of her class wasn't in evidence as she'd packed up, so she'd skipped the formal goodbyes and caught the shuttle bus to Crenshaw.

Out of the frying pan and into the napalm. Part of her wasn't convinced last night's recruitment pitch hadn't been a tequila-fueled delusion, but she supposed she'd find out soon enough.

The cavernous hanger did contain a ship, but it was smaller than she'd expected. An older patrol model, its hull pockmarked and pitted and the heat shield on its underbelly scorched and blackened. But as she looked closer, she realized that there were no signs of corrosion or other serious structural issues and no damage beyond the cosmetic. No name was stenciled on its bow, but there was a registration number in what looked like fresh paint.

It's in better shape than it looks.

In the middle of the floor sat a pair of chairs. Both were occupied. By the same person. He leaned back in one, eyes fastened on a tablet in front of him, while his boots – black and worn, but unmistakably military – were perched on the seat of the other. Unlike the footwear, the rest of his attire was decidedly civilian: a long-sleeve crew shirt and trousers.

Raising a fist to her mouth, Addy gave her best attempt at a polite cough.

Blue eyes flicked over the top of the tablet in her direction. "Uh. Hi." He glanced around, the telltale look of a junior officer trying to find someone more authoritative to pawn off responsibility to. Seeing no one, he laid the pad down on his chest. "Can I help you?"

"Yeah, I'm supposed to meet someone here."

The man craned his neck, taking in the hangar. "Is it me? I hope it's not me, because I am *totally* unprepared for that." The tablet slipped off his chest and clattered to the ground, and he swore under his breath.

Addy forced down the heat rising in her chest. This was too elaborate to be a put-on, she reminded herself. Besides, Mathis wasn't smart enough to pull it off. She cracked a smile at that.

The man had replaced the tablet on the chair, where it slid out the gap between the back and the seat. Cursing again, he bent to pick it up, then evidently decided better and waved it off.

"Anyway, uh, yeah," he said, looking up at her again. "Who did you say you were looking for?"

"I...uh...I don't know his name. Older guy. Square jawed. A little shorter than you? Mostly brown hair but a little bit of gray here." She tapped her temple.

The man opened his mouth in an "ah", then called back over his shoulder at the ship. "Boss? You got a visitor." He looked back at her and smiled. It wasn't a bad looking smile, as such things went.

"He's not big on sharing," said the man, lowering his voice to conspiratorial levels. "Personally, I think he likes to look as though he knows everything."

Addy nodded as though she had any idea what the hell he was talking about. She was about to ask his name and, more importantly, what the hell unit this was, when a familiar voice came from the direction of the ship.

"Oh good, you're here." The man from last night descended the ramp of the ship, one hand on the bulkhead. He ducked out of the ship, and crossed the hangar floor towards them.

A woman trailed behind: high cheekbones, dirty blonde hair pulled back into a functional ponytail, a pale face highlighted by sharp blue eyes. Addy felt those on her, scanning her up and down and silently appraising – she'd seen it in many an officer over the years. *She's wondering just how far she can throw me.* Like the two men, the woman was dressed in civilian gear with a slight military timbre: an open-collared blue shirt and casual charcoal gray trousers tucked into boots.

"Glad to see you two have met," said the man as he joined them. The woman hung back slightly, arms crossed. "There should be an open locker in one of the cabins for your bag," he said, eyes alighting on Addy's duffle. He jerked a thumb over his shoulder. "We're on a bit of a schedule," he glanced at his sleeve, "so we'll be raising ship in about fifteen minutes."

The woman behind him coughed, politely. "Simon, I do believe you've neglected to make introductions." Her voice was rich and deep, and had an accent that made Addy think of schoolmistresses and nuns. She smiled vaguely in Addy's direction, though it was decidedly lacking in warmth.

"Oh, right," said the man. He nodded at Addy. "This is Specialist Adelaide Sayers. She'll be joining us on a provisional basis."

Provisional? Addy's hand tightened on her duffel bag. *Another set of hoops to jump through.* She should have figured that the job offer was too good to come without its own series of contingencies. Whatever. She didn't need this.

"Specialist Sayers," the man had continued, "this is my executive officer, Lieutenant Commander Natalie Taylor." He gestured to the woman, who gave a cool nod in Sayers's direction, if anything frostier than the smile she'd offered a moment ago. *Lieutenant Commander? That makes her Commonwealth Navy.*

"And I see you've already met our pilot, Lieutenant Elijah Brody."

"Eli," said the blue-eyed man, extending a hand. "Welcome to the team."

After a brief hesitation, she shook it. His hand was warm, slightly calloused, but without the telltale marks of weapons or combat.

"Good," said the man. "That's taken care of."

Addy drew her eyes away from the pilot, back to the man himself. "Except one. Who the hell are *you*?"

The man had the good grace to look embarrassed. "Of course. My apologies. Major Simon Kovalic, at your service."

"And what exactly is this unit?"

"I'm really falling down on the job here," Kovalic muttered, more to himself than anyone else. He cleared his throat. "The Special Projects Team is a small covert direct-action unit. We report to the Commonwealth's Strategic Intelligence Adviser, who in turn is responsible directly to the Commonwealth Executive. Our brief is to identify and intervene in matters of strategic importance, places where even a small adjustment can make a difference. Basically, we find a way to put our thumbs on the scale."

Special Projects Team? Strategic Intelligence Adviser? "Besides the Commonwealth Executive, I've never heard of a single thing you just mentioned," said Addy.

Kovalic grinned. "If you had, we wouldn't be very good at our jobs."

"And this is it?" said Sayers, waving a hand at the hangar and the assembled personnel. "This is your team?"

"No, of course not," said Kovalic. "That'd be ridiculous."

"Of course," said Addy. "Ridiculous."

"There's one more."

In less distinguished company, Addy might have slapped a hand to her forehead, but as it was, she merely tried not to goggle. Were they having her on? Seemed like an awfully big area of responsibility for a four-person team – five-person, she corrected herself. *What the hell have I gotten myself into?*

"We're still waiting on Sergeant Tapper, but like I said, there are some open bunks onboard. Make yourself at home."

The blonde woman cleared her throat, and tilted her head towards Kovalic. "A word, major?"

Kovalic's smile froze, but he returned the nod. "Pardon me." The two of them meandered away, towards an unoccupied corner of the hangar, speaking in tones too low for Addy to make out.

"So," said the pilot – Brody – leaning back in his chair again. "Where do you come to us from? No, wait, let me guess," he spread his hands wide, as if painting a panorama, "the elite Advanced Warfare Group. Covert insertions? High-altitude jumps? Sneaking silently through jungle and desert alike?"

Addy shook her head.

"Hm," said Brody, rubbing at his chin. His blue eyes sparkled. "Marine Special Operations, then. Fighting ship-to-ship against superior odds?"

"Not so much."

His expression had turned crestfallen. "I'm usually really good at this game. CID's Activities Division?"

"Sorry."

"OK then," he said, scratching his head. "I'm just going to pretend it's some outfit so shadowy and elite that word of it has never reached my ears."

"Yeah, I think you just described you guys," said Addy, glancing around. Granted, there were probably plenty of teams like this between the Commonwealth military and its intelligence agencies. She just wasn't sure how she'd ended up on one of them.

"I think I'll go stow my gear," she said, hoisting her duffle bag again. "Nice to meet you."

"Sure," said Brody, reclaiming his tablet from its spot on the floor, and wiping it on his sleeve. "Just a word of advice?"

He nodded at the ship. "Don't touch any of Tapper's stuff. He gets cranky."

"Uh. Got it."

"What the bloody hell were you thinking?"

Kovalic glanced over his shoulder, but Sayers had gone aboard the ship, and Brody was engrossed in his tablet again. "Permission to speak freely granted, commander."

Nat's eyes flashed. "Oh, *now* you want to hide behind discipline and formality?"

Raising his hands in surrender, Kovalic gave a slight nod of acquiescence. "Fair point. Look, there were a limited number of candidates to choose from."

"And she was the best of the lot?" Disbelief suffused every syllable.

"She was… the most qualified," Kovalic said, choosing his words with care.

"On what scale?"

"Look, what exactly is the problem?"

"She's young, Simon."

"So was Page."

Nat bit her lip. "Firstly, she is not Aaron Page. Secondly, look at what happened to *him*."

It seemed to Kovalic that her words echoed off the hangar walls, rebounding until they came back at him from every direction. *Look at what happened to* him. "She's for real, Nat. I checked her out. Expert marksman, experience with–"

"That's not the point, Simon."

He threw up his hands in his exasperation. "Then what is?"

"You keep doing this." Her voice was flat, but Kovalic could hear the anger simmering beneath, and it cut his heart out from under him. "Making decisions without me. Practically going behind my back on this one."

"It *is* my team." He knew the words were a mistake the second they were out of his mouth, but it was done. There was no taking it back.

Her jaw snapped shut. "You're right. I'm only the *acting* executive officer. But the point of an XO is that they're part of the decisions made about the team. Like new personnel. You want to make a different choice, then fine. But when you're working with someone, you need to include them in these decisions. You can't pull bullshit moves like this and just expect everyone to be onboard." She heaved a breath, her eyes darting away. "Just as well this is my last mission."

Something lodged in Kovalic's throat. "Last mission? What are you talking about?"

Her gaze still wouldn't meet his. "A position opened up back at NICOM. Chief of staff to Admiral Chatterjee."

"Back at NICOM? Out of the field?"

"It comes with a promotion to full commander. One more step up the ladder. We both knew the secondment was only temporary. This is best for everyone."

The conversation was spinning away from him. "Nat, wait–"

"I'm going to make sure our new team member is feeling at home." She turned on her heel and strode towards the ship, leaving Kovalic standing in the hangar.

Brody cleared his throat. "Sooo, you want me to prep for takeoff or… you know what, I'm going to go prep for takeoff." He slowly backed up the ramp, leaving Kovalic alone in the middle of the hangar.

Oh, yes, this was going to go well.

While not cramped, the ship was definitely close quarters. Addy had located the bunk rooms, and though the lockers weren't labeled – not so much as a piece of tape to identify their owners – there was one that was unlocked. There were four racks between two small rooms, but given the nature of the outfit it seemed unlikely that all five personnel would be sleeping at the same time. Irregular schedules, keeping watch, hot bunking, that sort of thing. Nothing new for her.

She dropped onto one of the bunks, staring at the barren cabin. No decorations, no personalizations. On the one hand, the more elite units often tended to have more leeway when it came to breaking from the traditional rank and file; on the other, this was clearly a working ship and, in the eventuality that someone other than the team was onboard, it was probably prudent to not have anything that was too easily identifiable.

Still, not exactly the most friendly of places.

A sharp rap at the door got her attention and she looked up to find the blonde woman, Taylor, leaning against the doorframe. While her expression hadn't gained much in the way of warmth, it at least didn't seem out-and-out frosty as it had been earlier. And there was something else in her eyes now – appraisal.

"Not the most comfortable of quarters, I know."

"I'm used to it. Slept in plenty of worse places than this." Let her appraise away.

"Where was your last billet, specialist?"

"Before the School? C Company, 37th Infantry."

Taylor raised a slender eyebrow. "Infantry? Didn't think we had many of those left."

"Somebody's got to fight the ground war while you lot are dropping the heavy stuff from upstairs." Addy pulled a few fatigues from her duffle and jammed them into an empty locker with somewhat more force than was probably required.

"You like it there?"

"Like it? Not sure that was a requirement."

"Why'd you get into this line of work, then?"

Addy glanced up from her empty duffle, which she folded up and stowed in the locker along with her clothes. "Due respect, commander, but what is this? Some sort of head-shrinking exercise?"

Cocking her head to one side, Taylor's eyes narrowed. *There's that appraisal again.* "Just trying to get a feel for the personnel I'm responsible for, specialist."

Addy snorted. "Most XOs I've met aren't big on chatting." *Unless they're chewing you out.*

"I think you'll find that we don't do things the way that most people do, specialist. For better or worse."

Rocking back on her heels, Addy frowned. "The major… Kovalic. What's his deal? He make it a habit of going around dragging burnouts out of the gutter?"

Something flickered across Taylor's expression, almost too fast to catch, but Addy was as familiar with it as she was her own features. *Pain and regret.*

"Not a habit…" she paused, frowning and glancing back out the corridor in the direction of the ship's cockpit. "Major Kovalic is one of the best officers I've ever had the pleasure of working with." Whatever she was going to say after that was swallowed as she glanced at Addy and seemed to remember who she was talking to. "The unit's a bit, let's say 'unorthodox.'"

Yeah, that's the impression I'm getting. If I can't make it here, I can't make it anywhere...

"Well," said Addy, rising to her feet and brushing her palms off on the thighs of her trousers, "I guess I'll get acquainted with the rest of the ship. Good chat, commander." She made for the doorway, but Taylor didn't shift aside. The blonde woman placed a hand on her shoulder.

Addy tensed at the hand but she pushed the feeling down and forced her gaze to meet Taylor's. The blue eyes had frozen over again.

"We might be unorthodox, specialist. And the major likes to play things fast and loose. But just remember, underneath all of that, we're still a team. We need to be able to count on each other to get the job done. And like it or not, you're a part of that team now. Understood?"

Addy tilted her head in acknowledgement and Taylor dropped her hand, then turned and strolled down the corridor towards the fore of the ship.

Like it or not, thought Addy, watching her go. Somehow she didn't think the commander had been referring to her.

CHAPTER 5

At least I'm not stuck in the car this time. Eli Brody dutifully took his seat in the ballroom, trying not to rub at his left eye, which was feeling increasingly itchy by the moment. A wash of murmurs and chattering rolled over him as he surveyed the crowd. *For a secret black market auction, this place is pretty packed.*

There were close to two hundred people in the ballroom of the Citadel Hotel on Tseng-Tao's Divide, more than Eli had expected, given that the auction was invitation-only. They wouldn't even have gotten in the door themselves without Kovalic reaching out to Zaina Vallejo at the Bayern Corporation and reminding her that his team had been all that stood between their planet and Imperial occupation, so a few invitations to an exclusive event were hardly too much to ask in return.

Most of the attendees had dressed for the occasion: finely tailored suits, elegant dresses, and attire somewhere between the two. Others had taken a decidedly more casual approach – the truly wealthy didn't need to flaunt it. And then was the third group, arrayed around the perimeter of the room: half a dozen extremely visible security personnel, provided by the auction firm, wearing matching black suits.

The event's rules had required weapons and personal security remain outside, to avoid any… misunderstandings, though Eli imagined some of latter might have made their way in under other pretenses.

For his part, Eli had decided to try and blend with the elite as best he could, digging out one of the suits he'd kept from his Elias Adler cover identity – the one that wasn't too much worse for wear after the events on Bayern. Taylor, meanwhile, had chosen a smart suit: chic, but with no compromise to mobility.

Their new recruit, Sayers, was wearing the same clothes in which she'd appeared at the hangar: casual, close-fitting trousers, a loose shirt, and a lightweight jacket. Her dark, short hair was brushed back from her forehead, and her brown eyes tracked the room on high alert.

Tapper and Kovalic had hung back; the sergeant was ostensibly running point, and the major had made noises about being too recognizable in this crowd. But Eli had a sneaking suspicion that he was trying to give Taylor some space to operate. Not to mention seeing how Sayers handled herself in the field.

Eli, for his part, wasn't quite sure what to make of their latest addition. He couldn't help but overhear some of Taylor and Kovalic's… "discussion" on Sayers's relative merits. As far as he could tell, she seemed a bit tightly wound. But then again, coming into a group as close-knit as theirs was bound to be a challenge for anyone. Anyway, with three months of experience under his belt, he was hardly an expert on what made a great covert operative.

Taylor's voice came through his earbud. "How's the view, Hotshot?"

Ugh. Another terrible codename. I'm sensing a theme. He'd expected comms to be jammed in the ballroom for security, but Taylor had explained that many of the attendees would be proxy bidders who might need to take instruction from their remote clients.

"I guess everything's fine?"

"Remember, you and Bullseye are just here to watch the crowd. See who else is bidding on the lot we're looking for and try to get a clear image."

Right. Eli tried not to rub at the contact in his left eye. Putting it in had been one of the most uncomfortable moments in his life, and after being almost killed in a space battle, locked in a military prison, and having had to scrub toilets for four years, that was saying something.

But the camera embedded in the contact would let them capture the faces without looking too much like they were doing, well, exactly what they were doing.

He blinked twice in rapid succession and watched as the bright heads-up display flared into existence. Turning to his left, he smiled at the person next to him – a woman in her forties with light brown skin and inky hair – and nodded politely in greeting.

The camera isolated the face and sent it to his sleeve, which started to run it against Commonwealth databases. After a moment, a matching image came up on his HUD: Elena Avastrios. Employed by Gemini Collections, a shell corporation that traced back to a prominent Novan business.

"Trieste van Sant's company," said Taylor, who was seeing their feeds routed to her own HUD. "She's a hardcore collector – never one to let legality stand in her way."

OK, sure. Rubbing elbows with the rich and famous had never particularly been on his bucket list. And, after Bayern, he'd had about enough of the upper classes.

The reminder of that mission's end sat uncomfortably in Eli's gut. Or at least what he knew of it. Kovalic had said little, other than that the taciturn lieutenant wasn't coming back, leaving the rest of the team to read uncomfortably between the lines. And every time Eli thought he'd worked up the nerve to confront the major about it, he found himself coming up with some excuse not to push the issue.

But sometimes, when Eli closed his eyes, he could still see the gun that Kovalic had taken to his meet with Page, and the empty holster upon the operative's return, pointing him towards one obvious and inescapable conclusion.

As "evidence" went, it would hardly hold up in any court of law, but more importantly, try as he might, he just couldn't square it with the man he knew. Kovalic had been hard on Eli, sure: dragged him from his self-pity on frozen Sabaea, forced him to confront his past, and thrust him into a life he wasn't particularly ready for. But physically threatening? Never.

Not that Eli had any doubt Kovalic was capable of killing. The man had been a covert operative for years, and a soldier in a shooting war before that. But there was a difference between taking a life in the heat of battle and the cold-blooded murder of a teammate.

Wasn't there?

And if that *wasn't* what had happened, then why hadn't Kovalic said so? Didn't he owe them that much? They were a team, after all.

Eli found himself glancing over his shoulder at Addy Sayers, a half a dozen or so rows back on the other side of the room. It was strange not being the freshest face on the team anymore. He felt *responsible* somehow. Someone had always been looking out for him; now it was time for him to pay that forward.

But what was he supposed to tell her? *Watch your step? Do a good job or you might get whacked?* Paranoia and veiled warnings weren't exactly the image of confidence he was hoping to project.

A voice over the public address system interrupted his thoughts. "Please be seated. The auction will begin shortly."

Settle down, Brody. He had a job to do, and worrying about Kovalic and Page and a mission that was already over wasn't going to help anything. He focused back on the task at hand.

Auctions turned out to be a lot more boring than Eli had hoped. The first several lots went by quickly. There was a Grecian urn, followed by a painting by a Dutch artist that he was pretty sure he remembered having been stolen from a museum on Earth, and a twenty-second century abstract sculpture that looked like somebody's impression of a body that had gone through a black hole.

Each of them went for more money than Eli had ever seen in his life.

He'd almost started to drift off, lulled by the comforting monotony of the auctioneer's calls for higher and higher bids, when the numbers he'd been listening for percolated into his brain.

"…lot 2187," the auctioneer was saying. "I have the honor of presenting this, the most singular item that we at Brougham & Weng have ever had the privilege of bringing to auction. It has recently been released from a private collection, and this marks the first time it has ever been available at an open sale. I give you... the Aleph Tablet."

A hush, appropriately unearthly in nature, fell over the room. Kovalic had briefed them on the objective, but even so, Eli felt the hairs on his arms and the back of his neck going up. He'd heard the stories of course: a little more than a century ago, surveyors on a moon in the Trinity system had uncovered a mysterious, featureless slab – perfectly rectangular in shape – about the size of the top of an end table and supposedly made of a never before seen ultra-durable yet incredibly light material. Sure, human history had its fair share of mythical artifacts, but the Aleph Tablet was unique, because it was believed to be the work of an intelligence that *wasn't* human.

Legends and whispers held that the tablet was somehow the key to unlocking the knowledge of whatever advanced civilization had left it behind, though Eli had never been sure exactly how one got information out of a blank slab of metal. Even the alien origin of the tablet had never been certifiably established. The relatively few pictures and videos of the tablet that had made the rounds had only contributed to its mystique: they were all of dubious quality, with believers arguing that whatever unique material the tablet was supposedly composed of couldn't be imaged, while skeptics pointed out just how convenient that was.

All of this was complicated by the fact that the tablet had never been subjected to rigorous scientific study – at least not publicly – in large part because it had never spent long in the hands of any legitimate owner. Instead, it had circulated amongst less reputable collectors, many of whom kept their ownership so quiet that the tablet often seemed to disappear for long stretches.

Many of those owners had also died under mysterious circumstances. That, in turn, had spawned additional conspiracy theories: that the tablet was cursed, or that whatever strange material it was composed of emanated deadly radiation, or even that a secret society had sworn themselves to protecting it by assassinating everyone who possessed it. As far as Eli was concerned, the deaths were more likely the result of people in dangerous lifestyles owning something that a lot of other people – many of them dangerous – also wanted.

"While the provenance of this item is... unique and somewhat difficult to ascertain," the auctioneer continued, "its radiological signature is consistent with the attested location where the artifact was discovered." He looked around the room, his gavel waving in a lazy figure eight. "As such, I'd like to begin the bidding at 275 million Commonwealth credits."

Eli's mouth dropped open. It was the highest starting bid so far – an outrageous price no doubt out of the range of all but the wealthiest people in the galaxy. Several of whom were probably represented in this room. The kind of people who, even if they couldn't conclusively prove it was actually an alien artifact, would still buy it just to say they had.

Around him, he heard the murmurs and tapping as the proxies whispered to or messaged their patrons. Most of them had clearly had advanced warning on this item, saving their pennies for the moment it came up.

Taylor's voice cut through the hubbub. "Hotshot, Bullseye, start tagging the bidders."

Right. Right. Eli tried to steer his attention back to the job. Hands were flying up everywhere, and no sooner was one bid accepted but another quickly topped it. The numbers being bandied about could have covered the costs of a couple luxury space yachts. Hardly pocket change, even for the richest of the galaxy's rich.

He focused on a bidder, a scrawny pale man with a sheen of sweat on his bald head, and blinked to run the facial ID scan, watching as a name appeared on the screen. Blinking again, Eli turned his attention to another: a woman with long, gray dreadlocks, who was identified as a broker with ties to the Harani government. Marking them as possible persons of interest, he caught sight of a hand flashing up from the middle of the room. As his eyes slid over the crowd towards them, his vision blurred suddenly, as if he'd teared up. He tried to blink it away, rubbing at his eye with the back of a hand, and frowned. The HUD itself was still crystal clear. His eyes scanned over the crowd again, and once again, his vision got cloudy as it passed over one specific section of the room.

Breath caught in his throat. "Uh, Peregrine, Bullseye, are you seeing this?"

"Shit," said Taylor. "That's an ocular diffusion field. Not exactly something you wear unless you're up to no good."

Out of the corner of Eli's eye, he saw Sayers was already moving with purpose down the aisle, everything about her carriage screaming combat-ready.

Taylor evidently had seen her as well. "Bullseye, do *not* eng–"

A high-pitched squeal suddenly interrupted Eli's train of thought and he slapped the cutoff switch on his sleeve. *Jamming field*. All around the room, there were yelps of surprise as the feedback took all the proxy bidders by surprise, and people started rising to their feet in alarm.

"It, uh, appears we are having some technical difficulties," the auctioneer was saying, trying to maintain control. People were looking around, getting to their feet, just a few steps shy of panic. *This whole place is about to go up.* Where the hell was the security? More than half of the guards who had been standing around the room's edge had conveniently vanished; the two that were left were trying valiantly to calm the crowd, but without much luck. Here and there, a few assistants had taken up protective positions around their principals – seems some folks had indeed brought in bodyguards, despite the rules. But none of them were conspicuously armed.

Eli stood, struggling to see through the mass of people, trying to find the blur, but he'd lost track of both it and Sayers amongst the throng.

Then something shimmered through his vision, heading for the dais and the tablet.

The lights went out.

The second Addy had seen the blur, she started moving. Her pulse quickened as she strode down the aisle, even as she faintly heard Taylor say something in her ear. Then there was nothing but static and she pulled her earpiece out with a growl.

The mission was the auction item. The tablet. Something about it triggered a vague memory in her head, like she'd heard of it once upon a time. Maybe something Boyland had said to her once? She couldn't remember, and anyway it wasn't important. What was important was stopping whoever the hell that blur was from getting it.

She was here to do a job. *Get to the tablet.*

Around her, the crowd had started surging to its feet, the background murmur of discontent rising to a higher pitch. Not quite at panic yet, but they'd get there.

Even as her eyes insisted on trying to blink away the impossible blur in front of her, she stayed focused, resisting the urge to wipe them clear. It was like trying to see through privacy glass; she could make out the vague outlines of a figure – head, arms, torso, legs – but none of the features. Taking out the contacts would have let her see them clearly, but she didn't exactly have that kind of time.

She shoved her way past a few people who had stumbled into the aisles, hearing one or two of them yelp as they reeled into chairs or other people. Didn't matter. Nothing mattered except getting to the tablet before the blur did.

Then all the lights in the room died, plunging them into blackness. A moment later, emergency lighting whined to life, blanketing the room in a deep crimson.

Addy was suddenly free of the crowd, standing right in front of the dais that held only the auctioneer, who was now cowering behind his lectern, and the plinth on which stood the gleaming slab of metal, now painted blood red.

She blinked and held her eyes closed for a split second – when she opened them, the contacts had detected the reduced light level and compensated, amplifying the meager light levels into a bright, if grainy image.

Just in time to see the blur shift directions and come after her.

Oh, you want to go? She felt the grin crossing her face, unbidden. *Let's do this.*

One blurred fist lashed out at her and she juked to her right, letting it pass harmlessly over her left shoulder. The follow-up jab came from the other direction, but she blocked that easily with a forearm. *They're testing me.* Fine, let them test her. Her teeth bared.

A knee came up towards her stomach, and she spun away from it, using her momentum to bring her leg around and deliver a kick to her opponent's left shoulder, with enough force to bring them down.

But the blur had seen her spin and ducked under the kick, then came up and under during the split-second that she had been off-balance with a hard jab to her gut.

The wind went out of Addy in a *poof* and she staggered backwards, one hand on her stomach. Her spine refused to straighten, even as she insisted to her body that she was fine, that it felt worse than it was. But before she could catch her breath, the blur had pressed the advantage, raining down a flurry of blows that had her put up her arms, shielding her face from the worst of it.

Son of a bitch. Anger burned, hot white, in her chest as she blocked the punches, waiting for the cramp in her stomach to subside. *This is not how this goes.* Panic had seized the crowd now and they rushed the exits, jostling each other as they all tried to get out. In her peripheral vision, she caught a glimpse of Brody and Taylor fighting their way upstream towards her.

A hook broke through her block, glancing off her temple. Her ear rung, high and sharp, and then everything around the blur was equally distorted, flashing as the contacts tried to compensate. A roaring filled her ears, blocking out even the wall of noise from the rest of the room's occupants. Addy wavered, nausea seizing her stomach, then thrust it down and let that supernova of fury explode in her chest.

With a deep, bass growl she launched herself forward, plowing right into the blur's mid-section. It took them by surprise, and while her mass was a lot less than her target's, her force was enough to knock them both to the ground, leaving her straddling the other's chest.

Hit me, *motherfucker.* Her punches flailed into the blur's face, knocking his head back and forth until, with a crackle and a spark, the ocular diffuser winked out, and she was left staring at a bruised and bloody man's face. Breath heaved from her chest in ragged gasps as she stared down into the eyes, one swollen shut, the other rolled back into the head.

A hand seized her shoulder, and she started.

The rest of the room snapped back into focus, loud and bright as the main lighting came back on. An alarm blared in her ears, punctuated by shouting from the room's occupants. Taylor was looking down at her, anger shot through with horror on her face. Grim was not a tone that Addy had heard in Taylor's voice before, but the otherwise stoic commander looked like she might have blown a fuse. "What the *fuck.*" Brody stood behind her, and even his normally upbeat expression had acquired a distinct look of shock. A lump rose in Addy's throat.

"I– I stopped him," said Addy, resting back on her heels. "That was the mission."

"No, the mission was the tablet," said Taylor, pointing one finger at the plinth on stage, which Addy quickly recognized as the source of the alarm.

The plinth that was now empty.

Shit. He'd had a partner. Maybe more than one. Addy swallowed, but the lump in her throat wouldn't go away.

So much for last chances.

*

Kovalic put his hands up. "I know what you're going to say."

They'd regrouped after the mission, and he and Taylor had repaired to one of the few private spaces on the *Cavalier*, the closet-turned-medbay. Even with the hatch closed for privacy, Kovalic had a feeling that nobody on the small ship was going to have much trouble hearing them.

"Do you? *Do you?*" Nat's blue eyes were glinting. "You probably think I'm going to tell you that your new pet project just cost us our mission. But no, I'm just going to tell you that Adelaide Sayers is a liability to this team and that you should send her packing."

Kovalic grimaced. "We all make mistakes." The second the words had left his mouth he wished he could bottle them back up.

Nat's eyes widened. "*Mistakes?* Are you kidding me with this, Simon?" She waved a hand at the door. "Not only did she disobey orders, she was so busy almost beating a man to death that she took her eye off the ball, and we lost the mission objective."

"But she didn't kill him. That shows a certain amount of judgment." The sound of the ice giving way under his feet was almost audible.

There was a squeak as Nat sat down heavily on the medbay's gurney, her hands massaging her temples. "Are you even listening to yourself? What is going on, Simon?" She looked up at him, and the anger in her expression had faded into concern. "What the hell is this all about?"

Kovalic leaned against the bulkhead. "Look, I know she's lacking some discipline." He ignored Nat's scoff. "But if we drum her out, she's got no place else to go."

"I'm sympathetic, Simon, I am. But if she keeps pulling stunts like that, we're going to be the ones with no place else to go. She's putting us all at risk." Her mouth set in a line. "And maybe we're seeing *why* she has no place else to go. Maybe… maybe she doesn't belong here at all."

It was Kovalic's turn to frown. He gave a curt shake of his head. "I'm not ready to accept that. She can do good work here, I know it. Look at Bro–"

"Brody was half-drunk when you found him, and yeah, maybe he had some black marks on his record, but he also wasn't flying off the handle and assaulting people." Her lips pursed. "God, don't let him know I was in here defending his virtue. I'll never hear the end of it."

Kovalic chuckled but it died in his throat as he saw the mirth dissipate from Nat's expression. "OK, we'll consider this mission a trial period. If she doesn't work out, she doesn't work out. But I think she can be helpful on this job, so let's give her a chance to prove that."

Nat eyed him for a moment, then got to her feet. "Look, it's your call. As you've pointed out. But for now, I'm still your XO and as far as I'm concerned, she gets one last chance." She raised a finger.

"One more chance," Kovalic agreed. "But we do have more pressing matters to deal with. The tablet's in the wind."

"Hell of a job. Smash and grab was hardly elegant."

"But it was effective. A couple ocular diffusers, cut the power to disable the security systems, and disappear into the crowd. Left a lot of pissed-off buyers in their wake, but even if Tseng-Tao's Divide had any authorities worth the name, who's going to report a theft from an underground antiquities auction?"

"At least we got one of them," said Nat, her expression tightening at the reminder of Sayers's behavior. "Citadel security might have him under lock and key for now, but it's even money whether Juarez enforcement or that Hanif baron who owned the tablet gets to him first. And honestly, in his shoes, I'm not sure which one I'd rather."

"Best not waste any more time, then. I'm thinking divide and conquer: if you talk to Sayers, I'll see if I can persuade Citadel security to let me have a chat with our would-be thief."

"Why do I get all the fun jobs?"

"Delegation?"

Her lips thinned to a line, Nat stalked out of the medbay. Kovalic let out a breath he didn't realize he'd been holding.

It was entirely possible that he'd gotten himself in over his head.

Addy sat on the edge of the ship's ramp, staring at her hands. They looked fine now, sure, but an hour ago they'd almost killed a man. She waggled the fingers experimentally, and they responded well enough. Sometimes, though, they just seemed to take on a life of their own.

But it's not really the hands. It's the person they're connected to.

Losing control was bad enough, but giving an opening for the partners of the man she'd jumped to make off with the mission objective made it that much worse. The SPT had failed to get the tablet, and it was *her* fault. She should have been paying better attention.

Footsteps sounded behind her, and she felt the ramp flex and bounce slightly from the pressure. Eli Brody settled down next to her, elbows on knees, and the two of them sat and looked out over the grassy meadow where they'd parked the ship. A breeze rippled through the tall grasses, eddies whirling as though wakes left by unseen creatures.

"Rough morning, huh?" said Brody. If any of his shock from seeing what Addy had done lingered, it wasn't evident in his expression.

Addy gave a noncommittal grunt, neither an invitation to continue talking nor one that suggested he should get up and walk away.

"They read you the riot act?"

That had been the more worrisome thing: so far, they hadn't. Taylor and Kovalic had been closeted in that, well, closet, and the acoustics of the ship being what they were, she'd retreated out here. When they'd made a decision, she imagined she'd find out soon enough. She shook her head.

"Well I wouldn't worry about it too much," said Brody, leaning back on his elbows. "They're not going to drum you out because of one, uh, incident. If they had, I'd have been out on my ear my first mission."

Yeah, but what about on the eighteenth *incident?*

"Taylor's got a hell of a bark on her, but she's not a bad sort when you get right down to it," Brody continued, undaunted by her lack of participation in the conversation. *He could probably talk for three or four without breaking a sweat.* "And Kovalic, well, don't tell anyone, but he's a big softie. How do you think I ended up here?"

She eyed him sidelong. She'd met a few flight jockeys in her day, and while most of them projected the devil-may-care attitude he'd demonstrated, he'd yet to display the overinflated ego that usually seemed to accompany it.

"How *did* you end up here?"

Brody grinned and she was reminded once again that it wasn't an unpleasant sight. "Long story," he said. "Kovalic helped me out of a jam… and then kinda got me into another one. Or, well, maybe I got myself into that one. Anyway," he said, waving a hand, "I think we're about even now. Point is, if you've already gotten this far, they're not about to cut you loose on job one."

Whatever hidden depths were lending confidence to Brody didn't seem to echo in Addy. But he seemed sure of himself, and that wasn't nothing.

"Thanks."

Brody shaded his eyes against the sun, which had begun to drop lower in the sky. "'Course. We're on the same team, after all. That means something." For a moment, it sounded like there was a catch in his voice, but before she could say something, the sound of a throat clearing came from behind them.

Addy stiffened, though she resisted the temptation to jump to full attention. Brody lolled his head back, not leaving his comfortable perch on the ramp. "Commander."

"Lieutenant. Can you take another look at that port stabilizing thruster? It's acting up again."

"No rest for the wicked," said Brody, his cheerfulness returned unabated. Clambering to his feet, he gave Addy a friendly smile, and then traipsed back up the ramp and into the ship.

Addy got to her feet, turning to face Taylor at the top of the ramp and adopting a parade rest. "Commander."

"Specialist," said Taylor, her voice even. "Major Kovalic and I have discussed your actions this morning and while they were far from satisfactory, we have agreed that, for the time being, you will continue in your capacity on this team."

The hope rose in her chest slowly, but she kept one hand firmly atop it, waiting for the implicit "but" that was surely on its way.

"*However,* any further behavior of that kind will not be tolerated, and will see you dismissed from the SPT and likely from the service altogether. Am I understood?"

Addy swallowed, and nodded. "Yes, ma'am."

Once again those eyes, cold and calculating, were on her, though she wouldn't call them malicious. Whatever Taylor was looking for, she evidently found it, because she gave a curt nod, and then disappeared back into the ship.

The breath Addy had been holding whistled out of her, shoulders slumping. She turned to look back at the wide open plains all around, letting the breeze run its fingers through her close-cropped curls. *Thin goddamned ice. And the cracks are already showing.*

CHAPTER 6

Dust settled in Kovalic's wake as he trudged back to the *Cavalier*, which they'd docked just outside of the only thing that passed for a town on Tseng-Tao's Divide. Beyond the Citadel Hotel, the moon didn't have much to offer, other than the administration of the Juarez system generally turning a blind eye to the goings-on here.

As he crested a rise, the small ship came into view, its battered exterior not even a little out of place amidst the scrub vegetation and dirt. Like the most competent operatives he'd known, its exterior painted a misleading picture: it had already been in excellent condition when they'd first started using it, before the Bayern mission, and over the last three months Brody had spent all his spare time further tweaking the ship's performance. They'd been working missions out of it non-stop since then, spending far more time aboard than back at home on Nova.

Each member of the crew had carved out their own favorite spots on the ship, so he was unsurprised to find Tapper stretched out on the *Cavalier*'s lowered entry ramp, a boonie hat tipped over his eyes. To somebody who hadn't served with the sergeant for as long as Kovalic had, it might look like the older man was taking a nap, but Kovalic knew he was just resting his eyes. If there were danger anywhere within a half mile, Tapper would be the first one to know.

"Boss," he said, without twitching a muscle.

"Tap. All quiet on the western front?"

"More or less. The commander's glued to a relay screen. Brody's playing with the flight control systems."

"Sayers?"

Tapper pushed the hat back from his forehead, squinting one-eyed at Kovalic. "Last I saw her, doing pull-ups in the bunk room. Looked exhausting. I left her to it. How'd things go with you?"

"The Citadel's security office was nice enough to give me a few minutes with the thief we nabbed after I flashed them a Commonwealth Security Bureau badge." He doubted the Commonwealth's chief law enforcement agency would be happy about spies appropriating their authority, but what they didn't know… "The crew were pros, and well-funded to boot: They bribed or suborned most of the private security brought in for the auction, which gave them all the inside information they needed to avoid and subvert the protections around the tablet. According to the one we nabbed, payment was blind, so he doesn't even know who hired them. Delivery's a drop on Jericho Station; he assumed his partners were probably already on their way there."

A whistle escaped through Tapper's teeth. "Mercenaries, eh? Surprised you got that much out of him."

"Well," said Kovalic, "I might have pointed out that it was a better deal than he was going to get from either the Juarez authorities or a certain Hanif baron. Plus, I jammed his door open and made sure Citadel security was on a coffee break."

"You're a generous man, boss," said Tapper. "Still, Jericho's a pretty big haystack. I dunno, maybe if that guy hadn't been beaten to a pulp, he would have been more cooperative."

Kovalic leaned against one of the ship's landing struts. "Something on your mind, sergeant?"

"You know me, boss. I'm the introspective sort."

They both chuckled, but Kovalic sobered first. "Seriously. You've been doing this longer than me and Nat put together. I value your advice."

Tapper's lined face wrinkled even further. "I read her jacket. Sayers. I have to ask: is she really the best person for the job?"

"Define best."

"Least likely to get us killed?"

"When was the last time you saw someone with this many certifications?"

"There's a difference between certified and *certifiable*."

"She may have some black marks here and there, but who doesn–"

"*Seventeen*? Insubordination? Gross misconduct? Failure to follow orders? How she's escaped a court-martial so far is beyond me."

"Hey, you didn't like Brody either when we brought him onboard. But you can't argue that he's been an asset."

"Look, the kid can pilot pretty much anything you sit him down in front of," said Tapper, putting his hands up, "but we both know that he's *still* no operative, even after Bayern. And he's a pain in the ass. Specifically, my ass."

Kovalic pressed a palm against the stubble on his jaw, feeling the bristles stand up as he ran his hand over them.

Tapper eyed him sideways. "Boss, you wanted to put together the best unit in the service, and you've done that. But this…this makes us a joke. They hear we're taking washouts, and pretty soon every unit is going to be trying to dump their problem children on us."

It wasn't that the sergeant didn't have a point, but Kovalic could care less what everybody else thought about his unit. As long as they got the job done, everybody could think they were total screw-ups, for all he cared.

"Look, I know what happened with Page threw you."

Kovalic's jaw set. "This isn't about that."

"Could've fooled me," said Tapper, eyes to heaven. "Page was a hell of an operator and he was part of this team. You say he betrayed us – hard as I find that to believe, you're the boss, and whatever happened on Bayern, I trust you had your reasons to do what needed to be done."

Kovalic's hand twitched at the memory of a heavy pistol there. Tapper was his most trusted confidant – they'd served together for more than twenty years. Keeping him in the dark was almost physically painful. But the decisions Kovalic had made were his and his alone; if the time came when someone had to answer for them, it was going to be him. No one else.

"If anything, maybe Page was too good," Tapper continued. "He was playing us and we all missed it. I guess it's not too hard to see why you'd seize on the person least like him to fill his spot."

Kovalic ran a hand through his hair. "You didn't see the rest of the candidates, sergeant. Qualified, sure, but cookie cutters, all of them. Not a single one ever had an original idea that didn't come from their CO. That's the last thing we need."

"Well, what's the damn hurry for replacing Page anyway? With you, me, Taylor, and–" he stifled a sigh, "–Brody, we're still at operational capacity." His eyes narrowed. "This isn't about the commander, is it? Because she and I may not always see eye to eye, but she's damn good."

"No, it's not about her," said Kovalic. He almost believed it, too. "Nat and I are fine."

"Oh sure," Tapper muttered. "If only you could decide whether you were married or not."

Kovalic ignored him. "But we're not going to have the commander forever; she's leaving at the end of this mission."

"What?"

"Her secondment is up, and there's a job waiting for her back at NICOM. So we need to start planning for the future."

"Don't take this the wrong way, but have you considered asking her to stay?"

He could. But Nat had always been ambitious, and he didn't want to get in the way of her goals. Besides the two of them not just working together, but her working *for* him? Seemed like a recipe for disaster, and they'd made that one before.

"I would feel better if we had some new talent. And sometimes people deserve a second chance, don't they?"

Tapper's *tch* of disgust didn't leave much room for interpretation. "I'm not so sure about an *eighteenth* chance. But you're the boss. You want to waste your time with this burnout, then that's your call."

"And here I thought there was nothing holier to you than the chain of command."

"Never kept me from speaking my mind to a damn fool decision before." He tilted his head. "I kind of figured that's why you kept me around."

With a laugh, Kovalic slapped his sergeant on the shoulder, and rose to his feet. "I keep you around because we both know there's no other unit that would put up with you. I

guess you and Sayers have that much in common." With
that, he climbed the ramp into the ship, ignoring the glare
Tapper shot after him.

It only took Brody about fifteen minutes to prep the *Cavalier*
and get lift off clearance; Tseng-Tao's Divide was not exactly a
stickler for traffic control. The trip to Jericho would take eight
hours or so, and once they'd broken atmo and were en route
to the system's gate, Kovalic headed for the ship's galley. He'd
laid in a store of produce before leaving Nova, because if he
had to eat one more ready-cook meal, he was going to crash
the ship himself.

Besides, cooking had a way of relaxing him. His father
had been a baker, and a busy kitchen had been one of the
hallmarks of his childhood. The bigger challenge was having
the time, space, and energy to do it, especially in his line of
work. Half the time he bought food to make at home, it ended
up going to waste when he got called away on a job. But he
still tried to make time for it when he could, and the *Cav*'s
galley was surprisingly well-equipped. If the outside ramp
was Tapper's domain, the galley was his.

That said, they were still aboard a ship, and subject to the
usual constraints: no open flames meant food was cooked via
an induction range or convection oven; every implement and
utensil had to be latched into place, covered, or magnetized;
and the stovetop was mounted on gimbals to account for
maneuvering. At least the invention of artificial gravity had
made cooking in space feasible: trying to prepare food in
zero-g was only a recipe for a mess.

Fortunately, the long, straight line trip to the Juarez gate from Tseng-Tao's Divide provided ample time to prepare a simple meal. And it quickly proved that nobody could resist the wafting aroma of garlic and onion. It only took about half an hour for Nat to wander in, rubbing at tired eyes that had spent way too long staring at a screen. At the sight of the pan on the induction range, she perked up.

"Wait, is that your eggplant parmesan?"

Kovalic gave a modest wave. "Just thought everybody could use a decent meal after the last day or so we had."

"You're not wrong," said Nat, reaching over and plucking a handful of shredded cheese from a dish, depositing it directly into her mouth. At Kovalic's glare she returned a look of pure innocence. "What? Quality control."

With a snort, Kovalic turned back to his pan, unlatched the cover, and stirred the sauce simmering there. "Tapper says you've been deep in the nets all afternoon. Any promising leads?"

"Well, uh, I might have gotten distracted and fallen down a bit of a rabbit hole."

He smiled to himself, his back still to her. You could take Nat out of the intelligence analyst department, but you sure as hell couldn't take the intelligence analyst out of Nat. "Oh yeah? What enthralling subject?"

"Aleph Theory."

"Please tell me you haven't been watching conspiracy theory videos from too earnest kids with way too little grasp of scientific rigor."

Nat gave him a look. "Please, Simon. Give me a little credit. Respectable and vetted sources only."

"I wasn't aware that xenoanthropology had become a peer-reviewed field."

Taking a seat on one of the stools bolted to the floor by the counter, Nat rested her chin on a palm. "I fully admit that hard evidence is sparse, but there are some interesting points nonetheless."

Kovalic sighed, scraping at the sauce in the pan. "I'm going to regret asking this but, 'Such as?'"

"Well, of the wormhole-connected systems that we've discovered, around eighty-five percent of them have at least one planetoid capable of supporting human life. Eighty-five percent! That's absurdly high, especially given their astronomical dispersal."

"Coincidence?"

"Coincidence?" Nat scoffed. "That we just *happened* to discover wormholes leading to habitable planets. Pull the other one."

"It doesn't exactly prove the existence of aliens."

"Ooh, you guys talking about aliens?" said another voice.

Kovalic glanced over his shoulder to see Eli Brody emerging from the direction of the *Cav*'s cockpit, brushing a lock of sandy hair out of his eyes.

"Also, something smells amazing." The pilot hopped up on a stool next to Nat, peering over the counter with the kind of hungry eyes usually reserved for teenagers.

Nat rolled her eyes, but her heart wasn't in it. She'd grown fond of Brody over the past few months since the Bayern job – protective in a big sister way. Kovalic suspected that was because he reminded her a little bit of her actual brother: slightly hapless, but generally cheerful.

"And what exactly do you know about Aleph Theory?" Nat asked.

"Well, there was this video about an ancient Earth site at a place called Stonehenge and how aliens–"

Kovalic sidled over to Nat. "Oh, yes, your case is looking

better and better," he murmured, unable to keep a smug edge out of his voice.

She cradled her head in her hands as Brody continued to ramble. "There's booze on the ship somewhere, right?"

"Ask Tapper."

Thirty minutes later, Kovalic was dishing out fried eggplant to Tapper, Nat, and Brody, who'd gathered around the cramped table in the ship's lounge. Sayers was nowhere to be seen, but he'd set a portion aside for her, just in case she got hungry.

Despite Kovalic's best efforts to change the subject, Aleph Theory had continued to be the topic of the day, with even the sergeant venturing an opinion.

"Look," said Tapper, "I'm just saying I've been around. And I've never seen *anything* to make me believe that super-intelligent aliens ever existed. Where's the proof? They never left *anything* behind? No buildings? No civilization? No ships?"

"Maybe you're just judging them based on our own limited human perspective. What about a dozen planets with human-breathable atmospheres, water, and around one g of gravity?" Nat said, punctuating the questions with jabs of her fork. "That not enough for you? What about wormholes between those systems?"

Tapper threw his hands up. "Oh come on, now the aliens made the wormholes? I suppose they built black holes and stars too."

"Maybe," said Nat. "I'm just saying that if humans were able to devise a way to artificially prop wormholes open, there's no reason to believe that an advanced intelligent species couldn't have figured out how to build the wormholes themselves in the first place."

Brody piped up through a mouthful of food. "I saw this

one thing that said maybe the Aleph were actually giant space worms who *burrowed* through…"

If there was a back half to that sentence, it didn't register with Kovalic. He didn't have a horse in this race. It didn't matter if the Aleph Theory or the tablet were real. The only thing that mattered was perception, like the general had said. If *anybody* thought the Aleph Tablet was real, then Kovalic and the team had to treat it like it was, just to be on the safe side – and the fact that the tablet *had* been stolen certainly supported the theory that someone out there put stock in its value.

The sudden silence in the conversation brought him back to the present, and he looked up to see Adelaide Sayers pause on the threshold of the room.

Kovalic got to his feet. "Hungry?"

"Uh, sure," she said, her eyes going to the crowded table.

"Pull up a chair," said Brody, sliding his own to one side.

Kovalic pulled the tray out of the oven, smiling to himself while his back was turned. Brody's value wasn't limited to the cockpit.

"It's fine," Sayers was saying. "I can just take it back to my bunk."

"Nah, plenty of room."

With the look of someone who expected a trap to be sprung at any moment, Sayers took a seat. Kovalic put a bowl in front of her, along with a fork. "Hope you like eggplant."

Sayers poked at it dubiously. "I'm not sure I've ever had it before."

"Fry it up with enough cheese and tomato sauce and it's pretty passable," said Tapper.

"Thanks," said Kovalic. "Don't think I won't remember that next time it's your turn to cook."

Spearing a piece, Sayers gave it a tentative bite and seemed to come to the conclusion that it wasn't poisonous.

"So," said Brody, leaning back in his chair. "We're having a very important discussion on Aleph Theory. Care to weigh in?"

Sayers blinked, cornered, and Kovalic could see the panic in her eyes. "Uh…"

"Commander Taylor and I are of the opinion that millions or maybe billions of years ago super-intelligent aliens built wormholes between systems in which they'd terraformed planets to support human life, paving the way for humanity's expansion into the stars," Brody waved a hand, as if painting a picture. "Major Kovalic and Sergeant Tapper are, on the other hand, unenlightened heathens."

Sayers's eyes darted back and forth, going from the pilot to her superior officers, her jaw slowly working as she chewed. Finally she swallowed, took a deep drink of water, and looked at Brody. "That is the stupidest thing I've ever heard in my life."

Tapper barked a laugh. "She's got your number, kid."

Brody laughed too, not seeming particularly hurt by the pronouncement. Kovalic envied the younger man's ability to let things roll off his back; Brody had been through a lot and he'd clearly learned to not sweat the small stuff. But despite that, Kovalic couldn't shake the feeling that something was eating at the kid.

Sayers seemed surprised by the reactions, but a smile – a genuine one – tugged at the corner of her mouth, and the tension with which she'd held herself since the first moment Kovalic had met her, relaxed, if only slightly. He felt his own stress ebbing along with it.

"Well, the good news is that we finally have a tie-breaker," said Tapper. "All these two-to-two votes have really put a crimp in things."

"How long have you been a unit?" said Sayers.

"The major and I go back a ways... longer than is worth mentioning," said Tapper, helping himself to a second piece. "But the commander and Brody here have only been with us about three months. Officially."

"Three months?" Sayers echoed, wide eyed.

"Seems like longer most days," said Brody. "Especially when you have to put up with Tapper's snoring." He was saved from a retort by the sergeant's mouth being full. "What about you? How long have you been in the service?"

And just like that, it was as if a blast door had slid closed over Sayers. Her expression was once again wary, careful to not give anything away. "A few years."

If Brody sensed the change, he didn't show it. "What'd you do before that?"

"This and that."

"A woman of mystery! Where'd you grow up?"

Sayers's eyes narrowed. "Why do you care?"

Even a frontal assault wasn't enough to ding Brody's enthusiasm. "We've got a real hodgepodge here. I grew up on Caledonia, during the Illyrican occupation... the commander here's from Centauri." He lowered his voice to almost conspiratorial levels. "Sergeant Tapper's from *the moon*. We think that's why he's so cranky all the time."

Kovalic methodically sliced up his dinner, eating each piece slowly and thoroughly. Sayers didn't have to open up to them if she didn't want to, but she'd need to if the team was ever going to gel. Their missions might be secret, but they shouldn't be keeping secrets from each other.

There was a twinge in his stomach at that: it was an ideal that even he wasn't living up to right now, keeping what happened with Page from the rest of the team. But that was different. That was for the good of everybody, not just himself.

Brody's persistence finally dragged an answer out of Sayers. "I grew up on Nova."

"Commonwealth born and bred, eh? No surprise you joined up."

Sayers's lips thinned into a line and, abruptly, she stood. "I'll be in my bunk." She started to collect her food.

With a sigh, Kovalic waved her to sit back down; she didn't look thrilled by the prospect. The chitchat hadn't paid off, but they still had work to do. "Sorry, specialist. Afraid we'll need you here a little bit longer." He cast a glance around the table. "We'll be at Jericho in a few hours, and we need to have our next move ready. What have we got?"

Nat tugged at her ponytail. "Not much, frankly. Whoever paid our thieves made a point of being discreet about it."

"And we've ruled out the crims?" said Tapper. "We know they want the blasted thing."

"Those mercs could have been cutouts, sure," said Kovalic. Every intelligence agency used third-party go-betweens for deniability. "But Eyes has the resources to grab it themselves, and I feel like they wouldn't be shy about letting us know."

"So, who does that leave?" said Brody, picking at his teeth.

"Other governments," said Nat.

"Big corporations," added Kovalic.

"Anybody with money," said Tapper.

"Well, we're going to Jericho Station," Brody pointed out. "That place is huge. Don't you guys know people in low places?"

The kid had a point. His instincts were improving. Do anything long enough, and Kovalic supposed that you had to get better at it. He glanced at Nat. "Itzkovitz?"

She shook her head. "He left Jericho six months back; retired to someplace in Hanif space."

"What about Warsame?" said Tapper. "She helped us out on that Centauri gig a few years back."

"Dead, I heard," said Kovalic. "Got caught in a tight spot between rival gangs." He scratched his head. "There was that woman... Harjo?"

"No," said Nat and Tapper simultaneously, then exchanged a surprised look.

"Uh, had a bad experience," said Tapper, staring pointedly at the ceiling.

"Yeah," said Nat slowly, eyeing the sergeant. "Me too."

Kovalic drummed his fingers on the table. "This doesn't leave us with a lot of options. The timetable's pretty tight; we don't have time to develop another asset." Much as he preferred the surgeon's scalpel to the sledgehammer, this was starting to look like some drywall that needed to come down.

"I might be able to help."

It was as if everybody had drawn a breath at the same moment. Sayers had spoken, but she was still staring down at her food, her entire body language conveying nothing but an intense desire to be left alone.

Kovalic suppressed a sigh of relief. The direct approach with Sayers seemed to be hit or miss – he'd been hoping she'd offer something of her own volition instead of him having to pry it out of her. Her background, checkered as it was, was one of the main reasons he'd recruited her for this job in the first place.

He nodded in her direction. "Go ahead."

Looking up from her bowl, she focused on him, ignoring the rest of the team. "There's an old friend of mine – well, friend might be putting it strongly. We used to run together when we were kids in Salaam. She's kind of plugged into this whole scene. If anybody knows who stole this artifact, it's her. And, last I heard, she was on Jericho."

Kovalic nodded to Nat. Last mission or not, she was still the team's XO.

She glared daggers at him in return, but summoned her equanimity. "Thank you, specialist. That sounds promising. Give me her name and I... we can check up on her. If the boys wouldn't mind cleaning up dinner," she said, turning a too-sweet smile towards Kovalic.

"Cooking *and* cleaning?" he said. "Hardly fair."

Tapper rolled his eyes. "I think I know a thinly veiled order when I hear one. Come on, kid." He nudged Brody, rose from his seat, and started collecting plates.

Reluctantly, Sayers followed Nat over to the relay terminal. Kovalic imagined that Tseng-Tao's Divide probably didn't have the most up-to-date databases around, but hopefully they were at least fairly recent. He leaned back and took a rare moment of having absolutely nothing to do.

As Brody and Tapper loaded the dishes into the washing unit, Kovalic put his feet up and checked the newsfeeds on his sleeve.

Things really had been quiet since their mission to Bayern three months ago. The Crown Prince Hadrian had taken a step back from his belligerent posturing, withdrawing from the spotlight almost entirely. His brother Matthias – widely regarded as competent, if unambitious – had apparently taken over much of the day-to-day politicking as his father's representative, while their sister Isabella had only redoubled her programs providing aid to the less fortunate communities on Illyrican worlds.

Meanwhile, the emperor's ill health was still a matter of rumors and whispers. Nothing new there – even Erich von Denffer, the former leader of Hadrian's honor guard, whom the Commonwealth had debriefed extensively after his role in the Bayern incident, couldn't shed much light on Alaric's current condition. All in all, business as usual.

Kovalic flipped over to his messages, skimming through the latest dump from the relay on Tseng-Tao's Divide. Nothing of import in his main inbox, so he tapped in the code to access his secure dead drop, trying to ignore the anticipatory tightness in his chest. He checked the headers for a specific code string, but there was nothing. Still. Swiping it off his sleeve, he took a deep breath.

"Ah *ha*," said Nat, sitting back from the terminal with a satisfied air. "Got her. Henrietta Schenk. Looks like she's still on Jericho."

Sayers, leaning over Nat's shoulder, shook her head. "Hard to believe. Never really saw her as a stationsider."

"Jericho's hardly a station," snorted Tapper. "Especially with all that jiggery-pokery they do to make you believe you're actually on a planet. Fake skies, sunrise and sunset, even *weather*. On a space station!" He shook his head and grumbled something about not putting up with those kinds of shenanigans when he was younger.

Kovalic joined them at the terminal. "She's on our watchlist?"

"Our good friends at the Commonwealth Intelligence

Directorate have apparently been keeping tabs on her as a known associate of... well, about three-quarters of the criminal elements on the station, apparently."

"Useful person to know," said Kovalic, raising his eyebrows at Sayers.

"Schenk always did have a way of making friends wherever she went," said Sayers, arms crossed. "Or, at the least, she always knew the right friends to make."

Kovalic glanced at Nat. "What do you think?"

"It's the best lead we've got."

"It's the only lead we've got."

"Can't argue with that. All right, specialist, you got yourself a show. Make contact with your friend Schenk, but keep your cards close. Let's see what she knows."

Something flitted through the woman's eyes, some look of regret and maybe even a tinge of nervousness, but she nodded anyway. "Yes, sir." And then she was up and gone, practically leaving a dust cloud in her wake.

"You sure about this?" murmured Nat. "Can we trust her, after what happened back there?"

"If this is going to work, we're going to have to start to sooner or later." And, he didn't add, if it didn't work, they were hardly any worse off than they'd been before. "Here's hoping I'm a hell of a judge of people."

CHAPTER 7

The last time Addy had been on a space station was during infantry training. Since the artificial gravity generators could simulate different g-forces, stations were ideal for prepping soldiers for environments with lower or heavier gravity. That base had been spartan and very military, all uniform gray corridors and harsh fluorescent lighting, bereft of decoration or any personality.

It had been nothing like this.

Jericho Station, a massive floating cylinder that was home to fifteen thousand people and a roughly equivalent transient population, was not only the biggest self-sufficient human-built habitat, but also occupied the single most strategically important location in the known galaxy.

The Jericho system – or the bottleneck, as it had been dubbed – had no habitable planets of its own, but it was the only bridge between the dominion of the Illyrican Empire and the independent systems of the Commonwealth. Its administration maintained a staunch neutrality in the conflict between the two superpowers, making it fertile ground for commerce, espionage, and even tourism.

A gondola drifted by on its repulsor field, propelled by an oarsman in a striped shirt and straw hat. The hat made

Addy snort: despite the golden colors of the late afternoon overhead, the artificial sunlight in here would give you less of a tan than the background radiation.

Out of curiosity, Addy knelt on the stone pavement – plasticrete made to look like stone, her brain concluded as she touched the pitted but warm surface – and dipped her fingers in the water of the canal.

The surface shimmered as she touched it, dissipating without a ripple. A hologram, naturally. Nobody was going to be piping valuable water through a space station for decoration.

She shook her head and stood, brushing her hands on her pants out of muscle memory.

"You're not here to sightsee, Trapshot," said Commander Taylor in her ear. Addy's jaw muscles tightened. God forbid she take five seconds out of this precious mission. "Any sign of your contact?"

Addy scanned the piazza again. It was all fake, from the red tiled roofs to the cobblestones on the ground. So much money spent aping a place light years away that most of the people here had probably never seen. Bizarre and self-indulgent, to her mind. Give her the honesty of that military station any day of the week.

"Negative, Sparrowhawk." At least the rest of them had codenames just as ridiculous as the one she'd been handed.

People sat at metal tables around the square, drinking coffee out of tiny cups and eating overpriced – and not terribly good – pasta and red sauce.

Tourist digs, tourist food. Some things were universal. At least the gelato didn't look half bad.

Addy set out on another perimeter walk, strolling like

she was merely taking in the sights, but keeping her eyes on the plaza's half dozen entrances. The message she'd sent Schenk had said to meet at half past noon; the woman was late. Not that Schenk had ever been the most punctual. But Addy hadn't even gotten a reply, so there was the chance that Schenk hadn't received the message. Or simply wasn't coming. Maybe Addy had misjudged whatever connection she had thought they'd had, or maybe, just maybe, Schenk didn't give a shit about her.

Her lips tightened. Just another failure for Taylor to lay on her shoulders. This didn't pan out, the team would be scrambling for another lead. And Addy would be out on her ass again.

Pressure constricted her chest, and she saw the colors in her vision go too sharp, clashing wildly. She fought down the rising tide of panic that pounded in her ears.

Had it not been for that, she was sure she would have heard the footsteps behind her, caught movement out of her peripheral vision, maybe even picked up the distinctive scent of sweat mixed with grease. But the panic washed away everything, so that when the voice came, her heart pole-vaulted into her throat.

"Didn't expect to hear from you ever again – much less see you in the flesh."

Only the barest vestige of self-control kept Addy from whirling and planting a fist in the woman's stomach. She imagined herself in a cold shower, rivulets icing their way down her body, dripping from her hair, quenching the hot wave of anxiety. It didn't entirely eliminate the panic, but she regained enough poise to turn and face the woman with at least a veneer of calm.

"Schenk."

Henrietta Schenk was a beefy woman, arms as thick as oxygen canisters and a large muscular torso to match. Doughy cheeks flanked a nose that had been broken one too many times beneath iridescent blue eyes. A pink mohawk bristled from her pasty scalp, and her navy blue jumpsuit was zipped open to the waist, revealing a grimy once-white tank top.

"What are you doing here, Addy?" Nothing about Schenk's expression was warm. "Think we said everything needed saying way back when."

All that and more. Addy's heartbeat had ratcheted back down to a merely fast pace, no longer thumping against her chest. "This isn't about the past, Schenk. New business."

One eyebrow, pink to match the mohawk, went up. "Business? Last I heard, you were out of the life."

Addy had been vague with Schenk, but if her old partner wanted to think she was still running cons and thieving, well, that was just fine by Addy. "Looks like the life wasn't done with me."

"Funny. You never had much of a taste for it. I seem to recall you calling me a shit-eating bottom-feeder. Which was both insulting *and* redundant."

"Mistakes were made."

That earned a snort from Schenk. "Aren't they always."

"Look, I know you're pissed at me. Fine. But this is for real. You want to talk business or you want to rehash ancient history?"

"Oh, I can do both, honey."

Addy's fingers curled into fists but she kept them at her side, all too conscious that Taylor and the team were listening in. "Fine. Maybe we can go somewhere a little more private?"

Schenk looked around and huffed a laugh. "Yeah, only the tourists spend any time in Venezia. Anyway, I've got a little time before my shift starts. We can go somewhere with fewer eyes. Come on."

"Not too far," said Taylor's voice in her ear. "Don't blow your backup."

Addy's instincts told her that Schenk wouldn't looking for a tail, but the specialist realized she was still a little spun up from earlier. Heeding Taylor's advice was probably a good idea, much as it rankled.

Schenk led her down one of the passages, away from the piazza. They passed a few vacant storefronts, dusty glass framing what used to be a pastry shop and a restaurant.

The architecture grew more practical as they went, shifting into modern plastiglass and steel, but still the fake sky lingered overhead, complete with the occasional sounds of chirping birds. A cool wind ruffled Addy's short hair and for a split second she wondered if it was going to rain.

"Gets you, don't it?" said Schenk. "Even after five years, I sometimes forget we're hanging in the middle of empty space."

"What planet isn't?"

"Fair point."

Addy followed Schenk around a bend and up to what looked like a white wood trellis, ivy spidering outwards towards neighboring wall panels. Glancing around, Schenk reached down and triggered a catch; the panel swung open, revealing a dark space beyond.

Warning bells rang and Addy tensed. None too subtly either, as she caught an amused look on the other woman's face.

"Relax. Just looking for someplace quiet."

It wasn't the most reassuring explanation. *Hope the team's getting this.*

"What is this, some sort of secret hideout? A door hidden behind a bunch of plants? A little cliché, even for you, Schenk."

Schenk gave her a sour look. "You want to talk? Step into my office."

Addy considered her options: take a risk on an old friend or turn around and admit that she'd failed.

No choice at all.

The panel swung closed behind them, plunging the room beyond into total darkness. But at a click, it flooded with blue fluorescent light.

The space was small: a junction of maintenance crawlways, with a spaghetti-jumble of conduits and piping. Some radiated heat, others were rimed with frost. Above a ventilation fan whirred, sending downdrafts across Addy's scalp.

Her earbud hiccuped and hissed, and she reached up to tap it under the guise of scratching her ear. No dice. Interference from the conduits must be jamming the signal.

The mohawked woman leaned against a wall and crossed her arms. "So, let's make this fast. My break's only twenty minutes."

Guess the foreplay's over. Schenk had always valued straightforwardness.

"You heard about the auction on Tseng-Tao's Divide a couple days ago?"

Schenk's eyes narrowed. "Maybe."

"Oh come on, Schenk, don't be coy. A brazen robbery in broad daylight? The theft of a priceless artifact? If you haven't, you're losing your touch."

"Yeah, OK, I heard about it. What's it to you?"

"I need to know who was behind it."

Schenk stared at her as if she'd asked for the deed to a small moon, then threw back her head and laughed. The sound reverberated off the metal walls, bouncing all the way up to the fan and then back down, a hideous distortion of itself.

"Sure. Somebody with that kind of muscle and reach, you just want me to point you in their direction? You haven't changed, honey. Always did like punching above your weight."

Addy's teeth ground against each other. *I'll show you punching.* "I know the delivery was set for Jericho. All I need is a name. And I can make it worth your while." Taylor had told her they had a line of operational credit, up to a number with more zeroes than Addy had ever seen in her life. She was pretty sure that whatever Schenk asked for, they could pay.

"Sorry, honey, but you don't have enough money for this." For the first time Addy saw something else beyond the self-assuredness in her old friend's eyes. Something that she couldn't recall ever having seen there before.

Fear.

"Look," said Schenk, "you want my advice–"

"I don't."

"–you walk away from this. Before you get hurt."

"Is that a threat?"

Schenk shook her head. "No, it's a warning. For old time's sake. The Aleph Tablet might be a hoax, but it's a hoax people are willing to kill over. This whole thing is bad news."

"No can do."

"Well," said Schenk, "I'm really sorry to hear that." Her hands fell to her sides.

Addy's alertness had been on a low simmer, but the second Schenk's hands moved, everything spiked, her own hands coming to the ready, hips setting, body dropping into a stance with a lower center of gravity.

Then she hesitated.

She'd been wrong back at the auction, and she'd paid for it. The nagging doubt tugged at her brain: what if she was wrong again? What if she blew another lead?

Schenk hit a valve and steam hissed out of one of the pipes overhead towards Addy's face. She had just enough time to feel the heat blossoming on her skin before she ducked down and out of the way, throwing up her arm to take the brunt of the gas.

There was a barrage of clanks and bangs and by the time Addy got her eyes open, she saw the soles of Schenk's boots disappearing into one of the crawlways.

Shit. Addy dropped to her knees, but one of Schenk's feet lashed out and hit a lever, dropping an emergency pressure hatch that nearly took off Addy's fingers as it slammed shut.

Double shit. Her fingers scrabbled across the hatch, but if there were a release it was on the other side. Maintenance was Schenk's specialty; Addy had seen her rig everything from hydraulic lifts to electrical conduits. This little office made a lot more sense when you considered that it had given

Schenk plenty of escape routes. Damn it, she should have thought about that *before*.

Spinning around, she found the trellis panel they'd entered through and barged through it, almost bowling over the man peering closely at the ivy-covered walls. Addy caught a flash of light brown hair out of the corner of her eye, but she was already looking down the passageway towards the main drag, trying to rotate a three-dimensional model of the space station in her head, suss out which direction Schenk had gone – she could be anywhere by now.

A hand touched Addy's shoulder and she whirled, drawing back for a strike.

"Whoa, whoa, whoa," said Eli Brody, hands raised. "What happened?"

No, no, no. This wasn't happening. Addy knotted her fingers in her hair. Calm. She forced herself to breathe. This was still salvageable. Somehow. "I need a station schematic."

Brody jerked a thumb over his shoulder. "What about your friend?"

"She... she ran."

"Well, shit. We should call in reinforcements." He lifted a hand to his ear.

Addy snaked out a hand and caught his wrist before he could trigger the comm. "No. Not yet. I can fix this. I can find her."

Brody's eyes softened and Addy bit her tongue. She didn't need pity or favors. She just needed a minute to get her bearings so she could figure out how to track Schenk down. "Please."

After a moment, Brody lowered his hand and gave her a nod, his expression turned serious for once. "What's your plan?"

Addy almost heaved an audible sigh of relief. "Thank you."

"Don't thank me yet. We've got less than ten minutes before the commander will want an update. You know this Schenk pretty well – where would she go?"

She *had* known Schenk pretty well. Once upon a time. They'd crewed together on Nova, when Addy was a teenager who was small enough to get into the kind of tight spaces that opened up possibilities: ventilation ducts, cracked windows, maintenance tunnels. Schenk had helped Addy learn how to case likely targets, jimmy her way inside, and find and disable security systems. Generally all while Schenk waited in the comfort of a nicked hovercar a block away. Because she'd always had an escape plan – at least for herself.

"Someplace she feels safe."

"It's a big station. That doesn't really narrow it down."

Not just *safe*, though. Schenk was a woman of creature comforts. She wasn't going to hole up in, say, a sanitation tunnel. No, she'd built a life for herself here, and she wasn't going to throw that away.

Raising her sleeve, Addy tapped a command and a holoscreen flickered to life, displaying the station directory that had automatically been loaded when they arrived on Jericho. At a swipe of her fingers, the display morphed into a three-dimensional model.

On one end of the station's long cylinder was the Imperium's embassy; the Commonwealth's sat on the opposite end. Like the rest of the galaxy, Jericho Station was balanced between the two superpowers, with a lot of innocent people in the middle.

Brody peered over her shoulder. "The maintenance crawlways aren't on there."

"Not looking for them," said Addy. Her eyes scanned through the listing of establishments that she'd pulled up and sorted into categories. There had to be a place on the station; it was far too well populated to not have one–

"Gotcha," she muttered, staring at the glowing blue letters.

"A coffee shop?" Brody said.

"Two levels down, near the arboretum. Nearest lift is around the corner." She dismissed the screen with a snap and turned on her heel, Brody continuing to dog her track.

"Great," he said. "Perfect time for a coffee break."

Addy sighed, part of her wishing she'd just kept going after she'd knocked him over. But he hadn't ratted her out to Taylor or Kovalic, so she supposed he was OK. "Look, Schenk's a creature of habit. As long as I've known her, she never went without her morning cup: beans from Phayao Province, dark roasted. It's only carried by a few places – like this one. If she's a regular, they might know her."

"Uh huh," said Brody, as they reached the lift tube and Addy punched the down arrow. "And the last time you saw her before this was…?"

"Before I joined up. Six years ago."

"And no chance she decided to change her ways between then and now. Make do with the artificial stuff? Maybe kick her caffeine fix altogether?"

A gentle chime sounded and the doors slid open. "Schenk? Not a chance." At least she hoped so. She punched the button for level 1 and the lift car smoothly zipped towards the lower level.

Leaning against the wall of the elevator, Brody drummed his fingers against the handrail. "So," he said. "What's the story with you and this Schenk character?"

Addy grunted. She was confident Kovalic had shared her record with Taylor and probably the sergeant too – but she wasn't sure about Brody. He hadn't treated her with the same standoffishness as the others. Maybe that was just the way he was, or maybe he was just really good at playing dumb.

"We grew up together," she said finally. "Got into a few scrapes."

"Ah. Been there."

Addy raised an eyebrow in his direction, trying to figure out whether Brody really had any idea what he was talking about, but the lift took the opportunity to arrive at their level.

They stepped out onto a bustling promenade, far busier than the old world dereliction of the Venezia district. Crowds milled among the boutiques that lined the walkway, awash with the wafting smells of cooking meat and spices. It made Addy's stomach rumble, but she focused in on one particular smell.

Coffee.

It didn't take long to track down the coffee stand: Lao's Bean Roasters had a line out its door. Addy, disoriented, glanced at her sleeve. Station time was half an hour into first rotation, meaning there were a lot of folks getting up and heading to work.

"We don't have time for this," she said, pushing her way into the store and earning dirty looks from the crowd.

"Pardon me," said Brody from her wake. He had a genial smile for all the people she had barged through. "Excuse me. Sorry about this!"

Planting herself in front of the delivery counter, Addy tried to catch the eye of the barista.

"I hope you've got a plan," Brody murmured as he caught up. "Because you just pissed off a *lot* of caffeine-deprived people."

"'Course I have a plan," said Addy, waving at the barista, a young woman with short black hair and a nano-ink dragon tattoo rippling on her arm.

The barista looked non-plussed at Addy flagging her down. "You can order over there." She jerked a thumb at the counter and the long line snaking from it.

"I'm looking for a friend of mine who comes in here. A few inches taller than me, big pink mohawk?"

The barista blinked. "What?"

Addy tried not to let her exasperation show through, an attempt with which she was not wholly successful. "Pink mohawk. Muscular. Works in maintenance."

"You station security or something?"

Before Addy could open her mouth, she felt Brody step forward beside her. "Someone's been going around clogging all the toilets in the public washrooms on Level 3. We thought she might be able to help us track them down before they cause more mischief."

Light filled the barista's eyes. "I knew it. Assholes. Every time I want to use one, it's always out of order. Just last week, I was—"

"It's a nuisance," Brody interrupted with a smile. "Do you happen to know where we could find her? It's really important."

"Oh," said the barista, instinctively smiling back. "Yeah, she comes in here every morning. I think I heard she works over in maintenance bay 7L." She leaned over the counter and pointed. "A couple sectors down that way."

"Thanks," said Brody. "You're a life saver." He made to take Addy's elbow, apparently thought better of it, and then just gestured back to the promenade. The crowd shot them more dirty looks on the way out.

"I could have handled it," said Addy, when they'd emerged from the throng.

"I know. But the point of a team is that you don't always have to."

Addy swallowed her objection and they walked in silence for a moment, passing by eating establishments from every old Earth country that Addy knew and a few that she didn't. There was even a place selling traditional Novan saucers: flat cakes studded with fruit. She'd stolen one once, as a kid. Hell, that's how she had met Schenk for the first time – the older girl had seen Addy nick it and tripped the shopkeeper chasing after her, letting them both make their escape.

Funny thing: she didn't even like saucers that much. She'd just been that hungry.

"Thanks," she said finally.

"For what?"

"For having my back. How'd you know that would work?"

"You could say I've had some experience on the other side of that equation. Nothing gets people angry faster than broken toilets. Trust me."

Not for the first time Addy found herself wondering exactly who the hell she'd fallen in with.

Maintenance Bay 7L proved to be in Jericho's docking ring. The hatch slid aside at their approach, opening onto a cavernous space. Engineers and techs in jumpsuits similar to the one Schenk had been wearing were clumped around panels and conduits, some conferring while others were buried elbows deep in wiring.

Near the hatch, one middle-aged guy with a black shoulder-length mane caught sight of them and frowned, pushing away from the panel he'd been working on. "Can I help you?"

Careful, or they'll close ranks tighter than armor plating. "Yeah, I'm from a bar up on 2. Our pay terminal's on the fritz, and my boss sent me down here to talk to someone named…" She furrowed her brow as though she were trying to remember a name. "Schott? Shank?"

The guy grinned. "Schenk. Yeah, that's one of her specialties." He scratched his chin. "She stepped out, but she should back any minute, if you don't mind waiting."

Addy tried on the smile she'd seen Brody use, hoping it didn't look too frightening. "We don't mind that at all."

They'd no sooner taken up a spot leaning next to the hatchway when the comm in Addy's ear crackled to life.

"Trapshot, what's your twenty?" Taylor's voice had taken on a sharp tone. Well, sharp*er*. Addy opened her mouth to respond but Brody beat her to it.

"Sparrowhawk, this is Tailwind. I've got eyes on Trapshot. She's reeling it in. Give us a beat."

There was a hesitation before Taylor's voice came back, and when it did, the irritation had turned to grudging acknowledgment. "Copy that, Tailwind. Give me a sitrep in fifteen."

"You got it. Out." Brody gave her a look. "That's as much time as I can buy us."

Something in Addy rebelled at the idea of owing anybody a favor, even if it was one of her new teammates, but she managed to tamp that down. "Thanks. The good news is it's all we'll need," said Addy, straightening up as the hatch groaned open.

A pink-mohawked figure strolled in, whistling a jaunty tune to herself, and Addy's mouth curved up. *Gotcha.* She slid off the wall, closing the distance as quickly as she could without drawing attention to herself.

"Hey, Schenk!" called the man they'd spoke to. "Got some business for you." He waved in their direction.

Schenk frowned and turned to face them, realizing her mistake even as she did so.

Addy dropped an arm around the woman's shoulder. Schenk stiffened, but caught sight of Brody, whose right hand was resting meaningfully in his jacket pocket. Addy stifled a laugh; Taylor hadn't let them go out armed – some policy of Kovalic's, apparently.

Then again, Schenk didn't know that.

Addy couldn't quite banish the smirk from her lips as she watched Schenk's face fall. "I don't think we were done with our conversation, *honey.*"

CHAPTER 8

It didn't take long for Sayers to get the information they were looking for out of Schenk. Eli leaned against the wall, watching, and reminded himself not to get on his new teammate's bad side. *If anything, she's enjoying this a bit too much.*

"Ofeibia Xi?" said Eli as they walked away, leaving Schenk glaring daggers after them. "Who the hell is that?"

Sayers gave him a sideways look. "Really? You live in a cave or something?"

Five years on a planet disconnected from the rest of the galaxy, but I won't split hairs. "Let's just say I'm not tapped into the whole 'criminal underworld' thing."

"She runs the White Star Syndicate."

"Ah."

She eyed him. "You don't know what that is either, do you?"

"That's a hard nope."

"Christ."

"Hey, do you know how to use a flier to stop a maniac from crashing himself and his extremely important passenger into the ground? We've all got our areas of expertise."

Nothing but a blank stare. *I probably shouldn't be talking about that, anyway.* "So, what's the White Star Syndicate?"

Sayers hung a left down the hallway, heading back in the direction of the lingering aroma of coffee. "One of the most powerful criminal organizations in the galaxy. Xi built it up herself, from scratch – which, in those circles, means she managed to take over at least two or three separate gangs on which to build her power base."

"Sounds like a real charmer."

"She's dangerous as hell is what she is," said Sayers, her brow knitting. "I can understand why Schenk was freaking out. If we're going to go after Xi, we're going to need to be extra careful. And cover all our bases."

"I wouldn't worry too much about that," said Eli, punching the button for the lift. "The major, he's a bit of a planner. Commander too, come to think of it. No wonder they make such a…" he trailed off, coughing awkwardly. *Definitely should not be discussing personal business.*

But Sayers's eyes had lit up. "They make a…?"

"Nothing," said Eli hastily. "Just a…a good team."

"Uh huh."

Eli punched the elevator button again. A couple times. He tried to ignore Sayers' eyes boring into his neck. "Anyway, where do we find this Xi?"

A chime announced the lift's arrival, and after the people inside emptied out, he and Sayers had the lift to themselves. He punched the button for the docking level.

"I know she has a ship," said Sayers, leaning against the wall of the lift.

"Head of a criminal syndicate? I should hope at least one."

"A big one, I mean. The *Queen Amina*. A starliner, packed with hotel, casinos, restaurants, the lot. Cruises from system to system, even through the bottleneck. Makes a great front for all her shady business."

"You seem to know a lot about her operation. Ever met her?"

A strand of brown hair fell into Sayers's eyes as she shook her head. "No. But I used to run in… similar circles. When I was younger." Her mouth suddenly snapped shut, her eyes darting away.

I'm not the only one saying too much, I guess. Not wanting to talk about the past was an impulse Eli understood well enough. But he'd also learned that the longer he kept things bottled up inside, the more likely they were to eventually explode.

"Well, at least we know where we're going and who we're up against. I guess that's something."

Sayers pushed herself off the wall, pacing around the lift compartment. "So now what? We sit around and wait?"

"I wouldn't worry about it. The major's not one to waste time."

Kovalic eyed the docking port with studied disinterest as he strolled past, casual as you please. As soon as Sayers and Brody had called in the intel, Nat had checked and found that, yes, Xi's ship, the *Queen Amina*, was indeed in the Jericho system, on the current stop of its galaxy-spanning cruise. A cruise which no doubt enabled Xi to do her *other* business at every port of call along the way. He'd grabbed Tapper to do a quick recon.

The guards on either side of the hatchway weren't obviously armed, but they carried themselves with the poise of training – they wouldn't have any trouble handling angry, entitled passengers on a luxury liner. The white five-pointed stars on their shoulders stood out in stark relief against their all-black uniforms.

"Professionals," said Tapper as they stopped by the window of the duty-free shop next to the gate. Kovalic focused on guards in the window's reflection; they were alert and standing at attention, despite the lack of any supervisory presence.

Then again, when Ofeibia Xi was your boss, it probably didn't take much motivation to be on your best behavior.

Kovalic knew Xi by reputation only, but it was a reputation that preceded her with bold and bloody action. The Phoenix Cartel and the Marfud had been the two biggest casualties of the gang war that had left Xi sitting pretty, controlling a huge chunk of arms deals and smuggling throughout the galaxy. Kovalic had seen the reports from CID and the Commonwealth Security Bureau: Xi made her living selling weapons to terrorist organizations like the Black Watch and Nova First, as well as doing business with governments, including the Hanif Collective, the Imperium, and – Kovalic suspected, though the reports he'd read had carefully not mentioned it – the Commonwealth itself. Politically discriminating she was not.

But apparently she was also, in her copious spare time, quite the collector of rare artifacts, which explained why she'd made a play for the Aleph Tablet. Or maybe she was intrigued as anyone else about whatever secrets it supposedly contained. The weapons of an ancient civilization could no doubt fetch a pretty penny, assuming the stories of the tablet were real *and* she could figure out how to decipher whatever information it contained.

"Huh," said Tapper, peering through the window. "Should we buy a bottle of Saltyre's for Brody? Surprisingly cheap."

"I think he's given up the hard stuff," Kovalic murmured, still studying the guards.

"Maybe I'll buy one for myself then."

Kovalic glanced up at the holographic display shimmering over the gate. The *Queen Amina* departed tonight at 23:25 for its next stop in the Hamza system.

He and his people would have to be on it.

He'd left Nat working on getting them berths onboard, though he was still running the numbers on how to divide his team for maximum usefulness – and maximum staying-out-of-trouble.

"Any idea how much security we're looking at onboard?"

Tapper shook his head. "I bought a round at my favorite dockworkers' bar, but all I found out – aside from the reminder that those bastards can drink – was that Xi doesn't hire outside firms for her muscle. It's all in-house, every guard personally vetted by her security chief, a guy named Cortez. The *Queen Amina* might be registered under a shell company, but I hear it's her pride and joy, so, long story short, I'm going to guess the security presence is heavy."

Great. That probably meant bribery and coercion were out of the question – someone with Xi's resources would make sure her security forces were well paid. Not ideal, certainly, but it could be worse: the heavier the security, the more likely it was to make a target overconfident. And that was an edge that Kovalic could use.

"What does the heavy security presence mean for getting fake IDs?"

"Well, that depends," said Tapper.

"On?"

"Whether you're willing to do business with Divya again."

"She overcharges. By a lot." Comparison shopping for forged papers wasn't really a thing, but Divya's rates were twice as high as what Kovalic had seen elsewhere.

"Yes, but she's also the best damn cobbler on Jericho. If you don't want red flags popping up the second we buy our tickets, we need her."

The SPT's operational slush fund was generous, but five fake IDs from Divya were still going to put a serious dent in it. And that was just the price of admission. They'd have to be a little more frugal for the rest of the job.

Kovalic rubbed his eyes. "Fine. Meet her quote. But not a credit over. What about schematics for the ship?"

Tapper raised his hands. "Don't look at me. That was the commander's department."

"Outfitting?"

"I put out some feelers. Seiji owes us from last time, when we took care of that shakedown artist. If I remember correctly, I think he promised to fit you for your next wedding."

Kovalic stuck his hands in his pockets and started walking again. "Oh good, because that's definitely been top of my mind."

"Things seem to be solid between you and the commander," said Tapper, falling into step with him. "Neither of you has shot the other yet, anyway."

"*That's* your definition of 'solid'?"

"Every relationship needs a strong foundation."

Kovalic steered them away from the docking ring and back onto the main promenade, and made some similar course adjustments to their conversation. "OK, send Seiji over some scans of me and Sayers. A couple of nice outfits each – the more expensive looking, the better. And it'll need to be a rush job." Clothes made the cover: give him the right suit, and he could walk all the way into the Imperial Palace on Illyrica. Probably. He hadn't tried that one yet.

"Got it," said Tapper. "I also got a line on some composite magnetic accelerator pistols. They ought to get past anything but the most stringent security scan."

"You know the drill, sergeant."

"For the life of me, I will never understand your weird hangup about not carrying weapons," Tapper said with a sigh.

"Less chance of us getting into trouble."

"Funny, we always seem to end up there anyway."

Kovalic crossed his arms, leaning back against the bulkhead. The rest of the crew was sitting around the table where only a day ago he'd been dishing out dinner. Now, it was strewn with equipment: tablets, sleeves, and half a dozen weapons that Tapper had divested from his person.

"Our intel on this op is limited," said Kovalic. "We do know that Xi is a collector and maintains an extensive private gallery aboard the *Queen Amina,* which we believe to be adjacent to her quarters. That's the primary target. The minute we step onboard, we're on the job. Got it?"

His gaze took in each of his team members: Tapper and Nat both tipped their heads in acknowledgment without a second thought, while Brody seemed to glance over to them to take his cue. Sayers looked least sure, but after a moment, she nodded too.

"Good," said Kovalic. "Your covers." He pulled out a stack of ID cards and dealt them out like a round of poker. Divya's prices had been exorbitant, but the results had been worth it: fully backstopped IDs that would hold up to all but the most detailed scrutiny.

"We'll be traveling in two groups: Commander Taylor, Lieutenant Brody, and Sergeant Tapper are Bravo team. We'll be inserting you as crew members in various departments. The good news is that starliners like the *Queen Amina* employ a lot of short-term sub-contract labor and Jericho is a common place for crew to leave or embark. The better news is that their on-station sub-contractor is much easier to hack than their shipboard databases. Your false identities have been positioned as qualified specialists in their respective fields who've already been vetted and hired on for the next couple legs – though once we're onboard, Commander Taylor will tweak the *Amina*'s database to make you don't have to show up for any actual shifts. Specialist Sayers and I, meanwhile, are Alpha team; we'll be posing as passengers, operating out of a suite in the executive staterooms."

"Aw, man," said Brody.

"Privileges of rank, lieutenant," Tapper said, patting Brody on the shoulder.

Kovalic ignored them. "Alpha's assignment will be to make ourselves known amongst the more prominent clientele of the *Queen Amina*: gambling, drinking, and generally having a grand old time. We'll be gathering intel about Xi and her collection, looking for an opportunity.

"Commander Taylor's team will operate as our eyes and ears, gathering intelligence from among the crew and working on specific tasks: Nat, we'll need a tap into the *Queen Amina's* main computer network for security and surveillance; your cover as a technician should make that easy. Tapper will be serving as our logistics and support specialist – if there's any equipment or other resources we need to scrounge up, that's him."

Brody glanced between the two. "What about me?"

"Transport," said Kovalic. "There's a good chance we're going to need a way off the ship under our own power. Navigational mechanics should provide the excuse for you to get where you need to go."

"So we're just leaving the *Cav* on Jericho, then?" His hands smoothed over the tabletop.

The commander shook her head. "It doesn't fit the profile of any of our covers," she said. "We'll have to leave it docked on the station, come back for it after the job. So if you need anything off it, pack it with you. Within reason," she said, catching the gleam in Tapper's eye.

The sergeant threw his hands in the air. "You ask one question about ordnance…"

Kovalic pressed two fingers to the spot between his eyes, right about where it felt like someone was slowly tapping a chisel in. "Contact between the two teams will be limited, so as to avoid anyone connecting us. In the case that one group is blown, the other will still be operational. Questions so far?"

"Yeah," said Sayers, raising her ID card between two fingers. "What the hell is my cover supposed to be exactly? You and I are…?"

Kovalic waved a hand. "We've made it flexible so we can play it by ear. Partner, illicit lover, colleague – there may even be some overlap there." She didn't look too happy about it, but Kovalic had more pressing matters than her happiness with their fake background. "Commander, any luck on schematics for the *Queen Amina*?"

Nat tapped her sleeve and a three-dimensional holo displayed over the table, showing a miniature version of the ship. "The *Queen Amina* is custom-built. Its frame is a modified *Aurochs*-class bulk freighter, but the similarities end pretty quickly. It has almost four thousand guest rooms, almost two dozen full-service restaurants, seven theaters, a shopping mall with fifty boutiques, and, of course, three separate casinos."

Brody whistled. "That's bigger than a lot of towns where I grew up."

"It's also a lot of ground to cover," said Kovalic.

"Not to mention the background population," Nat added. "We're talking several thousand guests; the crew and employees of the third-party vendors are going to double that, at least."

"Target identification's going to be a nightmare," said Tapper. He was leaning back in his chair almost casually, but Kovalic could see his eyes focused on the schematic, taking in all the details.

"The security onboard is no joke, either," said Nat. "It's an adaptive algorithm-based system. Basically, they build a profile of everybody using biometric information like face and gait, then link it to your sleeve. They search for you and can see not only where you are but everywhere you've been."

"That's why maintaining cover is especially important," said Kovalic. "We'll conduct communication primarily by dead drop – Commander Taylor will distribute the protocol. Encrypted comms for emergency only.

"I'm not going to give you a spiel on the importance of this mission – you know the deal. We don't take the small jobs."

"Yeah, kinda makes me miss the old days," Tapper muttered.

Kovalic surveyed his team. "If there are no more questions, I'm going to go check on our wardrobe delivery. The *Queen Amina* leaves in four hours. See you all onboard."

Seiji proved to be as good as his word. A small container arrived at the *Cavalier*'s docking port less than an hour later, delivered by a surly teenager snapping some gum. Kovalic signed for the order and deposited the container in the lounge.

Nat looked up from the tablet she was consulting as he dropped the box to the floor. "You never did know how to pack efficiently."

She smiled at him, and he couldn't help but return it.

"You going to be OK with Brody and Tapper?" he asked. "I know they can be a handful."

"Tapper and I don't always see eye-to-eye, but at the end of the day, nobody's ever accused him of not being able to take orders. Brody… he's been struggling a bit since Bayern. That cocky exterior covers a lot, but the whole thing with Page has been hard on him." She bit her lip. "On all of us."

A tightness enveloped Kovalic's chest. "Nat, I… I did what had to be done. To protect the team."

"That doesn't make it any easier for you, or for the rest of us. I just wish you'd talk to me. Or Tapper. Or *anyone*. You're not alone."

Kovalic couldn't stop the bitter laugh from escaping. Who was there to talk to when keeping it to himself was all that was keeping his team safe? Tell them the whole story and there might be no team left. "You know the job, Nat."

"I do. Better than most. But taking this all on yourself… it's going to eat away at you. And the team takes its cue from its leader. You wanted to know why the cracks are showing, well…" Nat combed her fingers through her dirty blonde hair in a gesture Kovalic knew all too well. "I just… I worry about you, Simon."

Kovalic gave her a crooked smile. "I worry about you too. And I'm going to miss your wise counsel when you're gone. There's nobody I trust more to have my back."

"Not even Tapper?"

"Not even Tapper. Don't tell him I said so. You know how he gets."

Silence hung over the room, and Nat looked around, her expression turning wistful. "I've enjoyed these last three months. I'd forgotten what it's like to be on the ground."

"So maybe… maybe don't go?"

Nat's lips set in a line. "But I've also remembered why I left in the first place. The secrecy and the ulterior motives… they're caustic, Simon. It's hard to do the job – much less be a partner – when you're never sure if you know the truth."

The sentiment twisted in Kovalic's gut with all the sharpness of a knife. He opened his mouth, ready to spill the entire story of Bayern and Page's suspicions about the general, and the decision that Kovalic had made, hard as it had been. He could feel the weight in his chest rising like a ship escaping a gravity well.

Brody picked that moment to wander into the lounge, eating something out of a plastic pouch. He stopped short when he saw the two of them, eyes going from one to the other.

He swallowed whatever he was chewing. Loudly. "Uh. Hi."

Nat stood. "I'd better go prep. See you before mission time."

Brody watched her go, then turned to Kovalic. "I totally just interrupted something, didn't I?"

The kid had a knack for timing. Not all of it good. "It's fine, lieutenant. We've got work to do anyway." He turned back to the container and started picking through the contents, trying to ignore the lingering lump of the words trapped in his throat. Controlling his breathing, he focused on what was right in front of him. The mission. That was all that mattered.

Seiji's work was second to none, even working under a time crunch. Unzipping one garment bag, he ran his fingers along the lapels of the charcoal gray suit within. Synthetic it might be, but without the benefit of a microscope you'd have a hard time telling the difference between a suit printed from an autofab and one made of real silk.

A crunch came from beside him; Brody was leaning over his shoulder. "Oh, great stitching on that. Looks good." He gave him a thumbs up, even as a cloud of unnaturally orange-yellow food dust drifted down onto his own shirt.

"Brody, if you get crumbs on my suit, I swear to god that I will have Tapper give you an 0530 reveille for two weeks. And you know he'll do it, because the man doesn't sleep."

Artificial orange dust around Brody's mouth only served to emphasize how pale he went. "Uh. Right." He took a step back. "Copy that."

Zipping the bag up, Kovalic draped it over the back of one of the chairs, and then continued sorting out the rest of their attire. The pilot apparently had no place to be, because he continued standing there – at a safe distance now – eating his snack.

Kovalic eyed him sideways. "How did Sayers do, in your opinion?"

There was a gulping sound followed by a bout of awkward coughing. "I mean, you saw for yourself. She came through."

Kovalic didn't turn around; he had a feeling his direct scrutiny might only make Brody more recalcitrant. "Yes, she did. I'm not asking 'what' so much as 'how.' Do you have any reservations about the way she handled the assignment? Anything unusual come up?"

"Nope. Everything was peachy. She probably could have done the whole thing blindfolded. I was just along for the ride."

It wasn't that Brody was a *bad* liar; he could be pretty convincing when he put his mind to it. But there were times that Kovalic swore the man had tried to learn fibbing from a book.

Something had happened with Sayers and Schenk – he'd figured out that much, even if he didn't know what. He'd let Nat run the op because it did him good to let go of things. One of the benefits of having her as his second meant he didn't *have* to oversee everything. Which, he had to admit, felt a little bit weird. Especially when it meant he didn't know everything that happened with his team. She'd told him that Sayers and Brody had been out of contact for a little under ten minutes, and her radar was telling her something didn't go quite as planned.

But whatever it was, he knew he wouldn't be able to drag it out of Brody. Say one thing for the kid, he was loyal. And given how tense Brody had been lately, Kovalic doubted that throwing his weight around would do their relationship any favors.

"Fair enough," was all Kovalic said, pulling out two more bags and hanging them over other chairs. "I'm going to pack.

One hour." He slung the bags over his shoulder and tipped Brody a meaningful look, then strode out of the room and towards one of the bunks.

Seiji hadn't just done well; he had outdone himself.

Truth be told, the styling of Kovalic's suit was more ostentatious than he liked. Pinstripes had never been his thing, and the dark blue of the backing material was a trifle too shiny. He'd donned a blue button-down shirt, open at the collar, and, with extreme reluctance, had even tucked a pocket square into the coat's breast pocket.

He straightened the jacket on his shoulders for what felt like the umpteenth time. It wasn't that it didn't fit – if anything it fit *too* well. He was used to cheaper, off the rack stuff that hung and bulged in weird places. But frankly if every suit wore like this one, he might have to make a permanent upgrade to his wardrobe. One that he definitely couldn't afford on his current salary.

Adjusting his cuffs, he turned and found Nat eyeing him like a perfectly-cooked steak. A slight smirk touched her lips, and her blue eyes danced as they met his.

"You're dressed nicer than you were at our wedding."

"That's because our wedding was in the chapel of a battlecruiser and neither of us even had dress uniforms."

Kovalic grinned. For her part, Nat was wearing casual attire more befitting a crew member: plain white shirt, brown loose-fitting jacket. Her hair was pinned up out of the way.

"Damn this damnable monkey suit!" growled Tapper as he stumbled into the *Cavalier*'s lounge, trying to pull on a sock.

Nat exchanged a glance with Kovalic.

"Problem, sergeant?"

"What?" Tapper looked up, mid-hop. "No, no problem, boss. I think Seiji's having one on; blasted socks are too small!"

Kovalic choked back a laugh. Sure, the man could handle a grenade launcher, lay down suppressing fire, or drive a tank, but one pair of dress socks was apparently enough to bring him to his knees.

From the other side of the compartment, Brody and Sayers joined the assembly. Like Nat, Brody was wearing casual clothes designed not to stand out. His face fell slightly as he took in Kovalic's attire. If nothing else, that mission on Bayern had evidently given him a taste for the finer things in life.

Sayers, meanwhile, had undergone a more substantial transformation. The black cocktail dress was light on ornamentation, opting instead for an elegance and simplicity that was timeless. A white shawl covered her bare shoulders, and the black leather flats on her feet were a concession to mobility and practicality. But she kept tugging on the knee-length dress, discomfort written plainly on her face.

Tapper finally conquered his sock, pulling his shoes on and clicking them experimentally together. His suit was somewhere between the chic of Kovalic's clothes and the casual of Brody's get-up, a plain black number with a white shirt that let him easily blend into the background.

"Well," said Kovalic, taking them all in. "Don't we look nice? What do you say we go find ourselves a priceless artifact."

CHAPTER 9

The *Queen Amina* was enormous. Easily the biggest ship that Addy had ever seen, though that wasn't saying much. She'd ridden a transport up to the station during training, and seen Commonwealth destroyers overhead on Nova, but it wasn't like she'd ever been on an Illyrican dreadnought or anything. Still, the starliner might give the famed Imperial warships a run for their money.

As they traveled all around the known galaxy, starliners like the *Queen Amina* had to be largely self-sufficient. The ship played host to thousands of passengers that were going from point A to point B in various levels of luxury – or the lack thereof – but there was also an equally massive number of crew to keep it running and see to the passengers' every need. And then the people who saw to *their* needs. It was less a ship than a city that just happened to move from place to place.

Even docking a ship of that size was a problem. Jericho Station was the largest space station humanity had ever built, but the *Queen Amina* made up a not inconsiderable fraction of the station's size and mass. There was simply no way for it to moor at the station.

Instead, half a dozen of Jericho's docking ports had been given over to tenders that ferried passengers over. Addy and

Kovalic were in the executive class; tickets there were pricey, but not out of the reach of their credit line. It also meant they had a dedicated boarding area on the *Queen Amina* and, as they stepped off the tender, Addy's jaw dropped.

The tender had been luxurious beyond Addy's belief, but the starliner surpassed even her imagination. Constellations of lights, seemingly untethered to any physical objects, floated above her, giving the impression of distant stars. Every surface was polished within an inch of its life, from the brass balustrades that swept up the curved staircases to the gleaming wood of the reception desks. Crushed red velvet rustled underfoot like autumn leaves. Even the air smelled enticing, a mix of sandalwood and vanilla that made Addy think of fresh cookies.

Maybe they actually have *fresh cookies.*

An attractive woman in black livery appeared at her side, silently sweeping her up to the first empty reception desk, manned by a handsome – Christ, was the whole staff this good looking? – man with a dark brown complexion and bright blue eyes.

"Welcome to the *Queen Amina*, madam," he said. "Just place your sleeve near the pad and I'll retrieve your reservation."

Addy placed her wrist over the pad, which immediately glowed green.

The man gave a brilliant smile and his eyes defocused slightly, flicking back and forth as he consulted an ocular display. "Thank you, Ms Bell. We've prepared a stateroom for you on the forward end of level 18, our executive floor. Your sleeve will act as your key, and can authorize lifts and trams as necessary. Likewise, you can charge any expenses to your room and we will settle them at the end of the journey to the account you have specified. You have full access to all our facilities, including the pools, gyms, and lounges, and we've granted you a complimentary ten thousand credits for use in the casino."

It was an effort for Addy to stop her eyes from widening at that. Ten thousand credits? *I haven't seen that much in my whole life, and they're just* giving *them to me?* Her mouth had gone dry, but she nodded in what she hoped was a most elegant manner. The fake IDs Kovalic had acquired for them had clearly passed muster – and then some.

"Of course, the safety and security of our guests is paramount," the clerk continued. "While we pride ourselves on having top notch security, if there are any belongings that you don't feel comfortable having in your quarters, you are of course welcome to store them in our vault, which is available at any time of day.

"Most of our facilities and many of our eating establishments are likewise open at all hours. For departure, we sync our clock with Jericho Station time, but we understand people may be on different schedules. Is there anything I can do for you right now?"

Her mind was awhirl with all this information, but she shook her head and offered up what she hoped was a pleasant smile. "Nothing that I can think of right now, thank you."

"Very good. In that case, you'll find the forward lift tram just to the port side here. Your luggage has been brought onboard and delivered to your room. If you need anything at all, do not hesitate to call upon us, any time of day. Please enjoy your stay."

With a murmured thanks, Addy drifted away from the desk and towards the heavily gilded sliding doors to her left. The display above the door was holographic but designed to mesh with its surroundings, the text in thin rounded letters and an old-school dial showing the slow approaching progress of the tram.

A moment later, she felt the flicker of a presence and looked over to find Kovalic standing beside her.

"Fancy meeting you here," he said. "You get the whole spiel?"

"Yeah. Still kind of taking it in. It's more than a little… overwhelming."

"I hear that," said Kovalic. "It can be tough to look past the trappings, but let's not forget what's beneath the surface. Just like in nature, the prettier things look, often the deadlier they are."

Should I be writing down these pearls of wisdom? Maybe Kovalic could print them on a calendar.

With a gentle chime, a soothing voice announced the arrival of the forward tram, the doors sliding open onto an empty car. They flowed in among the crowd of guests that had amassed, some chatting idly with their fellow passengers, others keeping to themselves, but all of them dressed in the latest fashions.

The tram was somewhat more functional and less ornate than the rest of their surroundings she'd seen so far – Addy supposed the cars must be in use by all the guests, not just the high-paying ones. It whisked them quickly and silently towards the forward end of the ship, its "windows" displaying holographic scenes of some old Earth city at night, all sparkling lights and gleaming towers. Addy rolled her eyes at that – she'd never quite gotten the Earth fetish. Nova's population had exploded after the Illyrican invasion of the homeworlds; it became the capital of the Commonwealth and absorbed an enormous population of Earth ex-planetriates, who had promptly set about trying to recreate humanity's home atop the work of the original colonists who had been building something new. It gave her some sympathy for the Nova First movement that had cropped up in recent years, arguing that the original colonists should have a bigger say in the planet's administration.

The tram stopped a few times on the way to the residential area; several folks got off at the esplanade, in search of a midnight snack or other entertainments, while more departed at one of the casinos, looking to get started on their vacations despite the late hour. The rest, including Addy and Kovalic, were deposited near the lifts for the executive staterooms. From there it was just another short lift ride until they were outside room 1817, which unlocked at a wave of their sleeves.

Even after all the luxury Addy had seen thus far, the stateroom drew an involuntary gasp from her. Her last room, at the School, had been a fraction of this size, and she'd shared it with Song. Also, it had been a *lot* emptier.

Sleek, elegant furnishings populated the room, from the glass coffee table seemingly hovering over the floor – an indulgent use of repulsor fields if ever she'd seen one – to the fully stocked walnut sidebar in the corner. Her feet sank noiselessly into the plush carpet, and she had a sudden urge to kick off her shoes and run her toes through it.

But the most impressive feature was the wall opposite her, which seemed to open onto the vast emptiness of space. Stars blared from far away, and vertigo threatened to take hold as her perspective wobbled; she leaned against the wall for support.

"Wow," Addy breathed.

Kovalic had to nudge her slightly farther into the room, though the indulgent look on his face suggested he'd caught the combination of awe and nausea on hers. He reached over and touched a control on the wall, and the starfield faded back into a solid bulkhead with a more soothing geometric pattern painted on it.

As she straightened up, he strode past her into the room, walking a path around the perimeter, waving his sleeve around as though trying to get a signal.

Addy raised an eyebrow.

"Just ensuring our privacy," said Kovalic. "I'm sure White Star extends their customers every courtesy, but I'm equally sure that the security staff wants to know what's going on in their patch."

Four different doors led off the main room to smaller compartments, and Addy couldn't resist poking her head in each. One held a spacious closet, complete with a clothes presser and various garment bags that could be sent out for cleaning. Another was a small washroom, clearly intended for guests – no shower or bathtub.

The next two led on to separate rooms, each spacious in their own regard, complete with their own large closets and washrooms, the latter of which had compact but very fancy showers with more spray nozzles than Addy could see the use for.

As she stepped back into the common room, Addy noticed that their suitcases had been carefully parked there, making no judgment about which bedroom they would be using, or what the sleeping arrangements would be. She looked over at Kovalic, who was finishing his perambulations. He glanced at the sleeve and seemed satisfied by the result.

"If there's any surveillance gear here, it's too good for me to find," he said. "I'll check the bedrooms next. Did you have a preference?"

Mutely, Addy shook her head. Either would be nicer than any place she'd ever slept. Kovalic started with the one on the port side, leaving Addy to claim the other.

Slowly, Addy unpacked her case, which mainly contained a few more outfits in a similar style to the one she wore. At least they'd all been designed using fabric with some give to it; clearly the tailor had been instructed to keep comfort and freedom in mind. It was nice to know she wouldn't be ripping a seam if she did, at some point, have to punch somebody.

As she hung her clothes in the wardrobe, she marveled at the lack of other equipment that they'd packed. She'd always imagined all these covert operative types loaded up with gadgets and hidden weapons, but if the team had any she'd missed out. That was just fine by Addy: the infantry had trained her on a variety of weapons but what she had taken away from her time at the School was that *she* was the only weapon she could ever really count on.

There was a rap on the doorframe and she looked up to find Kovalic. "Pardon me. Just need to finish the sweep. Settling in all right?"

Addy looked down at the rather paltry amount of clothes she'd just put in the drawer, then back up at Kovalic. "I'm worried there might not be enough space in here."

He laughed and stepped in, starting to circle the perimeter with his sleeve again. "Pack light..."

"...and nothing you can't afford to lose," Addy finished. "Colonel Benton?" The School's commandant seemed to have an aphorism for any and every situation.

"Some things never change," said Kovalic. "Is Musa still there?"

Addy rubbed at her neck, remembering a long list of throws onto exercise mats. "Sergeant Djalair? Yep. Ornery as a pissed off badger."

"So he's mellowed, then?"

Cracking a smile, Addy finished folding the last few clothes, then slid the drawer shut. "Sir, can I ask you something?"

"Shoot."

"Why... why did you recruit *me*? I'm sure Colonel Benton would have given you your pick of the School's candidates."

Kovalic kept scanning. "Who says he didn't?" The sleeve chimed and he consulted its screen. "Looks like we're all clear. I'll get out of your hair." He crossed back to the room's entrance. "Get some sleep, specialist."

"Yes, sir." Addy sat down on the bed.

"And Sayers?"

"Yes?"

"I picked you because you're the right person for this job. The rest of them, well, they may have what it takes on paper, but, if I'm being honest, I don't trust anybody who looks perfect on paper. I prefer my team with a few rough edges. Good night."

"Night," said Addy as the door closed behind him. She fell backwards onto the bed. Some people might have been nervous the night before a big job – pre-mission jitters. Not her. If anything she felt like she might have trouble sleeping from the excitement. Like the night before Christmas, or so she'd heard; most of the places she'd grown up weren't big on holidays.

She was ready to jump in with both feet – this mission was her chance to prove herself. To Kovalic, to Taylor, and most of all, to herself.

CHAPTER 10

To Eli, the lower decks of the *Queen Amina* somehow managed to look both exactly like – and entirely unlike – the dozens of other ships he'd been on in his life. There were the usual corridors studded with conduits and panels; that kind of thing was universal.

But the one big difference was that it wasn't a military ship. Those had been stark, spartan. By contrast, the lower decks of the *Queen Amina* teemed with activity: crew members and a couple of passengers bustling from place to place, waste and maintenance drones trundling past, and even a few small animals – mostly cats and dogs, though Eli swore he heard the squawk of a parrot. Large swaths of the levels below the esplanade had been transformed into informal markets: semi-permanent stalls selling coffee, food, and even trinkets and crafts. They blurred by too fast for Eli to take them all in, especially with the crowds bustling all around him, but he was pretty sure he'd seen one with jewelry made out of spare retaining clips and bolt fasteners.

It's like the bottom of the ocean: a whole different world. Wonder what it's like upstairs?

He trailed after Tapper and Taylor, following them through the many twists and turns, until they came to the first of their berths: a small cabin with two bunks. The commander was in another shared room a couple of doors down.

"And I thought the *Cav* was tight," said Eli, slinging his bag onto the top bunk. Besides the beds, the narrow room had a chair, tiny desk, and a viewpanel that showed some pastoral scene that was probably supposed to be soothing, but just seemed incredibly fake. Eli cycled through the options and eventually landed on a seascape, because at least it felt consistent with being on a ship.

"Ugh, you're going to make me nauseous," said Tapper, who'd dropped into the chair. "Just turn the damn thing off."

"No thanks. I've already lived in a windowless box."

Eli hopped up on the bunk and lay down, hands behind his head. *I guess you could call it cozy.* If you really, really wanted to overstate things.

"So, now what?" he said, with a glance at Tapper.

"Gotta be a bar around here somewhere," the sergeant said.

"Really? That's your veteran move?"

"Look, you want to find out what's really happening on a ship this size? Find the place where people spend their time drinking. No better option. Besides, I could use a beer."

Eli gave him a tired thumbs up that was not particularly enthusiastic.

At a rap on the door, Tapper opened it to admit Taylor.

"At least you two know who you're bunking with," the commander said, leaning against the one patch of exposed bulkhead. "Lady in mine sounds like she might be professionally-ranked for snoring."

"You haven't heard Tapper on a good night."

"What was that, kid?"

"Uhh, nothing."

"All right," said Taylor. "Let's get this show on the road. The *Queen Amina* will be departing the Jericho system in a couple hours, once they finish taking on passengers and supplies. I want a full report on logistics and transport options by the time we hit the Badr sector. I'll be working on getting access to the ship's computer system. Any questions?"

Yeah, way too many.

"Nope," was all he said, though. He'd learned from the last few missions he'd been on that he was expected to figure out these things on his own.

And with that, Taylor disappeared, leaving Eli with little choice but to follow Tapper to the nearest watering hole. It was that or go to sleep, and despite the late hour he wasn't quite ready to turn in just yet. Something about being on the mission had him feeling wired.

The bar, which catered to the ship's crew that called the lower decks home, proved to be a surprisingly nice stall a few junctions away from their room. It was a far sight from the kind of places that Eli had seen on Caledonia growing up: smoky joints with tables and chairs, a wood bar, and lots of music and carousing.

There was still plenty of carousing, to be sure; at this hour, it looked like the place was just starting to fill up as crew members came off shift. They managed to snag the last two empty seats at the bar, and Tapper ordered them both pints of the local, whatever that was.

It arrived in metal cups more appropriate for serving a milkshake, magnetized to a tray borne by a rolling delivery drone – no fancy glasses down here – and proved to be thin and bitter. Eli sipped it anyway, trying his best to blend in with the rest of the clientele.

Tapper, for his part, raised his drink in a salute, then disappeared into the burgeoning crowd, leaving Eli alone with the unappealing beer. *I wasn't even good at mingling when it* wasn't *for a mission.*

Surveying the rest of the bar, he played a little game with himself, seeing if he could figure out what the rest of the patrons' jobs were from their appearances alone. There were a few muscled types who screamed security, and the people with tool pouches hanging off their belts had to be engineers. Beyond that, it got a lot harder.

Picking up his drink, he vacated the seat at the bar and began a kind of aimless meandering around the establishment's fringes. Besides the counter itself, there was a small cordoned off area of tables and chairs, most of which were occupied. Loping through them, he kept on with his game.

Let's see. I think she's wearing chef's whites underneath that jacket. And he's got a hammer in his belt – carpenter? Do you still need a carpenter on a spaceship? I guess maybe there's wood somewhere?

As Eli wandered away from the main bar, a muffled shout caught his attention from around the corner. With a frown, he rounded the corridor junction and stopped short.

A dark-haired man and a woman with a splash of freckles had pressed a slim, androgynous figure with a mop of short, dark hair up against the bulkhead.

"We're being paid well for this job. So you're going to do this for us," the woman said, forearm laid across their neck. "Or else your secret isn't going to *stay* a secret."

The slim figure, for their part, was barred from any response by the forearm against their neck, but their eyes slid suddenly to Eli, followed quickly by the other two.

"What the fuck are you looking at?" growled the woman. "This isn't any of your business."

A firm hand clutched Eli's stomach, and for a moment he wavered. He knew bullies when he saw them, and years of staying out of trouble was telling him to turn around and walk away. But something else was shoving back at that, hard. *You're a goddamned covert operative, not some scared kid.*

"Let them go." It took a second for him to realize that he'd spoken.

The dark-haired man exchanged a glance with his partner, who stepped away from their victim. With a flick of her wrist, the woman produced a blade. "Beat it."

Eli tamped down his quickening pulse. A knife. Sure. Kovalic had been teaching him a little bit of self-defense. He could handle one assailant with a knife, probab–

Another click and the dark-haired man was also holding a blade; he'd taken the woman's place, one hand against the sternum of their victim, whose eyes had widened at the sight of the knives.

Eli's right hand clutched the flimsy metal cup. *Add another to my tally of miscalculations.* "Hey, this doesn't have to go this way. Just let them go and we can all walk away from this."

The freckled woman smiled, but not in a friend-making way. She advanced on him and it took everything Eli had not to back up. *Own your space.* That was step one. Confidence.

"I don't know who the fuck you are," said the woman, "but *you're* the one who should be walking away." The blade glinted in the fluorescent overhead lighting as she closed the distance.

"Look, I have a good friend in ship security," said Eli. "In fact, I was meeting him for drinks just over there. He's got strong feelings on people pulling knives."

"Oh, does he?" said the woman, her voice more amused than worried. "Too bad he isn't here." And with that she drew back the blade.

From behind the woman came a sudden *thump*, followed by a groan of pain as the person against the wall drove a knee into their captor's groin.

As the woman started to whirl, Eli took the opportunity to whip the contents of his cup into her face.

She shouted as the beer soaked her face and shirt, stumbling backwards. Her partner was on the floor, coughing; the person up against the wall started to bolt, but the man on the ground summoned enough wherewithal to grab their ankle and yank them to the ground.

Eli stepped forward to press his advantage on the woman, but his foot hit a puddle of his own beer and skidded, throwing him off balance.

The woman wiped the liquid out of her eyes and growled at him, actually *growled*. She lunged, knife first, and Eli tried to throw his weight backwards, succeeding a little too well as he tumbled to the floor.

With a smile that was overly pleased with his misfortune, the woman drew back her arm to plunge the knife down towards Eli. Ignoring the protest from his tailbone, Eli tried to scoot backwards throwing up an arm in defense.

The stab didn't come and Eli let one eye slide open. The woman was as surprised as he was to find a hand holding her wrist back with seemingly little effort.

"I leave you alone for *two whole minutes*," grumbled Tapper.

He yanked the woman's arm back further, and she yelped and let the knife fall to the deck.

Behind them, the dark-haired man was still getting to his feet, but his former victim gave him another kick, this one a little more hesitant, and he seemed to reconsider.

"So," said Tapper, looking between the two assailants. "Let me nicely suggest that you two find somebody else to pick on or I won't even *bother* calling security and you can enjoy being locked in a maintenance closet until somebody finds you."

With a grunt, the freckled woman gave a recalcitrant nod, and Tapper released her wrist. The dark-haired man slowly crawled to his feet, but remained slightly hunched over, the pain clearly written on his face.

"I won't forget this," seethed the woman, massaging her wrist.

"Jesus, I hope not," said Tapper. "I'd hate to have to do it all over again."

And with that, the woman put the dark-haired man's arm around her neck and the two of them limped away down the corridor. The sergeant gathered up the two knives that had been left behind and disappeared them somewhere about his person.

"Thanks for the assist," said Eli. "But I totally had it under control. Well. Mostly."

"Oh yeah? What was your next move: being a pincushion?"

Eli ignored him and walked over to the intended victim. "You OK?"

Hazel eyes met his, worry not entirely banished from them. "I... I think so? Thank you."

"No problem," said Eli. "You know those two?"

They scratched their head. "Cavanaugh, the woman, she's in the sanitation department; Romero too. They, uh, make a little extra cash by shaking people down."

A criminal element on a ship owned by a criminal. Who'd have thunk it?

"What'd they want with you?"

"Um, I... I won a bunch of scrip at the bar's maintenance trivia. Forgot to buy everyone a round, which I guess made me a target."

Tapper snorted. "Not your fault, kid. Assholes like that are just looking for a reason."

"Right. Thanks again."

"Sure," said Eli. "Eli Bishop, by the way." He put his hand out. "And that grumpy bastard is Trevelyan." He heard a grunt from Tapper, and lowered his voice. "He's all right, though."

"Oh! Yes." A hand clasped Eli's, pumping it enthusiastically. "Cary Maldonado. But everybody calls me 'Mal.' Or at least they used to where I'm from."

Eli's sleeve vibrated, and he glanced down to see Mal's smiling face appear on the smart-fabric display, along with his contact information: Cary Maldonado, ship tech's assistant, they/them.

Ship tech's assistant? I didn't even know ratings went that low.

"So," said Mal, as they walked back towards the bar. Behind them, a cleaning drone had already happened upon the puddle from Eli's beer, and was enthusiastically mopping it up. "You're new here?"

"Yeah," said Eli. "Just signed on at Jericho. Ship tech third class." That's what the cover said, though if anybody looked too close they might notice that he was still in the "unassigned" crew pool, and didn't have any responsibilities.

Just the way I like it. The good news was that with thousands of crewmembers aboard, the chance of being discovered was low – and they aimed to be long gone by the time anyone did. He jerked his thumb at Tapper, who was trailing behind them. "And Trevelyan's in logistics. Where are you assigned?"

"Uh, yeah, I move around a little bit, you know how it is when you're at the bottom of the ladder. Mostly, though I'm in the rear skiff bay."

Well, I guess it's my lucky day. Here Eli had been trying to figure out how he'd get a chance to scope out the transport options on the *Queen Amina*. "Nice. Haven't been back there yet – what have they got, Fischl 380s?"

"390s," said Mal, voice lowered to conspiratorial levels as the hubbub from the bar, still doing plenty of business, washed over them. "I didn't even think they were out yet, but apparently the boss," their eyes went to the ceiling, "made a… deal with the manufacturer."

I bet she did. "How many onboard?"

"Two there, two in the forward bay – is that where you're posted?"

"Yep. The forward bay. That's where I'm assigned." *Sure, why not.*

"You'll be working under Kwasi then," said Mal, nodding to a man with space-black skin at one of the tables. "Tough, but reasonable. Best tech on the ship. Somehow that idiot Vinson beat him out for running maintenance on the big boss's private yacht. That thing is *sweet* – custom from stem to stern. Shame that shmuck's always talking out of his exhaust pipe." Mal stopped short and flushed, looking down at their cup. "Uh. You didn't hear that from me."

"Sure. Good to know." Place this big, there was always scuttlebutt.

"I'm going to grab a drink," said Tapper. "Either of you want anything?"

Mal shook their head. "Been a long night, and I'm on early shift. I should probably head home. But find me tomorrow and I'll buy you both a drink. Thanks again."

"Of course," said Eli. "Stay out of trouble."

With a wave and an uncertain smile, Mal disappeared down the corridor, leaving Eli and Tapper standing alone.

"Nice kid," said Tapper.

"Yeah," said Eli, though he couldn't help but wonder exactly what Mal was mixed up in. That woman doing the shakedown – Cavanaugh? – had said something about a secret. Then again everybody had their secrets, and that probably went double in a place like this. But as long as Mal could get him into the skiff bay, it didn't really make a difference.

"What do you think," said Tapper. "Want a beer?"

Eli made a face at the memory of its taste. "I think I'm going to turn in too. Long day ahead of us."

"Suit yourself." And with that, he was off to the bar, leaving Eli alone with his thoughts. The good news was now he at least had an idea where to start. Oh, and he hadn't gotten stabbed. He could put that in the win column. Here was hoping his luck held out tomorrow.

CHAPTER 11

"Red 23!" called the green-haired croupier to a groan of disappointment from most of the crowd. Sweeping in the chips with their rake, they then removed the ball from the roulette wheel and looked around for any fresh takers.

Kovalic reclaimed his chips, up a few hundred from the amount he'd placed on the table, and slid one across the green felt to the croupier as a tip. They nodded to him in acknowledgement as he left the table.

Shipboard time had it at about eight in the morning and the casino was bustling, even if it wasn't quite full. The *Queen Amina* had pushed off from Jericho sometime in the small hours, after all the passengers and luggage had been loaded, and was now cruising at a modest speed towards the wormhole gate that led from Jericho to the uninhabited Badr sector.

Kovalic had hit the gym, watching the feeds during his workout, but the news was mostly quiet: a new trade deal between Haran and Sabaea had been nailed down, the Commonwealth Executive had downplayed concerns about the Nova First movement, and the Imperium was spotlighting relief efforts after a particularly brutal storm had hit the Centauri city of Yeni Ankara. There was a brief piece about the daring robbery of a black-market auction on a moon in the Juarez system, but the only mention of the Aleph Tablet described it as a "storied artifact with a questionable past." Credulity was in short supply these days, it seemed.

After having donned one of Seiji's more casual suits, he'd left a note for Sayers and headed down to the casino and withdrawn the chips reception had given them.

He idly flipped a chip over his knuckles as he walked towards a table playing rouge et noir. The card game had recently come back into vogue, since its relatively simple rules appealed to players more familiar with electronic and mechanical games of chance. Kovalic pulled up a chair as the dealer began flipping the two rows of cards.

The dealer had finished and announced the result – rouge et couleur gagne. An older couple and a man with long, gray dreadlocks had won; a pale woman pursed her lips in frustration as her chips were taken away. Kovalic nodded to the dealer, and tossed a chip on the inverse bet before the man began dealing out the next set.

Sitting back and idly watching the cards as they came up, Kovalic scanned the room with an eye for the White Star's security personnel. There were a few around the edges wearing the distinctive black uniforms, but the ship had evidently made an effort to keep obvious security to the minimum – it made people nervous. Naturally, each table had a dealer and every half dozen tables or so a floorperson; somewhere there would be a pit boss keeping an eye on everything. In some places the security presence was more overt – he'd passed the entrance to the high-rollers room, cordoned off by a velvet rope and a beefy-looking guard – but Kovalic had no doubt that there were more than a few plainclothes security around as well.

Security personnel were the least of his concerns. Nat's

warning about the surveillance system was still at the forefront of his mind, and he imagined it was even more pervasive in the casino, well hidden to help catch potential cheaters. Pinhole cameras concealed in the ceiling would be beyond even Kovalic's ability to find, but he was fairly certain he'd identified a half dozen decorative sconces that doubled as parabolic microphones. He was sure that thermal imaging and electronic scanning and jamming were in place as well; for all he knew, the drink service drones were packing full sensor suites.

"Rouge perd et inverse!" the dealer announced, and a few more chips were slid over to Kovalic's stake on a low-power repulsor field. He pocketed them and nodded to the dealer, sending a chip back in his direction. Tipping dealers shouldn't affect the outcome of the game, but a happy dealer would be more likely to share if Kovalic needed to dig up some intel later. Might as well spread the love around. He headed for the bar.

"Coffee, please," he said to the tender. "Black."

A steaming cup appeared in front of him, and he waved his sleeve on the payment terminal, adding a generous tip that was almost the cost of the coffee.

He sat, sipping the coffee for a few moments, until he felt a presence appear at his shoulder.

"Bartender, give me a double of what he's having." Sayers took the seat next to him.

"Uh, yes ma'am. I mean, it's coffee…"

"Yes, I got that. Just make it twice as big." Sayers had donned a simple, stylish pantsuit that blended well in the casino.

"She lives."

The younger woman pulled a face. "Space travel always knocks my clock out of sync. There's a reason I never joined the navy."

Kovalic covered a smile with his cup. "Don't let Nat hear you say that."

The bartender set a large mug of coffee in front of Sayers. "The biggest we had, ma'am."

Sayers nodded her thanks and waved her sleeve for payment, then blew on the coffee to cool it down. "So what's on the agenda?"

Kovalic took another sip of his coffee. The bar was far enough from the casino floor that the security wasn't as pervasive, but it paid to be paranoid. He'd packed the anti-eavesdropping baffle, but a random audio dead spot would draw unwanted attention. Just as effective to choose his words carefully. "I'd like to know more about our host's collection."

"Something tells me she's not about to let just anybody wander right into her showroom of priceless artifacts."

"Doesn't seem likely. The key, I would think," he lifted his coffee, "is to not be just anybody."

"Oh? What have you got in mind?"

He jutted his chin at the velvet rope and guard on the other side of the room. "How's your poker face?"

Sayers studied him for a second, then smirked. "I could beat you."

"Big talk."

"We'll have to have a game and see."

He suppressed a smile. Unconfident, she was not. "Maybe later."

"Suit yourself. I can take your money anytime. But I'll settle for theirs right now."

"All well and good, Ms Bell. But don't forget the job comes first."

She didn't look particularly chagrined at the reprimand. "Understood. It's probably going to take some cash to get in there. Any limit?"

"Charge it to the room and we'll figure it out when the dust clears." He didn't look forward to discussing with the general how they'd managed to kill a significant percentage of their slush fund on this mission, but then again, that's what it was there for.

"Got it. See you back at the ranch," said Sayers, downing the rest of her coffee in a gulp.

Kovalic glanced back at the cup he'd been nursing. Infantry wasn't the marines, apparently. Taking a last sip of his own coffee, he hopped off the stool and headed for the lift back to the esplanade.

He took a tram from a bank near the esplanade's mid-section towards the stateroom, drafting a communiqué to Nat along the way. A handful of people disembarked with him on his level, filtering off into side corridors, as he followed the lit placards back towards his stateroom.

A man with a shaved head turned down the opposite end of his hallway at the same time as him; nothing unusual about it, but Kovalic found his alertness kicking in. Something about the way the other man, who was tall and lean, carried himself: balanced, poised.

Military.

And not alone. The back of Kovalic's neck told him that someone else had been dogging his tracks. They were a few meters back, but between them and the man coming down the hallway, he was boxed in. His room was about halfway down and, at his current speed, he might *just* beat them there.

He quickened his pace – not so fast as to be obvious, more like someone who was in need of the facilities. The man opposite him had shifted slightly, almost imperceptibly, to wariness. Kovalic didn't dare risk a look over his shoulder.

As he closed with the other man, he made eye contact and held it a little longer than necessary, giving a smile and a nod of the head, as though recognizing an acquaintance. Kovalic could see the confusion in the other man's eyes at the look; the distraction gave Kovalic enough time to spring towards the other man, slamming him into the wall.

There was a resounding thud as the other man crashed into the bulkhead, which shuddered at the impact, the light panels flickering. Kovalic heard rapid steps behind him and lashed out with a kick, catching the unseen assailant with a glancing blow to a meaty part of the anatomy. He heard an *oof*.

The tall man was coming up off the wall, hands in a defensive guard. Kovalic feinted with his left fist, then brought up his right knee, but the man ignored the punch and blocked the knee with both hands, thrusting it away.

Kovalic stumbled to one side, off balance, and hit the deck hard with the same knee, feeling a dull, deep twinge of pain. Where the hell was ship security when you actually needed them?

A whine rose in pitch as he started to clamber up off the floor, and he had just enough time to glance in its direction and see the second of his assailants – a familiar-looking woman with jet black hair – pointing the business end of a KO-gun in his direction.

The rippling stun field caught him point blank and sent him into oblivion.

CHAPTER 12

The solemn-looking man in White Star livery guarding the velvet rope had clearly been picked for this job because of his impassiveness. Addy walked up and offered what she hoped was a disarming smile – she never could quite seem to master the fake pleasantry thing – and held out her sleeve.

Looking down at it and then back at her, the man didn't so much as twitch an eyebrow. "Can I help you, ma'am?"

Ma'am? How old do I look?

"Yes, you can. I'd like to go in there, please." *When in doubt, be straightforward.*

A curt shake of the head. "I'm sorry, ma'am. These games are by invitation only. May I suggest you try your luck at one of the many tables in the main lounge? Or, if you prefer, one of the several other gaming rooms aboard the *Queen Amina*."

Nothing made something quite so tantalizing as being told you couldn't have it. Addy crossed her arms over her chest. "Fine. How much is it going to cost me?"

"I'm sorry, ma'am, it's not a matter of money. This is an exclusive suite."

So much for our VIP tickets giving us all the access we need. There's always another level. A surge of anger spiked, her fingernails digging into her palms. Just another man playing gatekeeper and telling her what she couldn't have.

Easy, Addy. Calm. She forced herself to take a breath and code her anger as the annoyance of the entitled, letting it leak out through gritted teeth.

"I'd like to speak to your manager, please."

The man's eyebrow went up at that. "Yes ma'am. I'm afraid she'll tell you the same–"

"Let her tell me then."

Turning to one side, he raised his hand and spoke quietly into his sleeve. After a moment, he turned back and nodded his head. "She's on her way."

"Good," said Addy. Or so she hoped. *Or I've just jumped in the deep end.*

Not two minutes later a woman appeared from the door behind the rope. Unlike every other employee Addy had seen, she was dressed in civilian clothes: a sleek black dress that almost reached the floor set off her pale white skin and clung to her frame in ways carefully tailored to maximum flattery. A rich length of buttery blond hair was piled artfully atop her head, and when she smiled it reached her green eyes. She touched the man on the elbow and he stood aside to let her come face to face with Addy.

"Good morning," she said, her voice all spun sugar. "I'm Domina, the general manager. What seems to be the problem?"

Addy had, in the intervening moments, flipped through an extensive list of possible angles. Part of her wished that Kovalic had filled out their legend a little bit more – freedom to improvise was all well and good, but there wasn't much to backstop if anyone started digging. Hopefully it wouldn't come to that.

"Good morning," said Addy, drawing herself up slightly. "I'm here to play," she said, nodding at the door the woman had entered through.

Domina's teeth gleamed. "I'm sure Marcus here has explained that this suite is only for those guests who have been specifically invited. I don't believe you have been issued an invitation, Ms Bell."

Addy kept her gaze locked on the other woman without blinking. "An oversight, I have to assume."

"Oh?"

"I understand that you are invested in keeping the clientele exclusive, but I'll have you understand that I'm no tourist here to gawk." She waved a hand at the tables behind her in a desultory fashion. "These games are fine for the average passenger on your ship, but they are hardly up to my standards."

Domina's gentle smile had shifted gears to patronizing. "Ms Bell, I'm not sure you know quite what you–"

"I would have thought that the White Star Lines would have done its homework. I understand that using an alias might have been an impediment, but I expected better treatment nonetheless. I've played the tables from Sevastapol to the moons of Juarez, and this is the first time I've ever been turned away from a game."

The blonde woman's brow creased, as if by a sliver of doubt, but she held her ground. "I'm afraid our invitations are not based on considerations of other institutions."

"Well, that is your mistake," said Addy. "I can assure you I'll be telling my friends that they avoid the *Queen Amina* and other White Star ventures in the future, lest they be humiliated in such a fashion." She tried to keep the desperation out of her voice. *This could be going better.*

Domina tilted her head to one side in acquiescence, but irritation flickered over her features. "I'm sorry to hear that, Ms Bell. If there's anything else I can do to make your stay more pleas…" She halted in the middle of the sentence, her eyes unfocusing slightly as though hearing something Addy couldn't. She turned to one side, and Addy could hear the murmur of "Are you sure?" After a moment's pause, Domina nodded and said "Very well," then turned and tapped the attendant twice on the elbow.

Without a blink, he unhooked the velvet rope and stood to one side.

"My deepest apologies for the oversight," said Domina, and this time it was her teeth that were gritted. "We would be delighted to accommodate you in our executive lounge, Ms Bell. Right this way."

Trying to keep the surprise from her face, Addy nodded as if she'd expected this end result all along, and followed Domina. The door slid aside at a touch and the woman gestured her into what turned out to be an elaborate lift tube car, filigreed in gleaming chrome fixtures. With the touch of a control, it began to glide upward towards the "top" of the ship.

Domina stood silently by the controls, hands behind her back. Addy got the impression she wasn't used to escorting guests of such insignificant stature on a one-by-one basis – she wondered exactly who had been on the other end of that call. *Who does the general manager report to?*

The lift car slowed to a stop, the door sliding open on an oblong room lined with tables. A bar stood against one wall, resplendent in deep walnut, and staff in black uniforms moved between the tables, delivering drinks and food. The hushed atmosphere of a church hung over the room; nothing above a whisper came from the guests, when they spoke at all. At the other end of the room, twinned staircases curved up to a balcony where two more uniformed personnel flanked a pair of frosted glass doors.

Domina gestured her into the room. "Welcome to our executive lounge, Ms Bell. If you need anything at all, please don't hesitate to ask Raoul, our maître d'." She pointed out a man with carefully combed dark hair threaded with gray, who was bent over a nearby table, listening intently to a woman bedecked with jewelry worth more than all of Addy's possessions combined.

And with that Domina vanished back into the lift, the door sliding closed behind her. Immediately a holoscreen flickered over it, blending seamlessly with the rest of the wall.

Well, I'm here. Now what? She glanced around the room again, and drifted over to the bar. When in doubt, have a drink.

Before she'd even taken a seat, a napkin had been laid on the bar. The woman behind it smiled at her in a fashion that was more genuine than anything in her exchange with Domina.

"Good morning, ma'am. What can I get you? A mimosa? Bloody Mary?"

"Whiskey. Straight up."

If the order went against propriety, the bartender didn't show it. "Coming right up." She pulled a bottle off the shelf, poured two fingers into an elegant rocks glass, and placed it on the napkin.

"Cheers," said Addy, raising the glass and taking a sip. She hadn't specified a brand but whatever the bartender had poured was damn good. A sight better than whatever

Jonesy had stocked back at base. *Mud in your eye, Mathis, Kazuo, the whole lot of you.* Her next slug went down even easier.

"So," she said to the bartender, putting the half-empty glass down. "Between you and me, where's the real action?"

There was just something about the *click-clack* sound of a large pile of chips being slid over felt. Especially when it was in your direction. Money won was even sweeter than money earned, Addy thought as she picked up a plaque and tossed it towards the dealer. The poisonous glares she was getting from the other three players at the table was just the icing on the cake.

If there was one thing that there had been plenty of during her upbringing on the streets of Terra Nova's capital, it was gambling. Dice, cards, even dog racing. Kids would bet on whether or not it was going to rain, what the soup kitchens would be serving for lunch, and whether or not they'd be able to sneak their way into such and such a bar. Nothing was too inconsequential to lay a wager, even with the meager stakes they had at their disposal.

Addy had learned early that as important as it was to learn the game, it was far more important to learn the people you were betting against, so she had set about cataloging all the other kids' tells. Boyland had been a particularly rotten card player. Too honest for his own good. Naive, almost – and that was saying something for a cop in his fifties. But it was kind of endearing really. He was the type of guy who always got stuck with the queen of spades in a game of hearts or always drew to get that elusive straight. Hoping for the best. Addy guessed that was why he'd invested so much time in her.

She shook her head, realizing the dealer had said something to her and saw that the ante had come around to her. Tossing a chip in the pot, she waited as the cards whispered over the felt in her direction.

The cards weren't bad – good enough to bet on. Addy tossed a few chips in, sussing out whether the rest of the players at the table were likely to buy in. The carefully plucked eyebrows of the androgynous figure in the loud plaid suit to her right waggled as they held their cards close to their face. They had nothing. The woman in the low-cut green dress to Addy's right let her cards lie on the table, hands folded on her lap. Quiet confidence. Maybe just a bluff, but likely bolstered by good cards.

"Five hundred," said person in the plaid suit, throwing some chips in the pot, then leaning back in their chair. "So, I hear our illustrious host has added a unique piece to her private collection."

Addy's ears perked up, but she kept her attention on her cards.

The woman in the green dress sniffed as she raised the bet. "Her means of acquiring it were rather… unseemly. Poor Baron Rijal was most put out."

"It was nothing more than a payday for her," scoffed Plaid Suit, meeting the raise. "At least Madam Xi appreciates the history and significance of such a significant artifact."

"If you ask me, it's a lot of fuss over a piece of metal that's probably a fake anyway," said Green Dress, toying with a dangling diamond in one ear. "Aliens. I never."

As the bet went around, it quickly escalated beyond what

Addy's hand would bear. Knowing when to walk away was a good skill to have in the streets and at the table, so Addy dumped her cards and sat back to watch the rest of the hand play out and listen to the gossip. Intelligence gathering, she supposed Kovalic would call it.

Something about watching others made you acutely aware when you yourself were being watched. Eyes were on her from somewhere; probably from several directions, given the omnipresent security on the *Queen Amina*. *Well, good thing the point wasn't to stay under the radar.* To be fair, she'd bulled her way into this room, and that was likely to draw some attention.

So let's see who's interested. She indicated to the dealer to keep her stake on the table and rose, heading back towards her new best friend, Nina the bartender.

Nina had proved to be an excellent resource, pointing Addy in the direction of the table where she'd already cleaned up, and it was clear that she'd found her way into this exclusive locale by being superlative at her job. Another glass of whiskey was already poured and waiting for Addy as she took a seat.

Leaning her back against the bar, Addy let the booze singe a path down her throat as her gaze drifted around the room. There were maybe twenty-five people in all, including staff. Most had their attention focused on the tables, but at least one was clearly more interested in the players.

Seated in a plush banquette against the opposite wall, a man was doing his level best to look like he wasn't watching. A scar ran through one of his eyebrows, and even in his suit the muscled build of a fighter was apparent. Plainclothes security from White Star? One of the players' private bodyguards? Or just a guy with a combat background on vacation? Could be any of the above.

Well, let's see what we can find out. Picking up her drink, Addy walked over and sat down next to the man with the scar. He looked up as she did so and gave her a polite nod, with the barest hint of suspicion.

It took every fiber of Addy's being to not start by punching him in the throat. But Taylor's recriminations over the auction were still fresh in her head.

Not that she couldn't be direct in other ways.

"So," she said, swirling the whiskey in her glass. "Which one's yours?"

The man's brows knit. "Sorry?" His voice was higher pitched than she would have thought, and he didn't seem particularly sure of himself. Brawn, not brains. "I don't know what you mean."

"Oh, come now," said Addy, allowing a smile to flicker on her lips. "You're telling me you're not security for one of them?" She tilted her head towards one group, where a cavalcade of jewelry glinted amongst the immaculate clothes and elaborate coifs. "You and I, we don't really fit in up here, do we?"

The man huffed a brief, but strained laugh. "I hear that. Price of admission's more than I make in a year."

"Now, that's a shame," said Addy, glancing back over to the players, her voice turning warmly conspiratorial. "Which one's the cheapskate, then?"

He seemed to have found his footing, though, and smiled confidently. "Sorry, love, can't tell you that."

Addy's hand tightened around her glass, resisting the temptation to throw the whiskey in his eyes. *You just had to go and ruin it by being a condescending asshole.* Maybe the throat-punching opening wouldn't have been so bad after all. She forced herself to take a deep breath and smiled, though even she could tell it was far too wide.

"Of course," was all she said. "I expect the kind of high-paying clients in some place like this expect discretion."

He was looking more comfortable by the moment, putting his arms back along the top edge of the banquette. "Sure do. They pay for the best, and they get the best."

She barely caught herself from rolling her eyes, even though she was sure he was full of shit. This guy wasn't a freelancer – a real pro would have kept his mouth shut; no, he'd taken her cue and run with it because it was in the opposite direction from the truth.

And if he didn't want her to know the truth, then that was very interesting.

"So," she said, leaning a little closer to him. "What kind of person pays for this kind of top notch security? Wait, let me guess..." She raised one finger to her lips, neatly drawing his attention to them as well. She didn't normally wear lipstick, but it seemed like the kind of detail that her cover identity would use, and, well, she had committed to it. "A rich heiress?"

The man's shoulders rippled in a playful shrug. "Neither confirm nor deny, you know." As he did, Addy's eyes caught sight of the butt of a weapon holstered under his left arm. Her pulse ratcheted up at the threat, but her brain had already automatically catalogued it: a Rakunas 5000 knockout gun. Short range, but high impact. Good way to incapacitate a single target, or give several targets the worst hangover of their lives.

Either he's White Star security, or he figured out a very clever way to get that aboard. She filed that away to report back to Kovalic;

anybody running around the *Queen Amina* armed seemed like bad news.

"You're right. These surroundings are far too nice to talk business," said Addy, resting her chin in her hand. "Especially when we could be talking pleasure." She ignored the sour feeling in her stomach.

If he had been watching her, this was playing right into his hands; he ought to be suspicious that his mark was practically sitting in his lap, but she was guessing he wasn't thinking with his brain anymore. "Perhaps we could go someplace more... private?" With a last smile, she stood, turned on her heel, and walked towards the back of the lounge where the restrooms were, making sure his eyes followed her all the way back over. *Kovalic should have told me the job would have been this easy.*

The bathrooms were as lavish as she had expected. Marble floors, gold fixtures – even the stalls were a deep, rich mahogany that made them look more like changing rooms in some of the high-end department stores where Addy and her crew had used to pinch merchandise. She gave the room a quick scan with her sleeve, using the same package that Kovalic had to check their stateroom, but even a ship as surveilled as the *Queen Amina* seemed to draw the line at spying on people in the bathrooms – especially when it came to the exclusive clientele who frequented this level.

She leaned over the sink and stared at herself in the mirror, the brown eyes looking back at her with accusation. *Feminine wiles, Adelaide? Really? How original.* Well, it was like Colonel Benton had always said: you use whatever weapons you had at your disposal in the field.

The door to the restroom slid open, and the man stepped in, somehow looking both confident and totally unsure of himself. Addy turned, leaning against the sink and gave him what she hoped was a come-hither smile.

It apparently worked, as he closed the distance in what seemed like record time, enveloping her in the acrid mix of his sweat and some cologne that he'd poured on way too thick. Something about the scent was familiar, but before her mind could place it, he was pressing up against her.

Her heartbeat spiked. Cornered. She was cornered. Her vision started to tunnel and she felt her forehead turn clammy. *No. Not now. Keep it together.* Adrenaline flooded her system as everything told her to pummel this guy within an inch of his life. *I did not think this through.*

She forced herself to unclench the tight fist of her left hand, and put it on his chest, spreading her fingers and turning her head to one side as he leaned down to kiss her. Drums pounded in her ears.

"Wait…"

"Huh?"

"I'm not sure I want this."

His brow creased. "Oh?" His tone was playful, but there was an undercurrent of frustration underneath. "What *do* you want?"

She thrust him firmly away. "You're probably not going to like it." In her other hand, she raised the KO-gun she'd snagged from his holster and pulled the trigger.

The stun field splashed out, catching him mid-gape. His eyes rolled back into his head and he went down like a marionette with the strings cut, collapsing into a heap on the marble floor.

Addy's breathing came in ragged gasps, and she clutched the sink with her free hand. *Easy. Easy does it. No threats here. Not anymore.* She toed the man, but he seemed down for the count.

Her assessment of his muscled build had been spot on: he was pretty dense in every sense of the word. With some effort, Addy was able to drag him into a stall and prop him against one wall. Fortunately, the door and the partitions went all the way to the floor, so he wouldn't be spotted unless someone opened the stall.

Patting him down didn't reveal much beyond his sleeve – a generic burner model widely available on Jericho Station and elsewhere – and a connected earpiece.

As she searched him, she got a whiff of the cologne again, and this time, without the distraction of him pressing against her, it registered sharp and vivid in her memory. Mathis had worn the same brand back at the base on Nova: Illyrican cologne. Something about wearing the scent of your enemies to trick them. He'd bought it on the black market, bragging that it had cost a fortune.

Illyrican cologne. The military bearing. Back against the wall. Watching everyone in the room.

Oh. Shit.

Doing her best to jimmy the stall closed from the outside, Addy left the man – Illyrican agent? – within. Yes, she'd blown her cover, but if he'd been watching her there was a good chance he'd already known, or at least suspected, who she was.

Which didn't bode well for the rest of the team.

This wasn't the kind of thing you left for a dead drop. She needed to tell Kovalic and she needed to tell him now.

She weighed the KO-gun in her hands. Holding onto it would be the best play, but her slim pantsuit didn't exactly provide a lot of places to conceal a bulky weapon. Fortunately, she was able to mostly shove it into her clutch bag, which she could tuck under her arm. As long as nobody looked too closely.

Turning to the mirror, she touched up her makeup and mopped her brow. Fortunately, her short hair was already in the "artfully tousled" style, so her encounter hadn't left her too bedraggled. Satisfied, she stepped out of the restroom and back into the lounge.

She returned to the table at which she'd been playing. The man in the loud suit had departed in her absence, leaving only the woman in the green dress, who was playing the dealer with an air of boredom. Signaling to the dealer, Addy indicated she'd like to cash out and an attendant appeared to total up her winnings, minus the requisite gratuity. He presented her with a tablet, complete with her bar charges, and the balance of her chips credited to her room account.

She was about to press her thumbprint to the reader when there was a sudden change in the room's atmosphere, as though everyone in it were suddenly holding their breath.

It wasn't hard to see why: a woman in a floor-length red dress, striking against her dark black skin, was descending from the staircase opposite the lift. A pair of White Star personnel, weapons holstered at their waist, trailed several feet behind her.

As she reached the bottom of the stairs, the floor itself shimmered, rippling outwards. What had a moment before been a drab, camel-colored carpet sparked to life, explosions of color flaring outwards from the woman's dress.

Crossing the floor, the woman moved like liquid silk, nodding her head gracefully to the people she passed, though a smile never crossed her lips. Not even hushed tones heralded her passage; there was total silence. A few people gave respectful bows, but most just lowered their eyes, unwilling to look directly at her.

As the woman drew closer, Addy's breath caught in her throat. Rounded cheekbones flanked an upturned nose beneath eyes so startlingly dark it was hard to tell where the pupil ended and the iris began. Blood red lips stood out against her dark skin, a flash of white teeth appearing between them from time to time. Rubies dangled from her ears, shimmering and glowing in sympathy with the floor's fireworks display.

Addy froze, gawking, the tablet still held in her outstretched hand, until the woman was right in front of her, studying her with those impossibly dark eyes.

"Ah," she said, and her voice had a musical lilt to it, no less warming and rich than the whiskey Addy had drunk at the bar. "Just the woman I have been looking forward to meeting. Welcome aboard the *Queen Amina*, Ms Bell. My name is Ofeibia Xi."

CHAPTER 13

A hovertruck had backed up right over Kovalic's head and then dumped a couple tons of debris on top of it for good measure.

Or at least that's what it felt like. He blinked against the harsh lighting that wavered around him and tried to focus on something, anything, that wasn't moving back and forth.

He rubbed at his eyes to clear them and noticed that his hands were free. More to the point he noticed that he *noticed* his hands were free. Why had he expected them to be otherwise?

With a jolt, the last thing he'd seen came back to him: the two assailants in the hallway, the KO-gun. The ache from his knee flooded back, a deep bruise that was probably going to hurt for the next few days, but he didn't think there was any permanent damage.

As his vision stabilized he realized, with some surprise, that he was in his own stateroom, lolling in one of the armchairs in the main sitting room. It was hard to tell exactly how long he'd been out; he reached for his sleeve, but it was gone.

His eyes went to the end table, where a small black ovoid sat, a single red light pulsing red: his own anti-eavesdropping baffle. Sitting next to it, in a bunched-up pile, was his sleeve.

"I thought we'd want to keep this between us."

The clipped, precise voice brought back another memory: the woman he'd seen in the split-second before he'd been incapacitated. Her hair was shorter, her clothes less tattered and worn than the last time he'd seen her. But if there had been any doubt, the voice dispelled it.

"Mirza?" he groaned, searching around until he found her, sitting in the room's other chair, about ten feet away. The KO-gun was held loose in her hand, but not currently pointed at him.

"Kovalic." She tilted her head, hair falling in a dark curtain on one side of her face. Her clothes could have been taken from Kovalic's own wardrobe: casual trousers, a military-style jacket, plain white shirt. Simple, functional, efficient. A lot like the wearer.

"I take it you're not enjoying a well-deserved vacation. Because if you are, you're doing it wrong." He didn't need to ask why she was here. Commander Ekaterin Mirza of the Imperial Intelligence Service's Special Operations Executive didn't take days off any more than he did.

Mirza didn't laugh. He remembered that about her. "Let's skip the pretense, Kovalic. I know you're here for the tablet. You know I'm here for the tablet."

Kovalic rubbed his brow, trying to work away some of the lingering effects of the stun field. As his faculties returned, he became aware that they were alone in the room. Wherever Mirza's other officer was – posted outside maybe? – she hadn't felt the need to invite him to this meeting.

That was good.

"So what you're saying is what happened on Kameral IV stays on Kameral IV?"

Mirza's lips thinned, her tongue between her teeth. "Our *arrangement* against those marauders was temporary as you well know."

"And here I thought we had a special bond."

Now the KO-gun was pointed at him. "Need I remind you we are enemies?"

"No, I don't think you need to. And yet, I can't help but notice you stunned me instead of shooting me, and I'm not restrained in any way." He waved his hands.

Mirza held the gun on him for a moment longer, then lowered it a fraction. "I did not think it was...necessary."

A chink in the armor. Kovalic would take it. He leaned forward, elbows on his knees. "It wasn't. Thank you for that."

A scowl crossed Mirza's face. "Don't thank me. It's merely professional courtesy."

Kovalic put his hands up. "I understand. And I appreciate it. I'm hoping we can continue to talk this out as professionals."

Silence hung in the air and Kovalic let it sit. If he could play this just right...

"This is an... unusual situation," said Mirza. "I... I feel that I owe you. I would not have survived on Kameral IV without your assistance."

Kovalic inclined his head. "Nor I without yours."

"So consider this an attempt to pay that debt. A warning. I am here on a mission and I will not let anything interfere with that. If you or any member of your team gets in my way, I will not hesitate to do what needs to be done."

"Very generous."

"Don't mistake me for some doddering old fool, Kovalic. I'm not Harry Frayn, looking the other way while you walk all over the Imperium."

Kovalic thought about pointing out that he and Frayn working together had managed to stop the Imperium's crown prince from starting a shooting war, but something told him that Mirza wouldn't be receptive to the idea.

"Understood. How is Harry, by the way?"

Mirza made a *tch* of disgust. "Reassigned out of the field. He is a good officer, but his decision-making on the ground lacked judgment. Plus his soft spot for that traitor Adaj—" Kovalic could see the effort it took for her not to spit after saying his name, "—made it unwise to give him too much autonomy. No, he's better off someplace where an eye can be kept on him."

Which meant IIS headquarters on Illyrica. "I'm sure your director will be delighted to have him so close." A little delicate probing never hurt anybody.

Mirza studied him through half-lidded eyes. "I'm sure."

Oh well.

"So, where does that leave us, commander? I assume you're aware that I'm not going to just abort our mission."

Mirza smiled at that, but it was without mirth. "I didn't think you would. But, as I said, I thought I owed you the courtesy." She rose from the chair, the gun pointed at him once again. "And whatever else his failings, Colonel Frayn did provide a full report on the Bayern incident. So I know all about Commander Taylor, Sergeant Tapper, and your man 'Adler.'"

Not great. At least they hadn't discovered Brody's real identity – the cover job they'd put in place for Bayern seemed to be holding up. He still had a sister on Caledonia, which was under Illyrican control, and the last thing Kovalic wanted was for her to be put into any danger on their account.

"I can see you're well informed," said Kovalic. He scratched his head, something else occurring to him – he blamed the stun field for not thinking of it earlier. "How did you find me, anyway? There are thousands of passengers on this ship; you can't have been surveilling all of them just hoping to find us."

Mirza crossed to the door, keeping the KO-gun trained on him. She smirked. "You're getting sloppy, Kovalic. When we met on Kameral IV you were going by Sam Richardson; on Bayern you were James Austen; and Major Shankar documented his encounter on Caledonia with the mysterious Mr Fielding. It didn't take a genius to find the pattern. I cross-referenced the passenger manifest with early British novelists, and 'William Godwin' was one of only a few possibilities. Once I saw he was traveling with 'Charlotte Bell,' well, that confirmed it."

Kovalic gritted his teeth and cursed himself inwardly. Mirza had him dead to rights. Not reusing work names was the first thing they taught you in covert ops. Using a pattern had been stupid, and too cute by half.

Mirza tapped the door release. "Good to see you, major. I hope we don't have to meet again." And with that, she disappeared into the hallway.

This time, Kovalic kept his eyes open for tails.

Mirza was right about one thing: he'd been sloppy. So worried about the rest of the team – Nat's secondment, Brody's mood, Sayers's temper – that he'd forgotten to pay attention to himself. Focused in the wrong direction, just as he'd been with Page.

Nat had set the dead-drop location across from a noodle shop on one of the *Queen Amina's* lower levels, below the esplanade. Nestled in among machine shops and cargo holds, it was an area frequented by the ship's crew. Not the kind of place where you ought to find a well-dressed gambler.

So Kovalic had ditched Seiji's luxurious suits for one of his own inconspicuous outfits: work trousers, a plain gray shirt, and a gray jacket. He'd have swiped a maintenance jumpsuit if he could have, but there just wasn't time.

Getting down to the maintenance level required a combination of lifts, old school drop tubes, and even a stairway, which let him out in a cramped corridor, lined with conduits and pipes.

The section wasn't off-limits to guests, per se; it was open to passenger and crew alike, though it counted on the former choosing not to venture far from their comfort zones.

He turned right down the corridor, squeezed past a sweeper drone doing its duty, and walked by a variety of stalls, makeshift affairs compared to the carefully designed stores on the main drag above. Everything seemed to be on sale here, from spare mechanical parts to carefully woven cloth spun from leftover insulation. A micro-economy inside a micro-economy.

There were plenty of food stalls down here too, though only a few were more than a cart or stall. Radomski's Ramen occupied a coveted corner spot on a junction; half a dozen people sat on stools, slurping away at bowls of broth piled high with a mix of noodles and pierogi.

He'd made a pit stop on the esplanade to buy a new sleeve – the old one he'd tossed into the recycler as soon as he'd left his stateroom, on the assumption that any communications device left alone with an Eyes operative had obviously been compromised.

The new one was still finishing its setup sequence, but that was fine. All Kovalic needed was the encrypted chip reader. He plugged in the key code he'd committed to memory – no safer place to keep it – and leaned against the wall kitty-corner from the noodle shop, just like anybody else sitting around waiting for someone, reading the news. The sleeve scanned for a narrowband low-power signal among the conduits.

An icon on the screen blinked as he located the signal. The dead-drop chip, hidden in the wall, was the safest way to pass information to the rest of the team. Kovalic typed in his message, the codeword they'd designated for an emergency all-hands meet: EXARCH. Nat would relay that to the rest of the team and slag the chip afterwards, just in case anybody found it and tried to pull ghost data off it.

But there was no telling when Nat might actually check the drop; for security reasons, the chip was restricted to low-power local transmissions, so she wouldn't be alerted that there was a message for her. He'd hang around for a little bit, just in case she happened by.

He took a vacant seat at the counter of the noodle shop and ordered a bowl of the local specialty. A good meal was one of the better ways to banish any lingering effects of a stun field and he could feel his head starting to clear after a few mouthfuls.

So, Mirza was here for the tablet. No surprise there: the general had said the Illyricans would want it. Right now she had a leg up on them: she had identified his team and even where they were staying, while they were in the dark about her. He had to find a way to level the playing field.

An idea was starting to percolate in his head, but it was in the early stages. And it had a lot of moving pieces, which meant a high degree of risk. *'Risk is just opportunity by another name'* is what the general would say, with that trademark twinkle. It would be annoying if he didn't end up being right so often.

Downing the last of the broth directly from the bowl, Kovalic wiped his face with a napkin and swiped his sleeve to pay for the food.

The pad blinked red.

With a frown, he tried again. Same result: charge rejected.

He double-checked his sleeve. There ought to be more than enough credit there to pay for lunch, unless this was the most expensive bowl of noodles ever sold in the galaxy.

Or unless somebody had tampered with it.

Mirza.

It was a nice move; exactly what he should expected after seeing her in action on Kameral IV. Mirza was a pragmatist: she hadn't teamed up with Kovalic to take on that band of marauders because they were terrorizing the moon's small settlement of colonists, but because she knew she'd never be able to survive on her own. No atheists in a foxhole, and no enemies when you're all up against the wall.

Speaking of up against the wall.

Putting on his most ingratiating smile, he caught the eye of the server, a large man who looked like he could moonlight as a professional wrestler. "I guess you better show me to your sink."

An hour later, he stepped out of Radomski's Ramen, rolling down his sleeves. He was a little damp around the edges, but nothing that wouldn't dry.

Nat was leaning against the bulkhead opposite, a self-satisfied smile on her lips. "Learning the value of a credit?"

"I'll have you know washing dishes was my specialty back when I was a private at Salinas."

"I clearly did not take enough advantage of that skill."

"Your loss." He glanced around. "You got the drop, I take it?"

"Yeah, I got it. Then I caught sight of you hard at work, and figured I'd wait around to pick up my man. Anyway, the chip's toast and I brought you a present." She tossed him an earbud. "Encrypted backchannel's up and ready to roll."

"You always pick the best gifts," he said, tapping it to his sleeve to link and activate it. He tucked it into his right ear.

"All right, Updraft, Bruiser," said Nat. "Corsair's on the line."

The comm crackled to life in Kovalic's ear, with the gruff tones of Tapper. "Good to hear from you, boss. We sideways already?"

"When aren't we?"

"I'm still not sure I've seen *any* of your plans go right," came Brody's voice.

"All right, all right," said Kovalic, glancing at his sleeve to check the time. "Rendezvous in an hour at location Charlie and we'll do a full sitrep. Keep a close eye on your six and it's probably best not to go back to your rooms."

Nat's expression had lost any hint of joviality. "That bad?" she murmured.

"Worse."

"Oh. Great."

"Boss?" Brody piped up. "What about Maverick?"

Kovalic rubbed his chin. He'd left Sayers to the high-rollers suite and he didn't have an easy way to find her since he'd ditched his sleeve. "She'll probably go back to the stateroom. Bruiser, go keep an eye on the place – but keep it low profile, huh?"

"At his height, his profile's always pretty low," Brody cracked.

"Shut it, kid," said Tapper. "Bruiser out."

Kovalic tapped his earbud off, ignoring the tightness in his chest. That sort of surveillance job was the kind of thing Page had excelled at, but they had to use the resources at their disposal, and that meant having Tapper try to act inconspicuous.

Nat leaned against the wall. "I don't love the idea of having her out of pocket."

"She can take care of herself."

"That's not exactly what I meant."

No, it wasn't. He knew that. But right now Sayers was on her own, and one way or another, they'd be finding out whether she was up for the job.

CHAPTER 14

At a flick of Xi's fingers, Addy's bag was plucked deftly from her grasp by one of the security officers. Maybe she could have put up a fight, but this wasn't the time or the place.

The security officer removed the KO-gun and checked the charge, then offered it to Xi, who waved it away. "I hope you don't mind, Ms Bell," she said. "I understand that personal safety is important, but we do of course have a strict policy against weapons onboard. For the safety of all our passengers."

Easy come, easy go. She just hoped the stunned Illyrican wouldn't pick this moment to come charging out of the bathroom or there would be even more questions.

"Of course," was all she said.

"Thank you," said Xi, giving her a dazzling smile, and then linking an arm through Addy's. "In that case, as I said, I'm most interested in talking with you. Perhaps I can offer you some light refreshment in my personal suite?" Not waiting for Addy's answer, she steered them both back towards the staircase. Addy couldn't help but notice the looks cast her way – they were pretty evenly split between those who looked envious at the attention and those who looked relieved that it wasn't them.

Not that I'm totally sure how I should be feeling about this myself...

At the top of the stairs, the guards opened the doors onto yet another strata of the *Queen Amina*. Beyond, a small entryway led into a much larger room that looked like a museum gallery.

Which was because, Addy realized after a moment, it *was* a museum gallery.

Xi's collection.

Peppered throughout the room were pedestals and glass cases holding everything from clay pots to bronze sculptures to full suits of armor. Paintings lined the walls, some famous enough that Addy even recognized them.

"Wow," she breathed. "Are these all..."

"Real?" Xi's eyelids lowered as she smiled. "Yes. They are *very* real. And very expensive." She gestured with one hand, a series of gold bangles jingling on her wrist. "You might say I'm a bit of a collector."

"Of what?"

"Of everything. Or anything. Whatever catches my fancy." She continued leading Addy by the elbow, gently but firmly, through the gauntlet of antiquities. "This amulet of Anubis dates back to at least 300 years BC," she said, pointing to a blue-green glazed ceramic of a jackal-headed figure. "I acquired it three years ago because something about it spoke to me." She lingered, contemplating the figure, then shrugged. "I wanted it, so I bought it."

Continuing down the aisle between the cases, Addy's gaze jumped to each new item. A full suit of samurai armor – "worn by Tokugawa Ieyasu himself," Xi murmured – then a collection of Roman coins – "from Caesar's time" – to watercolors from the late twenty-second century – "Alazar's green period was his shortest, but perhaps his most brilliant." Her head spinning with the sensory overload, Addy was aware that she ought to be paying closer attention to her guide and less to the surroundings, but she was craning her neck this way and that, trying to take it all in… and trying to find one particular item.

The tablet. It must be here somewhere. But even as she cast her gaze over the room – faking a look of awe wasn't proving difficult – she didn't catch sight of anything that looked like the item she'd seen at the auction.

As they reached another pair of double doors at the far end of the gallery, Addy finally managed to clear her head. *Don't get tunnel vision.* "This is truly amazing, Madam Xi. But why exactly am I here?"

Xi raised a finger as if suddenly remembering something. "Ah, yes. Of course, of course. Come with me and let us have some tea." At a snap of her fingers, the doors opened into an elegant sitting room, an impressive simulacrum of a fire flickering to life – at least, Addy assumed it was a hologram, as she couldn't imagine even the most self-indulgent person would be daring enough to risk open flame on a spaceship. A pair of leather sofas flanked a glass and steel table. As Xi lowered herself into one, her dress flickered orange in sympathy with the fire.

Addy cast a last, reluctant glance over her shoulder at the gallery, but trying to linger there when Xi clearly had something else in mind was going to look suspicious. She'd have to make another opportunity.

From behind a rattan screen, an attendant in White Star livery appeared bearing a tray with an iron tea pot, a strainer, and a pair of cups. Bowing to Xi, he placed them on the table between them and then withdrew.

Xi smiled again, graciously, and poured the tea through the strainer into the cups. "I wanted to meet you, Charlotte – may I call you Charlotte? – because, frankly, I was impressed." She raised the cup to her lips and eyed Addy over the rim. "I am not often impressed."

"Um… thank you?"

Taking a sip, Xi held the cup in her hands, as though warming them. "You wouldn't take 'no' for an answer when it came to getting into the executive lounge. And, once you were there, you proceeded to handily clean out a few top players without breaking much of a sweat." One of her carefully sculpted eyebrows rose a fraction.

Great, I've gotten the attention of an arms dealer. "I've had a lot of practice."

"So it would seem. Where else you have played? The Montserrat on Jericho? Kipling's *Starburst*?"

Addy vaguely recognized those as casinos, even though she'd never set foot in either. "Oh, here and there. You know. Mostly self taught."

"Ah," said Xi, her dark eyes lighting up. They almost seemed to shift towards a brighter auburn color as they did so, flecks in them turning iridescent. "A self-made woman. Even more impressive." She took another sip of tea, then nodded at the other cup.

Addy's cheeks flushed and she nipped her tongue beneath her teeth. She was doing a super job of blending in here. Couldn't even remember to take a drink when it was offered. Picking up the cup she took a sip. It was surprisingly smooth, with only a hint of astringency underneath.

"Another of my little luxuries," said Xi, raising the cup. "Did you know all tea – real tea, anyway – comes from a single species of plant? *Camellia sinensis*. It's a tree that can grow up to five stories tall, but only the top inch or two of leaves are used for tea. The plants are routinely trimmed back so that those leaves can grow again. I have sympathy for that kind of work." Her bangled hand waved at the museum gallery through which they had passed. "My collection is much the same. Only the choicest artifacts from human history." Those intense eyes landed on Addy once again, their lids lowering, revealing a gold tint. "And I take the same approach to people. I only want to know the very best."

Addy swallowed as heat rose to her cheeks. "I'm flattered, Madam Xi." The last time this much scrutiny had been fixated on her had probably been her final juvenile court appearance. Not a memory she wanted conjured up right now. "Your reputation precedes you."

"Oh?" said Xi, her voice taking on a playful tone. "What do they say about me?"

Just what I need: a gangster fishing for compliments. Not for the first time, Addy missed problems you could solve with punching. "That you're smart. Obviously. And perceptive. Demanding, but fair."

"Is that all?"

Oh well, take a shot. "Nobody mentioned that you were beautiful."

Xi's eyes widened, but feigned modesty quickly reasserted control. Addy covered with a sip of tea. Maybe she wasn't so bad at this after all. It helped, though, that the sentiment was far from false.

"Confident and capable, and we can add charming to the list too," said Xi, a smile curving across her lips. "I think I would like to get to know you better, indeed."

Addy's heart give a hard thump. But she was saved with having to come up with a clever response when the attendant reappeared from behind the screen, then bent down and murmured something to Xi. Annoyance flitted across her face and she shooed him away, turning back to Addy.

"I'm sorry to cut this short, my dear, but I'm afraid I have another appointment. I've most enjoyed our conversation, though. Perhaps we could continue it over dinner this evening?"

There was a buzz in Addy's head, equal parts relief and disappointment, but "exploit opportunities" had been another of Colonel Benton's maxims, and, more to the point, Xi didn't seem like the type of person who took 'no' for an answer.

"I'd be delighted," said Addy.

"Splendid." Xi rose, all elegance and grace as colors rolled across her dress like a waterfall.

A cough came from over Addy's shoulder, and she saw another flash of irritation dart through Xi's eyes. A man stood in the doorway, halfway in and halfway out, as though he couldn't decide which direction to go.

"Come in, doctor," said Xi, not quite heaving a sigh.

"Pardon me, madam. I'm so sorry. I didn't mean to interrupt." His voice was soft and cultured, and he wrung his hands slightly.

"It's quite all right," said Xi in a tone that suggested it wasn't. "Ms Bell, Dr Seku al-Kitab."

The man bowed. He had a kindly lined face with a neat black mustache and goatee. A gray tweed suit, worn at the edges, overlaid a matching waistcoat and an open collared shirt. Not the kind of man Addy would expect to find in Xi's company, but if he was a doctor, perhaps that explained it.

The real question is what does Xi need with a doctor?

"Nice to meet you," said Addy, extending her hand.

Al-Kitab shook it quickly, his hand feathering in and out of Addy's grasp like a frightened bird.

"Well, I'll leave you to it," said Addy. "I hope it's nothing serious, doctor."

The man looked confused for a moment, then his expression cleared. "Oh, not that kind of doctor. Actually, my speciality is—"

"Now, now," said Xi, interposing herself between the two, "let's not bore Ms Bell with all the details."

"My apologies," said al-Kitab, looking crestfallen.

"Ms Bell, I look forward to seeing you later," said Xi, reaching out to press her hand. The woman's grip was smooth and warm, and it sent a thrill through Addy that she couldn't entirely explain.

The attendant reappeared, but as he escorted Addy to the door she could hear al-Kitab mounting a wavering protest. "Madam Xi, I must once again respectfully request access to your vault if I'm to be able to do the job I was brought here—"

The rest was cut off by the door sliding shut.

Back in the executive lounge, Addy collected her bag – sans the KO-gun – and had her winnings deposited into her account, then headed back to their room to report in.

But the stateroom was empty when she returned. She swapped her outfit for something more casual, then tried to call Kovalic, with no luck. He'd want to hear everything about her contact with Xi.

Doubt nibbled at her, though. What had she really learned so far? Not much beyond Xi's penchant for collecting, which they'd already known, and maybe that she liked tea. Not exactly critical intelligence. After the chewing out she'd gotten on Tseng-Tao's Divide, anything Addy delivered was going to need to be gift-wrapped if she were going to start climbing out of the hole with Kovalic and Taylor. Dinner would hopefully prove a fruitful opportunity to learn more about the ship's dynamic proprietor, and she had to admit that she found herself looking forward to it on both professional *and* personal levels.

At the thought of dinner, her stomach gurgled, reminding her that all she'd had today was coffee, whiskey, and tea. No use trying to think on an empty stomach, and sitting around just waiting for Kovalic to show up wasn't going to get her anywhere. She imagined she could be trusted to get some lunch.

When she reached the esplanade, it was already packed with everyone from people in suits on their way to the casino or important meetings to kids running around the stalls and stores while their parents chased gamely after them.

As she made her way through the mass of people, Addy caught a whiff of spices – chili, cumin, za'atar – from a paquet stand, instantly transporting her back to her childhood, navigating the streets and crowds of Salaam, stealing food off the carts, and most importantly, avoiding the cops.

The cops. Kovalic said he'd chosen Addy because she could think like a criminal, but maybe she needed to start thinking like a cop instead. *Boyland would have known what to do.*

The paunchy cop had collared her one day when she was running with Schenk and Ali; they'd slipped away before he could nab them, but she hadn't been so lucky. Boyland had given her scrawny frame one look and sighed. *'Too small. Going to have to throw you back.'* He'd taken her to a paquet cart, not too different from this one; she'd been worried, at first, that he was one of those sketchy adults that Schenk and the others had always warned against, but if there was one thing the street had instilled in her, it was a judgement of character. It became clear pretty quickly that Boyland was the rare person who was exactly what he purported to be: world-weary, but always willing to see the best in people. He'd done right by her then, and he'd continued to do so for the rest of his life.

Must be too many onions, Addy thought as she got to the front of the line, wiping away the stinging in her eyes. She ordered a trio from the man behind the counter.

When the paquets arrived, they were spicy and savory, but just a little bit bitter – not as good as the ones she'd had when she was younger. Or had they always tasted that way? She sat in one of the parklets on the esplanade and watched the crowd go by.

She wasn't sure how to reconcile all these civilians and families with Ofeibia Xi. The woman she'd met an hour ago didn't seem like the type to concern herself with amusements, or, for that matter, meet with academics. But Boyland would have said to see who someone *really* was, you had to dissect the image they wanted you to see.

Her pulse quickened when she thought of Xi. Why was the head of a galaxy-spanning crime syndicate so interested in *her*? That kind of attention ought to have Addy ducking for cover, but instead she just found herself... curious. Nothing about Xi was what she'd expected from the woman's reputation;

she didn't seem so much ruthless as she did driven. And why shouldn't she be? The woman had climbed her way to the top of an empire. There would always be some people who saw her as a threat, no doubt, but it didn't necessarily mean she was a villain.

And someone that driven didn't make a business move or meet with someone without a reason.

Addy's breath caught and she nearly dropped the last of her paquets in her haste to bring up her sleeve. A search for "Seku al-Kitab" yielded only one result in the ship's onboard databases: a faculty list for Rizkin University on Hamza, the department of archaeology, where he researched *extraterrestrial* archaeology. Next to the name was a picture of the man she'd met in Xi's quarters an hour prior. *It was right in front of my goddamn face.*

So focused was Addy on the screen that she didn't at first register the man who sat down on the bench behind her. But suddenly he was there, and she cursed herself for letting her guard down. He hadn't been particularly subtle; she should have seen him a mile away.

"That smells delicious," said Tapper, nodding at the paquet. "Hope you brought enough for the whole class. Come on, the boss wants us."

CHAPTER 15

Location Charlie was a supply room on sub-deck 12 that Nat had picked out. It was long-term storage: mechanical parts and extra furniture that shouldn't be needed while the ship was in flight. It wasn't comfortable, but what it lacked in amenities it made up for in total anonymity.

"Nice digs," said Brody, looking around. "I still think this might be an upgrade from the bunk room."

Kovalic figured it better if he didn't mention the luxuriously large stateroom he and Sayers had so recently vacated.

There was a triple rap at the door, followed by a shorter double rap. Nat glanced at her sleeve; they'd bypassed the security feed in the hallway, sending a looped image to the main system while intercepting the live feed for themselves. She gave him a nod.

Kovalic punched the door control and the hatchway slid open, admitting Sayers and Tapper, then closed after them with a hiss.

Nat gave him the high sign. "We're secure."

"Good to see you all, though I wish it were under better circumstances," said Kovalic.

"So," said Tapper. "How fucked are we, on a scale of one to totally fucked?"

"That depends on how you feel about a little not-so-friendly competition."

Tapper scowled. "Goddamn crims are here, aren't they?"

"Got it in one."

"Well, we knew they'd want the tablet as much as we do," said Nat.

"We did," Kovalic agreed. "What's got me scratching my head is that they decided to pay me a visit."

That earned double-takes around the room.

"And you're still here? Sounds like you had an interesting morning, boss," said Tapper.

"You could say that. What we're dealing with is an SOE team run by Commander Ekaterin Mirza."

"Mirza?" echoed Tapper. "From the Kameral IV recon mission that went south?"

"Oh *really*?" said Nat, eyeing Kovalic. "So you're old friends?"

"Not unless a friend is someone who warns you that they'll kill you next time they see you."

Nat waggled her hand in a so-so gesture.

"Look, the SOE are Eyes' elite, and from what I saw on Kameral, Mirza's one of their best," said Kovalic. "We can't afford to underestimate her. Yes, Brody?" The pilot had raised a hand.

"For those of us who don't speak fluent military jargon and have no idea what an SOE team is, care to fill us in?"

"That's the Illyricans' Special Operations Executive, kid," said Tapper. "Small covert direct action teams that report to the head of IIS. They specialize in sabotage, assassination, and high-risk black operations."

Brody blinked. "Uhhh, that kind of sounds like–"

"Like us?" said Kovalic. "It should. The SPT was built on the SOE model."

"Hoo boy," said Brody. "So this makes this Mirza what… the Illyrican you?"

It wasn't an unflattering comparison: Mirza was hypercompetent, dangerous, and smart. Then again, she was also merciless and unforgiving. Kovalic hoped he might have the advantage in that department – if it was in fact an advantage.

"We need to identify the rest of Mirza's team," said Nat. "Simon, you said you saw another man with her."

"Only briefly," said Kovalic. "They got the drop on me, and he didn't stick around for the post-knockout chat. Tall, shaved head."

"And we're estimating at least two more."

Sayers cleared her throat. "I may have run into one of them up in the executive lounge."

"Oh?" said Kovalic, exchanging a look with Nat. "What happened?"

"There was a guy watching me. Solid build, stubble, a scar just here," she said, indicating her temple. "Reeked of Illyrican cologne. I took a knockout gun off him in the bathroom."

"In the bathroom?" said Brody. "What were you doing in there?"

Sayers eyed him. "What do *you* do in the bathroom?"

"OK," said Kovalic, interrupting before Brody could provide an answer that he was pretty sure he didn't want or need to hear. "That's three. I'd guess one or two more. Nat, we're going to need a tap into the security system. First priority is to find footage from outside the stateroom before my attack or from the executive lounge around the time of Sayers's run-in. If we get lucky, we might be able to tag the SOE team's biometrics and retrace their steps."

The commander chewed her lip. "The executive lounge will be tougher; there are limited cameras in there and they're on a discrete network with additional layers of security. The high-rollers pay for their privacy and they pay well."

And, she didn't need to add, around here you got what you paid for. "Understood. See what you can do." It was a long shot; Mirza would be at least as careful as Kovalic had been. "But Eyes isn't the main event here. Their presence just means we need to get to the tablet, and fast."

Tapper snorted. "Getting it off the ship is going to be a trick and a half. Even if Eyes weren't gunning for us, White Star's security is top notch from what I've seen."

"If it were easy, sergeant, they wouldn't have sent *us*." Kovalic spread his hands. "I'm open to suggestions."

"Do we have any idea where the tablet is currently?" Nat asked.

"We've been operating under the assumption that Xi's keeping it in her private collection, up on the executive level."

"No," said Sayers. "It's not. I'm pretty sure it's in the *Queen Amina*'s vault."

Four pairs of eyes swiveled to the specialist, who blanched under the attention. For a moment, there was no sound at all in the storage compartment.

"Well," said Tapper, exhaling and seemingly speaking for all of them. "Shit."

All five of them traipsing into the vault access room on the esplanade would have pushed well past the limits of staying inconspicuous. So Kovalic went in alone while the rest of the team staked out positions at cafés and parklets nearby.

The attendant at check-in had briefly mentioned something about storing valuables in the ship's vault, and Kovalic chastised himself for not paying closer attention. Even he could be distracted by the opulence of his surroundings.

He was hardly immune to errors, but he made a point to at least learn from them. He'd be extra vigilant this time – but he'd still left his comm channel open for the rest of the team to listen in, just in case he missed something.

The open archway was marked with the icon of a safe, and led into a vestibule with a reception desk, hallways curving back around each side. It was, unsurprisingly, empty of other passengers. Not exactly the kind of place that people hung out when there was eating and gambling to be done.

A woman with a swirl of purple-silver hair stood by a display emblazoned with a white star and the word *Queen Amina* in flowing script, and gave him what Kovalic had begun to think of as the Company Smile.

"Good morning, sir. How may I help you?"

"Morning. I've got some valuables in my stateroom that I'm considering putting into the vault. Could you run me through what that would entail?"

"Of course!" said the woman brightly. "Right this way." She led him around the curve to a long white hallway lined with frosted glass panels, a red or green light above each. "You may choose any vacant compartment, indicated by the green light. Just hold your sleeve near the access panel." With one hand, she indicated the panel next to the door.

Kovalic hesitated before waving his sleeve at the panel. Nat had looked into unfreezing his credit, but it seemed Mirza hadn't hacked the system, rather taking the much simpler route of flagging his identity with a red notice from the Illyrican government. Clearing his record would mean talking to the security department, which would not only take up valuable time, but also require putting his false identity, good as it might be, under the microscope. They'd taken the interim solution of cloning a sleeve from a passenger who bore a superficial resemblance to Kovalic while they figured out something more permanent.

Fortunately, it appeared that this system only checked to see if he was a valid passenger. The frosted-glass door slid aside to reveal a room containing a console and a small hatch in the wall that reminded him of an old dumbwaiter. In front of the hatch sat a small metal table.

"So," continued the woman, "you just wave your sleeve over the console and it will pull up the secure enclave for your room – if you need more than one, that can be arranged. The empty container will be retrieved by our automated system and delivered here," she said, pointing to the door. "Place whatever you want in the lockbox and seal it with an access code of your choice and a biometric facial scan. After you've locked the box, simply activate the return system on the console, and the lockbox will be sent back down to our vault."

"Hm," said Kovalic, clasping his hands behind his back, and peering at the door in the wall, which was probably three or four feet high and as many wide. "How exactly are the boxes transported? Mechanical convenience of some kind?"

"Oh, no. We have a state of the art repulsor field system that helps prevent any damage to more fragile items. A laser grid scans and verifies each lockbox as it passes through, to maintain a record of custody."

"I see," said Kovalic. "And where is the vault actually located? Is there any other way that it can be accessed?" He injected a note of concern into his voice: the cautious and security-conscious consumer.

"No, no, that would be impossible during flight," said the woman, clasping her hands. "The vault is located near the ship's engines and there's a solid foot of composite shielding in between them and the rest of the ship."

Kovalic made a suitably impressed noise. "Very good. And the security on the consoles and lockboxes?"

"State of the art encryption. The lockboxes maintain their own local security and are not networked in any way. Compromising one box wouldn't compromise any of the others. Likewise, the console systems are on an isolated circuit, inaccessible from the rest of the shipboard systems."

"And surveillance systems?" said Kovalic, raising a circling finger at the ceiling.

"We respect our customers' privacy. The only cameras are in the hallway and the reception area."

"Very impressive. One last question: if I have something *particularly* valuable to store, would this be the most secure place on the ship?"

"Oh, absolutely, sir," she said, eyes wide. "I can't think of any place else that even comes close."

Kovalic hemmed. "I mean, I understand you *have* to say that – your job and all. But you can't tell me that the crew keep their valuables in the same place as passengers?"

"They absolutely do," said the guide, a mix of pride and rebuke in her voice. "I can guarantee that our own staff – all the way up to the *Queen Amina's* owner – use the vault system. We treat our guests as we treat ourselves."

"Well," said Kovalic. "That's the best news I've heard all day."

Ten minutes later, they'd reconvened in a private meeting

room the level above the esplanade. Nat had hacked their way in, so that Mirza – or anybody else paying attention to them – wouldn't know it was them, and Kovalic had flipped on the baffle for good measure.

Nat flicked a holoscreen into existence above the table, displaying the starliner's schematics. The *Queen Amina* had forty-two decks, but the engines occupied three decks on the ventral side, plus a huge chunk of the rear of the ship. As Nat zoomed in on that area, a small box appeared, nestled amidships, just fore of the engine compartment and aft of what looked to be the ship's main power plant. It was surrounded on all sides by thick borders.

Tapper let out a low whistle. "They are not kidding around here." He waved a hand at the lines. "Like the lady said, we're looking at a heavy-duty composite of titanium, lead, and probably even some plasticrete in the mix. Even if we could get down to it – and the nearest access looks like it's about three decks away – drilling or burning through it would take heavy duty equipment and time that we don't have. Not to mention all the alarms we'd likely set off."

"So directly cracking the vault is out," said Nat. "What about the shafts used to transport lock boxes to and from the vault? Could we send someone down one and then pull them back up with the box?"

"It's a tight fit, but the real problem is that laser scanner grid," said Tapper. "We *might* be able to trick it into thinking a person is a lockbox, but even then we're still going to need someone to wait in the vault access room to pull them out. Might raise eyebrows from the staff if we're in there for thirty or forty minutes, and last thing we want is them checking in on us."

Kovalic made a face. "How about hacking our way into the console?"

"Maybe, but it's not going to be easy," said Nat. "The air gap means you'd need to be in the access room, and the three-factor authentication means we need Xi's sleeve, face scan, *and* access code."

"Sweet Moses on a log roll," said Tapper. "I've seen banks and royal palaces with less security."

"Anybody else think this thing is basically uncrackable?" said Brody, looking around.

"There's no such thing as an uncrackable system," said Sayers. "As long as people need to get things in and out, there's a way to exploit it."

"Sound like you have some experience with that," said Tapper.

"Enough."

"If you got a suggestion, specialist, now's the time to put it out there," said Nat.

With the expectant glances leveled from all sides, Sayers leaned over to the holoscreen, enlarging the section at the very bottom of the ship. As it zoomed in, a small rectangle appeared. "There," she said. "Service hatch. That's our way in."

Tapper squinted at it. "That's an *exterior* service hatch. Not that I don't appreciate outside-the-box thinking, but that is *literally* outside the box."

"Which also means that they probably didn't spend as much time securing it."

"Because it's *outside the ship*."

"You wanted a way in," said Sayers, frustration mounting in her voice. "Now you want to complain about it?"

"OK, OK," said Kovalic, putting a hand out towards each of them. "Settle down. Sayers is right – that hatch is probably our best way in."

"And how in the name of the almighty are we going to get to it?"

Nat panned the schematic. "The closest airlock is on subdeck 17. From there, it's about a hundred and fifty meters across the hull to the service hatch. I should be able to bypass the cycle alarm on the airlock, but the bigger problem is the ship's outboard sensor array. It's going to pick up an anomaly the second anyone sets foot out there."

"We can't hack those?" asked Kovalic.

Nat shook her head; with a flick of her fingers, she'd zoomed back out to a view of the entire ship and overlaid a second set of lines on the schematic. "Command and control systems are separate from the rest of the ship. I'd need to be on the bridge or at an auxiliary control station."

Kovalic didn't need Nat to add that gaining access to either of those would require a lot more time they couldn't spare and a lot more risk of getting caught.

"What if we didn't have to hack their sensors?" Brody said slowly.

"What if I was the king of all the universe?" said Tapper.

"No, I mean, what if the sensors are already scrambled?"

"What are you thinking, lieutenant?" said Kovalic.

Brody tapped his sleeve and brought up a different display: the ship's course. "We're currently about four hours away from the Hamza gate, at which point we'll make the wormhole jump from the Badr System to Hanif space." He zoomed in, focusing on a dot at the end of the line.

"Holy shit," Nat muttered.

"What am I missing?" said Tapper, looking back and forth between them.

"The gravitational and electromagnetic effects of a wormhole play havoc with sensor arrays," said Brody. "There's way too much interference; you get false positives all over the place. Most pilots ignore them or even shut them down during transit."

"He's right," said Nat. "Commonwealth Navy SOP is to suspend sensor systems during wormhole transit. Not like there's much to detect there anyway."

Brody was shaking his head. "Going outside in a wormhole...that's a pretty risky play."

Spacewalks were dangerous enough on their own, but performing one in a wormhole was a whole different story. One wrong move and the gravimetric currents would sweep you away – and that was far from the worst case scenario.

But if it was the best option, the risk was worth it. The job was too important.

"How long does this jump take?" Kovalic asked.

Brody's eyes rolled up in thought; most pilots ended up memorizing a lot of data about intersystem travel. "Badr to Hamza's a short one. Fifty-six minutes, seventeen seconds."

"That's a tight margin," said Kovalic. "Fifty-six minutes to pop the airlock, make it across the hull, get inboard, find the right container, retrieve it, and get back to the airlock – with the container in tow."

"Not to mention the whole separate problem of actually opening the damn box once we've got it," put in Tapper.

"One impossibility at a time, if you don't mind, sergeant." His mind was already compiling lists of resources and running down the timetable. It was doable, if just barely. But there were a lot of variables. "We'll need an EVA suit."

"Should be able to snipe one from the maintenance department without too much attention," said Tapper. "Who's going?"

Kovalic surveyed his team. "Commander Taylor and I have logged the most EVA time, but she'll need to be at a terminal to override the service hatch lock and just in case any alarms crop up. So I guess I'm drawing the short straw on this one? Tapper will watch my back at the airlock. Brody, how's transport coming? As soon as Xi discovers the box is missing, the ship's going to be in full lockdown. I don't want us stuck without a way out of here."

"The best option is probably one of the four maintenance skiffs," said Brody. "Both the tenders we came in on and the lifeboats are slower than a snail riding a turtle, and neither can break atmosphere. The personal passenger vessels docked in the *Queen Amina*'s cold storage are better ships, but they're not easily accessible: they just get loaded in one after another by an automated system. And the hangar doors will be sealed during wormhole transit."

"Well that's easy enough," said Tapper. "We blow the doors."

Brody looked at him in horror. "That'd decompress the entire compartment and eject everything in there into the wormho... Have you ever met a problem you haven't tried to fix with explosives?"

"So far I haven't met one they couldn't fix."

"*Anyway*, no matter which ship we use, we can't launch until we clear the wormhole."

"So what I'm hearing," said Kovalic, "is that we can't start the op until we're *in* the wormhole but we can't finish it until we're *out*."

"That's about the size of it."

Right, no problem. They had their work cut out for themselves, that was for damn sure. "We're going to need to figure out how to crack that lockbox without destroying the tablet. Which means we're going to need access to Xi herself: face scan, access code, cloned sleeve, the works. Sayers, you think you can handle that?"

A mix of hesitation and pride warred on the young woman's face, as though she wanted to say something, but eventually she nodded. "I should be able to record her biometrics and clone her sleeve – getting her to give up her access code is going to be harder. Can we override it? There must be a failsafe, just in case someone forgets their code."

"Maybe," said Nat. "But any override or code reset would likely require Xi provide proof of her identity. And since it's her ship and everybody knows her, any sort of impersonation play is going to be incredibly risky."

"Sayers, work any angle you need to," said Kovalic. "We'll look for some sort of vulnerability in the system to exploit as a backup, but if we can get legitimate access to the system easily, I'd rather do that."

"Aw, you're getting soft in your middle age, boss," said Tapper.

"What about the Illyricans?" said Nat. "We might not be the only belles at the ball on this one."

They were the wild card here, for sure. Mirza was smart – maybe smarter than they were – but he'd lay odds that she definitely wasn't as crazy. "Nat, if you can find them on the internal security systems, we can keep tabs on them, but until then we can't predict their actions. So the best thing we can do is have our contingencies and be ready for anything."

"That seems… vague," said Brody. "How can you have contingencies for everything?"

"Don't worry, kid," said Tapper, slapping the younger man on the back. "I've seen just about everything by this point."

"Somehow that doesn't make me feel better. Look, I know I was going on about extraterrestrial life and advance civilizations, but this seems like an awful lot of trouble to go through for a piece of rock that might be total garbage."

"Much as it pains me, I have to agree with Brody on this one," said Nat. "I'd feel a lot better if we could figure out whether or not this is the genuine article before we try to steal it."

"If there even *is* a genuine article where tablets created by ancient alien civilizations are concerned," said Tapper.

"Actually," said Sayers, "I might know somebody who could help us with that."

Some part of Addy hadn't wanted to share her encounter with Xi – and, by extension, Dr al-Kitab – with the rest of the team. Mostly because she'd wanted to provide it with a bow on top, delivered as a fait accompli. But a deeper part of her had felt weirdly possessive. After all, *she*'d been the one to make contact. This was her asset. She and Xi had developed a rapport, and she didn't want Kovalic or Taylor taking that away from her.

But after she'd related most of what had transpired, she started to realize that had been a tactical error. "So this Dr al-Kitab must be here to authenticate the tablet, right?"

Taylor's gaze was less appraising than hostile. "When exactly were you going to share this information, specialist?"

Addy flared. "I shared it when it was relevant, which is now." She could feel Tapper and even Brody eyeing her from either side, and it seemed like the temperature in the storage compartment had dropped a few degrees.

But this is what I was supposed *to do.*

"OK," said Kovalic finally. "I'll take the professor, see if there's any more information he can give us on the tablet. Nat, see if you can dig up anything on the guy. Maybe there's something we can use as leverage. Turn him to our side."

"I'll see what the ship databanks have, but there's no guarantee he'd be in the local cache. And I won't be able to get a real-time query back from any on-planet systems before we need to move on this."

Tapper was leaning against the bulkhead, arms crossed, and pointedly avoiding looking at Sayers. "Now that we have this *vital* information, shouldn't we just wait and grab it from the egghead when he's studying it? Would save us cracking the uncrackable vault."

Addy bit back a rejoinder that without her, the team would never have known about al-Kitab in the first place. *Not like that would particularly help my case.* She glanced at Brody, but the pilot was uncharacteristically quiet, eyes on the deck.

Kovalic hesitated. "We'll keep eyes on him once we've made contact, but there are too many unknowns: we don't know when or where he might get access to the tablet. I don't like the idea of sitting on our hands; it leaves Mirza and her team an open field. We've established that there's a window of opportunity while we're in the wormhole – we need to make our move while we can." He turned to Addy. "Specialist, you keep working Xi. We're going to need that security information if we have any hope of cracking the lockbox."

Addy swallowed. Cloning a sleeve was one thing; getting close enough to steal biometrics or convincing Xi to give her an access code was another entirely. It had been a long time since she'd pulled that kind of con, and back on Nova she'd had a crew she'd trusted. Or, more importantly, a crew who had trusted *her*. Right now, it didn't seem like her stock with the rest of the team was particularly high.

But "I've got it," was all she said.

Kovalic didn't say anything to that, just nodded, then turned back to the rest of the team, doling out responsibilities. "Brody, go with Tapper and scrounge up the rest of what we'll need. Try to keep it quiet."

"Quiet's my middle name. Well, I mean, legally it's Hamish, but I think you'll find that…" The rest of whatever the pilot was going to say was lost as the sergeant dragged him bodily out of the room, leaving Sayers alone with Kovalic and Taylor.

Something unspoken passed between the two of them, that ended with Taylor rolling her eyes.

Addy sighed. *Time for the mom and dad talk.* Or so she figured – not like she'd remember firsthand. She slipped into parade rest, hands behind her back, ready for the dressing down.

Kovalic sat on the edge of the conference table. "Specialist, I want you to know I don't doubt your capability in this matter. And though this isn't the infantry and I value your initiative, you still need to keep us in the loop when you have intel – especially when it's this critical.

"More to the point, though," he continued, without waiting for her to respond. "I want to make sure you're being *careful*. Xi is dangerous, even if she likes to play coy. And we know she's smart and manipulative."

This time Addy did jump in, one hand clenching the other behind her back. "Due respect, sir, but I can handle myself. I know when somebody's playing me."

Taylor threw up her hands. "God forbid anybody try to express concern or tell you anything."

"We don't all have the luxury of growing up someplace where safety is an assumption. Ma'am."

"I can see why that mouth has gotten you into trouble," Taylor snapped.

"That's enough," said Kovalic. What his voice lacked in volume it more than made up for in firmness. "We're on the job, which means putting aside our differences for the moment and getting this done. The mission comes first, understood?"

"Yes, sir," said Addy, resisting the urge to click her heels together.

"Understood," said Taylor, though a part of Addy was relieved that her glare was turned for once on Kovalic.

"Good," said Kovalic, ignoring the icy look. "Sayers, you'll make contact with Xi at the appointed time. If anything seems wrong, I want you to get out of there as fast as you can – signal the abort code on your sleeve, and we'll get you out. Got it?"

Abort code. Of course. For when I can't hack it. Addy's mouth set in a line. She wasn't going to give anybody – not Xi, not Taylor, and not Kovalic – the satisfaction of seeing her turn tail and run. But she nodded all the same. "Yes, sir," she repeated, trying to keep the frustration out of her voice.

"In that case, good luck," said Kovalic. "See you on the other side."

CHAPTER 16

"I can't believe she held out on us," Nat said as they made their way to the esplanade. "What the hell is that about?"

"For what it's worth, I don't think she was trying to mislead us," said Kovalic. "She just seems to like keeping her cards close to her chest."

"Oh, come *on*, Simon. This is a mission, not a poker game. She needs to know how to work with a team."

He couldn't argue with that. Teamwork had, so far, not been Sayers' strong suit. She'd proved her ability to do the work, her reported contact with Xi had proved that much. Everything that he'd seen in her jacket back at the School had been true – the bad and the good. She just needed to learn that there were some situations you couldn't just fight your way out of.

"There's only so much we can do about it right now," Kovalic pointed out. "You go in the field with the team you have."

"I can't believe you're OK with this," she said with a sidelong glance. "A year or two ago, you would have cut her loose after that incident on Tseng-Tao's Divide. Now you're all in for fifth chances?"

Kovalic's shrug was carefully constructed, but something

about Nat's words went sub-dermal, resonating with what Tapper had said to him. *I know what happened with Page threw you, boss.* He'd sniped it down quick, but it was still lying in wait there, like a tripmine. Page had been a team player… until he hadn't. If even the perfect operative had proven to be untrustworthy, then maybe what you needed was someone who was decidedly imperfect.

"I guess I'm embracing forgiveness. I'd have thought you'd be all in favor of that."

"I'm not about to take that bait."

Kovalic smiled. "Back to the issue at hand, then. What'd you pull on our doctor friend?"

For a moment, Nat looked like she was about to push back on the change of subject, but she seemed to decide better of it. "I ran a quick query, but the shipboard database didn't have anything beyond what Sayers already turned up. Dr Seku Al-Kitab, PhD in Ancient History and Archaeology from Magdalen College, which apparently he decided to put to good use by researching aliens."

"He wouldn't be the first person with bona fides to buy into conspiracy theories," said Kovalic. "How do we find him?"

"I've only got limited access to the security system, and his profile is above the clearance I've wrangled. I'm running my own facial recognition search now, but it's going to take a while."

"What about our other friends?"

"Haven't cracked the executive level," said Nat as they stepped on to the esplanade. "So I can't find the guy Sayers ran into – assuming he *was* an Illyrican agent, anyway. As for your attackers, it looks like there was a 'fault' in the security cameras in your hallway right around the time they jumped you." Her tone of voice suggested exactly what she thought of that coincidence.

Kovalic scratched his chin. "Some sort of signal jammer, probably. Though Mirza did use my baffle for our little chat. Is it possible that they've compromised the *Queen Amina's* systems as well?"

"I assume their playbook's not that different from ours."

"Well, in that case, what if we stop looking for them and start looking for their footprints? Maybe we can figure out how they compromised the system and backtrack the hack to them."

Nat's eyes swept back and forth rapidly. "If they're smart, they'll have covered their tracks. But I might be able to narrow it down a bit."

"I'll take any edge we can get. If we can figure out where they're holed up, we might be able to get the jump on them."

"I'll see what I can do."

Late afternoon was a sparse time on the esplanade, as people took in the shows and other entertainments before dinner rolled around. There were still plenty of folks about, but it wasn't the madding crush that Kovalic had seen earlier in the day. That cut both ways: the smaller crowd made it harder to hide, but also made it harder for anybody following you to stay unseen.

Spotting the people following them proved to be even easier, because they were all wearing the black uniforms of White Star employees.

Kovalic glanced in a shop window as they passed, catching the reflection of two White Star security personnel, hands on sidearms, trailing about fifteen feet behind them.

"Two on our six," he murmured.

"And that's not all," said Nat, taking his arm and tapping three fingers against it. "Two ahead and one to our three o'clock."

That was a whole lot of muscle for two people, especially in a public place. He felt confident he and Nat could hold their own in a fight, should it come to that, but taking on the shipboard security was going to make a lot of problems for them in the long run.

"This is less than great."

"How do you want to play it?" she asked.

Kovalic scanned the route in front of them. It was easily a hundred meters to the next bank of lift tubes, and the cordon was tightening as the two behind quickened their pace.

"We need more information. And better ground."

Ahead, the esplanade branched into two smaller passages, one leading to the main level's theater, the other to more shops. Kovalic veered left towards the former, glancing at the holoscreen floating by the fork. The current show was approaching its end, the area empty aside from a few custodial workers and cleaning drones, sweeping up the detritus from the showgoers.

The doors ahead were closed and sealed – no admittance during the performance – funneling them to a dead end.

"I hope I know what you're doing," Nat said under her breath.

"So do I, most days."

As they strolled up towards the doors, Kovalic's peripheral vision picked up the guards fanning out around them. There were five, as they'd counted, and each seemed to have a weapon at their side; none drawn yet, so it was hard to tell if they were simple knockout guns or something more lethal.

"Mr Godwin," called a voice. "Please stop where you are and turn around slowly."

Kovalic exchanged a look with Nat and they dropped their hands to their sides and did as requested.

The group's leader, an older man with a curly mop of dark hair shot through with gray and a few days of gray stubble, stood with the stiff formality that came with a higher pay grade.

"I'm Chief of Security Cortez. May we have a word?"

The other four officers had split into two pairs and taken up spots on either side of the room, each about twenty feet away from where Kovalic and Nat stood. That was a hefty advantage for them with their ranged weapons. No way he and Nat could even close half that distance before getting shot from at least one direction.

Kovalic made a point of taking in each of the guards in turn. "Looks like you have me at a disadvantage, Mr Cortez. In more ways than one. What can I do for you?"

Cortez stepped closer and though his face was neutral, his eyes were pure steel. "Your account has been flagged for potential fraud, something we take very seriously. Would you mind handing over your sleeve, please?"

"I would, actually. Do you have anything more than a vague allegation?"

"I'm afraid I must insist."

Nat jumped in. "I believe we're still in the Badr system, which is not under the jurisdiction of the Commonwealth, Imperium, or any other government entity. But intersystem law – which does apply here – holds that we don't need to surrender any property without a warrant."

Kovalic pushed back his smile. Cortez seemed like the kind of guy who wouldn't respond well to smugness. "If you have a warrant, Chief Cortez, I'll be more than happy to comply. But until then, I think we will be on our way." He took a step forward towards the security personnel, then stopped as he heard the whine of KO guns charging from either side of him.

Cortez came closer, his own hand draped loosely on the pistol on his belt. "You are a guest on the *Queen Amina*, Mr Godwin. If you had closely read our passenger agreement, you would see that it requires you to comply with all White Star security procedures while you are aboard the ship. That includes confiscation of any personal property that may violate the policies of this ship or its parent company."

Ah yes, the fine print. "I think you and I both know that won't hold water."

"You're welcome to appeal it to an intersystem magistrate when you reach Hamza. I believe their queue time is only a matter of weeks. For now, though, I'll need your sleeve." He put out his hand.

Kovalic could feel Nat tensing beside him. He glanced up at the holoscreen floating behind Cortez's head. Too much time. He needed to stall. "May I ask where you came by this information?" As though he needed to ask.

Cortez didn't blink. "Anonymous tip."

Flagging his account had given the SOE team time to plan their next move while slowing down Kovalic. Slick, effective, and requiring very little effort on Mirza's part. He expected no less from her.

Slowly, Kovalic peeled his sleeve off his forearm and held it loosely in one hand. "I'm certain this is all a misunderstanding, but I would like to retain shipboard counsel anyway."

"I'm sure you would. I'll be happy to direct you to them. *After* you hand over your sleeve."

Kovalic turned the device over in his hand, making a great show of thinking about it, but all the while watching the holoscreen floating behind Cortez. Any moment now. He just had to ride this line between seeming like he was going to comply and not provoking Cortez into just stunning them both and taking what they wanted.

With a sigh of resignation, Kovalic slapped the sleeve into Cortez's outstretched hand.

"Thank you for complying, Mr Godwin. Now, if you don't mind–"

There were a series of *clunks* as the doors at the end of the hallway slid open. Kovalic watched Cortez's gaze sharpen over his shoulder, his expression shifting into one of wariness as the crowd began to flood out of the theater.

In the second that Cortez was distracted, Kovalic brought his other arm up and grabbed the hand in which the security chief held his sleeve. He twisted it around as Cortez winced and tried to call to his officers.

But the flow of the crowd was too thick and the rest of the guards were pushed to the outer edges of the hallway; if they wanted to shoot Kovalic, they'd be firing into a group of passengers. None of them seemed about to make that decision without a direct order from their boss.

Kovalic wrenched Cortez's arm further and heard a strangled cry as the limb went in a direction it wasn't supposed to go. Reclaiming his sleeve, Kovalic neatly pinned the man's arm behind his back. "Let's take a little walk, shall we?" said Kovalic, deftly snaking his free hand down to pull the sidearm off Cortez's belt.

Sparing a glance over his shoulder, he saw Nat, who had also used the sudden appearance of the crowd to her advantage, closing the distance with the pair of guards against the wall to their right. She'd disarmed both quickly and quietly, leaving them slumped on a bench against the wall.

The remaining pair were trying to wade through the crowd towards Cortez, but Kovalic let the crowd's momentum sweep them back to the esplanade.

"Take a left," he murmured to Cortez, following him around the corner and away from the main drag. Nobody seemed to be paying them any particular attention, instead chatting about the show or about which bar they'd be going to for drinks.

Just off the esplanade, Kovalic found a quiet little parklet under an arbor and shoved Cortez down on a bench, out of the way of prying eyes. Taking a seat across from the security chief, Kovalic leveled the weapon at him, relieved to see it too was a knockout gun. He wasn't looking to rack up a body count.

"So," said Kovalic pleasantly. "You were saying earlier. An anonymous tip?"

Cortez, for his part, had gone from steely to grim in the space of about fifty meters. Nobody liked having their own weapon pointed back at them, a feeling that Kovalic could sympathize with. But people reacted in different ways – some pled, some clammed up, some just passed straight out. The question was, which kind was Cortez?

"Two options," said Kovalic. "One, you really don't know who the tip was from. Two, you do and just don't want to tell me. In the case of number two, I'd ask you to reconsider." He held the gun steady, but it wasn't really a threat – just insurance if Cortez decided to make a move. Frankly, the security chief was probably going to get stunned at the end of this no matter what.

"I'm not telling you anything," Cortez bit off. "You're a criminal."

"Takes one to know one."

The man drew himself up, as much as was possible while on a park bench at gunpoint. "I'm the chief security officer of this ship. I report *directly* to its owner. Before that, I spent thirty years in law enforcement."

"Working for an arms dealer is an interesting career choice, then."

Cortez's eyelid twitched, but otherwise his expression was stony. Kovalic wondered just how much he knew about his boss's affairs. Enough, he wagered, to feel at least a little bit uncomfortable.

Kovalic leaned back and rested the gun in his lap, though he kept his hand on it. "Come on, Cortez. The White Star is a crime syndicate that spans half a dozen systems and runs weapons – and who knows what else – through the bottleneck. They sell to the Commonwealth. They sell to the Imperium. They sell to anybody who can pay. All this," he said, waving a hand at the ship around them, "is nothing more than window dressing. Cover. A way to launder credits. That's got to bug you a bit."

Cortez crossed his arms over his chest, but he wouldn't meet Kovalic's gaze.

"Yeah," said Kovalic. "I thought it might."

His earbud crackled to life and Nat's voice came through. "Ditched the rest of those guards. I'm assuming you're good but probably best if we split up for a while. Rendezvous back at your dishwashing job in an hour."

Kovalic gave his earbud a double tap of acknowledgment. Nat had the right of it; if security was looking specifically for him, she'd be better off on her own for the moment.

"Look," said Kovalic. "Maybe you're complicit in your boss's crimes, or maybe you're just a guy caught in a bad situation. Not my place to judge. But we might be able to help each other out."

Cortez snorted. "I don't need your help."

"Sure, you say that now. But what about twenty-four hours from now, when the rest of your security team finds you hogtied in the middle of the esplanade in your underwear? I feel like that kind of thing makes it hard to maintain respect."

The security chief couldn't quite decide whether he wanted to laugh or look genuinely worried, so he settled for a suspicious nervousness. "Who the hell are you?"

"Somebody who's got a job to do, just like you." Kovalic pretended to study his fingernails. "And maybe somebody who'd like to see your boss taken down a peg or two." Now came the question of whether he'd read this guy right.

Cortez still had an air of suspicion about him, but Kovalic thought he caught a gleam in the man's eye. Yeah, he'd read him right. He wasn't sure how Xi had maneuvered Cortez into her service, but this guy wasn't here because he was an immoral piece of shit – that wasn't the kind of person you put in charge of your security, unless you wanted them to turn around and stab you in the back.

"It can't find its way back to me. I may not love this job, but I need it."

"Wouldn't dream of it."

The security chief drummed fingers on his thigh, then seemed to come to a decision. "Fine. What do you want to know?"

"I'm looking for someone aboard the *Queen Amina*, and who better than the ship's security chief to tell me where I can find them?"

"What are you, some sort of private investigator?"

No better cover than the one that got handed to you. "Of sorts."

"Ah. One of those independently wealthy detectives I've read so much about, then," said Cortez dryly. "Well, before that red flag froze your funds, anyway."

Kovalic gave a modest shrug. "It seems a rival of mine is working the same case, and she decided to make life difficult for me by cutting off my resources *and* sending you after me."

A flicker of recognition shot through Cortez's eyes. "A woman with dark hair? Not much of a sense of humor?"

"I see you've met."

"Yes, I've had the... pleasure."

"So you know what I'm up against here. She can be pretty ruthless."

"I know the type. Who are you looking for?"

"A professor of archaeology. His name is Dr Seku al-Kitab."

Cortez hadn't entirely banished his suspicion. Once a cop, always a cop. "Why? What do you want him for?"

"It's a... personal case. It seems he may not have paid his child support. Not glamorous work, but it does pay the bills." An oldie, but a goodie.

Cortez nodded knowingly, though a bit of his old superiority had returned. Fine. Let him think he had an edge; that'd suit Kovalic's purposes just fine. "I know this man. An oblivious academic, single-minded in his pursuits. It doesn't surprise me that he might have neglected his family."

"Perhaps you know where he spends his time? I'd love to get a chance to speak with him – before my 'colleague' does."

Now that he had something to offer, Cortez had relaxed a bit into the bench. "This may be possible. And, in return, perhaps you will do me the service of returning my weapon? And, of course, not speaking of this again?"

"Naturally. I'd also appreciate it if you could purge our name from whatever wanted list got your attention in the first place. Oh, and unfreeze my room funds."

Cortez rubbed his chin. "Suppressing the flag on your profile is possible – all security matters onboard are subject to my discretion. But I'm afraid dealing with your financial problem is more challenging. If you can give me a day, I should be able to put through a request quietly. To do it quicker would mean overriding the purser, who also reports directly to the owner. And you must forgive me, but I don't wish to answer questions from those quarters."

The security chief had a point: keeping off of Xi's radar was a high priority and a request to free up their funds after they had so recently been frozen would be sure to raise an eyebrow or two. But they didn't have a day to wait – they'd have to make do with the meager funds they had on hand.

"Fair enough," said Kovalic. He flipped the weapon over and handed it, butt first, to Cortez. The barrel pointed directly at Kovalic's own mid-section; if Cortez wanted to renege and stun him where he sat, well, now would be the time.

As Cortez's hand closed around the grip he hesitated, as if he himself were thinking the same thing. But after a second, the sidearm went back into the holster. "Should I ask about my officers?"

"Bruised egos mostly. I'd have them checked over, but my guess is they'll be OK."

"Perhaps it's time I raised my hiring standards. I don't suppose you're available?"

Kovalic chuckled. "I try not to consider job offers while I'm working, but I appreciate the sentiment."

Cortez slapped his thighs and rose to his feet. "A shame. I feel like perhaps I should enjoy working with you, Mr Godwin."

Kovalic wasn't sure the feeling was totally mutual, but he took the compliment where he could get it. "Thanks. Now: Dr al-Kitab?"

"Of course, of course. You'll find him most evenings at a little coffeehouse down on sub-level three. Café Turek."

"Appreciate it."

Cortez turned to walk away then looked back over his shoulder. "A word of advice, Mr Godwin? The doctor is a personal acquaintance of the owner of the *Queen Amina*. Tread carefully."

"I appreciate the warning, chief." Getting to his feet, Kovalic tipped him an informal salute, and walked in the other direction.

They were going to get Ofeibia Xi's attention sooner or later, of that much Kovalic was confident. And if it wasn't from tracking down Dr al-Kitab then it would probably be when they stole the Aleph Tablet right out from under her nose.

CHAPTER 17

What does one wear to a dinner with a notorious gangster?

Addy's current attire, though it would probably pass muster, had the distinct disadvantage of being the same thing she had worn in her encounter with Xi earlier in the day. It would probably be polite to at least give the appearance of having freshened up.

But their stateroom had been seized in the wake of their funds being frozen, so all the other clothes that Kovalic's tailor had made for her were under lock and key in a room being watched by ship security. And the lack of funds meant that buying new clothes was out of the question.

Like you've never stolen clothes before. But this wasn't like when she'd been a teenager, nicking a new top to impress her compatriots.

No, this required a decidedly more delicate touch.

The stores on the esplanade ran the gamut from casual apparel all the way up to the most formal of wears. Addy picked one of the higher-end ones – the kind of place that catered to a demanding clientele – and swept in with her best aura of entitlement. She idly perused the racks until a clerk with a sunny disposition appeared next to her.

"Good day, ma'am. Can I help you find anything?"

"Oh, yes!" Addy said, injecting a note of breathlessness. "I have this tremendously important dinner tonight and simply *nothing* to wear!" She fluttered a smile.

"No problem at *all*," the clerk assured her. "I'm sure we can put together an outfit in no time. What kind of dinner is it? Business? Pleasure?"

"I guess you could say starting as one and, hopefully, ending up as the other, if you know what I'm saying?"

The clerk gave a knowing smile. "I think we can find something. Give me just a moment."

Five minutes later, Addy was ensconced in the dressing room with an armload of clothes. As she tried on the third dress, a flattering white and black number, she had to admit that the associate – Tess, her name tag said – had a good eye. All of the outfits she'd picked out were cut to flatter Addy's figure.

Damn, if I'd had any of these back when I was running short cons on the streets, I could have waltzed my way into the fanciest restaurants in Salaam.

"Honestly, these are all marvelous," said Addy, as she stepped into the hallway, her skirt swishing. "Thank you so much for your help."

Tess looked her up and down thoughtfully. "We'll take that one in a little bit at the waist, but it really shows off your arms, which you absolutely should."

Addy flushed. *All those push-ups in training counted for something, I guess.*

"We can of course have these altered and delivered to your room," said Tess. "I'll just need your sleeve for payment."

The moment of truth. "Of course!" said Addy. She started sifting through her bag. Letting a frown cross her face, her groping got more frantic, but she produced only a makeup compact, a hair tie, and a few sticks of chewing gum. "It's not here," she said, despondent.

"Oh dear. Perhaps you left it in your room?"

"Maybe? Or I lost it again, how *clumsy* of me." In her experience people couldn't resist a sob story. As a kid, turning on the waterworks in front of the cops had gotten her out of hot water more than once. Had never worked on Boyland, though; somehow he'd seen right through it.

"I could look up your room account," said Tess helpfully. "Your biometrics should be on file."

Which is going raise more flags than a gravball match.

"Oh, please, no," said Addy, clasping her hands. "William – he can't know about this. It's… it's not him I'm meeting, you see."

Tess's eyes widened slightly. "Ah."

"He's very sweet, but I was so young…" *I don't know where this is coming from, but keep it up, brain.* "And then I met Helena…"

There was a softening in Tess's expression and she patted Addy on the shoulder. "It's fine. Look…" She glanced both ways, as if checking to see if anyone was watching. "Give me just a moment."

Addy sat down on one of the armchairs in the dressing room area, resting her chin on her hand, and plucked at her skirt disconsolately. It was a nice dress; she wasn't sure she'd ever owned anything quite this beautiful. Not to say that it was the kind of thing she'd want to wear everyday, but to have *the option*, well, that was something new.

Tess reappeared. "All right, here's what we're going to do. I'm putting this dress on hold for you. As long as you return it within twenty-four hours, it'll be fine."

"No, no," Addy protested. "I can't let you do this."

Tess took her firmly by her arm and walked her to the door. "I insist. You shouldn't have anything less than what makes you feel like who you are. Just promise me you'll come back for the rest of them – we work on commission around here." She winked at Addy.

"Oh…oh, *thank you*," said Addy, gathering up her things. "You're too kind." She felt a pang of regret; here Tess was, helping out a total stranger, with nothing to gain. And here Addy was taking advantage of the woman's trusting nature. Once upon a time, she wouldn't have thought twice about it, but this time it was eating at her.

Tess shooed her out of the store with a smile and no trace of remorse, and Addy found herself on the esplanade, clutching a bag containing the clothes she'd had on this morning, and wearing a dress that she hadn't owned a mere ten minutes ago. *This job is weird.*

That lingering thought ringing in her head, she turned on her heel and made her way towards the casino, her stride growing more confident with each step. After all, she had a dinner to get to.

This time there was no impediment to Addy's trip to the executive lounge. The guard at the lift swept the velvet rope aside for her.

She'd stowed the bag containing her old clothes in a storage locker right off the esplanade and reclaimed her "missing" sleeve. A nearby restroom offered an opportunity to apply a little judicious makeup and made herself look generally presentable, despite the lack of a shower in the last day or so.

A myriad of her reflections scattered every which way in

the lift's mirrored walls, and she gave her hair a last minute touch-up, but keeping it short had its advantages.

The executive lounge was much as she'd left it, though with different passengers playing the tables. She exchanged a smile with Nina the bartender, who was mixing a complicated orange drink with a perfectly formed sphere of blood red floating in the middle. Security personnel met her at the stairs, escorting her up and into Xi's private quarters.

The lights in the gallery had been dimmed, though phosphorescent panels along the walls glowed a deep purple and individual cases were uplit in green or orange. Sparkling jewelry pieces and burnished brass sculptures gleamed in the light, taking Addy's breath away anew.

The guards had remained outside, she realized suddenly, leaving her alone in the room. Well, almost alone.

"It's quite something, isn't it?" Ofeibia Xi drifted into view, wearing a gown that sparkled from chest to floor. Even more scintillating than the one she'd worn this morning, this one picked up the lights around the room and refracted them back, glittering like starlight.

"It's... beautiful," said Addy honestly.

Xi bent her head, her neck a graceful curve. "Thank you. I do believe in collecting beautiful things."

Addy felt heat start to rise to her cheeks. *Keep a grip on it, Sayers. You're here for the mission.* She clutched her purse tighter. Taylor had helped her slip a femtoweave antenna into the lining of the bag; get it close enough to Xi and it ought to be able to clone her sleeve. Meanwhile, the ocular scanners she was wearing as contacts would be building a three-dimensional model of Xi's face throughout the evening. She just had to maintain eye contact.

Which might be dangerous in a different way. She swallowed, her throat suddenly dry.

Xi shimmered closer. "You look lovely, Charlotte. Is that dress from Chez Matisse?"

"Yes. I didn't have anything else that I thought was quite appropriate in my luggage."

"Well, it was an excellent choice." Turning, Xi hooked Addy's arm through her own. "Let's go have a drink, shall we?"

Xi led her out of the gallery and through another set of doors into an elegantly set dining room. Above a black lacquered table floated a pair of spherical flames, flickering and glowing.

Addy peered closer at these decorations. These were real fire, not merely holograms – she was sure of it. *So much for not risking open flame on a spaceship.*

"You like them?" Xi asked. "A fascinating use of microrepulsor fields. I saw something similar in an art exhibition on Illyrica, and I put my engineers to work recreating it. I think the effect is rather stunning."

Addy nodded mutely, still staring at the flames dancing and writhing.

"Don't worry," said Xi, tracing a fingernail down Addy's arm. "They're perfectly safe. Still, it brings a little thrill, doesn't it?"

Goosebumps rose on Addy's skin along the path of Xi's finger, and she barely managed to suppress a shiver.

"Ah," said Xi. "I believe our drinks are here."

Nina, the bartender from downstairs, had appeared, bearing two of the drinks that Addy had seen her preparing. If anything, they were more impressive from close up, the blood red globe sitting in the middle like the pit of a peach. Nina gave Addy a look that was part surprise and part knowing glance, then withdrew.

Xi pulled out a chair for Addy, then took a seat at the head of the table, so that they were next to each other, but with the corner of the table decorously in the way. Addy hung her bag on the back of her chair, angled in Xi's direction – this ought to be close enough for the cloner to do its job.

Leaning back in her chair, languid and sinuous, Xi raised her glass in Addy's direction. "Santé."

Addy raised her own glass and then took a small sip. A melange of flavors swept across her palate: a deep, strong citrus married to the bite of alcohol and with just a hint of real spiciness that left a burning sensation on her lips. Wide-eyed, she stared at the drink, then back to Xi. "What is this?"

Xi shrugged, and Addy watched, mesmerized, as her collarbone rose and descended like a ship sinking beneath the waves. "My bartender created it. She calls it a Sabaean Sunrise."

"It's delicious," said Addy. She hadn't spent a lot of time drinking alcohol for the taste; maybe it was time to start. "What's in it?"

"Trade secrets, my dear. Shall we eat?"

As if summoned by the question, a pair of attendants in White Star livery appeared and deposited bowls in front of both of them, filled with a steaming dark brown soup, topped with what appeared to be crispy noodles.

"Manchow soup," said Xi. "I hope you don't mind spicy." Her eyes danced.

Addy smiled. "I'm game."

The soup was spicy as promised, but also deeply savory, with a broth of scallions and vegetables that was thick on the tongue.

"So," said Xi. "You must tell me more about yourself,

Charlotte. What brings you to my little corner of the galaxy?"

"A little bit of this, a little bit of that," she said, trying to match the other woman's playful tone.

Xi's carefully sculpted eyebrows went up, but the amusement hadn't vanished. "You told Domina that you'd played the casinos of the Juarez system. Surely, you must be acquainted with my old friend Jaime Agbaje?"

Addy bought time with another sip of her drink. Xi was testing her, waiting for a misstep. Best to short circuit that. "I may have… exaggerated my qualifications."

Xi didn't say anything for a moment, one fingernail tapping on her cocktail glass. Her gaze on Addy was level and unwavering.

Shit. She's going to have me hauled out of here, isn't she?

"Well, I suppose that makes you quite the gambler, indeed," said Xi. "But a woman of your skill, well, you really ought to try Juarez one of these days. Jaime is the manager of the Praetorian, one of the most sumptuous casinos in the galaxy – present surroundings excluded, of course."

The meal proceeded through a variety of opulent courses, Xi proving a captivating conversationalist, though Addy suspected the cocktail and subsequent glasses of wine were playing a part. *Keep your head, Addy. You're supposed to be working, not being worked.* She tried to focus, but the candlelight kept sparkling in her vision, and every time she looked over at Xi, her breath caught anew.

"So, what was life like for you, growing up?"

"Oh, it wasn't so bad," said Addy. "I guess you could say I learned about life the hard way. The haves and have-nots. Anyway, I did all right for myself."

"That you did," said Xi, leaning back in her chair. "As a

matter of fact, I'd say you... Yes, what is it?" she said, her voice turning sharp as an attendant entered. He leaned over and murmured something in Xi's ear, and the woman's smile tightened. Waving him away, Xi sighed and turned to Addy. "I'm so sorry for the interruption, my dear, but there's something I must take care of. It will only take a few minutes, but I insist you continue with your dinner. I wouldn't want it to get cold." She beckoned with one bangled hand and another attendant appeared to refill Addy's wine glass. Reaching across the table, Xi laid a warm hand on her arm. "Forgive me."

"Oh, of course," said Addy, a bit more waveringly than she would have liked. "I understand completely."

Xi smiled, squeezed her wrist, then rose, her gown shimmering in the light of the floating flame bulbs. "If you need anything, don't hesitate to ask." And with that, she disappeared behind one of the screens.

OK, Addy, concentrate. You've got a minute.

As she dug into her bag for her sleeve, she blinked twice and looked out of the left corners of her eyes to access the ocular camera Taylor had given her. The HUD flickered to life.

Come on, come on, she thought, as she flitted through the cumbersome menu. After a moment a map of Xi's face appeared in her screen: most of it was in photorealistic detail, complete with contour mapping, but a few last portions of it – mostly on the right side, which had been facing away from Addy during dinner – were still missing. It shouldn't be too much trouble to fill it in once they left the dinner table.

A quick glance at the sleeve's display showed that it had cloned about fifty percent of Xi's sleeve so far – in order to not be detected, the antenna used a low-power signal with limited bandwidth. She slid the sleeve back into her purse.

Blinking the HUD off again, she rubbed her shoulder and took another sip of wine.

Of course, capturing Xi's face was the easy part; tricking the lockbox into believing that the 3D model they created was the real Xi was where the fun began. But that was Taylor's problem.

Even that was a stroll in the park compared to getting Xi's access code. How the hell was she supposed to convince her to do that? Kovalic had told her to work any angle, and she could think of *one* way, but that raised the question of how far she was willing to go for this particular job. *Not that it would be much of a sacrifice, with those eyes.* She shivered slightly, and eyed the wine. *Enough of that. Gotta keep my head about me.*

True to her word, Xi returned about ten minutes later, looking apologetic as she sank back into her chair.

"Everything all right?" Addy asked.

"Quite," said Xi, setting her napkin back in her lap. "The *Queen Amina* is, as you can see, a full-time job. I prefer to delegate as much as I can, but some matters are…unavoidable."

"I can't even imagine. I'm not sure I'd be cut out for it."

"These are hardly skills one is born with – there's no substitute for on the job learning."

Addy snorted, then covered her mouth in embarrassment. "Excuse me."

Xi laughed. "No need. But I'm serious. All this has taken me a lifetime to build. And what it required, more than anything, was the will." Glancing at Addy's plate to confirm she was finished, she rose from her chair and extended a hand down at Addy. "If you're up for it, I'd like to show you exactly what will can accomplish."

CHAPTER 18

Café Turek was a level up from the noodle shop where Kovalic had done his brief stint as a dishwasher, but still three levels below the esplanade – close enough that its clientele was a mix of passengers and crew, though weighted more towards the latter. The walls were green with geometric decorations and wooden screens partitioned off the main seating area, filled with worn armchairs and threadbare pillows.

Sitting at the bar, Kovalic sipped a very black and very hot coffee. Nat had generously transferred a few credits from her account to a wallet on his new sleeve, along with a barely suppressed smile and an injunction to not spend it all in one place.

As he drank, he scanned the room for Seku al-Kitab. The picture on the Rizkin University website had been of a man with light brown skin, thick black hair, and a pencil mustache. Somehow he looked nervous even in the still image.

"You trust Cortez's intel?" said Nat's voice in his ear.

Turning on his stool, Kovalic peered past the screens and into the main room, where the commander was sitting in one of the overstuffed armchairs, pretending to read from a tablet.

"He seemed truthful," said Kovalic, covering his comment

with another sip of coffee. He saw the minute shake of Nat's head that signaled a suppressed laugh. "What?"

"You always did pride yourself on your ability to read people."

"And I'm usually right."

"But not always."

"Who is?"

Even from his spot at the bar, Kovalic could see Nat's mouth set in a line as he punched a button on the tablet.

"This still about Maverick?"

"It's your team, you made that very clear."

Kovalic sighed. "I may have spoken too hastily. What I meant was, I appreciate any input you have to give on personnel."

"It's fine. After this job, I'll just head back to the old grind and leave you all to it." She said it with a deliberate carelessness that was in itself indicative of just how much she cared about it.

"Look, I don't think–"

"Heads up, on your six. I think that's our man."

Even after years of working in covert operations, Kovalic still had to actively tamp down the urge to look directly at the man who had just entered the café. Instead, he turned back toward the bar and watched the mirrored panel that hung below the menu.

It was hard to tell completely in the reflection, but the man who had entered certainly did bear a striking resemblance to the image on the university's website. He wore a tweed jacket, plaid bowtie and, unusually, a pair of round spectacles.

Having ordered, with precision, a cup of rooibos tea, brewed for exactly seven minutes, with one teaspoon of sugar, the man took an empty seat near Kovalic, then set down a tablet, straightened it on the bar, and began to read.

Kovalic reached up to double tap his earbud, then studied the man out of the corner of his eye.

It was al-Kitab, of that he was certain. The same face, the same carefully trimmed mustache; and that nervous energy from the picture was clearly conveyed in his carriage and behavior. Kovalic continued to watch him as he sipped his coffee and idly watched the video feeds that hung over the bar. He didn't want to seem too interested in the man – and, more to the point, he wanted a chance to make sure that nobody else was too interested either. Seven minutes ought to be plenty of time to suss out anybody tailing the good professor, whether it be White Star security or Mirza's team.

When al-Kitab's tea arrived, he very precisely aligned it to the upper right corner of his tablet, turning the handle to a ninety-degree angle so he could hold it with his right hand while continuing to read. At the end of every page he would reach out, tap a control on the tablet to move to the next page, then move his hand to the tea cup and raise it to his lips for another sip.

"No sign of babysitters," said Nat in his ear, her assessment jibing with his own. "You want this one? Or should I make an approach?"

The woman who had been sitting between Kovalic and al-Kitab got up and left.

"Me," Kovalic murmured. "You're the hard sell if we need it."

"Copy. On you."

Kovalic slid over towards al-Kitab, taking his coffee with him. He peered over at the tablet, trying to make out what was on it.

The text was in small print, too fine for Kovalic's eyes to at this distance. No wonder the man needed glasses.

Only, as Kovalic glanced up at al-Kitab's eyes, rapidly zipping back and forth like a game of world class table tennis, he realized that al-Kitab *did* need the glasses precisely for this reason. The text on the page wasn't really text at all, but computer-generated codes that the glasses displayed as text, video, three-dimensional models, and so on. What al-Kitab was looking at through the glasses was far more informationally dense than text on a page.

"Must be riveting stuff," he said.

At first, al-Kitab didn't respond; not rout of rudeness, but because he was so enraptured in what he was reading that he either didn't hear Kovalic or couldn't imagine anybody was talking to him.

When his brain did register, he looked up and blinked through the glasses at Kovalic, his eyes disoriented as they focused back on what was in front of him. "I'm sorry?"

Kovalic nodded at the tablet. "Whatever you're reading. Must be pretty interesting."

"Oh. Yes." He turned back to the tablet.

"Never was much of a book learner myself."

Smiling politely, al-Kitab continued reading.

"What's it about, then?"

Drawing the deep breath of everybody who has been bothered by a stranger while trying to read their book, al-Kitab turned back to Kovalic. "A paper on archaeological finds on Earth in the late twenty-first century."

"Oh. Sure. You a professor then?"

"Indeed."

"Of archaeology?"

Al-Kitab sighed, clearly resigning himself to the fact that Kovalic wasn't about to leave him alone. "Yes. Archaeology." He gestured at the tablet as if the answer should have been self-evident.

"Wow. That must be fascinating. You ever find any dinosaur bones?"

One of al-Kitab's eyebrows began to twitch. "That's paleontology. An entirely different field, though there is occasionally some similarity in techniques."

"Gotcha, gotcha. So what kind of old bones do you look at?"

"Mostly human," said al-Kitab, his intense gaze seeming to suggest he might enjoy studying Kovalic's skeleton in the distant future. "If you'll excuse me, I really must get back to it." He gave another polite smile.

"Of course, of course. Say, I had an argument with a friend – maybe you could settle it."

Al-Kitab's shoulders drooped and he cast a wistful look at his tablet. "What kind of argument?"

"Well, my friend, he thinks some ancient alien civilization terraformed all of the planets that humans now live on; me, I think if that were the case, we'd definitely have found some evidence that there used to be aliens, you know? What do you think about that, doc?" Kovalic took a slow sip of his coffee, his eyes locked on al-Kitab.

The professor blinked, the glasses making his eyes especially owlish. He took off the spectacles, produced a cloth from the inside of his coat, and began wiping the lenses. "That... is a very interesting question, Mister... I'm sorry, I didn't catch your name?"

"Godwin."

"Mr Godwin. You've stumbled on one of the fundamental discussions in my field of study."

"What a coincidence," said Kovalic, his voice level.

Al-Kitab hooked the glasses back over his ears. "There are those who believe – and I count myself among their number – that a sufficiently advanced alien civilization might not have left behind any traces that human science is capable of detecting. Perhaps, for example, their technology was largely organic, or maybe they deliberately obfuscated any evidence of their existence so as not to influence later civilizations. Maybe they never lived on these planets at all, merely terraformed them from afar, creating conditions ripe for human life."

"Hmm. I guess that's all plausible. But, if it is true, I still have one question."

Al-Kitab gave a chuckle, smoothing his mustache with a finger. "Just one?"

"Well, one that I can think of right now," Kovalic admitted. "If their technology was undetectable, or they wanted to hide it, then why would they leave behind a single artifact like the Aleph Tablet?"

Halfway through raising his tea, al-Kitab froze. When he set the cup down, it rattled. He took a moment to compose himself, carefully aligning the mug once again. "Who are you?"

"An interested party."

"It would be unethical for me to discuss the business of one of my clients."

Kovalic gave him a hard look. "Dr al-Kitab, your client is an arms dealer and criminal. We're about twelve parsecs away from ethics."

"I am a scholar and an academic, Mr Godwin. My goal is the truth."

"Didn't stop you from taking her money."

At that, the man's shoulders sagged. "The truth doesn't come cheap these days, I'm afraid."

"It never did."

Raising his tea, al-Kitab took a long, thoughtful sip. When he set it down again, he seemed calmer, fortified. "The Aleph Tablet is a singular artifact, that much is true. I've made extrasolar archaeology the focus of my career, much to the dismay of my many advisors and administrators, and I have never found substantiated proof of any other extrasolar artificial objects. The accepted conclusion is that humanity is alone in this corner of the cosmos."

"Accepted."

"I'm sorry?"

"You said 'accepted' conclusion. Which I assume means that you continue to disagree with it."

A tight smile crossed the professor's face. "The Aleph Tablet is an outlier, Mr Godwin. We know it exists, though nobody has ever conclusively proved whether it is actually the work of an alien intelligence or simply a random occurrence of nature."

"It's had plenty of owners, from what I hear. Nobody ever studied it?"

The smile transmuted into a scowl. "Those who have possessed it certainly never had scholarship as their design. It was, rather, a trophy to be possessed and whispered about, an indication of power and wealth. As such, it would regularly disappear and then resurface in the hands of a completely new owner."

That meshed with the general's brief. The tablet never seemed to stay in one place long enough for anybody to get a proper look at it. Otherwise maybe this whole mess could have been avoided.

"The fact that you're here, though," said Kovalic, "tells me that *you* believe in it."

Al-Kitab plucked at the sleeve of his coat. "It is the work of my lifetime, Mr Godwin. To get even a single moment's chance to be in its presence would be the culmination of all that I have worked for and sacrificed." His left thumb pressed against the base of his third finger, rubbing a faint band of lighter skin there.

Kovalic let out a sigh. "Look, professor, I deal with the here and now. The kind of things you can see in front of you. I'm having trouble understanding what's so important about a block of – I don't even know what it's made of. Metal? Stone?"

"Most accounts suggest an incredibly dense metallic alloy, unlike any other we've discovered."

"OK, sure. Anyway, say you found it and studied it. What's the big deal?"

"The big deal? *The big deal?*" Al-Kitab's fist came down in a muted thump on the bar, rattling the cups and earning them side-eyed glances from around the cafe. Out of the corner of his eye, Kovalic saw Taylor tense but he flashed a surreptitious "hold" hand sign in her direction.

"Proof of other advanced civilizations would change *everything*, Mr Godwin. Who were they? Where did they go? Why isn't there more evidence? Fields from biology to sociology to religion would be fundamentally altered forever. We would have to recontextualize our entire *existence*." Al-Kitab turned his gaze back toward Kovalic, shining tears magnified by the lenses. "We thought we were alone, you see. But we weren't, all along."

Kovalic didn't say anything for a moment as the professor collected himself and took another sip of tea.

"I understand," said Kovalic finally. "But my concern is something a little more... tangible."

"Ah," said al-Kitab with another sad chuckle. "You mean the secrets it's said to hold. Well, in normal circumstances we might call that the sixty-four million credit question, but here it's merely one among many."

"I take it there are theories."

"As many as there are stars in the sky. I've heard that it's everything from the Aleph's version of *Voyager*'s Golden Record, to schematics for their advanced technology, to a recipe for goulash."

"You have a favorite?"

"I have to admit, I've always had a taste for goulash." This time the professor's smile was genuine. "But yes, I do."

"Care to elaborate?"

Al-Kitab drained the last of his tea and gathered up his tablet. "While this has been a most illuminating conversation, Mr Godwin, as I said, I must respect the wishes of my client. I'm afraid I can't discuss these matters any further at present." He paused. "However, if you are still interested in the subject, might I suggest you look up the recording of the lecture I gave at the Centauri City University? You'll find it in their database: index number 7113. It's a good overview on the subject – only... half an hour?" He rose and nodded to Kovalic. "I bid you and your *colleague* a good day." And with that, he was gone, leaving only his empty cup behind.

After a few moments, Nat sat down in the doctor's recently vacated seat, and reached over to toy with the discarded tea cup. "So... was that what I think it was?"

"I believe so," said Kovalic, finishing the last of his coffee. "I have to say, for a professor, his spycraft isn't too shabby. Shall we?"

"After you."

Thirty minutes later, having assured they weren't followed from the café, Kovalic knocked on the door to room 7113. He'd assumed that the professor's mention of his colleague had been an implicit invitation for Nat to join them, which just as well: whatever al-Kitab had to tell them, he had a feeling she would have a much better chance of understanding it than he would.

Al-Kitab opened the door, but was careful to stay well inside as he ushered them in. "Please, come in, quickly."

The professor scurried around the room, throwing a pile of clothes off one chair and dragging it to the middle of the room. His gesture to Nat was gentlemanly, and she looked amused at the formality, but smiled as she sat down. Kovalic leaned against one wall.

"I apologize for the subterfuge," said al-Kitab. "It was a bit theatrical, I must admit, but when your patron has a reputation for possessiveness, it's best to be careful."

"Frankly, I'm surprised you're willing to talk to us at all," said Kovalic.

"I do not believe in locking away knowledge, even for a fee," said the professor, drawing himself up. He deflated slightly. "Though, I must admit, I have an ulterior motive."

"Oh?" said Nat. "And what's that?"

The professor cocked his head to one side. "I suspect your interest in the tablet is not purely *hypothetical*. Let us say merely that I am... preparing for all contingencies."

Kovalic rubbed his mouth to hide a smile, but merely dipped his head to al-Kitab. "Very practical."

"So," said al-Kitab. "Where was I? Oh yes!" At a wave of his hand, a holoscreen appeared, showing a schematic of circles and lines instantly familiar to anybody over the age of seven, no matter where in the galaxy they lived, because it *was* where they lived.

"The known galaxy," said al-Kitab. "Systems where humans have discovered wormholes leading to other systems. Most – but not all – of which have contained planets suitable for human life." Many of the rings glowed green.

"I've heard this one," said Kovalic. "The conspiracy theory that the Aleph supposedly terraformed all these planets to support human life."

"That is one theory. I'm not sure about the 'conspiracy' part, but, for my part, I would suggest that as an explanation, it does not go quite far enough."

Oh, great. Kovalic made sure he knew where the exits were. Al-Kitab didn't seem like the kind of guy who bought red yarn in bulk, but sometimes you just couldn't tell.

"If you're going to posit that the Aleph actually created the wormholes between the systems, then we've heard that one too," Nat added.

Al-Kitab tilted his head towards her. "Indeed, I do believe that to be the case. But the bigger question is 'why?'" With another flourish, a second image appeared, similar in composition to the previous one, but the circles were distributed much less randomly; one was all the way off on one side of the display. Three more were clustered very closely. "This is not as instantly recognizable, but perhaps you can figure it out."

Nat leaned forward, her brows knit in the expression that Kovalic knew meant she was unraveling a particularly thorny puzzle. "It's the same thing, but in actual stellar geography."

"Very good," said al-Kitab. He flicked a finger at the display and a conventional image of the galaxy appeared behind it. "You'll notice that our commonly used schematic misrepresents the actual locations of these systems – Jericho and Badr, for example, are considered to be adjacent because of their wormhole connection, but in reality they are halfway across the galaxy from each other."

"Right," said Nat. "Nobody's ever discovered any pattern to their locations."

"There is not," al-Kitab confirmed. "*But* let us take a step back in our assumptions. What if the Aleph did *not* terraform planets to support human life? What if, instead, they used the technology they *did* have – creating space-time disruptions to bridge disparate galactic locations – to connect systems which *already* had planets suitable for supporting human life? A similar hypothesis, to be sure, but one that changes the conversation a great deal, because then we have to ask a different question altogether."

Kovalic's head was spinning a bit at this point. "I don't get it. How would they know which systems had planets that could support human life?"

Al-Kitab pointed a finger at Kovalic. "Yes. *That* is the question that we should be asking. Not *why* but *how*. If the Aleph were operating on a purely trial-and-error basis, we ought to be finding discarded wormhole cul-de-sacs to support this theory. But every single wormhole we have discovered has led us, eventually, to more human-habitable planets. That is a surprising degree of precision, unless…"

"Unless they had a map," said Nat slowly.

"Unless they had a *map*," al-Kitab echoed, his voice triumphant.

Kovalic stared at the schematic. Something gnawed at his stomach like a hamster working at its straw. Humanity had discovered fewer than twenty systems: a lot, when you considered the diaspora of their species, and yet an infinitesimal fraction of the number of stars in the galaxy, much less the universe.

Nat voiced the thought running through his own head. "This can't be all of the habitable systems in the galaxy."

"The odds are certainly against it," said the professor.

"So we've only seen part of the map," said Kovalic. The gnawing had intensified. Was this what an ulcer felt like?

"That is my theory, yes."

"And the rest of the map?"

Professor al-Kitab pushed his spectacles back up on his nose. "Mr Godwin, I believe this map was the most treasured information that the Aleph possessed. And I believe they deliberately left it behind on one of the planets they connected, for whatever life would come after them. In other words, I believe the complete map – a map that would show every star system in this galaxy, at least, where human life could be supported, as well as how to travel between them – is onboard this ship right now: the Aleph Tablet."

CHAPTER 19

Access to the skiff bays was what the Illyrican navy would have considered "lax," given that Eli and Tapper were able to walk right in behind a crew of maintenance techs coming on shift.

In general, security on the crew levels seemed much less intrusive than on the passenger levels. Then again, during Eli's time as a lowly maintenance tech on the frigid tundra of Sabaea, finding workarounds for annoying security protocols had practically been de rigueur: doors propped open, passwords written on sticky notes, even guards who'd wave you past after your tools set off the scanners. *Everybody is just looking to make their job easier.*

The bay was dominated by the two skiffs moored there. Each was about half the size of the *Cavalier*; they were intended for short hops between ships, outboard work on the *Queen Amina* itself, or excursions of small groups of passengers to planetary surfaces. The perfect vessel for them to make their exit: not flashy, but they would do the job. Once they installed the data spike Taylor had given them, they'd be able to access and control it remotely, powering it up so they could make a quick getaway.

One of the skiffs was being actively worked on, but the

techs barely spared a glance for Tapper and Eli, and the drones rolling past, carrying tools and spare parts to the various workstations, didn't give them any more notice.

"All right," said Tapper. "Let's get this done."

They crossed the bay to the unattended skiff. Eli studied the underside as they went. From what he could tell, the ships were in good shape and well looked after. *Not that I'd take them over the* Cav, he thought with a slight tinge of guilt. He didn't like leaving the ship behind, though the practical considerations had been undeniable. But that didn't stop him from missing it.

The entry ramp was, thankfully, down, making it the work of a moment for the two of them to stroll onboard. Eli had never been on this particular model before, but the layout was fairly standard, and he had no trouble locating the cockpit. He palmed the door control and it slid open.

A startled yelp issued from the dark compartment, and Eli jumped back, nearly colliding with Tapper.

"Sorry sorry sorry," said a voice. "I know I'm not supposed to be here, I just fell asl... Wait.... Bishop?"

Eli opened his mouth to automatically correct the misapprehension, his mind still on the job in front of him, until he remembered that was the name he'd given the other night at the bar. A slim, familiar figure stepped into the dim light of the corridor, brushing the dark hair out of their eyes.

"Maldonado? What the hell are you doing in here?"

"Uh... well, I was checking the results of a test I was running – faulty O2 sensor reading, you know – and I just sat down for a minute, I swear, then I must have drifted..." The tech frowned as their brain evidently caught up with their mouth. "Wait, What are *you* doing here? I thought you were assigned to the *forward* skiff bay."

"Logistics got reports that parts were going missing across the ship," Tapper broke in, before Eli could even open his mouth. "Doing a quick inventory during downtime to see if we can figure out what's going on. I asked Bishop here to help me check out the skiffs, because he knows them so well."

Mal's brow creased. "But I thought you just came onboard."

"Generally," said Eli hastily. "I know skiffs in general. Trevelyan here is just a support guy, you know. Doesn't know his pitch from his yaw, if you get my drift. So if you don't mind, we actually just need to pop in there for a sec..." Eli started to move past Mal, who quickly shifted to block his view, leaning against the doorframe with a studiously casual expression that Eli recognized all too well from having seen it on his own face.

They really do not *want me looking in the cockpit.*

"Maybe a little later?" said Mal. "I'm kind of just in the middle of something."

"Didn't you say you were asleep?" said Eli.

"Er, yes! But that's because I was waiting for this report to finish running, and I–"

Tapper huffed an angry sigh that signaled the end of his patience and strong-armed his way past both of them into the cockpit, where he suddenly pulled up short.

He glanced back at the tech, eyebrows raised. "Are you *living* here, kid?"

Mal's face fell and Eli followed Tapper into the compartment.

A rumpled blanket sat in the chair for the navigational station; on the console beside it was a takeout container full of noodles. A satchel was shoved into one corner, clothes peeking out from underneath its flap, and hanging from a handle on the piloting computer interface was a toiletry bag.

"Well, er, that is," Mal started, looking desperately like they wanted to bolt through the nearest wormhole. "There was a problem with my berth and it hasn't been fixed, but the quartermaster keeps telling me 'soon,' and…"

Tapper had taken on the look of a parent disappointed in his kid's math grade. "You're a stowaway, aren't you?"

"What? No, I… I'm totally supposed to be here." Mal slid possessively in front of the toiletry bag, as though Eli and Tapper might try to steal their toothbrush.

Oh, kid. You want to live in between the cracks, you're going to need to be a lot better at lying.

With a sigh, Tapper glanced at Eli, then stepped over to the console and slotted in the data spike.

Eli held Mal's attention, but the tech had started to fold in on themselves, arms encircling their body as though they were cold. "Look, I just needed a job. Any job. Anything was better than where I was. But they were full up on ship techs here… so I just called myself an assistant and, well, nobody's bothered me about it yet. I've been trying to pull my weight! Fixing things that need fixing, you know. Hoping somebody might take me on as a legit assistant at some point." A glance between the two of them. "You're not going to turn me in, are you?"

Eli shot a look at Tapper, but the sergeant was studiously examining the progress of the data spike at the console. *And, technically, as he loves to remind me when it comes to making the difficult decisions, I outrank him.* "No," said Eli. "We're not going to turn you in."

He thought he saw Tapper nod to himself out of the corner

of his eye, but he was too wrapped up in the relief that washed over Mal's face.

"I really appreciate it," Mal was saying. "I owe you guys one. Anything you need, anything I can help you with, let me know. I've had to work around a bunch of systems – food vouchers from the crew commissary, laundry stations, empty crew berths when I could find them. Not a system I don't know at this point." If the kid had any regrets about scamming the ship's resources, it wasn't evident.

Ripping off a notorious gangster sure doesn't seem like a great idea if you want to live to a ripe old age.

"Don't worry about it," said Tapper, who had retrieved the data spike from the console, and pocketed it. "But you better pack up your stuff, because you definitely can't stay here. And the next people who find you aren't going to be as understanding as we are. Christ, don't you even know whose ship this is?" He shook his head.

They made it to the base of the entry ramp, each of them carrying one of Mal's bags, before Eli realized that the skiff bay was strangely quiet for a place where people traditionally worked on noisy machinery.

It didn't take long to figure out why.

The maintenance crews that had been on shift when they'd come in had vanished. Four people stood in a loose array opposite the bottom of the ramp. Eli recognized the pair that had braced Mal outside the bar the night they'd met. The other two didn't look familiar but Eli swore he caught their eyes widen as they met his, as if they recognized him somehow.

"You again," spat the freckled woman – Cavanaugh, Eli somehow recalled Mal saying. "I'm going to enjoy this."

"Bloody hell," Tapper muttered, one of Mal's overflowing bags occupying both hands. "You try to do something nice."

"This must be our lucky day," said one of the others, a man with a white scar running through his brown eyebrow. "Three birds, one stone."

"You know these assholes?" said Cavanaugh.

"By reputation only," said the scarred man. "But it's nice to finally make their acquaintance."

Who the fuck are these guys?

"Oh, hey, Cavanaugh. Romero. How are you guys doing today?" Mal said, bright eyes darting between the two, their voice doing absolutely nothing to conceal their nervousness.

Cavanaugh's teeth bared. "I told you you'd be doing this job, Maldonado. One way or another."

"OK, OK," said Mal, trying to put up their hands, despite the bag cradled there. "It's fine. I'll do it. Just, you can let them go, OK?"

"Not going to happen," said the other new addition, a woman with short, curly brown hair. "They'll be coming with us." She reached back and produced a pistol, holding it loosely at her side.

"You don't want to do anything for them, kid," said Tapper. "Those two are Illyrican agents, and trust me: they're not about to let you walk away after they're done with you."

"Wait, what?" said Eli, looking back and forth between Tapper and the other two.

"Unless I miss my guess, Handsome over there is the one who took a nap in the ladies' room," said Tapper, nodding to the scarred man, who scowled in return. "Anyway, yeah, none of us are going anywhere with you."

"I don't recall offering you a choice," said the brown-haired woman.

"That's fine. Here's one for you: walk away now, and you can skip that embarrassing talk with your boss about how you blew this."

The cocksure tone of Tapper's voice had all of Eli's muscles tensing.

"I don't think the cavalry is about to ride to your rescue," said the scarred man. "So put down the bags and we'll all walk out of here real quiet like." Tapper looked back at Mal and Eli, then shrugged. "You heard him, boys. Turn and burn."

Turn and... oh no.

As the sergeant laid down the duffel bag he was carrying, Eli saw him surreptitiously tap his sleeve. A thrumming coursed through the deck plates and up into Eli's boots – almost unnoticeable at first, but as it grew louder, Eli saw the Illyrican agent who was holding the gun frown.

The weapon barrel rose towards them. "What did you...?"

And then the skiff's engines fired.

Had he been asked his opinion on this plan, Eli would have strongly advised *against* starting the main engine sequence while in an enclosed space like a hangar. For one thing, the engines weren't particularly efficient while in atmosphere. For another, they made a hell of a noise.

Then again, that might have been the point.

The skiff lurched drunkenly forward, with just enough time for Eli to let the armful of bags topple out of his hands as he hugged the ramp's hydraulic strut. Out of the corner of his eye, he caught Tapper and Mal doing the same.

Straining against its umbilical connections, the skiff bucked like an amusement park ride, jumping up in the air a foot or two before slamming back down to the deck. The vibrations sent Cavanaugh, Romero, and the Illyrican agents sprawling.

And then, as suddenly as the engines had fired up, they whimpered to a stop, flaming out. The skiff dropped to the deck with a crunch, its landing struts creaking under the sudden weight.

Eli staggered off the ramp, legs wobbling. "Holy shit, was that a terrible idea."

"Worked, didn't it?" said Tapper, surprisingly upright as he helped Mal off the ramp. "Get moving." The sergeant glanced over his shoulder at the Illyrican agents, who were also getting to their feet. "Go!"

Without any further need for encouragement, Eli stumbled at the best speed he could manage towards the hangar's door, ignoring the shouts in his wake. A shot pinged off the bulkhead to one side, but the Illyricans' aim was clearly still shaky.

The door slid open at their approach, and Eli bolted out, followed closely by Tapper and Mal. The tech darted to the control panel beside the door, fingers flying over the screen as several green icons blinked to red. Klaxons blared to life around them and amber lights began to flash around the door's frame. With a look of satisfaction, Mal slapped a large red control and the door slammed shut, just ahead of another shot from the Illyricans' weapon. The alarms cut off abruptly, though the warning lights continued blinking.

Mal heaved a sigh of relief, slumping against the wall. "That was too close."

"What did you do?" said Tapper, eyeing the panel.

"I convinced the system there was a hull breach in the hangar. That triggered the emergency decompression protocols. It'll slow them down, but only until the damage control team shows up and lets them out."

"So we should make ourselves scarce," said Tapper. "Come on."

Summoning their best nonchalance, the three sidled away from the door, making their way into the ship's lower levels until they were sure they weren't being followed.

"What did those guys want from you anyway?" said Eli, when they were well away from the hangar.

"Uh, well, not *officially* being part of the crew has its challenges," said Mal, scratching at their scalp with a slight hint of embarrassment. "Cavanaugh and Romero figured out that I'd been manipulating the systems. They said they wouldn't tell ship security about me as long as I did a few jobs for them; those other two hired them to get access to the ship's systems."

"So you're what, a sub-contractor?" said Tapper.

"Sort of?"

The sergeant shook his head. "Yeah, well, that job definitely wasn't going to come with any benefits beyond death and dismemberment."

Mal's face took on a decidedly greenish hue. "So, what do those guys have against you, anyway? You just got here!"

"Let's just say we've got some history and leave it at that."

But the tech was on a roll. "And did you install a *data spike* in that skiff? Why'd you do that? What is going on?" Their breath was starting to come in quick, short puffs.

Tapper put a reassuring hand on Mal's shoulder. "You know, I'm betting you didn't get a single good night's sleep in that skiff cockpit. Seems like you could use a rest. Come on, we'll let you borrow our bunk."

That seemed to console Mal a bit, and a few minutes later, the tech was securely ensconced in Tapper's bunk, which the sergeant had cleaned off. All the adrenaline seemed to have ebbed out of their system, and they were snoring less than a minute after their head hit the pillow.

Tapper and Eli stepped into the hallway, the sergeant closing the door behind them.

"You really think dragging Mal into our mess is helping them out?" Eli said.

"The kid'll be all right. Better than where they'd be when the Illyricans start tying up their loose ends. And hey, it might even slow them down a little."

"Yeah, well, now we've got a new problem. Our exit plan just went up in smoke, and there's no way we'll get back into the skiff bays with both the Illyricans and White Star on high alert."

"That's the job, Brody. Roll with the punches."

Roll with the punches?! That's the best he can do? Eli opened his mouth to object, but Tapper had started off down the corridor, leaving Eli little alternative but to jog after him.

"So, now what?"

"Now we go secure the airlock for the EVA, like the boss asked us. And you start thinking about a new way to get us the hell off this ship."

CHAPTER 20

One of the benefits of being the owner of a ship the size of the *Queen Amina*, Addy discovered, was having your own private lift tube. Xi led her out of the dining room and Addy, her head still a little fuzzy from the drinks, just barely remembered to grab the purse on the back of her chair. But the right side of Xi's face – the part she still needed to capture – faced away from Addy, and she hadn't figured out how to maneuver into a better position.

So close.

A panel in the wall, indistinguishable from those around it, slid aside at Xi's approach and they stepped into the lift tube. Unlike the rest of Xi's quarters, this was more utilitarian than ornate, with stark metal paneling. Elegant and sleek, but no frills.

There were also a decided lack of controls. Instead, Xi pressed something on one of the bangles on her wrist and the door slid closed behind them. The lift tube drifted into motion, though the ride was so subtle Addy had trouble figuring out which way they were going.

"You know I was born on Trinity?"

Addy blinked at the non-sequitur. "The Commonwealth colony?"

Xi's nose wrinkled. "The Commonwealth wasn't formed until later, and we certainly didn't see ourselves as its colonists. My parents were amongst the first generation of settlers; when they arrived, it was a habitable world only by the slimmest of definitions.

"My mother was an agricultural engineer, developing strains of common crops that could survive the harsh environment. She was very good at her job, but Trinity proved a tough nut to crack. Towering dust storms in the summer, ferocious blizzards in the winter. Underground pests that liked to eat all the roots and tubers. Every time one problem was solved, it seemed as though three more reared their heads.

"My father was an astronomer who studied quasars. She was looking down, he was looking up." Her smile, wistful at first, twisted with an injection of sadness. "Neither of them were particularly political. When the Illyricans invaded Earth, it seemed so far away – we thought we'd be insulated. But then the Earthers fell back to Terra Nova, a short wormhole jump away from us, and Trinity was conscripted into the Commonwealth.

"I was fifteen. At first it didn't mean much: new flags, a small garrison. We never even saw any fighting. But the Commonwealth still insisted on everybody 'doing their part' for the war effort. So my mother started working even longer hours, trying to raise crop yields. My father was drafted into some military research program. They left me to take care of myself, which I was perfectly capable of doing."

Xi stared at the wall, lost in thought. "There was nothing anyone could have done to predict the freak dust storm that killed my mother. Didn't stop my father from blaming himself. He drank himself to death within a year. Then I really was on my own."

There was a pause, the first real opening for any sort of interjection. "I'm so sorry," said Addy.

Reaching down, Xi squeezed her hand, flashing a smile at the same time. "Thank you. It was a long time ago. I didn't know much of anything at that age, but I knew I didn't want to be there anymore. So I took what little money they had left – they were not the best about saving for the future; we all think we have more time left than we do – and headed for the stars."

The lift slowed to a stop, the doors opening into a large, dark room.

Great. Addy tried to keep her breathing under control. If Xi was going to off her for some reason, she could have done it back in her apartment, and nobody would have been the wiser. This whole ship was hers, no need to be picky. Still, at least there wasn't plastic sheeting on the floor.

Their footsteps echoed through the space and when the lift door closed behind them, they were in near total darkness. When they came to a stop, the only sensation Addy could detect was Xi's hand, warm, on her arm.

"I was determined to make my own way," said Xi. "The money ran out by the time I reached Jericho Station, and I realized I'd need more, because what I wanted, more than anything, was to not live under someone else's thumb. I wanted the galaxy at my fingertips."

There was a flare of light from another of Xi's bracelets, followed by a loud groan of hydraulics as the ceiling split along its length. Massive shutters tessellated open, revealing a tapestry of stars.

Addy's eyes had adjusted to the pitch blackness of the room, making the scattering of stars all the more stunning. It wasn't just a projection: something about it was too... imperfect. Some shone brightly, while others were little more than faint spots seen out of the corner of her eyes. Her hand reached out of its own accord; they seemed so close, it was almost as if she could pluck one from the void.

"It's the largest transparent aluminum lattice ever installed on a ship," said Xi. "Cost a fortune. Just a thin layer of material between us and the vacuum of space."

Holy shit. Addy clenched her fists as the vertigo began to kick in and the stars spun in her vision. Her knees buckled and she started to waver.

Strong hands caught her. "Hey. Hey. It's OK. Look at me. Down here."

With an effort, Addy forced her eyes down to meet Xi's. The brown eyes were soft, sympathetic. "You're OK. Everything's all right." Xi smiled and pressed her hands against Addy's cheeks. "Just breathe."

Addy closed her eyes, took a deep breath in through her nose and let it out through her mouth, trying to quell the bass drum pounding in her chest. There was the sound of machinery once again and when Addy opened her eyes she saw that the shutters above had closed. Soft lighting had flooded the room, revealing an assortment of couches and lounge chairs, all angled to provide unobstructed views of the ceiling.

"I realize it can be a little intense," said Xi, withdrawing her hands from Addy's cheeks, which felt unaccountably cool and lonely in their absence. "I'm sorry for springing it on you like that."

"It's fine," said Addy, taking a seat on a couch. "Amazing, but also a little… terrifying." Getting that word out required pushing it past a large lump in her throat, and she felt her cheeks burning once again. *It's not the same thing as scared. It's not.*

"I understand," said Xi, sitting next to her. "I come in here sometimes because it reminds me of how small and alone I felt when I first left home. But now, well," she jangled the bracelet on her arm, "now it's at the touch of *my* finger. The universe at my beck and call." Xi's mouth set in a firm line, and those brown eyes hardened into ironwood. "And how did I accomplish it? Hard work. Perseverance. Force of will. I *wanted* it. So I took it." Xi reached over and pressed Addy's hand between her palms. "It doesn't matter where you come from. It's all there for the taking."

Addy's heartbeat was running like quicksilver. *What is happening here?* In the corner of her eye, a lone green dot blinked suddenly – with Xi's face turned towards her, the biometric scan was complete. "I see a lot of me in you," said Xi, and her tone was a mixture of hope and sadness. "The galaxy has let you down, hasn't it? It's hard to find a place where you fit in, and nobody ever seems willing to give you a break. Some days – most days – it feels like everybody's against you. I know that feeling. And this is your opportunity."

"What do you mean?"

Xi smiled. "I want to give you a break. I could use somebody like you. Fearless, confident. Somebody who knows that sometimes rules get in the way of doing what's necessary."

Is that me? She flushed at Xi's description. It sounded like someone else entirely. A better version of her, not the short-fused and lonely version that she saw in the mirror every day.

"I think you could be a valuable addition to my organization," Xi continued.

"I… I can?" Addy's head spun, though not from the vertigo of the star field this time. Left was right, up was down. The green dot continued to blink, insistent. She held her head between her hands and fought back the urge to burst into tears. *That wouldn't be very confident or very fearless.*

"Absolutely," said Xi, squeezing Addy's hand tightly. "You have so much potential, just waiting to be tapped. I think we could do great things together. The galaxy would never see us coming. The *Queen Amina* is just one part of my operation. I have contacts in every system: Commonwealth, Imperium, independent. There's no place I don't do business, no one I don't do business with. You could be a part of that, and with it, the rewards are... well, endless." She looked up at the ceiling again. "You *deserve* all this."

Addy swallowed. *The mission, Addy – the mission.* Kovalic, Taylor, Tapper, Brody were all depending on her. But that was a small voice in her head, droned out by the blood rushing in her ears. "What could I possibly do for you?"

"Let's start small. Just one little thing to begin. To prove you're the person I believe you can be. Do you think you can do that?"

Maybe the air mix in the room was off and there was just too much oxygen, but Addy found herself nodding, lightheaded. "OK."

Xi broke into another of those brilliant smiles, and reached out to take Addy's hand, squeezing it. "Excellent. I'm so glad to hear that, Adelaide."

The smile overwhelmed Addy, so much so that it took a moment before she understood why all the hairs on the back of her neck had gone up. And by the time she realized that Xi had used her name – her *real* name – it was too late to do anything about it. The abort code was on her sleeve, out of reach in her bag. *Too far.*

"What I'd like to know is exactly how many of your team are onboard, and what their plan is. Do you think you can help me with that?"

CHAPTER 21

"A map," Kovalic was still muttering to himself, fifteen minutes later, as he and Nat took a lift car to the esplanade. More importantly, a host of new planets, all human habitable, and no doubt with resources ripe for the taking. That wouldn't just be a leg up in the war – it would be an insurmountable advantage.

"So, no chance we're letting the Imperium have that," said Nat.

"If we do, it's game over," agreed Kovalic, checking his sleeve. If he could have called in the navy to just impound the *Queen Amina* and the tablet, he'd have considered it, but they'd already left Commonwealth space behind, and it would take the better part of a day for a message to make its way back to the general and from him on to the nearest available naval unit, ceding precious time to Mirza and her team. Not to mention the political ramifications of the Commonwealth seizing a civilian ship outside of their jurisdiction.

No, the general had sent the SPT because he believed they could get the job done. This was down to them.

"Less than two hours until we hit the Hamza gate," said Kovalic. "Can we be ready to go by then?"

"I'll check in with Brody and Tapper."

"Any word from Sayers?"

Nat shook her head. "She'd better be well on her way to getting Xi's biometrics or this is all going to be for nothing."

"I trust her. She'll come through."

"You say so."

"Let's just say I'm feeling more charitable toward her than I am toward our good friend the professor. If he decides to tell Xi about us, then this whole thing is over before it begins."

"Look, I'm not going to argue for the altruism of academics, but this is his life's work. From what he said, I don't think he's about to turn down a chance at the tablet in his hands, no matter how exactly that comes about."

Privately, Kovalic had to agree with her. If al-Kitab was willing to make a deal with someone like Ofeibia Xi in the first place, changing his allegiance was hardly beyond the pale... provided they had the tablet.

More to the point, they needed the professor. There was certainly no one else aboard the *Queen Amina* – and quite possibly nobody else in the galaxy – who knew as much about the tablet as he did. If anybody was going to be able to authenticate the artifact *and* decode any data that might be stored on it, Kovalic was willing to bet it was Seku al-Kitab.

But first things first: they had to get the tablet.

Nat had tapped her earbud and was leaning against the wall, listening to a report from Tapper and Brody. "Copy that, Bruiser. We're en route to your location and will be there in about fifteen."

"Everything OK?"

"Brody said Tapper threatened to lock him in a supply closet."

"The usual, then."

The lift car slowed to a stop and Kovalic stepped up to the door as it began to slide open.

His ears popped suddenly and amid a deafening whooshing of air he felt a pressure differential pull him towards the door and the dark, empty void of a lift shaft beyond.

Nat grabbed his belt with one hand and a handrail with the other as his foot hovered over thin air, then managed to haul him back into the car, throwing them both to the floor.

"What the…" Kovalic managed.

"That first step's a doozy," gasped Nat, climbing to her feet while keeping a tight grip on the handrail. She punched an emergency override button on the control panel. Nothing happened. "Goddamnit," she yelled, over the air whistling from the shaft, "somebody sabotaged the car."

"*Somebody*," said Kovalic.

"Your friend Mirza is quite the pain in the ass," shouted Nat as she started to pry off the control panel with one hand.

"Can't argue with that," said Kovalic, unthreading his belt and lashing it through the waistband of Nat's trousers and the nearest rail so she could use both hands. "What have we got?"

"I'll have to do a local bypass," said Nat. "Eyes clearly has a backdoor into the *Queen Amina's* systems too, and it looks like they've been able to monitor us via the security feeds." She raised her sleeve, then tapped a few commands as she waved it towards the control panel.

The doors on the lift car jerked closed and Kovalic let out the briefest sigh of relief. At least they wouldn't be falling hundreds of feet towards an uncertain end. It was a hell of a lot quieter without the constant rushing air, too. He wiggled a finger in his ear.

"OK, I think I've got control," said Nat. "I'm disabling the cameras and microphones in this particular car so they can't keep tracking us, but there's a good chance they'll pick us up whenever we get off."

"Great," said Kovalic, retrieving his belt. "So I guess we need to find a blindspot in their coverage. The esplanade's right out. Service levels?"

"I'll see if I can reroute, but it's going to play havoc with the lift tube traffic network."

"So, we'll have some angry passengers who can't make it to the casino," said Kovalic. "I think they'll live." Possibly more than could be said for them if Mirza had her way.

Mirza. Did she know exactly what she was jockeying for here? Al-Kitab had said he hadn't told anybody else, not even Xi, about what the tablet might contain. It was, as he had stressed, a theory, even if he seemed to have personally bought into it.

But if Mirza did know what the tablet was – after all, the general had said Emperor Alaric had been after it, so he might have had an inkling of its true nature – then it was them or her, and all things being equal, Kovalic was going to choose them, thank you very much.

"Got it!" Nat said, and the lift car sped into motion. "Even if Eyes is tracking the car, I've spammed them with so much garbage it'll take them a while to figure out where we've gone."

Kovalic rubbed at his mouth. "Damn it, Nat, we're still playing defense. We need to get a step ahead of Mirza and her team. We can't be watching our backs while we're trying to break into the vault; somebody's going to get hurt." Something tickled at his brain, something he'd missed. But the more he reached for it, the less substantial it seemed, like a dream that had already started to evaporate.

The lift tube slowed to a stop and Nat tapped a control on the panel to open the doors. This time, Kovalic made sure to check there was actually a floor to step onto.

"Where the hell are we?"

Nat swept a hand expansively. "You wanted off the grid, I give you off the grid. Sub-deck 19. Security coverage is sparse down here, and I've mapped out a path that avoids most of the cameras between here and our rendezvous. Just remember to keep your head down. And here." Producing a mini tool, Nat unscrewed a couple of bolts and handed one to Kovalic. "Put this in your boot."

"In my boot?" said Kovalic, eyeing it dubiously.

"This should disrupt the gait analysis part of the *Amina*'s security system."

Twenty painful minutes later, when they limped into the locker room that Tapper and Brody had secured, Kovalic said nothing, just sat down on a bench and dumped the bolt out, then massaged his foot.

"I knew it," said Brody.

Kovalic, Tapper, and Nat all eyed him.

"He's, uh, got a screw loos… OK, tough room."

"Well," said Kovalic, "I've never fired anybody in the middle of a mission before, but I guess there's a first time for everything." He fished the baffle out of his pocket and flipped it on, feeling his ears pop.

"All right, boys," said Nat. "Show us what you've got."

Tapper popped open a locker behind him. "Ta da. Kim Industries Mark VII environment suit, rated for hard vacuum. Built-in reaction control system, radiation shielded, primary and backup air supplies, high-power gravboots. This is the luxury groundcar of vacsuits."

"I might never take it off," said Kovalic, checking his sleeve.

"Any word from our inside woman?" Tapper asked.

Kovalic shook his head. "Maverick is still on radio silence. But we've got to assume she's doing her job, which means we need to do ours. Run me through what else we've got."

"The airlock the commander identified is just through there." Tapper pointed at a hatch on the far end of the locker room.

"We've got just under an hour before the *Queen Amina* hits the wormhole," said Brody, tossing up a holographic screen displaying a countdown timer. "I've sent it to your sleeves so we're all on the same mission clock."

Kovalic glanced down at his sleeve and thumbed an authorization to accept the clock sync request from Brody. "Copy that. Commander, where are we with accessing the vault maintenance hatch?"

"It's not designed to be opened remotely. I'll need to patch through an override via your comms once you're in position."

"Didn't you say something about tremendous amounts of interference from the wormhole? Won't that affect our communications?"

Nat exchanged a glance with Brody. "We're hoping that it's short range enough that it won't get jammed."

"'Hoping' isn't quite as much assurance as I'd like. Do we have a backup plan?"

She glanced over at Tapper. "Sarge, show him the backup plan."

Tapper popped open an equipment locker. "Plasma torch and an emergency airlock seal. Set up the e-lock, burn through the outer door, then cycle the airlock and pop the inner door. On the way out, secure yourself and pop the seal. Piece of cake."

Kovalic pinched the bridge of his nose. "I'm loving this less. Tell me we've got some good news in here somewhere? Brody?"

"Uh, I thought the commander's news was pretty good?"

"Exfil, Brody. We all set?"

The lieutenant's eyes darted, nervous, to a characteristically unflappable Tapper. "Uh, we had a minor setback there. But we're working on a backup plan."

As reassurances went, it barely qualified. "Do I want to know?"

"It'll be fine, boss," Tapper interjected, giving Brody a hard stare. "We've got it under control. You worry about the spacewalk, we'll have the exit plan ready."

Brody didn't look any more confident than he had a minute ago, but if Tapper said they had it, then they had it. He'd been in enough jams with the sergeant to trust him.

"Any further run-ins with Eyes on your end?" Tapper asked.

"They already tried to kill us once in the last hour. I'm sure it won't be the last attempt." Still that weird memory in his brain. Something about Mirza's team, about her warning. He didn't like leaving her at their backs. It wasn't like she was spending all of her time messing with them; somewhere in this she had her own agenda, but Kovalic was still groping around the edges, trying to figure it out. He just needed a different angle and a little more time – he could almost feel it ticking away on his wrist.

The Illyricans had already gotten the drop on them. If it were Kovalic, he'd be pressing that advantage, not making half-hearted attempts to kill them and definitely not warning them... off.

A bass drum thumped, once, in his chest. Shit. He'd missed it. He'd taken his eye off the ball, too wrapped up with the drama with Sayers and navigating things with Nat. Idiot.

He patted his coat. Where would it be? He'd ditched his sleeve. Changed clothes.

The rest of the team were watching him now, quizzical looks on their faces. He'd taken all possible precautions, hadn't he? Watched for tails. Used eavesdropping countermeasures. He glanced at the ovoid on the bench in front of him.

And froze.

That clever...

"Simon?" said Nat. "You OK?"

Not even remotely. His brain spun as if trying to rebalance a particularly difficult equation, moving variables from one side to the other. Maybe he could still salvage this. "Yeah, just... I had an idea. Nat, where's the closest lifeboat station?"

Frowning, Nat tossed up the schematics and tapped a square. "About a hundred meters away. Standard cluster of five."

Kovalic nodded. "OK, here's the deal: once we bring the lockbox back onboard, Nat will disable the surveillance systems in the cluster, and we'll stow the tablet in one of the lifeboats. As soon as we enter the Hamza system, Nat, you'll fire all five lifeboats – make it look like some kind of malfunction. Nobody but us will know which one has the tablet, so we have time to make our escape and scoop up the lifeboat on our way back through the gate."

Tapper's brow furrowed. "That seems like a lot of moving pieces, boss."

He wasn't wrong, but he also wasn't seeing the same big picture as Kovalic. "Trust me, sergeant. It's the safest play. We get grabbed or separated, we still have the tablet. That's the priority."

The sergeant looked like he wanted to argue, but they'd worked together long enough that he recognized when Kovalic had made a decision. "Yes, sir."

OK. Good. That was that sorted. Fingers crossed. "All right, let's get this show on the roa–" A chime sounded on his sleeve, echoed by the same alert from the rest of the teams' sleeves, followed by an alert box displaying a single word: CRUSADE.

One word that blew away all those careful plans like somebody had opened an airlock into hard vacuum.

"That's Maverick's abort code," said Kovalic. "She's in trouble."

CHAPTER 22

"In trouble?" said Eli. "What the hell are we waiting for?" He started for the door, but Tapper slid in front of him, one hand raised towards Eli's chest.

Kovalic silenced his sleeve, his eyes taking on that faraway look that Eli had learned meant he was working on an idea.

I hope he works fast. We can't hang Sayers out to dry. His jaw clenched. Not after what had happened to Page. He couldn't sit idly by again.

"What's our move, boss?" said Tapper, not moving from Eli's path. "Are we aborting?"

The major seemed to arrive at a conclusion. "No. We go on."

"Simon," said Taylor, "that's the abort signal. We can't just go on with the op."

"This job's too important. We can't afford to cede the tablet to the Illyricans. Besides, if she felt safe enough to send up a flare, then there's still time for us to help her. Mission proceeds. But," Kovalic said, holding up a hand to forestall Eli's objections, "I'll go help Maverick."

Taylor's brow creased. "Who's doing the EVA, then? I'm going to need to quarterback this in case we run into problems, and Tapper's watching the airlock, so..." she trailed off.

The hair on the back of Eli's neck went up as three pairs of eyes swiveled to him. "Whoa, wait just one second..."

"You were in the Illyrican Navy," said Kovalic. "Surely you've had EVA training."

"I mean, like emergency training *once*. And that was like seven years ago."

"Good news: they haven't changed space that much."

"You're a pilot," said Tapper. "You should be totally fine."

"See, the thing about being a pilot is that generally you're *inside* the ship."

"OK," said Kovalic. "Settled."

"No! Not settled! Why doesn't Tapper do it?"

"No can do, kid. I get claustrophobic in the spacesuit. Then agoraphobic in the vacuum. It ain't pretty."

Kovalic pulled the vacsuit out of the locker and tossed it to Eli, who mostly caught it. "Suit up."

"Come on, I'll give you a hand," said Tapper, dragging him over to the staging area while Kovalic and Taylor continued to hash out the rest of the changes to the mission plan.

Eli's stomach did somersaults as Tapper helped him struggle into the vacsuit, which hung baggy on his lanky frame. He hadn't been kidding: it had been at least seven years since the last time he'd had to suit up and go outdoors.

And he'd never done so while in a wormhole – hell, he wasn't sure he knew anybody who had. He'd heard, back when he'd been in the academy, of those foolish enough to venture outside in a wormhole, contorted by gravity pockets or just vanished into subspace; ghost stories told around the bar late at night.

Ships the size of a cruiser or the *Queen Amina* could plow through the eddies of real-space anomalies without too much trouble. By yourself in a spacesuit it was a different story. Get too far away from the ship's mass, and you were in for a rough ride; like shooting the rapids without a boat. And the chances of making it out alive were... well, "not great" was putting it lightly.

Taking a deep breath, Eli tapped a button on the suit's sleeve and the smart fabric constricted to fit his body as though it had been custom made for him. But he couldn't stop his eyes from flicking repeatedly back to the heads-up display status, double- and triple-checking the indicators for the suit seals. No matter how many times he looked, they remained green. *Easy, Brody. The seals are fine.*

"You're good to go, kid," said the sergeant, his voice muffled through Eli's helmet. "Locked up tighter than an Illyrican prison."

"That's not the most reassuring metaphor you could have picked."

Tapper chuckled. "Relax. I got your back."

Eli nodded inside the suit, his forehead bumping against the plexisteel of the faceplate. *Cramped as a prison cell, too.*

Kovalic came up behind the sergeant, looking over Eli's suit, his eyes taking in all the details and making sure Tapper had checked all the boxes. *This feels weirdly funereal.*

"The commander's setting up to get access to the ship's systems," said Kovalic. "It's going to be OK, lieutenant. Just remember your training."

Training. Right. Eli racked his memory for that long discarded information. Something about establishing a frame of reference.

"See you on the other side," said Kovalic, reaching out and clasping Eli's arm. He turned to go.

"Major!"

Kovalic glanced back.

"Just… make sure you get Maverick, OK? She's one of us."

Something flashed across Kovalic's face too fast for Eli to process, but the major dipped his head before walking away. Eli worked to get saliva back into his dry mouth. *Damn it, Kovalic. Get her back.*

"All right," said Tapper, "switching you over to your oxygen pack now." He tapped a button on the Eli's chest and the quality of the air in the helmet changed, its taste a little more stale and plastic than it had been a moment ago. "You've got two hours' worth of air in the tank, plus a thirty minute reserve in the suit. Plenty to get you to the vault, inside, and back."

Eli took a deep breath, feeling the air fill his lungs, and gave the sergeant a thumbs up that was more confident than he felt.

"Aegis, we're good to go here," said Tapper. "Pop the can."

Taylor's voice filtered through the suit's comm system and into Eli's ears. "Copy that. Two minutes out from the gate. Opening inner airlock door now."

Eli turned around, slightly unbalanced thanks to the utility pack laden with the plasma torch and emergency airlock seal, and watched as the red indicator lights above the circular portal turned green and the door rolled aside, opening onto a small, white compartment.

He felt Tapper's hand land on his shoulder, and turned – he had to turn all the way around; craning his neck in the suit would only give him a crick.

"Good luck, kid–"

Eli swallowed. "Thanks."

"We're all counting on you."

No pressure. Er, hopefully just the right amount of pressure, he amended, glancing at the suit diagnostics on the heads-up display.

He maneuvered the bulky suit into the airlock, and faintly heard the doors groan close behind him. It seemed quiet, just the usual whirring of the ship underneath him, until suddenly, a moment later, the only thing he could hear was his own breathing, loud in his ears.

"Atmosphere's been evacuated," said Taylor, startlingly loud in the silence. Eli dialed down the volume on the comms.

"There's an anchor point for your tether right outside the airlock. Once you've clipped in, you can switch on the gravboots," said Tapper over the channel.

Eli looked down at the toes of his boots, currently glowing red. The gravboots were based on the same technology as repulsor coils, but inverted; basically, very small versions of the same tech that allowed for artificial gravity onboard ships. A localized, miniature gravity field that should keep his boots stuck to the hull; you just didn't want to use them inside, because their effects when you were *already* using artificial gravity generators could be... unpredictable.

With a tap on his sleeve, Eli brought up the mission clock. The wormhole jump should be happening imminently, plus or minus some time to negotiate with the gate control.

As if summoned by his thoughts, Taylor came back on the channel. "External sensors say we're at the gate. Wormhole jump in thirty seconds. Sit tight everyone."

Eli reached out, grasping the handhold near the airlock's external door, and tried to calm his breathing. His old therapist, Dr Thornfield, had instructed him on using breathing exercises to quiet his anxiety over flying and, well, it had worked, hadn't it? No reason it couldn't work here.

Beneath his feet, he could feel the vibration of the ship's engine. And then it was gone, vanished, as the *Queen Amina* cut its main engines while it entered the wormhole. *Jump time.* A wormhole jump didn't *feel* like anything – at least, not outside of the slightly mind-bending experience aboard the Illyrican prototype jumpship Project Tarnhelm, where it felt a little bit like the world's worst ice cream headache.

"Jump complete," came Taylor's voice, breaking Eli's train of thought. He'd been so distracted thinking about the jump he hadn't even noticed it. "External sensors are offline; opening outer door now."

Silently the airlock door in front of him rolled open, washing the white interior of the compartment in the eerie blue-purple of the wormhole. Eli's mouth opened. He'd seen the inside of a wormhole plenty of times, but there was something different about knowing that you were about to step into it. The colors rippled and washed in almost hypnotic undulations.

"No time for gawking," said Tapper. "Get moving."

"Uh, right. Roger, I mean."

Taking a deep breath, Eli pulled himself over to the opening using the handholds set in the wall, and then flipped himself over and out of the ship.

Gravity literally went out the window.

Disorientation was familiar enough from all the hours he'd logged in fighters and sims – that was the name of the game there – but he hadn't had to deal with weightlessness in the same way. Even though fighters lacked artificial gravity, you were almost always strapped in and under thrust.

He hung there for a moment, re-acclimating to the feeling. *It's just like you're in a swimming pool, Brody. Easy.* Swimming pool? When the hell was the last time he'd been in a swimming pool?

Static crackled over his comm system along with Taylor's voice. "Don't forget to clip your tether."

Right. Good as the gravboots might be, redundancy was the name of the safety game. Always have a backup. He looked down at his waist and found the tether reel, pulled out the safety cable – a flexible carbon nanotube weave – and secured the carabiner clip to the anchor on the hull.

"Locked and ready to go," he reported. Raising his sleeve, he tapped a few controls and a red path appeared overlaid on his HUD, showing the way towards the maintenance hatch.

Positioning himself at the edge of the airlock, he clicked his heels to activate the gravboots and felt the *zip* as they glommed securely onto the hull. He tested one foot; it released on the upward motion, then grabbed the deck plate again on descent. Slow, but it would work. "Updraft is en route to target. ETA…" he glanced at the HUD, "ten minutes."

"Good luck," said Taylor's slightly garbled voice.

Thanks, thought Eli, as he started to work his way across the hull. *I hope that's enough.*

The abort flare that Sayers had sent up had logged her location at the time: the esplanade. Kovalic frowned as he found the nearest lift tube and punched the control for the ship's main level. He wasn't sure what had brought her there – maybe she'd been on the move. All that mattered was finding her before Xi's people did.

He kept coming back to the look in Brody's eyes, a combination of guilty and reproachful. The pilot didn't know the whole story with Page, but he'd clearly formed some version of it in his head, and Kovalic wasn't in a position to disabuse him. No matter how wrong it was, there was a grain of truth there: despite Page's betrayal, he'd been one of them. Kovalic had owed him something more.

He shook his head. Not the place or time for recriminations. They had a job to do.

The lift slowed to a stop, the doors parting at the esplanade, about a five minute walk from Sayers's last known location. From the ship map on his sleeve, it looked to be one of the small parklets that dotted the area.

The wormhole jump was happening during the night shift, which meant that the esplanade was quieter than usual, but on a ship this big it was rarely empty. Revelers stumbled their way home from the casinos or a late dinner; amorous couples stole away to a late-night rendezvous; a man bounced and cooed at an infant strapped to his chest. Security patrols were in evidence as well, and Kovalic gave them a wide berth – he may have an understanding with Cortez, but he wouldn't be so presumptuous as to think that extended to carte blanche.

The parklet came into view around the curve of the ship: a five meter square stand of shrubs and medium-height hedges, fed by the ship's irrigation system. Good for scrubbing some of the carbon dioxide exhaled by all the people on the ship, and a nice aesthetic touch to boot.

Head on a swivel, Kovalic stepped into the middle of the parklet, then did a quick circle. Nothing. Maybe Sayers had made a run for it, or maybe she'd tried to hole up somewhere. But she sure wasn't here now.

He tapped his earbud. "Aegis, this is Corsair. I'm at the flare location – no sign of Maverick. You got anything?"

There was a pause before Nat's voice came back. "Her sleeve still registers at that location. Can you find it?"

Kovalic frowned; it wasn't as if there was anyplace to hide. He ducked to look under the parklet's sole bench. Casting an eye around, he caught sight of an object amidst a tangle of hedge branches.

"Aegis, got it," he said, plucking the sleeve from amongst the branches, the sharp leaves pricking at his wrist. It lit up at his touch, still pulsating with the abort signal. "But just the sleeve. Can you scrub back through the video security logs and see where she went afterwards?"

"Checking now. Wait one."

Kovalic's fingers curled around the sleeve. At least she'd been alive to dump the sleeve. He hadn't let her down yet. There was still time.

"I've got a figure dumping the sleeve about twenty minutes ago, around the time we got the abort code. I *think* it's her, but she's wearing a hood and not facing the camera. Cameras show her heading astern, towards the main plaza, but then I lost her."

"Copy that, Aegis. I'm heading there now."

What else could he do? Kovalic chewed his lip and took another look around for anything he'd missed. Irritation gnawed at him. He shouldn't have let Sayers go off without backup. Anything happened to her, and it was on him.

He only hoped Brody was faring better on the EVA.

The first snag came eight minutes into Eli's walk across the hull. A red icon flashed on his HUD and he spent a solid thirty seconds trying to figure out what a cylinder-with-an-X-through-it meant before, mid-step, he suddenly spun around as though jerked. His right foot flailed in the air and all the muscles in his left foot strained to hold him to the hull.

"Jesus *Christ*," he yelled, thankful it didn't trigger the comm system.

OK, OK. First things first, get anchored. He managed to maneuver his right foot back down to the hull and felt the boot clamp into place again. Once that was secured, he had a moment to get his bearings.

It didn't take long to figure out what had happened: the tether cable stretched out behind him, tracing a path back along the hull to where he'd exited the airlock.

It was taut.

"Uh, Bruiser, Aegis… how much tether cable do these suits carry?"

The static had gotten worse the farther he'd gotten from the airlock. "Up… peat … didn't copy."

He checked the HUD. Almost fifty meters left to the vault hatch. "I'm gonna guess about a hundred meters." Looking back along the cable, he gave it an experimental tug, feeling it vibrate and writhe against his gloves like a live snake. "Tether cable is at the limit. Please advise."

Once again, he got a crackle of garbled audio back. He glanced at his sleeve; the signal strength had dropped to twenty percent. Next to it, the mission clock continued its inexorable countdown.

Shit.

It wasn't like he had a lot of options. He could reel himself back in to the airlock, but this was their opportunity – there might not be another.

He checked his belt, but there was no way to release the tether from this end, because why the hell would you want to do that, unless you were totally nuts? *They really ought to have foreseen the situation where you can't reach the access hatch for the secure vault you're trying to rob.* And the carbon nanotube weave was not going to be something he could just snip through with a pair of scissors, even if he had some. It was going to take some serious industrial equipment, like a...

Like a plasma torch.

He couldn't see behind him, but reaching back he found the gear pack that Tapper had given him, just in case he needed to cut his way through the vault hatch. That ought to make short work of the cable.

He swallowed and toggled his comm on. "Aegis, Bruiser, I'm cutting my tether."

If there was a response or an acknowledgment, Eli didn't hear it. He even waited a few seconds, in the hope that they'd try to talk him out of it, or maybe call for an abort. But there was nothing.

The mission clock, ticking away on his HUD, said they had fifty minutes left in the wormhole transit; there wasn't a lot of time to agonize over this decision. He needed to get moving.

Bracing himself, he unslung the small, handheld plasma torch. Even in his bulky gloves, thumbing it on was the work of a moment, and a bright blue-white jet appeared at the nozzle. His visor tinted automatically, shielding his eyes. Taking a step back, he let the cable slacken, gathered a fistful in his hand, and then applied the torch to a spot a few inches away.

The torch cut through the cable in a less than a minute, and the ship's forward movement caused the loose end to start drifting outward. *Well, I hope that doesn't cause any problems.*

No time to worry about it now. Flipping the torch off, he stowed it once again in his pack and started out towards the access hatch again, very carefully making sure that each foot gripped securely to the hull before taking his next step. Right now, his gravboots were the only things keeping him from spinning off into the abyss.

The hull is down. The hull is down. He repeated the mantra as he went, trying not to pay attention to the swirling vortex above him. That was how you got lost in these things – you lost your frame of reference, got vertigo, and then it was throwing up in your spacesuit and hoping the internal vacuum system had been cleaned out before you put it on.

So intently was Eli focused on his feet that he almost walked right past the access hatch. It wasn't particularly well marked; if it hadn't been for his HUD blinking that he had reached his destination, he might have kept going until he was at the bow of the ship.

"Aegis, this is Updraft. I've reached the hatch. Any time you want to pop this thing is OK by me."

A buzz of static was the only response.

"Aegis? Bruiser? Corsair? Anybody out there?"

Shit. The interference from the wormhole was playing havoc with the comms. He glanced at the mission clock. Forty-two minutes. He only had a couple of minutes of leeway until he needed to be inside. If Taylor couldn't find a way to punch through the static, he'd have no choice but to burn his way in.

Come on, commander. Help a guy out.

"Corsair, we've got a problem," came Nat's voice in Kovalic's ear as he followed the esplanade towards the main plaza.

"Is it Maverick?"

"Uh, no," said Taylor. "We've lost contact with Updraft. I haven't been able to get in touch with him since shortly after he went outside."

Something caught in Kovalic's throat. "Do we have any way of knowing if he made it to the hatch?"

"The same sensor interference that's keeping him shielded from the *Queen Amina*'s crew is screwing us too," said Nat, frustration welling up in her voice. "But assuming that he continued on at about the same pace, he should be there."

Should be. Where Eli Brody was involved, things that "should" happen had a way of not always going quite according to plan.

"So, no communications means he's on the contingency plan, right?"

There was a hesitation before Nat spoke. "Yes… but…"

"Oh, I love the sound of this already."

"It seems the outer hatch was recently reinforced for security – it didn't show up on the older schematics we were looking at. Cutting through it with the plasma torch is going to take way too long."

Kovalic bit off a swear. "Tell me you've got a solution."

"I can trigger the vault's emergency fire protocol, which will open the inner and outer airlock doors simultaneously – but that will also depressurize the vault, which means alarms. I should be able to suppress them, but I can't keep them from registering in the system."

Kovalic checked his sleeve. Forty-two minutes left on the wormhole transit, according to the mission clock. There wasn't a lot of time left to debate this. Damn it, *he* should have been the one out there. "Pop it."

"Copy that."

Taking a deep breath as the plaza came into sight, Kovalic hoped he'd made the right decision, otherwise this whole plan was dead in the water. And Kovalic was the sitting duck.

Eli had just pulled out the plasma torch to prep it when there was a shuddering that resonated through his boots. A light glowed green on the panel next to the hatch and the door started to slide open. He staggered backwards as a torrent of air started venting from the opening, but the bulky vacsuit wasn't exactly designed for quick movements.

Oh no.

The airflow caught his arm and it started to flail; the plasma torch was snatched from his fingers and spun away into the abyss. Eli's whole body started to lift away from the hull and his leg muscles once again screamed as they were stretched farther than they ought to go. He tried to pull himself back, but his only point of anchorage were the gravboots, which valiantly tried to keep him locked to the hull.

Holy shit. Hold on hold on hold on.

Orange indicators flared on his HUD: the increased strain on the gravboots was weakening their seal. As he tried to re-establish his toe grip and pull himself down, he saw one orange indicator turn red as the grav unit in the left boot ramped up and burned out. That foot flailed and came loose, twisting him into a knot and putting even more strain on his other foot, in turn ramping up power to the remaining gravboot – which quickly started to overload.

WARNING, flashed the onscreen display. LOCK LOSS IMMINENT.

This is not g–

And then he was spinning off the hull, cartwheeling into a massive whirlpool of blue and purple.

Set in the middle of the esplanade, nearly smack dab in the center of the ship, the plaza was the largest open-air space aboard the *Queen Amina*. An atrium had been carved out above it, with a mezzanine that overlooked the square. In the center of the plaza stood a small fountain that burbled amongst rocks, endlessly recycling its own water.

Even at this late hour, Kovalic saw a handful of folks scattered throughout, seated on benches or leaning against trees. Some were enjoying a drink, others were reading from tablets, and a couple were even tossing around a flying disc.

But his eyes went immediately to the figure sitting on the plasticrete wall around the fountain: the short, dark hair, and the military bearing.

Sayers.

He made a beeline for her, keeping an eye on the other denizens of the plaza, but none seemed to give him a second look. That unsettled feeling in his stomach, that something was just plain wrong, hadn't dissipated, but he was chalking it up to feeling antsy about being out of the loop.

Kovalic forced himself to draw a deep breath: he'd built his team for this. He needed to trust them. Even Brody.

As he took a seat next to her, Addy Sayers looked up. Tension he hadn't realized he was holding washed away in a tide of relief. Maybe things were starting to break their way.

"Gotta be honest, I was a little worried," he said, with a grin. "I hope you got what we needed, otherwise this is all going to be for nothing."

Before the specialist could open her mouth, another voice spoke from behind Kovalic. "Oh, I think you'll find that this *was* all for nothing."

He turned to find a dark-skinned woman in a flowing dress. Where she had come from, he wasn't sure – he hadn't seen her a moment ago. But he recognized her instantly and his stomach-sinking feeling returned with reinforcements.

Her dark eyes took him in at a glance. "You're shorter than I thought you'd be."

"I get that a lot. Madam Xi, I presume?"

She bowed her head. "You presume correctly."

Looking around, he was surprised to find that she seemed unaccompanied. Bold move.

Getting slowly to his feet, he spared a glance at Sayers. She was sharp; she'd pick up on any play that he might make. They'd make a break for the nearest lift. This was fine, totally fine. Completely salvageable.

"So," said Kovalic. "What was it? Did we miss an alarm somewhere?"

"Oh, no. You're asking the wrong question. It's not *what* gave you up, Major Kovalic," said Xi, taking a step back. "It's *who*."

From behind Kovalic, he heard the telltale sound of a knockout gun charging and he looked over his shoulder to see Sayers pointing the business end of a pistol in his direction. As if on cue, a pair of armed White Star security personnel emerged from concealment on either side of the plaza, weapons leveled at him.

Sayers, for her part, looked resigned but not particularly upset. "Sorry about all of this. I guess there really isn't any honor among thieves."

CHAPTER 23

This is it. All Eli could see through the visor was a swirl of blue-purple that was spinning faster than a carousel. Every once in a while, he caught sight of the giant gray mass that was the *Queen Amina*, but then it spun away too fast for him to focus. His stomach went from the ceiling to the floor and back again.

His HUD blinked red, red, red, with so many different icons that he couldn't possibly focus on a single one. Alarms blared in a cacophony of tones and pitches.

"Gravitational lock system disengaged," the suit's robotic voice chimed. "Emergency tether not functional." *OK, that one's on me.* "Recommend re-establish lock immediately."

"Yes, I *know*," he shouted, trying to dismiss the alerts while also not throwing up. "Shut *up*!"

Something beeped and the alarms shrank into a smaller portion of the screen. But he was still spinning wildly. *Training, remember your training.* Spin was the enemy – that was the first thing you learned in piloting a ship.

A ship.

He swallowed down the bile rising in his throat. "Status of reaction control system?"

"RCS online."

Now we're talking. "Give me manual control."

"Manual control engaged."

He worked his fingers in his gloves, identifying pitch, roll, and yaw controls. *I can work with this.* Spreading his arms and legs as widely as possible to slow his spin, he started firing the opposing thrusters to counteract it. Even then, it took a while for him to slow to a stop.

But then all he was looking at was the inside of a wormhole, which was only marginally less undulating now that he wasn't being spun around.

"Where the hell is the *Queen Amina*?" he asked.

A small holoscreen appeared in one corner of his display, showing an image of the ship from the suit's rear-facing camera, and red blinking arrows appeared on his visor, pointing towards the right edge of his field of view. Using the RCS, he slowly rotated himself around until he faced the ship.

The good news was that he hadn't lost the starliner entirely. The wormhole's gravitational "current" was still propelling him in the same direction, and he was only about fifty meters off the ship's flank.

But the bad news was that he'd been thrown backwards about a hundred meters from the access hatch, not far from the airlock where he'd first emerged.

"Oof," he exhaled. All that ground, lost. He pulled up the mission clock on his sleeve. Forty minutes left. "How long is it going to take me to get there on RCS?"

The computer projected a path, but it wasn't quick – the suit's RCS was designed for short bursts of maneuvering thrust, not propulsion, and a glance at his HUD showed that he'd already burned through most of its limited fuel reserves by stopping his spin.

Getting to the access hatch was a different story. Even if he could reach the ship, from his present position it would mean another long, slow walk across the hull. That was going to take time they didn't have: the rest of the team was already in motion, waiting on him.

OK, so figure a way out of it, Brody. Use that pilot brain of yours.

There had to be something else on the suit that would generate some form of pressure or energy. He reached back for the gear pack, and then remembered that he'd lost the plasma torch when he'd been blown off the hull. Not that it would have provided much in the way of thrust, unless he'd used it to combust something. But that would require oxygen, which he didn't...

Oxygen.

"What's my current air level?"

"Oxygen reserves at 75 percent."

How much oxygen did he really need for this job, anyway? Plus, if he didn't make it back to the *Queen Amina*, then all that air would be good for was letting him die more slowly, watching the ship slowly dwindle into a speck of nothingness as he was condemned to an eternity of floating though a wormhole.

He shivered.

Well, that settles that.

"Can we do a controlled vent of oxygen?"

"Venting oxygen not recommended. Oxygen is essential to life support systems."

Stupid onboard systems. Never can think outside of the box.

"I know it's not *recommended*. Can you do it?"

A red X blinked on the screen, along with a warning text in about a dozen different languages.

Goddamn it, this fucking safety system is going to kill me.

He reached behind himself, trying to grab at his oxygen pack, but his gloves scrabbled at it ineffectually. There weren't any exposed hoses anymore; they'd internalized everything in hard packs to reduce the risk of damage or accident. But the suits were still modular systems; there ought to be a way to detach the pack. Glancing down at the front of his suit, he spotted a pair of yellow-and-black pull tabs labeled EMERGENCY ONLY.

I'd say this qualifies.

Yanking the tabs, he heard a hiss and a click in his helmet, and felt the pack come off in his hands. A warning flashed on the screen: SWITCHING TO INTERNAL OXYGEN – SUPPLY LIMITED. Next to it, a clock started running down the amount of air left in the suit's built-in reserve, which wasn't at all anxiety-inducing. Sweat beaded on his forehead and he willed it not to drip into his eyes.

He pulled the oxygen pack around in front of him and started turning it over in his hands. The only connector he could find was the one that plugged into his suit; there was a mechanical valve that he could open by hand, but he wouldn't be able to do that *and* have the pack on his back.

He was going to have to do this backwards.

Oh, it's been so long since I had this *bad of an idea.* But it wasn't like he had any other options, and the *Queen Amina* was getting further away with every passing second.

Shifting the pack in front of him, he enfolded it in a bear hug. Then he brought up the rear-facing camera again, and used the thrusters to put the *Queen Amina* behind him.

"Plot me a course towards *Queen Amina* access hatch 31-2E."

The curved dotted line appeared on the rear camera's

image, which he enlarged so that he could see more clearly. Hopefully he had enough thrust to get him there.

All right, Brody. Now or never.

He opened the valve.

Nothing seemed to happen. He glanced down, in so far as he could through his helmet, and confirmed that a small cloud of gas was coming out of the valve. But with little frame of reference in the wormhole, it was hard to tell if he was even moving. In theory, slow but constant thrust was his best chance of catching up.

But fast it wasn't. And if he was wrong – if the suit's computer miscalculated in the slightest, or he missed his chance, he was out of fuel, air, and luck.

It wasn't the first time Kovalic had found himself at gunpoint, and he would wager it wasn't going to be the last. His eyes went from the barrel of the weapon, to Sayers's own eyes – hard, like ice – to Xi.

Slowly, he raised his hands. "I see."

"Don't get me wrong," said Xi. "I admire what you've done here. Infiltrating my operation isn't easy – I should know. I've had any number of would-be spies thrown out an airlock."

"And I'm sure that doesn't hurt when it comes to inspiring fear in the rest of your crew."

"That is where you're mistaken, major. I don't trust fear to keep my employees in line – they *love* me. I look out for them."

Kovalic glanced at Sayers, but if there was any wavering of conviction in the young woman, it didn't show on her face.

Stone cold. For the first time, doubt started to worm its way into the cracks of his mind.

It wouldn't be the first time he'd been betrayed, either.

"Adelaide here understood what I was offering," said Xi, laying her hand on the other woman's shoulder. "Around here, we *reward* people for a job well done, instead of just trying to knock them down with the next challenge."

"Plus, you pay well," added Sayers, a smirk on her face. "Can't say the same about him." She waved the gun at Kovalic.

"Money? That's what this is about?"

"It doesn't hurt. Have you seen how they live around here? It's a hell of a lot better than that shithole you dragged me out of. I could get used to being pampered for once in my life."

This was not going exactly the way Kovalic had planned.

"So," he said, looking between the two women and then at the guards lining the railing above. "Now what?"

"Now," said Xi, with a smile borrowed from a shark, "we probably toss *you* out the airlock. Unless, that is, you think your government would be willing to ransom you?"

Kovalic donned his sunniest smile. "What government?"

"Then I guess there's no profit in keeping you around." She pointed two fingers in his direction.

"If I may," Kovalic interrupted, before the guards could move in. "Obviously, you're perfectly capable of kicking me into a wormhole. But, if I may suggest, that might not be the most *prudent* course of action."

Xi cocked her head. "Oh? I am *so* looking forward to hearing this rationale." She waved a manicured hand, light glinting off gold nails. "Please, continue."

After a quick check to make sure he wasn't about to be

shot, Kovalic lowered his own hands, making a surreptitious check of the mission clock on his sleeve. Thirty-eight minutes and counting.

"Here's the thing," he said, straightening his cuffs. "If you *do* throw me out the airlock, you'll most assuredly never see your prized Aleph Tablet ever again."

Xi stared at him for a moment, then threw back her head with a rich, deep laugh. "The balls on you," she said, admiration tinging her voice. "You didn't tell me about the sheer bravado." The last was an almost reproachful aside directed at Sayers.

Kovalic held his breath, watching Sayers, but the young woman's brow only furrowed, as if she were deep in thought.

"I suppose I can indulge this a little further," said Xi, crossing her arms. "Entertain me."

Kovalic bowed his head at the reprieve. "Of course, madam. My team has already breached your security – I presume Ms Sayers has told you that."

"She has."

"Ah," said Kovalic, almost apologetic. "Plans have a way of being... fluid in this business, and her information's out of date. See, my team's already obtained the tablet from your vault."

Xi laughed. "Oh, come come. I expected better of you, major. If you've already gotten what you came for, why are we here having this lovely conversation?"

"I think it makes a pretty good diversion. After all, here I am and here you are. But the real show is taking place somewhere else."

"Why would you tell me this?"

Kovalic made a show of looking at the mission clock on his

sleeve. "Because the job's already done, madam. All I need to do is keep you here as long as possible while my team makes their escape."

At the corner of Xi's eyelid, Kovalic caught just the barest hint of a twitch. She wasn't buying his story, but he'd wedged in just enough of a lever to make her concerned. Someone like Xi didn't get this far in life without being careful.

"Anyway," Kovalic continued. "It doesn't matter if you believe me. Throw me out the airlock or in your brig. Either way, it's not going to stop you from getting robbed, because you've already *been* robbed."

By shades, Xi's expression had morphed from supreme confidence to barely contained anger. She stalked forward, past Sayers's outstretched weapon, toward Kovalic.

"You're bluffing," she said, sizing him up. "Badly."

"Am I? Then why was your vault's emergency fire protocol activated five minutes ago?"

Xi's jaw clacked shut, her eyes flashing, but she beckoned over one of her security team and murmured something to him before turning her attention back on Kovalic. "I don't think you understand the lengths I've gone to to secure the *Queen Amina*. The idea that your pathetic team could break it in a day is utterly unthinkable."

Kovalic grinned. "The bigger they are... Look, you want to check? Check. I've got nowhere else to be."

"Proximity alert," said the calm voice in Eli's ear.

What the–

His mind had wandered during his slow progress back to the *Queen Amina*, worrying about whether or not using his

oxygen tank had been the right decision, whether he'd ever
see the rest of the team again, and whether or not joining up
with Kovalic's outfit had been a good idea in the first place.
Now the gray hull plating of the ship suddenly loomed close –
too close – in the rear-view camera, and the distance readout
was ticking down way too fast.

*Continual thrust in the vacuum of space means you keep
accelerating, dumbass.* How could he have forgotten that?
Piloting 101.

"Proximity alert," the voice repeated. "Decelerate
immediately."

No shit! But with his arms wrapped around the oxygen
pack, he didn't have any way to slow himself down – and he
definitely didn't have time.

A moment later he slammed into the side of the hull,
knocking all the breath out of him. He bounced off, spinning
again, and felt himself cartwheel wildly, skimming along the
surface.

The spray of oxygen sputtered as the pack ran out of air. Eli
groaned, blinking away the rear-facing camera and watched
as his course reappeared on the HUD overlay. He was only
about twenty meters from the vault hatch, and moving in the
right direction, even if he was still spinning wildly.

Enough of this stupid thing. He released the oxygen pack,
watching it drift off towards the ship with its last dying gasp.
I've only got one shot at this. He caromed towards the hatch,
glancing at the RCS propellant tank – not enough left to
counteract his spin, but if he used it at just the right moment,
he might be able to give himself a nudge in the right direction.

The dotted line of his course angled closer and closer to the
dark open square of the hatch, and when he was just a few

meters away, Eli extended all his limbs and fired his starboard RCS thrusters.

He was close. The lip of the hatch caught his legs, whacking both his shins and sending him tumbling into the darkness of the vault, where he rebounded off a bulkhead. His fingers fumbled through the thick gloves of the vacuum suit as he tried to grab a handhold – any handhold – and halt his spin. There wasn't any artificial gravity in the hold from what he could tell, which made sense, since nobody was supposed to be down here while the ship was moving anyway.

At least he was inside. That was the good news. The bad news became apparent when he checked the gauge at the corner of his HUD and found that he'd just expended the last of the propellant for the RCS system. And, another warning reminded him, his in-suit oxygen was dangerously low.

The bad news is winning.

His feet skittered along a bulkhead, his boots failing to gain purchase. *The gravboots!* He clicked his heels, but then an alarm blurted in his ears as they failed to activate.

Shit, they burned out. He kicked a second time, harder, and the alarm sounded again. Being ripped from the hull might have permanently damaged them. A lump rose in his throat.

Oh come on. *Third time lucky...* This time he slammed the heels together as hard as he could, relying on that old tech maxim: when in doubt, use force.

With a *zip*, the gravboots sprung to life, glomming him to the deck with a satisfying thunk. He found himself pulled forward slightly by his momentum, but the lock held and he was able to steady himself.

Holy shit, I can't believe any *of that worked.*

With his position finally stable, he had the opportunity to look around. At first, he was slightly confused by the fact that somebody had bolted so much equipment to the walls, until he realized that *he* was on the wall. He slowly clomped his way down until he reached the floor, and then tried taking in the room from a more sensible perspective.

He had to admit, it wasn't as impressive as he'd hoped. When you heard "vault," you pictured a room with lots of little boxes and sacks full of money.

This place looked more like a warehouse. It took him a moment to realize that the enormous metal rectangles he was looking at were the ends of long shelves, mounted on repulsor fields that allowed them to move together, compressing for storage, or farther apart for access.

At the end nearest him stood a console and a robotic arm. To the right of the console was a short conveyor belt and a hatch that looked like a small version of a lift tube door.

He made his way over to the console, which lit up as it sensed his approach and prompted him for a secure login.

An alert chimed softly in his ear, letting him know that he had only five minutes of oxygen remaining in his suit.

I guess that's better than a klaxon blaring at me constantly.

Five minutes. What the hell was he going to do when he ran out of air? He spared a glance for the mission clock: thirty-five minutes to go. Too many clocks, all counting down. But the mission had to come first: the rest of the team was relying on him right now. Just like he was going to rely on them to figure out a way to get him out of here.

Toggling his comm on again, he crossed his fingers – metaphorically, anyway, given the thick nature of the vacuum suit gloves – that being back in the ship would cut through the interference.

"Aegis, this is Updraft. You copy?" He held his breath. Maybe that would help him use up less oxygen.

"Christ, you're alive, Br… Updraft," came Taylor's voice, and Eli could hear the relief in it. "Aegis copies you three by three. Still some interference. Status?"

"Good to hear your voice too, Aegis. I've got a console here, could use your expertise."

"Got an ID number on it?"

Eli poked closer at the console, looking around the edges until he found a plate labeled EK745J. He read the string off to Taylor.

"Looks like it's on an isolated circuit, like the rest of the vault systems," said Taylor. "Let's see if our signal's good enough for a remote link. I'm grabbing control of your comm systems."

An alert popped up on Eli's HUD, asking if he wanted to accept the remote connection. Tapping a button on his sleeve, he granted access, and a screen of text scrolled across, way too fast for him to read.

"Whoa, whoa, what are you doing?"

"Downloading my hack toolkit into your sleeve," said Taylor. "I should be able to use it to launch an exploit onto that console over a short-range wireless connection."

"Oh, sure. I mean, I could have done that."

"Uh huh. Pipe down and let me work."

Eli watched as the text window in his HUD miniaturized; another icon indicated the wireless connection in his sleeve, which was linked to his suit, had gone active, and a moment later, the console in front of him blinked off, then seemed to cycle through a restart. When it reappeared, there was no login prompt, just what appeared to be the device's standard user interface.

"OK," said Taylor. "You're in. See what you can do with that."

Leaning forward, Eli examined the controls. A pair of directional pads seemed to allow manual control of the robotic arm, but there was also a search box and keyboard for entering a particular container ID.

"Uh, we don't know which box is Xi's, do we?" said Eli.

"There should be a way to search by the name attached to the box."

Eli bent down and tapped at a few of the keys. It wasn't the most logically laid out system, but he supposed that it was mainly intended as a backup. Still, you ought to take pride in your work, even if was only going to get used every once in a while, say, by a team of special operatives looking to steal something out of–

"Got it!" he said as a search box labeled "Name" appeared. He typed in "Xi, Ofeibia" with smug satisfaction, but his face fell as it displayed a dozen hits. "Uh, looks like she has more than one." *Of course she has more than one, it's* her *ship.* Another chime reminded him about his low oxygen levels; he ignored it – it was hardly news.

As he watched, one of the items on the list started blinking. Movement registered in the corner of his eyes and he flinched backward, but it was only the robotic arm moving towards the shelves. As he watched, two of the storage units slid slowly apart and the arm trundled its way down the long aisle between them.

Eli looked back down at the display as he realized what was

happening. "Aegis, somebody just requested a box attached to Xi's name. 3263A27. Any chance that's not the one we're looking for? It's heading for vault access room six."

"Shit," said Taylor. "I've lost contact with Corsair, but his last signal put him in the vault access complex."

"Wait a second," said Eli, looking down at the console, and then back at the open square of the hatch behind him, his heart thumping in his chest. "If we could just retrieve the box from up there, why the *hell* did I have to go through all of that?"

"Updraft, he–"

"No!" said Eli. "I almost *died* out there. A couple times! You think that was easy? I could have been stuck in a wormhole forever. Well, at least until my air ran out, and then I would have just slowly suffocated!" His breath was coming in ragged gasps now. His eyes darted to his HUD, still counting down the amount of oxygen left in the suit's reserve – two and a half minutes. No wonder he was starting to feel dizzy. "Actually, I might still be suffocating in he–"

"*Eli.*"

He blinked past his lightheadedness. Taylor wasn't one to breach communications protocol. "What?"

"I'm trying to tell you: he *couldn't* have retrieved the box by himself. I think we've got a problem."

CHAPTER 24

Xi and two of her goons – each of whom looked like they could deadlift Kovalic with one hand while eating a sandwich – had frog-marched him into the vault access room, past the wide-eyed receptionist. Sayers followed, and if the KO gun in her hand wasn't pointed directly at Kovalic, it wouldn't be any trouble for her to stun him before he could act.

They had stepped into the first available vault access room and, without any preamble, Xi had waved her bespangled arm over the security console, then keyed in a box number: 3263A27.

There had been a whine as the system had powered up, red warning lights around the hatch alerting them that a lockbox was being retrieved, and then Xi had turned back to him, smile still firmly in place.

"So you decompressed the vault. Bravo. I'm not sure exactly what you thought you'd achieve, but it doesn't change anything: the access shaft's emergency airlocks will repressurize it and ensure the system continues to function normally." She spread her hands. "Consider your bluff called."

Kovalic kept his grin nonchalant, trying not to show too many teeth. Bluff called, indeed. Here's hoping that he was holding the right cards.

So far the deck seemed pretty stacked against him: Sayers might have loosened her grip on the KO gun, but it was still the closest weapon and he was still on the wrong side of it; Xi's two guards, meanwhile, were flanking the only door out of the room. The odds were most assuredly not in his favor.

Xi seemed to be enjoying Kovalic's discomfort with the utter serenity of someone who knows they have the upper hand. With a swish of her luminescent dress, she considered him.

"You're not the first to try and steal from me, you know. It's been attempted from time to time."

"Might want to up your insurance."

She laughed, this time a tinny jangling sound not dissimilar from the bracelets around her wrist. "None have ever succeeded. And generally they don't live to tell the tale."

Kovalic barely avoided rolling his eyes. Live to tell the tale? What was this, a pirate-themed amusement park ride? "Well, I'm sorry to break your perfect record."

"Let's not get ahead of ourselves, major," said Xi, running one finger across the console in an almost languorous manner. "The jury is still out."

"I hate to break it to you, Aegis, but he's not the only one in trouble," said Eli, watching his oxygen gauge deepen from orange to red. "I've only got two minutes of air left."

"Jesus, Updraft. What the hell happened to your... no, never mind. We've got to get you out of there."

"Yeah," said Eli, looking around the compartment again. Besides the console and the shelves there wasn't much in there. "My options are kind of limited. I can't exactly go back the way I came. Can you re-pressurize this compartment?"

He heard Taylor's teeth click together over the comm channel. "Not quickly enough. It's a lot easier to pull a fire alarm than to turn one off."

Eli swallowed and tried to push down the panic rising in his chest. "OK. OK." If there wasn't a way to get air in the vault, then he needed to get out. The only problem was that there was just one door: the one that he'd come in – hence the whole point of the spacewalk in the first place. Maybe there were some emergency suits in here? It was a halfhearted hope at best – nobody was supposed to be in the vault during flight. Just that stupid robot arm.

As if on cue, the robot arm whirred silently back in his direction, now bearing a metal box the size of a small suitcase.

Presumably the exact box they were looking for. Not that Eli had any way of getting it out of here. Or opening it. Frankly, he was going to be insanely lucky if he managed to survive the next two minutes.

The arm trundled over to the now-moving conveyor belt and laid the box down on it. Lights started blinking around the small hatch, which had slid open as the container rolled towards it.

Well, technically, he supposed there *was* another way out of here.

Wait a second, "technically" is all I need.

"Updraft, I'm going to get you out of there," said Taylor. "Just give me a minute."

"Commander, I don't have a minute," said Eli, watching the oxygen gauge plummet towards zero. "But I do have an idea."

*

A muted klaxon sounded in the vault access room as the hatch to the vault slid open. The conveyor belt in front of it began to move in expectation of the container that would shortly appear there.

Kovalic wasn't holding his breath exactly, but he did find himself unconsciously shifting weight to the balls of his feet, ready to act. He willed himself to relax, shook the tension out of his muscles. If he moved, Sayers would just stun him, and that would be the end of that. Without some sort of distraction, he was easy pickings. So his best option, for the moment, was to play this out, one way or another.

The lockbox hovered into view in the access shaft, then gently floated out and landed on the conveyor belt, which rolled it forward, depositing it on a metal table. Behind it, the hatch closed again.

Xi's lidded eyes roved to Kovalic, the carefully sketched brows rising. "Looks like my property is perfectly intact, Major Kovalic." She stepped up to the table and placed a possessive hand on the box. "A rather pathetic attempt at a bluff."

Kovalic fought blasé with blasé. "If you trust it's still in there."

A flicker of annoyance played in Xi's eyes. "You expect me to believe you somehow removed it *and* replaced the container? Really, major? Such superhuman feats!"

He couldn't resist letting a smile cross his lips. "Your words, not mine, madam. If you're satisfied, then we can all certainly leave," he said, gesturing to the door.

Xi's lips thinned, but she turned back to the box and pressed a button on the top; a grid of light splashed over her face. A beep sounded as she was recognized, a green light blinking. The box's display shifted to a keypad, on which she entered a code. A second beep, a second green light. Finally she waved a bracelet over the panel on top, and a third green light blinked along with the confirmation beep

Kovalic glanced at Sayers. Getting all three necessary factors to open the lockbox would have been nigh impossible. The container lid unsealed with a hiss as the pressure equalized.

"Corsair," his earbud crackled suddenly, Nat's voice coming through. "You're about to have company."

Kovalic's brows knit and he spared a glance at the door where the two thugs still stood guard. Company? Who else could possibly show up at this party?

Xi lifted the lid off the lockbox and placed it on the table, then reached in with both hands and removed a fabric-wrapped object about the size of a small painting canvas. She began slowly unwinding the fabric until it uncovered a rectangular tablet about an inch thick, with sharp, laser-cut edges. Despite looking to be made of some sort of metal, it was apparently light enough that Xi could lift it with ease.

She placed it down on the table next to the container and finished unwrapping the tablet; it gleamed where the light hit it.

Xi smiled, basking in the glow from the tablet and then turned to Kovalic. "The Aleph Tablet. Intact and unstolen. Despite your best attempts."

At that moment, a klaxon sounded and the lights around the vault hatch began to blink again. The small door slid open and the eyes of everyone in the room turned quizzically toward it.

"What the fuck is going on?" Xi demanded.

Something in Kovalic's mind clicked, which meant he was the only one in the room who was ready for what happened next.

A loud whoop echoed up the shaft, ricocheting around the room, and followed a moment later by what appeared to be a ballistic Eli Brody, who exploded out of the hatch like a cork from a champagne bottle. The force of his exit was enough to slam him, with a solid *thud*, into the empty container that had recently held the tablet. That in turn flew right into Xi, who was knocked to the floor.

Kovalic's body caught up with his brain and he whirled towards Sayers to wrest the KO gun from her grip, but to his surprise, she was already bringing the weapon to bear on the guards at the door.

The pair of goons reacted slower than everybody else, with perhaps the exception of Brody, who was lying on the table, hands scrabbling at his helmet.

Blue rings of force issued from the KO gun, but where the two guards should have been knocked insensate, the stun field dissipated harmlessly off them with a telltale shimmer. Sayers gaped at the weapon as if it had betrayed her.

Kovalic redirected his movement from her to the guards, launching himself at one before the man could draw the weapon from his own belt. His tackle caught the big man in the midriff, knocking the air out of both of them and sending them toppling to the deck. The guard's hand had gone to his sidearm, but Kovalic grabbed the wrist with both hands, trying to prevent him from clearing the holster. Behind him, he saw a blur as Sayers made a similar move, peppering the other guard with blows to the mid-section like she was working a body bag.

Leaning heavily on the arm of the guard, Kovalic tried to bring his right elbow around to catch the man in the jaw, but there just wasn't enough leverage to deal any significant amount of force. The guard's other hand, the one not trying to get to his gun, clutched at Kovalic's throat. He could feel the strong, calloused fingers trying to get purchase around his windpipe, and tried to pull his head back out of reach.

A heavy boot appeared from Kovalic's peripheral vision, hitting home on the guard's temple. Dazed, the thug's arm went limp to his side and Kovalic relieved him of his sidearm. Nearby, Brody, who had ditched the helmet of his vacsuit, was bent over, trying to catch his breath.

"What the hell was that?" Kovalic managed as he rolled off the guard.

"You're welcome!"

"Save it," said Kovalic, climbing to his feet. Sayers was still nimbly dodging the other guard's blows while trying to dart in whenever there was an opening, but she was getting tired a lot faster than the slab of plasticrete she was punching.

"Why the hell didn't the stun work?" Sayers yelled.

"Disruption matrix," said Kovalic, leaning over and yanking open the unconscious guard's tunic. A net of shimmering silver lay beneath, atop of what was clearly nanoweave body armor. "Not cheap, but it cancels out stun fields by broadcasting an equal and opposite wave of energy. Kind of like noise-canceling headphones."

"Thanks for the educational tip," called a breathless Sayers, narrowly ducking a fist the size of a softball. "Little help over here?"

"So we're on the same side again?"

"You told me to get close to her. Work *any* angle! I saw an opportunity!" Sayers protested, landing a kick to the man's gut. He grabbed the foot with both of his hands and swung her around into the bulkhead; she gave an *oof* as the wind was knocked out of her.

Brody exchanged a glance with Kovalic. "We *are* helping her, right?"

Kovalic sighed, but as the man was distracted with trying to throttle Sayers, he came up from behind and clubbed him hard on the head with the butt of the KO gun. The guard faltered, his knees weakening; Sayers broke his chokehold and slid down the wall, coughing and clutching at her throat. Her foot lashed up and caught the man right between the legs. He grunted and slowly fell to his knees; Kovalic pistol whipped him again and he went down for the count.

He glanced over towards Xi, but the box had clocked her hard, and she still wasn't moving.

"So," said Sayers, leaning against the wall, eyes closed as she rubbed her neck. "Was that all part of the plan?"

Kovalic glanced at the hatch. "Let's say yes?"

"It was the fastest way out of the vault," said Brody. "Good thing the console let the commander take control of the shaft's airlock systems *and* shut down the laser scanning grid, or I would be having a much worse day." He reached over to offer Sayers a hand up, but she waved him away and pushed herself up the wall, shaking her head.

"You guys are even crazier than I thought."

"I think that's what our unit insignia says," said Brody.

"Hey," said Kovalic. "Focus." He walked over to the table where the partially unwrapped Aleph Tablet sat, light glinting off of it. Upon closer inspection, it was a bright silvery metal, utterly smooth and flawless. With a slight thrill, he took it in both hands – maybe it was made by aliens and maybe it wasn't, but it was sure as hell a part of history. It was surprisingly light in his hands, but dense and solid nonetheless. History: never quite as weighty as you expected it to be. Maybe there was something in that, but now definitely wasn't the time to ponder it.

"All right," he said, rewrapping the object and stowing it under his arm. "Let's get a move on."

Addy's breath was still coming loud in her ears, and she prodded gingerly at her throat. *I don't think he did any permanent damage, but that's going to leave a mark.* She reached over and plucked the KO gun from the man's holster, the tension bleeding out of her shoulders at the familiar weight of a sidearm.

"We get what we came for?" she asked, nodding at the package under Kovalic's arm.

"Let's hope so. Otherwise, we just got ourselves in a shitload of trouble over nothing."

That oughta be my motto. She couldn't entirely banish the pleased feeling that washed over her. *But we're not out of this yet.*

"You won't get far," growled a voice, and Addy looked over her shoulder to see Xi, a nasty cut on her forehead, pulling herself up on the security console. She lifted her arm, where one of the bangles was now glowing bright red. "My security teams are all on alert." Her eyes moved to Addy, and almost softened. "I'm disappointed in you, Adelaide. You could have been something special."

"Oh, don't worry," said Addy sweetly, "I am."

"Maybe we should take her with us?" said Brody. "Might help us get past security if we've got their boss."

Xi bared her teeth. "I welcome you to try."

"Good idea," said Addy. "Sleep well." She raised the knockout gun at Xi and fired.

Another flash of a bangled arm and the stun field splashed off harmlessly. Xi grinned, her smile almost feral and flicked her other wrist at Sayers. A small barrage of flechettes zipped forth, but Addy dove out of the way as they implanted in the bulkhead behind her.

Xi rose to her feet, kicking off the heels she'd been wearing, and raised her hands into a fighting stance.

Oh, you want to dance? Addy returned the smile, and stowed the knockout gun in her waistband.

"This isn't the time to settle scores," said Kovalic. "She's stalling until her goons get here – we need to move."

Addy waved him off. "This won't take a minute." More to the point, she was going to enjoy the hell out of it. Like she could be bought with money and promises. Ofeibia Xi was going to learn that there was more to Addy Sayers than something broken that needed fixing.

"Addy," said Kovalic, and when she glanced over, his gray eyes were serious. "She's not worth it."

Her teeth ground together and she fought back the red pulsing at the edges of her vision. It would feel good, she knew, the impact of her knuckles into flesh, but as the throbbing started to fade, she saw it for what she was: another, separate part of her that reveled in the simplicity of violence.

"Yeah," she said finally, letting out a breath. "Let's go." She started backing towards the door to the vault room, Brody and Kovalic flanking her.

With another smile, Xi touched a different bracelet on her wrist and the vault room door slammed closed with the whine of a magnetic seal. "I'm afraid you won't be going anywhere. My security team has standing orders for just such a situation: they'll flood the room with a sedative gas and incapacitate all of us."

Behind Addy, Kovalic cursed as he tried to pry the door open. "She's locked it down."

"Oh good," said Addy, cracking her knuckles. "In that case, I don't mind having a go. You get that door open." She launched herself across the room at Xi with a feint-jab combination.

The gangster blocked the strike, then flashed a kick as her dress ruffled. Her heel took Addy in the thigh; there'd be a bruise there tomorrow. But it also gave Addy a moment to push closer, driving her other knee into Xi's mid-section. That one caught the gangster off-guard, and she doubled over, withdrawing outside of Addy's range.

Addy pressed her advantage, coming in with a low kick and following it with a swing at Xi's head, but the other woman straightened suddenly, her windedness evidently a ruse, and turned sideways to avoid the strikes.

She's fast, Addy just had time to think before a fist caught her in the shoulder. There was a click and a hiss and she felt something sharp pinch her; the arm went numb, flopping lifelessly to her side.

Fuck. She snarled at Xi, as she massaged her left shoulder.

Xi smiled, dancing away, then beckoned with one hand. "Come."

Glancing over her shoulder, she saw Brody and Kovalic trying to pry off a panel next to the door. She looked back at Xi and tried to figure out which of the many bracelets she'd used to trigger the lockdown. It had been that one, right? The flat, gold cuff? Maybe she could undo it, if she could just get close enough.

Well, if you ever bragged you could win a fight with one hand tied behind your back, now's your chance to make good.

Addy circled Xi warily. At least she'd managed to keep the usual blood-pounding ferocity at bay. This wasn't a fight that was going to be won by sheer strength or agility.

No, this time she needed to be smarter than her opponent.

There was a zap and a curse from behind her and she heard Brody utter a string of expletives, but there sure wasn't the sound of a door opening. Steeling herself, she charged at Xi.

Rotating her torso, she let her limp left arm flail towards Xi; there was no control behind it, but Xi couldn't afford to ignore it, so she turned toward it, bringing up a forearm to block it. As the dead arm bounced uselessly off her opponent's, Addy kept moving, bringing herself around into a spin kick, her opposite heel scything through Xi's block and into her shoulder.

Unbalanced by her numb arm, she landed in a stumble – Sergeant Djalair would have made her do it again – and followed it by coming up from her low center of gravity into a bullrush, taking Xi right in the stomach and slamming her back against the bulkhead.

Xi hit the wall with a grunt and Addy rebounded off her, both of them falling to the deck. Addy immediately tried to scramble upwards with her one good hand as leverage and launch herself on top of Xi in a pig pile.

It's not elegant, but it'll get the job done.

Xi's hands came up, her nails raking at Addy's face, raising long welts on her cheek and barely missing her eyes.

Addy dropped all of her weight on Xi, trying to pin her

down, but the other woman wriggled underneath her. That was just fine, though, because all Addy needed to do was grab Xi's wrist with her right hand and press her finger against the cuff there.

There was the clank of a magnetic seal releasing and the door to the vault room slid open, startling Brody, who was still working on the panel.

Trying to keep her weight on the flailing Xi, Addy looked over her shoulder at Kovalic and Brody. "*Go.*"

Kovalic started towards her. "Not without you."

"You said the mission comes first. Now *go,*" she said as Xi screamed, swinging again at her face. But Addy kept her finger on the bracelet even as the woman's fists caught her in the head, making her reel. Dimly, she saw Kovalic grab a protesting Brody and drag him out the door.

With a smile, she let go of Xi's wrist and heard the door slide closed again. A breath of relief left her and she let the other woman push her off.

"I expected better from you than playing the tragic hero," said Xi, drawing herself up into a crouch. She was breathing heavily, her perfectly coiffed hair thrown into disarray. Her dress was torn and grimy from rolling around on the floor, but despite that, she still managed to conjure an air of elegance.

Addy grinned from her place on the floor. "I don't know, 'tragic hero' has a certain ring to it."

"Your friends won't escape," said Xi, touching another control on her bracelet. "All you've done is doom them – and you – to a slower, more painful fate. I assure you, you *will* all live to regret this."

Oh good, thought Addy as she stared up at the ceiling. *Something to look forward to.*

CHAPTER 25

Eli watched the door slam closed behind him, his hand still outstretched. He stared for a moment, then whirled on Kovalic.

"Goddamnit, why didn't you *do* something?"

"Not now, Brody." The major was surveying the corridor, the wrapped tablet still underneath one arm. Red lighting flashed around them and all the screens in the hallway displayed the word LOCKDOWN. At least there weren't klaxons going off everywhere. Yet.

"When, then? Should I wait until after you've gone back and killed her yourself? Like with Page?"

Kovalic froze and suddenly Eli had that feeling you got when a foot went out from under you and your stomach was hanging in mid-air. *That may have been the red button.*

"You don't know what you're talking about," said Kovalic, without turning around.

"Tapper told me you don't leave people behind," said Eli. He pointed at the door. "But this makes *twice* just in the time I've been on this team."

"Brody, she stayed behind so *we* could get away, and you want to stand here jawing about it?"

"No, I want you to go back in, kick the shit out of that gangster, and get our *teammate* back." Eli crossed his arms over his chest.

The older man opened his mouth to respond when there was a loud clatter of footsteps from the direction of the vault complex's antechamber. Kovalic spun in that direction, then looked back at Eli. "Xi's security. We have to go."

"Not without– "

"Damn it, Brody, if we *don't* go now, then Xi will have all of us, and freeing Sayers will be the least of our problems. Now *move*."

Goddamn it. But there was the ring of logic to Kovalic's point, so Eli let himself be dragged along away from the vault door. *We'll get you back, Sayers. I promise.*

Kovalic tapped his earbud. "Aegis, we need another exit from the vault access complex."

Taylor's voice came over the comm. "Oh good, you're still alive." If it was intended as dry, the note of genuine relief undercut the attempt. "Checking the schematics. Give me a minute."

From down the hall, Eli could hear the tramp of boots. What sounded like a lot of them. And they didn't sound like they were walking puppies.

"There's a maintenance hatch about halfway down the main corridor, on the port side," said Taylor.

Kovalic snapped a finger at Eli and pointed at the wall. "I'll hold them off." He pulled out the KO gun he'd taken off Xi's guard and removed the power pack.

"But that thing didn't work on any of–"

"*Brody, open the goddamned hatch.*"

It took a moment for Eli to find the seam; the luxury liner took pains to disguise all the unpleasant necessities of space travel, instead aiming to convince its passengers that it ran on magic.

But Eli had spent a lot of time on spaceships by this point – he knew all the ins and outs of the *Cavalier* – and it didn't take him long to find the catch. He pulled the panel away from the wall, revealing a passageway just large enough to admit a person at a crawl.

Looking over his shoulder, he saw Kovalic lay the tablet down against the bulkhead, then do something to the KO gun's battery before shoving it back in place. The major rolled up his jacket sleeve, tore a strip off his shirt, and wound it through the trigger guard, tying it tightly.

A loud whine began to build from the weapon and Kovalic hurled it down the hallway, even as a half dozen White Star security in riot gear rounded the corridor. One of them shouted as the knockout gun slid towards them.

Kovalic grabbed the tablet from where it lay and ran towards Eli, hitting the deck in a slide. "*Go.*"

Eli didn't need any more encouragement. On his hands and knees, he shimmied into the crawlway. He could hear Kovalic following him and was about to ask a question when the hallway they'd just left exploded.

Shouts and cries came from behind him, Kovalic kept pushing him forward. The crawlway quarters were tight, lined with pulsing conduits and pipes covered in condensation. A couple times, Eli singed himself coming too close to those carrying steam or other heated gases. His knees and elbows began to ache from the repeated banging against the hard metal.

After five minutes of crawling, the tube widened into a four-way junction large enough to fit them both at a crouch. Kovalic rested the tablet between his legs.

Eli rubbed his knees. "What the hell did you do back there?" He raised an arm to wipe the sweat off his brow, only to remember he was still wearing the bulky vacsuit. *No wonder it's so hot.* The sweat reclamation system didn't work very well without the helmet on.

Kovalic was peering back down the crawlway. "Overloaded the KO gun's power pack and then jammed down the firing mechanism."

"And that turns it into a *bomb*? Where was that earlier?" Leaning against the wall, Eli yanked off one of the gravboots, letting it fall to the floor with a clunk.

"Not a bomb," Kovalic said. "Just a distraction. A loud noise, some bright light. It'll buy us a little time, but it's not going to be long before they figure out where we went, so we need to make ourselves scarce." He put one finger to his ear. "Aegis, we appear to be at junction T-16-425. Any idea where that is?"

No response came from Taylor. Kovalic frowned, then tapped his earbud again. "Aegis, you copy? Bruiser?"

Dropping the second gravboot, Eli glanced at the conduits lining the walls. "Too much interference from all this equipment, probably. All the shielding is in the bulkheads and we're behind them." He started peeling off the top half of the vacsuit.

"Great," muttered Kovalic. He seemed to ponder something for a moment, his eyes flicking back and forth rapidly. "OK, we're going to have to split up."

"That sounds like a terrible idea."

Kovalic flicked a holoscreen from his sleeve; the mission clock, bright orange, flashed at both of them. "Twenty minutes until we exit the wormhole, Brody. Time's not with us on this one. You need to find Tapper and figure out how we're getting out of here."

Oh good, the easy job. He let the rest of the suit puddle to the floor, then extricated his feet. "What are you going to do?"

Kovalic patted the tablet. "I'm going to find a safe place for this. Someplace nobody will think to look."

"That sounds nice. Can I go there?"

Ignoring the comment, Kovalic waved his sleeve at the junction plate, then eyed the display. "Looks like this one should lead back to the esplanade," he said, pointing to one of the other crawlways branching off the junction. "You take that one. I'll go this way. Check in with the commander as soon as you're clear of the interference."

Eli nodded and crouched down, then gave a look back at Kovalic. "We're going to get Sayers, right?"

Kovalic's gray eyes settled on his. "We're all getting out, Brody."

"I'm holding you to that."

Kovalic tilted his head in acknowledgement. "Get moving."

Wincing as his sore knees hit the deck plate, Eli tipped Kovalic an informal salute. *Should have brought kneepads.*

Once Brody had disappeared from view, Kovalic let out a breath. That jab about Page had hurt more than he thought it would, all the more so because he hadn't been expecting it from Brody, who usually seemed so upbeat and easygoing. But it just went to show that everybody dealt with pain in their own way.

Kovalic hadn't wanted to leave Sayers behind, but the specialist had made the call, and tactically speaking, it had been the right one. The mission came first. He looked down at the tablet. As long as this damn thing was worth it.

Taking a deep breath, he centered himself. The job wasn't over yet. He still needed to make sure the tablet was safe before he thought about getting his team – his *whole* team – off this ship.

Dropping to his knees, he pushed the tablet into the passage in front of him and started his long crawl.

Five minutes later, he'd come to another junction, this one with an actual egress port. Granted, if Xi's goons had figured out where they'd gone, there was every possibility that a squad of them might be laying in wait. But, tempting as it was, he couldn't live in the maintenance tunnels of this ship forever.

He wedged the tablet in between some conduits, then popped the hatch open and peeked out.

The corridor beyond was carpeted in a rough rust-colored weave and fortunately empty. He hoped Nat had managed to throw a wrench into the *Queen Amina*'s security system, or this was going to be over pretty fast. He retrieved the tablet, then replaced the panel.

Doors with frosted glass panes lined the corridor, each leading to what appeared to be private rooms for those who needed to get some work done while on vacation. Not, perhaps, the most frequented part of a ship that also contained casinos and restaurants, but that was just fine for Kovalic's purposes.

"Aegis," he said, trying comms again. "You copy?"

Still no response, and for the first time he started to feel something churning in his gut. It hadn't just been the interference. He tried Tapper too, but no luck from him. Or Brody. Or Sayers. Were all the signals being jammed, or just his? Maybe the lockdown was screwing with their comms somehow.

His grip on the tablet tightened. He still had a job to do. Getting the tablet to a safe place was his top priority; after that, he could worry about regrouping with the rest of the team.

Raising his sleeve, he brought up the schematics Nat had

downloaded and plotted a course to the lifeboat banks they'd
scouted earlier.

They weren't far: down a few junction corridors and around
a corner or two. The hallways were deserted, again probably
because of the lockdown, but as Kovalic rounded the last
corner to the lifeboats, he caught a glimpse of a pair of White
Star security personnel, armed with the heavy duty crowd
control weapons colloquially called "bouncers." About the size
of a shotgun, they used repulsors to generate concussive waves
that packed a much bigger punch than a KO gun. Nominally
they were less-lethal, but get thrown into a wall by one at
close range and you'd be lucky to get up again.

Kovalic flattened himself to the wall. These two didn't look
like they were on patrol – it seemed like they were stationed
at this junction, probably watching in case somebody made a
move on the lifeboats. He'd need a distraction.

He patted down his pockets, but all he came up with was
lint. Which just left the priceless artifact he was holding.

OK, so he'd have to do this the old-fashioned way.

Unwrapping the slab from its covering, he ran a hand over
the surface and marveled again at its smoothness. It was less
like metal and almost more like stone. Or glass. Regardless,
it ought to slide pretty well, especially as the short-weave
carpet of the corridor gave way to the slicker decking by the
escape pods. Hey, rugs were expensive to clean.

Winding up, he leaned around the corner and heaved the
tablet as hard as he could at the guards. It whooshed across the
floor, smooth as you please, getting the immediate attention
of the two security personnel as it slid right up to their feet.
They both looked down at it and then at each other.

That was all the opening Kovalic needed. By the time

they'd looked up again, he'd covered more than half of the distance, and they didn't have time to bring their weapons up before he'd closed. Leading with his knee, he caught the first guard in the stomach, knocking him back and to the ground.

Guard number two's jaw dropped, his gun almost forgotten as he watched his partner go down. Kovalic rolled off the man he'd knocked down, bringing his weapon along for the ride. The other guard didn't even have a chance to close his mouth before Kovalic squeezed the trigger on the bouncer and hit him square in the torso.

The concussion blast lifted the guard off the floor, almost into the low ceiling, and tossed him backwards ten feet before he hit the ground and slid into a bulkhead.

With his elbow, Kovalic jabbed the man he'd downed sharply in the face and heard his head bounce off the floor.

Sometimes the old-fashioned ways were the best.

Claiming the bouncer, he retrieved the tablet and secured it in its wrapping, then slung the weapon across his back.

There were, as Nat had reported, five escape pods in the bay. Above each lifeboat hatch shone a red light. While the *Queen Amina* was still in the wormhole, the lifeboats were locked down unless authorized by the command staff.

But there had to be a manual override for the doors somewhere. If the command deck was incapacitated for whatever reason, you couldn't leave people trapped on the ship. That was a quick route to mishap and, eventually, getting sued. Same reason that the lifeboats could be launched from the lifeboats themselves or remotely.

The manual controls weren't hard to find; it was the work of a moment for Kovalic to break the rather pathetic lock on the wall panel. Five large levers stared back at him; pulling the top one, he watched as the light above the leftmost pod switched from red to green.

Now unlocked, the lifeboat door ground open at his approach. As he entered, the interior lighting blinked on. It was a fairly standard layout: twelve crash couches that could, in a pinch, fit two people each; plenty of containers of food; and two self-sufficient refresher units. The facilities could accommodate full capacity for a couple weeks if need be, and there were compartments containing two dozen vacsuits – identical to the one Brody had recently ditched – in case of emergency.

Crossing to the second couch from the right, he started yanking up the memory foam pads there. If the standard layout held out, there ought to be a storage locker underneath this couch with a mechanic's tool kit. Hopefully not the sort of thing you ever really needed on a lifeboat, because if you had to repair something, chances were you were toast already.

But removing the toolkit provided a compact, well-secured niche where you could fit, say, a rectangular package a couple inches of high.

A crackle sounded in his earbud and he frowned, tapping at it. For a moment, he thought he'd heard a voice. Nat?

"Aegis? That you?"

If there was a response, he didn't hear it. He opened the toolkit and unpacked it, putting all the tools back, loose, under the foam pad. Even with the tools there would be just enough room to wedge in the tablet, though it'd be tight. Pushing the crash-couch's cushion down, he picked up the toolkit case and walked back towards the hatch. Wouldn't do for a loose case to be banging around if the lifeboat needed to be pressed into service.

Raising his sleeve, he brought up the mission clock. Five

minutes before the *Queen Amina* exited the wormhole. If they could make it that long, they ought to be home free.

"…sair… in."

He slowed. That was definitely Nat's voice, but the transmission was still garbled. He pressed the earbud tighter, as though that would improve the intelligibility.

"Repeat, Aegis. You're breaking up."

"…ch out… yricans…"

Kovalic stepped out of the lifeboat and back into the corridor where he'd left the incapacitated guards. Maybe he could get a better signal there.

"That's just far enough, major," said a voice that was most definitely not coming in over the comms.

He looked up to find the muzzle of the other downed guard's bouncer pointed directly at him. Behind it, Mirza wore a stony expression. "Put down the case and the weapon, then step aside."

Perfect timing. He'd expected nothing less from her. Slowly, Kovalic laid the case next to the lifeboat hatch and unslung the bouncer, placing it on top of the case. Then he raised his hands and stepped forward. "I guess my reprieve ran out."

Mirza gestured with the gun. "I told you what would happen next time I saw you, Kovalic. Fair warning."

"More than fair."

Closing the distance, Mirza kicked Kovalic's bouncer away; it skittered across the floor. "I have to say, hiding the tablet on the lifeboat was an inspired choice. Easy getaway and with your backdoor into the ship's systems you might even be able to convince the *Queen Amina* personnel that its launch was a malfunction or false reading. Then, what, you just swoop back later and pick it up, nice as you please?"

"I don't know why you're asking. You seem to have it all worked out."

Mirza stepped forward, motioning with the bouncer for him to turn around. "Hands on your head, spread your legs." When he'd complied, she quickly patted him down, checking his jacket and pants pockets.

"I can assure you, I'm otherwise unarmed," said Kovalic.

She removed a small black ovoid from one of his pockets and held it up, taking a step back. "Turn around. Keep your hands up."

"Just a baffle," said Kovalic, as he faced her again. "Nothing nefarious about it. It's not going to blow up or anything."

"Oh, nothing nefarious for you, perhaps," said Mirza, allowing a tight smile to cross her face. "But that's because you weren't looking in the right place. I have to thank you for stealing the tablet from the *Queen Amina's* vault; that was quite impressive. And it saved me a lot of trouble. Because if there's one thing we both know, it's far easier to steal from another thief. All you need is a good source of information." She clicked the baffle on, the red light on it glowing as Kovalic felt the pressure push in on his ears.

He frowned. "But the baffle should have stopped any listening devices you…"

Mirza clicked the baffle off and Kovalic's ears popped. "Which is why I bugged the baffle itself. Before we had our little chat in your stateroom. As long as it was active, it transmitted everything it could hear directly to my team."

"Damn clever," said Kovalic, tipping his head in acknowledgement. "So, what now?"

"Now you step aside, and I get what I came for." She motioned at him with the bouncer again.

"Well, when you make that convincing an argument." He stepped away from the hatch to the lifeboat as Mirza walked over, keeping the weapon trained on him. "You don't miss a trick, do you, commander? I did appreciate that aspect of our brief partnership."

"I prepare for every eventuality, major. You should understand that part of our jobs. But, then again, if you did, perhaps our situations would be reversed. Step into the doorway where I can see you, please."

Kovalic complied, hands still up. They were getting a little tired. "I find it next to impossible to prepare for *every* possible outcome. So I settle for the most likely ones." Another blurt of static in his ear, and he thought he could hear the faint sound of Nat's voice trying to punch through.

Mirza backed into the lifeboat, keeping her weapon on Kovalic as she peered around the interior. "And yet, the difficulty is figuring out which outcomes *are* the most likely, is it not? Who, for example, could have predicted that we would be where we are right now?"

Extending one finger, Kovalic pointed at her without lowering his hands. "See, that is a great point. I guess I've always thought of myself as a student of human behavior. People are, to a certain extent, predictable."

In front of him, Mirza's eyes alit on the slightly rumpled cushion of the crash couch. Kovalic cleared his throat, trying to draw her attention back to him. Keep her distracted. Just a little longer.

"Do you mind if I put my hands down, by the way? They're getting a bit tired."

"Keep them up," Mirza snapped, waving the bouncer at him, even as she reached back and pulled away the cushion, revealing the tablet's wrapping. She smiled again, but there was no mirth in it; just satisfaction in a job well done. Mirza wasn't the type to celebrate. "You're right," she said. "People are predictable."

Another blast of static in Kovalic's ear, and he tried not to wince, but then a voice came, thank god, crystal clear. "Simon? Goddamn it, tell me this worked. I've had a hell of a time fighting off one of Mirza's goons and cutting through whatever jamming they laid down, but I've got control back. Just tell me when."

Just in time, too. The mission clock was inching toward zero and they'd be out of the wormhole in moments. Kovalic smiled back at Mirza, though more one from relief than anything else. "So glad we agree."

Mirza's brow furrowed, but as she reached over to pull out the wrapping, realization started to dawn on her face.

Just not quite fast enough.

While her attention was elsewhere, Kovalic dove backwards out of the lifeboat hatchway, hitting the deck in the hallway. "*Now*, Nat. *Now.*"

A concussion blast and a curse came through the hatchway almost simultaneously, but the shot went over Kovalic's head. Then the lifeboat hatch slammed shut between him and Mirza, the light above it turning red again.

Kovalic climbed to his feet and returned to the hatch. A small porthole was inset in the door and through it he could see Mirza's face, contorted with anger as she yelled at him, but the material was thick, designed to withstand the rigors of space travel, and no sound penetrated.

Kovalic pointed to his ear and shook his head, even as Mirza waved the empty wrapping at him. He mouthed an "ah," then reached down and picked up the toolkit he'd been carrying and raised it in front of the porthole. Her eyes went wide as Kovalic opened the clasps and removed the tablet that he'd stowed there.

"Sim… Corsair? Did that work?" Nat's voice came across the earbud, sounding concerned.

Kovalic tapped his earbud. "Like a charm, Aegis. Get the lifeboat ready to launch on my mark. Oh, and can you patch me through to its intercom?"

"One sec." There was a squelch of static. "You're on."

"–uck you, Kovalic," came Mirza's voice across the comm. "Fuck you and your whole fucking team…" It kept going in a line of nearly unbroken invective and expletive.

Kovalic cleared his throat. "Language, commander."

"Kovalic? How the *fuck*?"

"We just agreed people are predictable, commander. I knew you'd have bugged the stateroom *somehow*. But then you made a mistake, with your strategy of a thousand little cuts. First you lock us out of our stateroom, so I knew the bug couldn't be in there. Then your subsequent plays were just a little too sloppy. Siccing Cortez on us? Trying to kill us in a lift car? Your heart just wasn't in it. It was enough to remind us that you were still out there, but not so much that it actually stopped us from doing the job. Why not? Because you wanted us to do your heavy lifting for you. Once I figured that out, it wasn't hard to deduce that you'd put the bug in the one thing that we'd assume wasn't a bug, that we would carry with us no matter where we went. So it was just a matter of feeding you a story that you'd believe." He waved a hand at the lifeboat. "And, of course, a little help from my friends."

"When I get out of here, I'm going to shove that tablet so far up your–"

"Let me stop you right there, because I've got good news and bad news. The bad news is you're not getting out of that lifeboat for a while. The good news is," he paused to glance at his sleeve, on which the mission clock was now running into negative numbers, "we've officially cleared the wormhole and you've got enough food for weeks. Emergency rations aren't tasty, but they'll keep you alive until someone finds the lifeboat distress beacon."

Mirza's eyes widened as she took in his words and she stumbled back from the porthole, raising the bouncer again.

Kovalic tipped her a salute. "Aegis, send her on her way."

"With pleasure."

The red light above the lifeboat door started blinking furiously.

Mirza's mouth opened in a scream as she pulled the trigger. "Kovaliiiiiiii–"

There was a muted *thwump* as the explosive charges fired, jettisoning the lifeboat into space and disconnecting the intercom connection. Through the porthole, Kovalic watched the pod spin away, quickly losing any sight of Mirza, though he thought he saw the rippling splash of a concussion shot against the porthole. It wouldn't be enough to cause any damage to the pod, but the recoil probably wouldn't do Mirza any favors at that range.

Kovalic tapped his earbud. "Nice work, Aegis. You need any backup?"

"Nope. Situation is under control here."

"Meet you at the rendezvous point, then. Let's just hope that the boys have done their part."

"Well," said Nat, "there's a first time for everything."

CHAPTER 26

It took ten minutes of crawling through junction tubes, climbing down ladders, and ducking into maintenance tunnels before Eli finally found his way back out onto the *Queen Amina's* deck. Kicking out a vent, he emerged into a disused corridor somewhere on the ship's lower levels.

There was, fortunately, nobody around to see him stagger out, somewhat grimier and worse for wear than he'd gone in. His shirt was ragged at the edges and stained with sweat, one trouser knee already torn through.

This is why I can't have nice things.

His hands started to tremble as the reminder of everything he'd done in the last hour finally caught up to him the way the sound of the explosion followed the flash. As if the spacewalk hadn't been bad enough, his body wouldn't be forgiving him for the trip up that vault shaft any time soon. Like riding a water slide in reverse. Which made it sound a lot more fun than it had actually been.

He gave himself time for three more deep breaths to settle his nerves, then got back to it. Kovalic had given him a job to do, and if they were going to get out of here – if they were *all* going to get out of here – he needed to do his part.

Leaning against the bulkhead, he raised his sleeve and

tried to initiate a direct connection with Tapper. "Bruiser, this is Updraft, do you copy?"

The sergeant came back immediately. "You're still alive, kid? I think I lost twenty credits to the commander."

"I'm not sure whether it's more upsetting that you were betting on whether or not I'd survive or the fact that you *bet against me.*"

"Gotta play the odds. And it didn't go quite as planned, if this lockdown's any indication."

"You don't know the half of it. We still need a way off this boat. Any ideas?"

There was a pause from the other end of the line, and then Tapper's voice came back with what, to Eli's ears, was a surprisingly cagey response. "Yeah, I got one. Where are you?"

"Uhhh," Eli eyed the wall until he found an ID plate. "Subdeck 13, section 21A."

"Copy. I'm just a few sections down. There's a bar back near the main hub; meet me there in ten."

Eli pushed his way through a pair of swinging doors and into a bar that felt like it had been jammed into an unused maintenance crawlway. Then again, that might have been the theme of the place. People were drinking out of tin mugs and whatever the bartender was pulling looked like it was coming straight out of one of the conduits in the wall.

Industrial chic?

Tapper was sitting at the bar, jawing with the bartender, a woman with bronze skin and a swept back fade of black hair. An abstract tattoo curled around one bare, muscled shoulder.

As Eli walked in, she threw her head back and laughed at something the sergeant said.

"Making friends wherever you go," said Eli, pulling up a chair.

Tapper raised his cup and took a swig. "That's my gift."

"Well, while you've been charming the locals, I had to spacewalk across the hull – fell off once, by the way – fight off some White Star goons, and crawl through roughly five klicks of maintenance tubes. But I hope you enjoyed your drink."

The sergeant smacked his lips. "Not much on taste, but boy does it have some kick."

The bartender reappeared and gave Eli an appraising look, at least until Tapper slapped him on the shoulder. "Friend of mine. He'll have what I'm having."

With a grin, the woman selected another cup – Eli hoped it had been washed sometime this month – and pulled a long stream of something dark that could have been coolant or maybe a porter. She put it in front of Eli, with an expectant look.

You know what? I was raised on Saltyre's whiskey. I can handle a little homemade ale on a luxury starcruiser.

He smiled, clinked the cup with Tapper's, and threw back a gulp.

Unlike the beer from the other night, which had been watery to the point of, well, water, this ale was strong, in taste and alcohol. The former was a mix of smoky and umami, with a mouthfeel that stabbed you in the sinus; the latter made itself known in a deep bitter aftertaste that felt like it would hang out in the back of your throat for at least a couple of days.

Eli hid a cough by wiping the back of his hand against his mouth. "Good," he rasped. "Really good."

The bartender's grin had only broadened as he downed it

and she gave him a look very near a respectful nod before going to check on her other customers.

Pushing the drink away, Eli turned to Tapper and lowered his voice. "So, what exactly are we doing here?"

"Working on our exfil. The lockdown's made things… complicated."

Eli looked around the bar, which, if not full, had at least a dozen people in it. "They don't seem too bothered by it around here."

"These are the staff and maintenance crews, kid. Essential personnel are all at their stations, but everybody else, well, they pretty much live here – it's their ship as much as Xi's."

"And she lets them?"

"She can't very well run the ship without them. They have a whatchamacallit… understanding."

Not a heart of gold, maybe, but a heart that understands exactly what gold is worth.

"So," said Eli. "What's this great plan you've got, then?" He'd been running through ideas since he'd left Kovalic, but none of them had felt like they offered odds any better than a coin toss.

"Well," said Tapper, cradling his cup, "it's going to take some work, and we'll need someone who can hack into some pretty protected systems. So I took the liberty of calling in a favor from a… friend."

A friend? Do we even have any –

"Oh, hey guys," said an unassuming voice from behind them. "Started without me, huh?"

Eli looked up into the sunny face of ostensible ship tech assistant – and actual stowaway – Cary Maldonado.

Oh, you have got to be kidding me.

Kovalic's place of temporary employment, the noodle shop, was closed up tighter than a defunct wormhole gate when he arrived there fifteen minutes later. He'd seen people out and about during the lockdown, but it wasn't anywhere near as bustling as it had been the other day. Still, at least he and Nat, when she showed up a couple minutes after him, didn't stand out.

"Everything good?" she asked.

Kovalic patted the toolkit. "Safe and sound."

"The boys?"

"Working on an exit now. They'll ping us when they've got something."

She nodded, but her expression turned troubled. "That just leaves our friend Maverick. She's really living up to that callsign."

Kovalic's lips pressed together. Sayers. She hadn't just left the rule book behind – she'd practically burned it. But you couldn't argue that she'd got the job done. And her reward was... well, Kovalic didn't want to think about the gory details, but Xi was not going to be pleased.

Nat hesitated. "In terms of OPSEC, Sayers doesn't know much beyond our names and unit designation. She hasn't even met the general."

"You're suggesting we burn her?" Kovalic said, one eyebrow going up.

Nat's expression hardened. "I'm looking at all the options, Simon. Like an XO should. We don't have the resources to mount a rescue right now. And that," she nodded at the toolkit, "is still our top priority."

Kovalic's grip tightened on the handle. There was a fine line between priceless and valueless, and the Aleph Tablet was skirted right along the edge. "Let's set Maverick aside for the moment. We need to get in touch with al-Kitab and see if he can authenticate it. But Xi's going to have eyes on him, and no doubt she'll have tagged at least me in the security system. Brody too."

"Oh, I wouldn't worry about that."

Kovalic blinked at the smile on Nat's face. "OK, I'll bite. What'd you do?"

"My access to the security system is still limited, but the bigger these systems are, the more security holes there are that don't get patched. I poked around a bit, and I can't remove your biometrics, but it turns out I *can* change your classification."

"Uh, do I want to know to what?"

"To something that can go pretty much anywhere and not get noticed. Congratulations, you're now a maintenance drone."

A laugh, the first real one he'd had in a while, bubbled up out of Kovalic, and he felt a small degree of tension lift from his shoulders. "Did you bring me a broom too?"

"Couldn't find one on short notice. But I also reclassified Brody, Tapper, and myself," said Nat. Her lips pressed together too. "And Sayers. Just in case."

Kovalic let out a breath. "Damn good work. That ought to buy us some breathing room. But Xi's not the only one I'm worried about. We got rid of Mirza, but some of her team is still unaccounted for."

"Down one, at least. I ran into the tall, dark-haired guy you saw in the hallway. He's enjoying the inside of a supply cabinet for the moment. I'm sure he'll find his way out eventually, though."

"But we still don't know how big her team is."

"Well, if the one Sayers took out in the casino was one of them, then it's at least three."

"I'd wager there's one or two more; and if we haven't seen them yet, that makes them especially dangerous. Let's keep our heads on a swivel."

"Always."

Eli tugged on the collar of his borrowed uniform as they rode the lift upward. It was a little tight, but neither of the White Star security staff who had showed up when they broke into the clothing store had been quite his size.

He still wasn't thrilled about being the bait in the first part of Tapper's plan. Mainly, he was lucky the guards hadn't stunned first and asked questions later. Their attention had been on him, hands on their weapons, when Tapper and Mal had stepped out from behind them and knocked them out with heavy bars repurposed from a clothing rack. Somehow, one of the security uniforms had fit Tapper perfectly. Of course.

Meanwhile, his own trouser cuffs didn't quite reach his ankles and he felt like he was about to pop the fasteners on the tunic. The good news was that the lockdown meant both had been carrying not only KO guns, but also less-lethal concussion grenades. Their sleeves were useless, however – the second they'd knocked the guards out, the devices had been locked and required an access code. And, being unconscious, they weren't about to generously supply said codes.

If Mal had any problem with knocking out a pair of security guards and stealing their uniforms, it didn't show. Currently, the tech was humming to themself as they consulted a small tablet.

"You really think this is going to work?" said Eli, trying to pull his tunic's cuffs down to his wrists. "I'm not sure this is going to work."

"Relax, kid," said Tapper, lounging against the back of the lift. "Trust me."

If he asks me to get in another spacesuit, I am out.

With the lockdown on, the lift hadn't been enthusiastic about accommodating them, but after a few moments of poking around Mal had convinced it that they had every right in the world to be there. And so they found themselves speeding upwards to a level to which normally they wouldn't have access.

Eli checked the charge on his KO gun for what seemed like the seventh time. Green. If he needed to use it, he could. But he hadn't fired a weapon in a long time, and he wasn't sure that he wanted to pick up the habit again. *Given that it's stun-only, and my training is probably almost a decade out of date, the likelihood of even hitting anybody – much less injuring them – is pretty low.*

They hadn't checked in with Kovalic and Taylor – maintaining radio silence as much as possible had been the order of the day, just in case Xi's personnel or Mirza's squad had compromised their frequencies. And, in part, because they weren't quite ready to let Mal in on the whole story yet.

Tapper seemed unconcerned about this sudden full autonomy, but his confidence hadn't bled over to Eli. *I would feel a lot better if I knew what the rest of the team was up to.*

The lift slowed to a stop as they reached their floor, and the doors slid open.

Eli hadn't spent a lot of time in the casinos onboard. It hadn't been part of his cover, and he didn't think that he'd be especially good at games of chance. *My luck has always been mediocre at best.* There was something about setting foot in the fancy surroundings that immediately made him feel like he was a salmon that had jumped right out of the water.

An elbow caught him in the ribs; Tapper was giving him a significant look. The older man nodded down at his torso – White Star livery. Right. They weren't here as guests.

So he followed Tapper's lead as the sergeant strode in like he owned the place, lock, stock, and barrel. "Who's in charge here?" he barked.

The lockdown had cleared out the guests, who had no doubt all been escorted back to their rooms, leaving only a pair of security guards, a bartender, a few waitstaff, and the casino staff, who were sitting around one of the gaming tables.

"I am," said a compact white woman with iron gray hair, pushing herself off the bar and crossing her arms across her chest. Eli tried not to let himself gawp as his eyes slowly went from her face back to Tapper's. *It's like long-lost twins.* "And who the devil are you?" She looked Tapper up and down with the scrutiny of an x-ray scanner.

"Is this what you call lockdown procedure?" Tapper bulled onward, ignoring her queries. "No defensive line at the lift door? Civilians lounging around? I bet that bar isn't even closed down. Dis*grace*ful."

"Now wait just a goddamned minute. I don't know who you think you are, but this is *my* floor."

"Not for long, once I report this woeful performance to Security Chief Cortez," said Tapper, seemingly pulling the name out of his unmentionables.

While the sergeant was holding the attention of the room, Eli had walked over to the bar, avoiding his natural inclination to smile at the bartender, who seemed the friendly sort. Instead, he tried to channel his best Tapper scowl as he peered around, as if in search of infractions. Mal, meanwhile, lingered by the door to the lift, doing an able impersonation of a tech dragooned into service by a couple of security guards.

"Well," said the woman, raising her arm. "Let's just see about that, shall we? I can call him right now."

"In the middle of a lockdown?" Tapper said. "Don't you think he has better things to do? That's why *I'm* here."

"I don't know you from Adam. And I sure as hell don't take orders from you. We'll let the chief sort this out."

Eli's eyes seized on an unstoppered bottle of rum just behind the bar.

"Boss," he said, waving to Tapper. "You were right. Liquor's not even secured!"

The sergeant made a loud *tch*-ing sound, shaking his head in disgust as he stalked over to the bar. "Next you'll tell me that they've got open flames!"

The woman had lowered her sleeve in favor of resting a hand warily on the KO gun at her hip. "Step away from the bar."

"Stand easy," said Tapper, waving a hand. "We clearly got off on the wrong foot." He swiped the bottle of opened rum, ignoring the bartender's stifled protestations, and turned around, proffering it towards the woman. "How about we have a drink and talk about this like civilized folk."

Iron gray brows knit over the security guard's suspicious eyes. "Drinking on duty is *also* against protocol."

Tapper raised the bottle in her direction. "I won't tell the chief if you don't."

She didn't make a move toward it, so Tapper turned toward the other security guard, a tall, rangy woman with dark hair. She opened her mouth to respond and then, at one glare from her boss, shut it again, and took a step backward.

"Oh, for fuck's... I've had just about enough of this," the gray-haired woman said, and out came the KO gun, pointed towards them. "I'm placing you both under detention for suspicion of dereliction of duty. Come quietly, or I will stun the *hell* out of you."

Tapper glanced at Eli, then shrugged and took a swig from the bottle. "Whew," he said, when he came back up for air. "That's the good stuff. No expense spared up here, kid. You want some?"

Eli looked at the bottle, then back at the woman aiming a weapon at them. "Uh. I'm good?"

"Suit yourself. Sorry, love, what were you saying?" This last was addressed back at the woman and seemed, if anything, to enrage her further.

"You know what? Fuck you. Nighty nigh–" Her finger pulled the trigger.

The next part happened almost too fast for Eli to follow as Tapper swung the bottle around by its bottom, spraying a stream of rum between them and the oncoming blue ripples from the knockout gun.

Where the two intersected, a crackling sheet of electricity flickered and sparked, miniature white bolts of lightning zapping and then disappearing, even as the liquid evaporated. The stun field never even made it to them.

Eli had already started to duck out of the way, but as the field dissipated, he found himself meeting the equally wide eyes of the woman who'd just tried to shoot them.

"I guess nobody ever taught you that stun fields don't play well with liquid," said Tapper, hefting the bottle. "That's why you can't use them underwater. They probably figure you don't need to know that on a starship." Before his opposite number could even react, he'd smoothly drawn his own KO gun and fired; the security officer's eyes rolled back in her head as she slumped to the deck. His weapon was on the second guard before she'd even managed to draw her sidearm.

"Two fingers," said Tapper, nodding to the guard's weapon. "And kick it over to me."

She hastily complied, and the sergeant stuck the other weapon in his holster.

Around the room, the rest of the staff had frozen, most doing their level best to fade into the filigreed wallpaper. The bartender had her hands up, eyes flicking back and forth between Eli and Tapper. Even Mal was staring at them, slightly agog.

It's all fun and games until the shooting starts.

"All right," said Tapper, waving his weapon at the remaining security guard. "You're going to give us the code for that door up there." He gestured to an entryway located at the top of a pair of winding staircases.

Color drained from the young woman's face and Eli could see a bead of sweat appear on her forehead, trickling its way in a saline path down her jawline. "I… I can't."

"Well, not with that attitude."

"But she'll kill me!" Her eyes went to the door and Eli had a pretty good idea that the "she" in question wasn't her unconscious superior.

Tapper lowered the KO gun. "Look, I ain't going to lie: I'm not going to kill you. And from what I've heard, your boss is a piece of work. But I can say with relative certainty that she's going to have bigger things to worry about, so maybe you'd better find a new job before she works her way down to you." He hooked a thumb in his belt. "I tell you what: you help us out, and I'll make sure you have a better offer by the time you hit port."

Her throat bobbed. "You... what?"

"This boat's headed to Hamza, right? I know the head of baggage logistics at Said Spaceport. Not glamorous, but it's an honest day's work."

"I... You're going to get me a job?" Befuddlement was writ large on her face, and Eli could sympathize. Tapper could have that effect on people.

There was a chime from behind them and Tapper looked over his shoulder at the lift that they'd arrived in, its door now cleverly camouflaged with the wall.

Oh shit, someone's coming up. One of the staff had probably hit some sort of silent alarm, but Eli wasn't sure which one; they were all maintaining bland looks of innocence. "Uh, we should go, right?"

Tapper stepped closer to the guard, hands up. "Look, I'm giving you an opportunity here. Change your circumstances."

The guard's eyes darted between the lift door and Tapper. "I'm sorry... I wish I could. It's just too risky."

Eli thought he could detect the regret in Tapper's face. *You can't save everyone.* His stomach twinged as the faces of Page and Sayers and even his brother Eamon flashed before his eyes. No, you couldn't save anyone. You just did the best you could.

"Understood," said Tapper. "Just... give us a head start, huh?"

"Sure," said the guard, looking down at the floor. "I didn't see nothing."

His face grim, Tapper nodded to Mal and Eli, and the three

of them made their way up the staircase. The guard they'd stunned was groaning and stirring, the stun already wearing off, so they didn't dawdle.

Tapper nodded at the tech. "Open 'er up, kid."

"Right, right," said Mal, fumbling with their sleeve and holding it up to the door lock.

Another chime from the far end of the room as the lift approached the floor. The staff were beginning to peel themselves off the walls, looking back and forth between the trio on the staircase and the approaching lift. *Calculating the odds.*

Eli glanced at Mal, who was slowly pressing controls on their sleeve; a drop of sweat splashed onto the fabric display, distorting the image, and they wiped it away, leaving a smeared blurry streak.

"Sorry," said Mal. "The lockdown imposes extra security layers. This is going to take a little bit."

"It's OK, kid," said Tapper. "Take your time and get it right."

Eli shot a glance at the gray-haired man. "We're about to have company here."

With a final, almost threatening tone, the lift door slid aside, and a contingent of six security guards fanned out, each of them carrying serious-looking weaponry.

Eli ducked behind the meager cover provided by the railing and reluctantly drew the knockout gun from his holster. He'd heard people say they felt reassured by the weight of a weapon in their hand, but it just made him feel like throwing up. The grip was warm and slick to his touch.

Below, the security team had established a perimeter around the room. Eli could hear a low voice ask something, but couldn't make out the words. He risked a glance over the railing in time to see the bartender point a wavering hand up at them; a security guard's eyes followed it towards Eli and for a moment their gazes locked. Her weapon snapped up and Eli ducked back down.

"*Any time now,*" he hissed at Mal.

"I'm going as fast as I can!"

A voice called from below. "You there! Throw down your weapons and come out with your hands up. This is your only warning; any other action and we will open fire."

Eli looked at Tapper, whose expression was unconcerned. The sergeant waved a hand dismissively. "Nah. That's just something you say."

Next to them, Mal wiped their arm across their forehead. "OK, almost got it. Just another minute."

I don't think we have another minute.

Tapper beckoned with one hand at Eli. "Gimme that conker on your belt."

Eli stared at him blankly.

The sergeant sighed. "The concussion grenade."

Patting his waist, Eli unclipped the small cylinder – cold, smooth, and heavy in his hand – and passed it over.

"Thirty seconds," said Mal.

"I repeat," the voice yelled from below. "Come out with your hands up and throw down your weapons."

Tapper fiddled with the grenade. "Hold on," he called over the balcony. "Do we throw down our weapons first or put our hands up first?"

There was a pause. "What?"

"Which order was it?" Tapper yelled, ripping off the grenade's safety tab.

"I... We... Just come out with your hands up!"

"Get ready to move," Tapper said. "Mal?"

"Ten seconds."

Tapper nodded and then started to stand. "I'm standing up. Don't shoot!" He rose from behind the balcony, the concussion grenade still clutched in one hand.

"Drop your weap... oh, shit!"

Several things happened at once. As Tapper hit the deck behind the railing, his hand now empty, Eli heard the sound of several people scattering, at least one of them shouting "Grenade!" Mal triumphantly tapped a button and the door in front of them clanked as the lock was released, then slid open. Below there was a tremendous bass *thwump* followed by an ear-splitting symphony of wood splintering, glass shattering, and screams.

Tapper belly-crawled his way through the door, dragging Mal, who had put their hands over their head, by the collar. Eli didn't need to wait for an invitation; he scrambled over and rolled in an undignified heap through the door.

The sergeant reached up and slapped the controls panel above him, the door sliding shut with a hiss. Pulling himself upward, Tapper pried the panel off the wall and pulled out a mess of wiring, which sparked and sputtered in his hand.

"There we are then," he said. "Done and dusted. Everything according to plan."

"That was, if anything, even stupider than you explained it," said Eli. "How the hell are you still alive after all these years?"

Tapper grinned. "Trust me, kid. This isn't how I go out. Now come on, both of you. We've got a job to finish."

CHAPTER 27

Not having to avoid surveillance cameras on the way to al-Kitab's cabin was a blessing, but it also proved to be the least of Kovalic and Nat's worries. White Star security personnel, some of them loaded for bear, were roaming the corridors, especially on the more exclusive levels of the starliner.

Couldn't have your well-paying guests put at risk, naturally.

Nat looked back from around the corner and nodded at Kovalic. "We're clear. But the patrol's on a two-minute loop, so let's make it fast."

Kovalic slipped around the corner and made a beeline for cabin A986, keeping his head down and strolling as casually as he could manage. He rapped softly on the door with a knuckle.

After a moment, a holoscreen flickered to life in front of him, the bearded face of al-Kitab staring at him with suspicion. "Who is it?"

Kovalic lifted his head just enough for the professor to get a look; the other man's eyes widened. "Oh, yes, yes. One moment."

The door clicked open and Kovalic jerked his head at Nat, watching from the end of the corridor. She double-timed it over to him and they disappeared inside just as the sound of the approaching White Star patrol made its way to them.

Al-Kitab was thrumming with nervous energy. His large, dark eyes darted from the kit to Kovalic and he pointed a hesitant finger at it. "Is that... it?"

Kovalic rested a hand on the case, watching as al-Kitab shakily clasped his own together. Coming face to face with something that you'd dreamt of your whole life had to be overwhelming. For Kovalic, it would be like setting foot on Earth again after all these years, but he'd found it better not to dwell on something that might never happen.

Without saying anything, Kovalic walked past the professor, placed the toolkit on the coffee table, and flipped up the latches to open it. A deep indrawn breath came from behind him as he lifted the tablet out.

"Oh my..."

He looked over his shoulder, and this time he could see glimmers at the edges of al-Kitab's eyes as the professor took in the tablet. And yet he made no move toward it, keeping the couch between them as if it were a defensive barrier.

Kovalic gave Nat a look and she placed a hand on al-Kitab's elbow. "Professor?"

"Hm? Oh yes. Pardon me. It's just... it's more beautiful than I'd imagined." Slowly, he rounded the couch, squeezing past Kovalic, and sitting down between him and Nat, the tablet before him. He reached out with one wavering hand and then extended an experimental finger, touching the tablet and then snatching it away as though it might burn him.

"I ought to be wearing gloves," he murmured, as if chastising himself. "But it's so smooth."

Nat's brow creased. "What's it made out of? It seems light for metal."

"I have no idea," said al-Kitab. His gaze remained fixed on the artifact. "It's survived for so long and in such good condition. There has been speculation that it's an advanced alloy unknown to us. Others have theorized an element that we haven't even discovered yet. I'll need to run tests."

Kovalic tilted his head. "First we need to establish its authenticity," he said gently. The auction house had supposedly proved the tablet's provenance, but it had passed through a lot of hands in the last few days – Kovalic would feel better if they made sure this was in fact the object they'd been sent to retrieve.

"Of course, of course. Forgive me." Dr al-Kitab broke eye contact with the tablet for the first time, then got back to his feet and stepped over Kovalic. "Let me just get my equipment set up. It will only take a moment." He disappeared into the bedroom.

Nat gave a quiet laugh. "Just like an academic."

Kovalic shook his head and checked his sleeve. No word from Tapper and Brody yet, but he wasn't expecting anything until they were in position. "You'd know better than I – my schooling got interrupted by an invasion."

Dr al-Kitab returned from the bedroom toting another case, roughly the same footprint as the toolkit containing the tablet, but three or four times thicker. Placing it on the coffee table next to the toolkit, he opened it to reveal a flat glass plate on the bottom half, a folding metal framework above it. Flipping a few switches, the device started to hum.

"That's a Naismith L3-25 portable scanner," said Nat, which was evidently impressive, gauging the tone of her voice. "Top of the line."

The professor was no less impressed. "You know your

equipment, madam. I've been lucky enough to receive some generous grants, and my needs are often fairly modest, so I felt justified in… splurging for this job." This time he did pull out a pair of latex gloves before removing the tablet from the toolkit and, holding his breath the whole time he handled it, placing it on the scanner. "I've tuned this equipment to my specifications, allowing me to perform mass spectrometry, thermoluminescence testing – likely not even applicable to this material – and X-ray fluorescence spectroscopy, as well as measure radioactive decay. It ought to be able to establish the provenance of the artifact beyond a reasonable doubt."

Kovalic scratched his head. He'd understood some of that, but it was definitely outside of his realm of expertise. "I'll trust you on that one, professor. Better get started. No idea how long we have." It was only a matter of time before White Star security started going door-to-door to find them.

Al-Kitab was staring at a holoscreen that had shimmered into existence above the device, stroking his goatee. He blinked and looked back at Kovalic. "Of course, of course."

Putting his hands on his thighs, Kovalic pushed himself up and gave Nat a meaningful look; she joined him as he made his way for the coffeemaker on the end table.

"Can you keep an eye on the security channels?" he asked as he unearthed a clean cup. "Maybe give us a heads-up if White Star's about to come knocking?"

"Sure," said Nat, frowning as she pulled her console rig out of her bag and started to set it up. "Something got you spooked?"

In truth, he wasn't sure, but there was something gnawing at him. Like there was still a bullseye on them, even with Mirza gone. "You think this thing's the real deal?" He punched a button and the coffee machine burbled to life.

Nat raised her shoulders. "Beats me. I understand the science of what he's doing, but I'm not exactly an expert in extraterrestrial archaeology. Hell, I didn't even know the field *existed* until today."

"I'm not sure how big of a 'field' it really is – may just be him," said Kovalic as the coffee finished pouring. He retrieved the cup and took a sip, biting back on the intense bitterness, then passed it to Nat.

"If it isn't real then we've all gone through a lot of trouble for nothing," said Nat, raising the cup.

Including sacrificing Sayers. Suddenly, Kovalic felt bone-tired. He rubbed at his eyes, blurred with fatigue. "I know I should be more concerned about the fate of the galaxy – that's the job – but I'm... uneasy about what we're trading for it. Leaving people behind. What's the point in ending the war if we lose our humanity along the way?" An image flashed in his memory: a park bench on Bayern, a gun in his hand.

Fingers touched his arm, and he looked over to find Nat's blue eyes on him. "As long as you're still worried about it, I think we're in fine hands."

With the door shut and locked behind them, Eli finally had a moment to take in their surroundings. Lights had warmed up at their presence, illuminating a large room full of display cases, pedestals bearing works of art, and paintings.

"Looks like your boss has expensive tastes," said Tapper, raising his eyebrows at Mal.

No kidding. Most of these things are probably worth more than the apartment I grew up in.

The firefight had clearly rattled the tech. Mal had started breathing heavily, looking around like a deer who saw hunters at every turn. "Oh, man, this is the private collection. We're dead for sure."

"Oi, none of that," said Tapper sharply. "Nobody's dying here. Come on." He started towards a door at the other end of the room, the only obvious exit from the gallery.

Eli followed the older man and, after a moment, Mal trailed after him, sweating profusely and trying to keep a lid on the moans.

Jesus, I hope I wasn't this bad the first time they recruited me. I guess I should say something encouraging?

"Buck up," said Eli, reaching over and slapping Mal on the back. "He knows what he's doing. He's never let anybody die on his watch." *Best leave Page out of it. And that pilot they had before me.* "Well, almost never."

Mal gulped.

"You two stop gabbing," said Tapper. "Mal, can you override this door?"

The tech's lip twisted in thought. "Most of this is secured to Madam Xi's private codes or her personal guard. I've never tried to crack anything that secure..."

Tapper turned back to the door. "There's got to be a manual override somewhere."

Eli frowned, turning back to survey the room. Maybe there was a panel hidden behind the wall somewhere. Or some sort of ventilation or maintenance shaft they could use to bypass the...

Huh. That might work.

Kovalic had always stressed taking the initiative and Eli's pilot training had never discounted one's gut instincts. Leaving Tapper and Mal at the door, he jogged over to the one of the displays, featuring a full-size suit of samurai armor, and drew forth the long, curved sword at the suit's waist.

The lights in the room immediately flickered red.

Tapper's head jerked up. "What the *hell* did you do?"

Sprinting back towards the door, Eli hefted the sword.

"Did you just steal a priceless artifact?"

Mal's jaw was working, but no sound was coming out.

"No," said Eli, "well, yes. I mean, *technically*. But you said you wanted a manual override, and I figured..." He held the sword out to the sergeant, who was staring at him with a mix of disbelief and respect.

"Worth a shot," said Tapper, snatching the sword from Eli's grip. "Shame to ruin a piece of history, but well, it's better than *being* a piece of history." He slid the sword into the crack at the edge of the door. "Usually there's an emergency release in here, just in case people lock themselves in. If I can just find the catch."

Bathed in red light, the room had taken on a sinister, eerie feeling, only compounded by a sound of hissing, as though a giant snake had been released. *I think I've just given myself nightmares.*

It took Eli a moment to see the translucent clouds issuing from the vents overhead. "Uh. Sarge?"

Tapper was grunting with effort as he attempted to lever the door open with the blade. The sword stood up impressively well for what Eli assumed was a several century old artifact. A testament to the blacksmith that had made it. "I'm a little busy, kid."

"Uh, I think maybe she put in some countermeasures."

"What?" Tapper followed Eli's gaze up to the vents. "Shit. There's no way that's good. Hold on." Bracing his feet against the door frame, he pulled with all his might.

Mal was looking up at the vents now too, their expression having turned more analytical than fearful.

Eli glanced over at them. "Uh, do you know what this stuff is?"

"Morphex," said Mal, blinking at the clouds as if reading a database entry. "Renders you unconscious within a minute. Which means we've got about thirty seconds, unless either of you has some sort of air filtration system."

Eli rubbed his eyes. They were starting to get blurry. *Damn it, should have held on to the vacsuit.* "Are there emergency respirators in here somewhere?"

Mal shook their head, slow and ponderous. "Only issued to Xi's personal security guards."

"So trusting. Sarge?" Eli stifled a yawn with his hand.

Frustrated, the sergeant was still pulling on the sword, to little avail. "Oh, come on, you stupid..." Wedging the sword in the crack between the door and the wall he kicked the handle, setting the sword vibrating back and forth like a tuning fork. "For fuck's sake..."

Eli found himself sitting on the floor without really realizing it, his head thick as though it had been wrapped in cotton. Maybe they needed more swords. There had been another over there, right? If he just crawled over, he could get a whole armful of swords and they could use them like acupuncture needles on the door's pressure points, convincing it that it really was in its best interest – health, really – to open...

He didn't even remember his head hitting the deck.

"Shit," said Nat, looking up from her console rig. "Security alarm."

Kovalic had been sitting on the arm of the couch with the bouncer he'd taken from the guard at the lifeboat, but at this he stood, aiming the muzzle toward the door. "They found us?"

Nat shook her head. "No, it's somewhere else." Her eyebrows went up as she read from the screen. "Xi's private quarters. Some sort of theft countermeasure got triggered. It just hit the central security system and everything is freaking out. As if they already weren't on high alert."

"Small favors," said Kovalic. "Maybe that'll keep their attention elsewhere." He glanced over at al-Kitab. The scanner was humming away, a bright line of light inching over every micrometer of the tablet's surface. "How's it going, doctor?"

The professor looked up. "I'm afraid it's too early to form any conclusions. I can tell you that this tablet is definitely a form of metal, though I'll need to wait until the mass spectrometer has finished its analysis to figure out its exact composition."

"But you think it's authentic?"

"I don't like to jump the gun, as you might say..."

"But?"

He looked around, nervous, as though somebody might be listening in. Kovalic hadn't swept the room for bugs or other surveillance equipment, but if there had been any, somebody probably would have already descended on them. Still, he couldn't fault the man for justified paranoia.

"But, yes," al-Kitab said in a low voice. "I think it is."

Kovalic's heart thumped in his chest and it felt as though the deck shifted under his feet. Might as well have been the whole galaxy. He drew a breath, and forced himself to exhale it slowly. There were still plenty of steps left. Even if this *was* an artifact as extraordinary as the Aleph Tablet was said to be, there was no guarantee that al-Kitab's theory about the map was accurate. They might decode it to find that it was nothing more than a plaque commemorating the species' existence or a long-lost greeting card to other intelligent life.

And that was assuming they had the right person for the job; his eyes went to the professor, who was still watching the tablet with rapturous delight.

"Doctor… the map?"

Blinking, al-Kitab looked up at him. "What?"

"The map. Can you retrieve it?"

"I'm afraid it's not as simple as opening a file on your sleeve, Mr Godwin. This artifact is the sum of our knowledge about the Aleph. If their intelligence was as far beyond us as has been theorized, then they could have stored the information in a way that would seem trivial to them – but might very well still be beyond our understanding."

"You said you had a theory."

The doctor tilted his head. "I've long suspected that the Aleph manipulated matter in much the way that you or I might write an essay or cook a meal. So, if they intended to store information in a way that would be resistant to corruption, they would have picked an appropriate medium."

Nat's eyes lit up. "You think they encoded it in the atomic structure of the tablet itself."

"Wait, what?" said Kovalic, his head spinning.

"With the right technology, you can treat atoms just like any other storage media," Nat explained. "If you're using binary, that means adjusting some aspect of an individual atom to represent a one or zero. We've been playing with it for centuries, but never had the technology to make it practical on an everyday basis. But if the Aleph were as advanced as people think, it could certainly have been within their power."

Dr al-Kitab raised hands in caution. "I will reiterate that it is just a theory. Testing it will require access to a lab with a scanning tunneling microscope. Even once we have a full model of the tablet's atomic makeup – which will be zettabytes of data at the *least* – we have to decipher the data. This is a matter not just of physics but of xenoanthropology, of understanding how the Aleph's minds worked. We don't know how the Aleph conceptualized math or physics, and with no other corroborating material, it might take years. If the theory even proves true."

Kovalic sighed. He doubted the general or the Commonwealth Executive would be satisfied with that assessment. Why was nothing ever easy? Would it kill the universe to give them a break just once in a while?

A high-pitched squeal blared into his earbud suddenly, resonating all the way down through his jaw. "The hell? Bruiser? Updraft? That you?"

The feedback died, replaced with a silky smooth voice. "Well, I suppose that means this is working. Hello again, major."

Kovalic's eyes went to Nat, her stricken expression confirming she was hearing it too. "Madam Xi." Even Dr al-Kitab perked up at that, peering over the edge of his scanner, his eyes worried.

"Oh, you remember," said Xi. "How flattering. Adelaide was kind enough to *lend* me her sleeve."

"I take it this isn't a social call."

Her laugh rang down the line, static bleeding around the edges. "No, my dear major, it isn't. This is business."

"I expect no less. What can I do for you?"

Reinforced steel replaced any playfulness. "You can return my property immediately."

Kovalic glanced at the tablet on the scanner, and al-Kitab's eyes widened. The professor laid a possessive hand on the device.

"And I know you'll need an incentive," Xi continued, "so I propose a trade. The tablet for your officer."

Nat made a slashing motion across her throat and raised her sleeve, tapping the mute button. Kovalic reached down and tapped the same control on his sleeve. A red line appeared through the microphone icon.

"Simon, we can't. Sayers will understand – she put the mission first."

Kovalic rubbed at his mouth, feeling the cords of his jaw tighten. Sayers had sacrificed herself so they could get the tablet; turning it back over to Xi would undo all of that. "Doctor? Where are we?"

"I need more time," said al-Kitab, concern written plainly across his face. "I've only scratched the surface of what's in here."

The tablet might hold potentially untold power for whoever possessed it; given enough time, it would shift the balance of the war. Were the millions of lives it could save in the future worth the one that hung in the balance right now?

"I'm sure you're probably thinking up some clever plan," Xi's voice broke in. "So allow me to simplify your decision process: bring the tablet to the observation deck in fifteen minutes or Adelaide dies." There was a crunch and a burst of static, and CONNECTION LOST blinked on Kovalic's sleeve.

"Well," he said, looking back and forth between Nat and al-Kitab. "She's not wrong about one thing: Now would be a great time for that clever plan."

CHAPTER 28

Xi made a great show of grinding her spiked heel into Addy's earbud with grim satisfaction.

"You're fucked if you think threatening me is going to work," said Addy, sitting a few feet away. A pair of White Star security guards stood just out of reach to either side, weapons pointed in her direction. "They're not about to turn over a priceless artifact to save some woman they just met." A pang in her stomach resonated with that note of truth. *I sure as hell wouldn't, anyway.*

"You'd be surprised," said Xi, taking a demitasse of coffee from the tray held out by one of her liveried staff. "I don't know your Major Kovalic very well, but he strikes me as a man to whom honor is a lifeline. I suspect letting someone die on his watch would be anathema to him." She took a sip. "Perhaps I'm wrong, but I hope, for your sake, that I'm not."

Addy gave a sidelong glance at the guard to her left. A pale blonde man, holding his weapon in a loose grip that suggested he was the less trained of the two; if there were a move, it would be on him. But the woman with the shaved head on the other side stood perfectly erect, and she held her gun like she meant it. Addy couldn't take both of them – not without some help, anyway.

Damn it, I'm not someone who needs to be rescued.

Xi oozed closer, bending down and putting one finger under Addy's chin. Addy resisted the urge to try and bite it.

"I am quite disappointed that we couldn't come to some sort of arrangement," said Xi. "You would have been a tremendous asset." The finger smoothly drew up her jawline, then tucked an errant strand of hair behind Addy's ear.

"Oh, fuck you," said Addy. "I saw you coming a mile away, lady. Don't play a player." She tried not to let her expression waver. Xi's offer *had* been tempting, but deep down she knew she never would have seriously considered it. She was just... tired. Tired of running, tired of being alone. But what Xi was offering her was more for the gangster's good than for hers.

Xi's face hardened and Addy winced as a fingernail gouged her cheek.

"So ungrateful," muttered Xi. She spun away, snapping a finger at one of her people. "Have a full complement of security posted around the perimeter of the observation deck. After I get the tablet back, I want Kovalic and his team *dispatched*."

The attendant snapped a salute and strode off. Addy looked around the observation deck; the metal shutters above were closed, the room lit only by the soft lighting from sconces around the edge. *Plenty of shadows for snipers*. This thing was a killbox, and if Xi was right, Kovalic and the team were going to walk right into it. And there wasn't a damn thing she could do.

Come on, guys. Don't fall for it. Stay the hell away.

Eli started awake with a gasp, sitting bolt upright.

Holy shit, I'm not dead. He patted at his chest and pockets, as though searching for his keys, and it took him a second to remember why he was dressed in an unfamiliar uniform.

The last thing he remembered was passing out in a… totally different room? He looked around, taking in the sleek white and stainless steel aesthetic of the compartment that he found himself in now.

"What the hell happened?" he said. A lightning bolt of pain shot through his temple at the words and he suddenly realized his entire body ached like he'd been run through an industrial washing machine.

A hand punched his shoulder. "You took in a healthy dose of Morphex," said Tapper.

Eli rubbed at the sting left by the sergeant's fist. "Ow. I guess I'm not hallucinating this, then."

Tapper reached down and helped him up. "No such luck, kid."

"How did we get out of there?"

"We've got our friend Mal to thank for that."

Eli blinked. Mal? He looked around and sure enough: the tech was crouched by another door, busily tapping away on their sleeve.

"Christ, how much of that shit did I breathe?"

"I'd be worried if I were you," said Tapper, "because it's not like you have a lot of brain cells to spare."

"You'd know, old man. But let's run this back: *how exactly* did we escape certain death?"

"Oh," Mal piped up. "The fire suppression system takes precedence over the security system. Madam Xi cares more about her collection than taking people alive. So I set off the fire alarm and it sucked all the oxygen out of the room – taking the Morphex with it."

Eli frowned. "Wait, so how come we didn't suffocate?"

"After the air's vented, it also unseals the doors, to introduce fresh air for safety reasons. Then I woke up and dragged you out."

"This kid's worth their weight in gold, let me tell you," said Tapper, with a tone of admiration that Eli had never heard in his voice. Certainly not directed towards *him* anyway. *Not that I'm jealous.*

"So, now what?" Eli asked.

"Now, what we're looking for is just on the other side of that hatch."

"I'm trying to convince the lock to open," said Mal, squinting at their sleeve. "But I don't have clearance for this. I still can't believe you guys are crazy enough to try this!" Their tone split the difference between awed and manic.

"That's kind of what we do," said Eli. "Any word from our…" he glanced warily at Mal, "…friends?"

Tapper's mouth set and he nodded at Eli, leading them away from the door. "There was a transmission about two minutes ago – you were still out."

"Kovalic?"

The sergeant shook his head. "Xi."

"On *our* comms?"

"She wants the tablet back or she's going to kill Sayers."

A whirlpool sloshed in Eli's stomach. *Oh no.* "What the fuck are we waiting for?" he said, starting back towards the door. "Blow this thing open already!"

Tapper grabbed his arm. "Easy, kid! We gotta be smart about this."

Eli whirled on him. "Goddamnit, you made me sit by when Page didn't come back. I'm not letting this happen again. She doesn't deserve it. Too many people have died. We need to save her."

"I'm sure the boss has it under control."

"Just like on Bayern?" In his mind, he saw Kovalic taking a pistol from the lockbox on the *Cavalier* before his meeting with Page; when he'd come back an hour later, it was with no Page... and an empty holster. *Maybe I don't know for sure what the hell happened, but what other conclusion am I supposed to draw?* Was that who they were? "We can't keep sacrificing people."

"It's the *job*, kid," said Tapper. "The mission comes first."

"Fuck your mission," said Eli, wrenching his arm free. "I sure as hell didn't let myself get drafted into *another* military just to watch more people die. Not when we can save them." He stalked back to the door.

With a triumphant crow, Mal hit a button and there was a beep and the control pad to the door's left glowed green. "Unlocked!" The tech gave a celebratory fist pump.

"Nice work," said Tapper, coming up behind Eli. "Now, all we need to do is–"

In that moment, something in Eli snapped. He reached over and snatched their one remaining concussion grenade off Tapper's belt, then slapped the control panel and yanked out the grenade's safety tab.

The door slid open on a pair of White Star guards, who looked wary but confused at their appearance. They flanked an airlock door, each holding a bouncer in both hands.

"Wait–" said Tapper.

"Hey," said Eli. "Hold this, would you?" He lobbed the grenade at them and one of the guards fumbled with his weapon as he instinctively went to catch it, even as his eyes widened. Eli hit the control panel again, crossing his arms and leveling a gaze at Tapper, whose mouth hung open.

A deep bass *thump* rattled the deck plates. Tentatively, Mal reached up and opened the doors again; both guards were splayed out on the deck, unconscious, their weapons by their sides.

"Well," said Tapper. "That's one way to handle it."

Eli grabbed Mal by the shoulders and pointed the tech towards the airlock. "Open that. Right now."

"OK, so we know this is a trap," said Nat.

"Definitely a trap," Kovalic agreed as he checked the power reserves on the bouncer. Still fully charged.

Nat, meanwhile, had unfolded a needleshot she'd acquired and was checking it over. When Kovalic asked her about it, she'd just shrugged. "Mirza's guy. I figured I needed it more than he did."

Al-Kitab, meanwhile, was just finishing up a scan of the tablet, his eyes wide as a kid waiting to unwrap a present.

"So, we're agreed," said Nat. "What's the play?"

Kovalic spared a glance at the professor and held back a sigh. He felt like something had fastened a cord around his chest and was pulling it taut. No good options. Maybe that ought to be the name of his memoir.

"Right now, I'm thinking we have to give her what she wants."

"Simon, you can't be serious. The tablet could let us end the war. We could be talking about dozens of new habitable worlds to colonize, raw materials for construction, maybe even launching points into the Imperium. It's worth *all* of our lives."

"*Potentially*. We don't know what's actually on it, and it might take years for us to figure it out," said Kovalic, slinging the bouncer over his shoulder. "Sayers' life is in danger *right now*. One life now for maybe millions later?"

"Sometimes we need to make the hard decisions."

"I *am* making it. We're not letting Sayers die today. Any problems with that?"

Nat opened her mouth as if to object, but then seemed to think better of it. "No."

"Good. Xi's listening in our comms, which means I need you to find a secure backchannel to Brody and Tapper."

Furrows appeared in her brow. "I might be able to bounce something through the *Queen Amina's* computer direct to their–"

"I don't need to know the details. We just need to be able to talk to them when the moment comes. Doctor?"

Al-Kitab looked up from the scanner, blinking. "Yes?"

"I'm afraid we're going to need you to pack all of that up and get ready to move."

"I don't understand."

"There's been a change of plans, I'm afraid. I'm going to need the tablet."

Fingers curled around the scanner. "But I've only just begun my preliminaries," said al-Kitab, panic flooding his eyes. "You can't take it away yet!"

Kovalic walked over and put a hand on the open lid of the scanner. "You are welcome to accompany it. But I'm afraid I'm going to have to insist."

Al-Kitab's eyes went from Kovalic to Nat, but he found no reprieve there. After a moment, he ducked his head in miserable acquiescence.

"Good," said Kovalic. "Let's get ready to move."

CHAPTER 29

Doors parted onto the dimly-lit observation area. Kovalic held the bouncer ready, finger resting above the trigger and muzzle pointing at the deck, as he surveyed the scene.

A glow of yellow-orange lamps doused the room in soft pools of light. There evidently wasn't much observation going on at present. A balcony, cloaked in shadow, ran around the room's circumference. If Kovalic were going to stage an ambush, that was definitely where he'd position his people. So at least he had a pretty good idea of where he'd be shot *from*.

Beside him, Dr al-Kitab shuffled warily, clutching the wrapped tablet close to his chest. He hadn't wanted to let the artifact out of his sight; separating them would have required more forceful measures, which Kovalic wasn't prepared to employ. He was here to save someone, not do more harm.

"Easy now, doc," said Kovalic, putting a hand out before the professor could step inside.

"Relax, major," called a voice from the other side of the room. "In my business, you're only as good your reputation."

Xi oozed out of the shadows, resplendent in a white dress that stood in stark contrast to her dark skin, like a bright moonlit night. She raised a finger and beckoned behind her.

Addy Sayers appeared, followed closely by a White Star

security officer with a weapon pointed at her back. A pair of heavy cuffs held her wrists in front of her and, even at this distance, Kovalic could tell she was pissed.

Granted, there was a fifty-fifty chance of that at any given moment.

Not taking his eyes off Xi and Sayers, Kovalic waved al-Kitab forward. "Nice and easy."

The professor's eyes were darting everywhere, looking for threats in every shadow, but never stopping long enough to see whether any actually existed.

"It's going to be OK," said Kovalic. "Stay with me."

Al-Kitab's eyes landed on Kovalic, and though they were nervous, there was something beneath that: a steely resolve that surprised him.

Xi's entourage had continued advancing; they drew to a stop about fifteen meters away from Kovalic and the professor. The gangster raised a hand towards Sayers and the security guard.

"I think that's about far enough," she said. "My tablet, if you please?"

Kovalic put out his own hand to stop al-Kitab's advance. "Certainly. As soon as you hand over my officer."

A laugh like glass breaking issued from Xi. "Come, come, major. You're on my ship – show a little courtesy. I'd hate to have to shoot Adelaide here in the head." She reached out and tousled Sayers's hair; the soldier gave her a look that was pure venom.

"What assurances do we have?"

"Assurances?" said Xi, with a thick veneer of innocence. She draped a hand on her chest. "Don't you trust me?"

Kovalic flashed a smile back. "Of course. Just as the frog trusted the scorpion."

A matching smile curved on Xi's lips. "I see we understand each other. Very well – once you have handed over the tablet, I will return Ms Sayers. You and your team will then be confined to a very nice stateroom until our arrival at Hamza in six hours, at which point you will all be able to disembark safely. You have my word."

Kovalic trusted her to stick exactly to the letter of her word. Sure, they would disembark safely. Probably in body bags. Or maybe handed over to some law enforcement official in Xi's pocket. Nice and safe – for Xi, anyway. He'd gotten better offers buying used hovercars.

Then again, a good deal wasn't the point here. The point was *time*. Specifically, buying enough of it.

Kovalic made a great show of thinking the offer over, poking at it as if it were a piece of dough he was testing. "I want your word that none of my team will be harmed in any way."

"You will be well taken care of. Now, if you please, I'd like to verify my property." Suspicion had crept into Xi's eyes, hardening them into flint. "Unwrap the package, major. Now."

Kovalic glanced at al-Kitab. "Do it."

Jaw set, al-Kitab began unfurling the cloth around the tablet. The artifact gleamed where the orange light hit it, the whole thing shining like the very idea of gold itself.

Xi scoffed. "I can't tell from here."

"Now *you* don't trust me?" said Kovalic. "I assure you, Dr al-Kitab here has authenticated it." Any time now.

"Very well," said Xi. "In that case, you will hand over Dr al-Kitab as well."

From Kovalic's side came a sharp intake of breath and, if anything, al-Kitab squeezed the tablet even tighter to his chest.

"Hold up. That wasn't part of the deal." Kovalic's heart

thumped in his chest. It wasn't supposed to take this long. Where was the signal?

Almost lazily, Xi reached out and ran a finger along Sayers's cheek. "I'm renegotiating. You want your officer back, those are the terms."

"Major," whispered al-Kitab, "you can't hand me over. She'll never let me leave!"

Kovalic laid a hand on the man's shoulder, trying to ignore the clock ticking away in his head. "It'll be OK," he said, more confidently than he felt. "She needs you. You'll be well looked after."

The professor shuddered and Kovalic swallowed his discomfort. Well looked after, perhaps, but still essentially a prisoner. If this didn't work, he was condemning the man to an uncertain fate, trading one soul for another. Just like he'd promised Nat – and himself – that he wouldn't. But Sayers was his responsibility. He needed to get her home.

He met al-Kitab's eyes, found a mix of fear and hope. "Please."

The professor swallowed, then let out a breath. "Very well, then."

"Thank you." Kovalic looked up at Xi. "Finally, you will ensure that Dr al-Kitab here–" a pair of clicks came over the comm in his right ear, about damn time "–is not mistreated in any way and that his freedoms will not be unduly impinged upon."

"Fine, yes, whatever," said Xi, her former impatience returning in full force. "Can we get on with this?"

"All right. Your terms are accepted."

Xi gave a sharp flick of her fingers to the security officer, who pushed their prisoner forward. Sayers stumbled and shot a glare at the guard as she started walking to the middle of the room.

At a nod from Kovalic, al-Kitab started forward as well,

the tablet still clutched closely to his chest. He looked smaller as he walked, hunched over, with his shoulders approaching his ears. A pang of regret stabbed at Kovalic's heart, but he pushed it down. Now was not the time.

They were nearing the midway point now, Sayers and al-Kitab both trudging towards the room's center. Kovalic could see the specialist still straining against her manacles, as if she thought she could slip out of them.

"One moment," said Xi, contemplatively, as Sayers and al-Kitab came abreast of each other. "It occurs to me that perhaps in addition to the Aleph Tablet, there is something to be gained from ransoming not one but *two* Commonwealth intelligence officers back to their government." She raised a finger and tapped her lips.

Kovalic's grip tightened on his weapon, his finger sliding onto the trigger. But even as he moved to raise it, he heard a chorus of high-pitched whines from overhead: weapons being charged and, in all probability, pointed in his direction from the balcony.

Called it.

"So, please kindly drop your weapon, major."

Sayers and al-Kitab had slowed to a stop at the sound of the weapons; they both looked toward Kovalic.

Too many shooters. Not enough time for him to target more than a couple. Xi had learned her lesson from last time, and compensated with overwhelming force. He was going to need some serious backup.

"All right, Aegis," he murmured. "On my mark."

Hell of a day, Addy thought blearily. Kovalic's appearance had left her awash with feelings, primarily anger that he'd showed up *with* the tablet; the whole point of giving herself up had been so the team could escape with it. That. Had been. The mission. But beneath that, something warmer was melting away at her cold fury.

He'd come back for her. Despite her many fuck-ups since she'd joined the team, they hadn't just cut her loose, even though she would have deserved it. Something stung at her eyes and she raised her manacled hands to brush at them.

Then she'd been shoved forward by the security guard and started the long walk across the room.

As they approached the midway point, Addy's gaze met Dr al-Kitab, who she hadn't seen since that first meeting in Xi's quarters. His eyes widened as he recognized her. When they came abreast, she heard him murmur something under his breath.

"He said be ready."

Despite the ordeal she'd been through over the past several hours, every adrenaline gland in her body suddenly pumped whatever it had left into her bloodstream; her eyes widened and muscles tensed.

Through the blood pounding in her ears, she faintly heard Xi tell her to stop, then order Kovalic to drop his weapon. *The balcony*, she thought, her eyes skimming across it, trying to pick out dark shapes against the even darker background. *This is why you weren't supposed to come, Kovalic.*

For a moment, everything was still, except for Addy's heart. Then the room exploded.

A needleshot zipped from directly over the observation deck's lift, lancing into the shoulder of the security guard standing next to Xi. He grunted and went down.

Then tremendous bursts of light exploded on both sides of

the balcony, blanketing the room in a bright whiteness that had Addy throwing up her arms to shield her eyes. Shots rang out, needles and concussion blasts; blinking her eyes against the glowing red afterimage from the flares, she made out a dark shape that she was relatively certain was al-Kitab and did the only thing she could think to do: knock him to the ground.

They went down in a heap, a surprised squeak coming from the professor as the tablet flew out of his hands and slid across the deck.

"Keep your head down," said Addy, trying to shield the man.

"The tablet!"

God, that stupid thing. Her vision was still flashing, but she peered around in what she thought was the direction the tablet had gone. A dark shape was crouching not far away and, as her eyes started to return to normal function, she thought she made out a sparkle of jewelry around their wrist.

Xi. Oh, I definitely *owe her one.*

"Stay here," Addy said, putting one hand on al-Kitab's back as she got to her feet.

Xi was rising, the tablet clutched in both hands, when Addy's running tackle caught her mid-section, sending them both to deck. The tablet slid away from them.

"Get *off* me, you bitch." A claw slashed at Addy's face, and she ducked back fast enough that only a couple of the nails scratched her cheek, gouging it with bright red flashes of pain.

Addy caught Xi's wrist, pulling her arm back against the joint, but Xi lashed out with a knee to her mid-section, knocking the wind out of her. Struggling against the manacles that still bound her hands, she tried to grab hold of Xi and pin her, but the gangster shimmied out from underneath, and reached for one of the bangles on her arms.

"Forget the ransom," Xi spat, "you're all going to die here."

"Promises," Addy tried to say, but it came out as more of a wheeze. *So much for the snappy lines.* Catching her breath, she settled into a combat stance, or as much of one as she could manage with the cuffs on.

"Oh, how cute," said Xi. "There's still some fight left in you." She pulled a bangle from each wrist over her knuckles, then touched them together. Blue energy arced between them.

Oh come on. Stun-gloves weren't uncommon amongst street muggers or hired thugs looking to dole out a little extra damage, but Addy had never seen them miniaturized into bracelets before. *Trust Xi to have all the fanciest toys.*

She barely had time to process that before Xi's hand was swinging towards her, crackling with electricity. Dodging left, Addy just caught the sharp whiff of ozone as the fist zipped past her.

But she'd focused too much of her attention on that hand; the second punch caught her by surprise as it glanced off her hip.

The searing shock elicited a yelp and Addy stumbled as her left leg turned to jelly, her knee rebounding off the deck; if there was pain from the impact, she didn't feel it, still preoccupied with the burning from her hip. She gritted her teeth.

Then there was a leg swinging through space, heel towards her face. She hit the deck, the breeze from Xi's foot ruffling her hair.

Feeling was starting to return to her left leg, along with spiderwebs of pain radiating out from her knee. Groaning, she rolled onto her back, just in time to catch an axe kick off her manacled forearms. *Jesus, she's vicious.*

Addy scrambled to grab Xi's ankle and use what little leverage she had to twist it and put the other woman off balance. She saw Xi hop and stumble, her expression startled, then rolled to one side to take the other woman's ankle with her.

There was a thump as Xi hit the deck and Addy tried to scramble back to her feet. Elegant this fight wasn't. She launched herself at the gangster, trying again to pin those dangerous hands to the ground.

Xi wriggled in her grip, growling and trying to free her arms. *Surprisingly strong too.* Addy felt the gangster pushing off the deck, even as the bracelets around her knuckles spat and sparked. *Come on, Addy, do something. Use your head.*

Without a second thought, Addy smashed her forehead into Xi's nose, knocking the other woman's head back against the deck. The gangster went limp, loosening her grip on the bracelets, which sputtered and died.

Addy slowly released her hold on Xi's arms, and toppled backwards on the deck, cradling her own head. Her hip and leg were still stinging from the shocks, but she didn't have time to take an inventory of every little ache and pain.

Stumbling to her feet, she caught sight of the tablet a few feet away. Al-Kitab was still cowering on the floor where she'd left him, though every once in a while he would look up from where he was curled, as if he were assessing the safety of actually getting up.

Addy limped towards the artifact, and hefted it in the awkward grip of the handcuffed. Not for the first time, she wondered whether or not a stupid slab of metal was really worth all of this. But it didn't really matter, because it was the mission. *Way above my pay grade.*

Click. A safety disengaging.

"Adelaide. Give it to me."

She turned to find Xi standing, if somewhat shakily – one of the gangster's shoes had gotten lost in the scuffle, her hair was bedraggled and there was a livid bruise across her nose and eyes. With the back of her free hand, Xi wiped away a stream of blood on her upper lip. But all of that was secondary to the weapon leveled at Addy. It wasn't a KO gun – no, this was a good old fashioned slug-thrower, small enough that Xi had been able to conceal it somewhere about her person, even in a dress that hadn't left much to the imagination.

"I don't want to have to kill you. But I will." Xi put out her hand, palm up. "This isn't irreparable. My offer stands: come work for me. You're everything I'm looking for in a partner: uncompromising, ruthless, and sharp. We could take this all so much farther. Together, we could be running all the organized crime in the *galaxy*. Just hand over the tablet."

Addy's hands clasped the artifact; she could feel her sweat making the surface slick and hard to hold. All this trouble over a big hunk of metal. When she could have the galaxy at her fingertips. It was a no-brainer.

"Thanks," she said. "But I've already got a job."

When Nat's needleshot lanced out from above, Kovalic bolted to one side, hitting the deck and sliding back behind one of the observation couches. A few shots followed him, pitting holes in the plastiform furniture.

In the middle of the room, Sayers had pushed the professor to the ground, then turned to take on Xi. The tablet slid to the middle of the room, unaccompanied for the moment. Kovalic might just be able to get to it.

A breath stirred behind him, enough warning for his combat senses to flare and for him to juke to one side as a fist hurtled through the air. He rolled, the bouncer sliding from his grasp, and found himself on his back, looking up into the face of the man who had helped Mirza grab him outside the stateroom. "Oh. Hey."

The IIS operative scowled, then lashed out with a kick at Kovalic's face. Didn't seem like he was one for conversation. Kovalic rolled again, coming up into a crouch.

There really wasn't time to be doing this whole mano a mano thing. He risked a sideways glance at the tablet. Sayers and Xi were still sparring around it. He suspected the specialist had only escaped being shot by the snipers around the balcony because she was too close to the boss. Hopefully that gave Nat more time to pick off the shooters.

More pressingly, the IIS operative charged towards Kovalic. He blocked the first punch, then ducked under the second strike, coming back with a jab at the man's gut. His hand connected with soft tissue, and he heard a muffled *oof*. Pressing his advantage, Kovalic followed up with a kick to the man's ankle, forcing him down to one knee, then brought his clasped fists onto the back of the man's neck.

With the IIS agent down for the count, he tapped his earbud. "Aegis, you ready for stage two?"

"Still a little busy up here, Corsair," Nat grunted, between shots. "Gonna need a minute."

Kovalic looked over to see Sayers had recovered the tablet, but Xi got to her feet and produced a slug-thrower from somewhere under her dress.

"I don't know if we have a moment, Nat," he said, scooping up the bouncer and raising it to his shoulder. At this range, the weapon's accuracy wasn't great; there was a good chance the concussion blast would hit both Xi and Sayers. "We're in now-or-never territory."

"You always want everything now!"

"I'm demanding, I know."

One more shot flashed overhead, and Kovalic watched as a woman with a gun tumbled off the balcony above him, felled by Nat. "All right, I've isolated the local grid. Standby, Corsair. In three... two... one..."

The tackle from behind caught him unaware, sliding both him and his assailant across the deck like so many hockey pucks, and knocking the bouncer out of his grasp. He had just enough time to register the face of the IIS operative he thought he'd knocked out before he careened, head first, into one of the observatory couches.

Addy watched Kovalic and the other man grapple even as Xi was lining up her shot, and she held her breath. The *thump* of the two men hitting the couch was loud and sudden; Xi whirled, gun still outstretched.

In that split second, Addy charged forward to take advantage of the opening, swinging the tablet into Xi's arm as best as she could with her hands still bound. The artifact hit the gangster square in the forearm, sending the gun spinning from her grip and across the room. Xi howled, clutching her arm, and Addy swung the tablet again – this time at Xi's head. The gangster hit the deck and stayed there.

Addy stood over her, breath heaving, tablet still clutched in both hands.

"Stop," said a voice. "That's enough."

She blinked and looked up to see the man who'd tackled Kovalic, the light from the observatory gleaming off his shaved head. He'd scooped up Xi's slug thrower and was pointing it down at Kovalic's limp form. "Give me the tablet, right now, or I will kill him."

Jesus, this is getting old.

"Who the fuck are you?"

"It doesn't matter. All I want is the tablet. Then you're free to go."

Yeah, sure. I've heard that one before.

Addy's eyes narrowed; she'd heard his description from Kovalic. "You're Eyes."

"The tablet. Now."

Hefting the artifact speculatively in one hand, Addy eyed the man. "You've got to know I'm not just going to give it to you, right?"

"I can take it off your body, if that would be preferable."

Oh, good, this one has a sense of humor. She let her peripheral vision widen, trying to see everything in the room at once, but the only things nearby were Xi's unconscious form and the White Star security guard that someone – Taylor, she had to assume – had shot. The latter had a KO gun and a concussion grenade on his belt, but if she so much as made a move she had little doubt the IIS agent would shoot her. What she needed was a distraction.

"Sayers!" shouted a voice from overhead that she recognized as Taylor. "Jump!"

She just resisted the temptation to ask "How high?", recognizing it for what it was: an order. The yell had been enough to get the attention of the Eyes operative, who glanced over his shoulder as Addy crouched and sprung.

As she did, the lights in the observatory flickered and she heard a sound that reminded her of nothing so much as an electronic version of water gurgling down a drain.

Then she was floating upward.

And not just her. Everybody and everything in the compartment that wasn't bolted down – Kovalic's limp form, a curled-up Dr al-Kitab, the unconscious Xi and her security guard – had suddenly gone weightless, as if the local artificial gravity had just died.

Taylor must have deactivated it.

Even as he bit off a swear, the IIS agent recovered impressively fast, snapping off a shot with the slug thrower. But Addy had already risen ten feet off the deck, and was still moving from her momentum. The slug hit the tablet, knocking it out of Addy's grasp, even as the recoil sent the IIS agent tumbling, heels over head, in the opposite direction.

Addy's fingertips brushed the corner of the tablet as it spun away from her, but with her hands still manacled she couldn't extend her arms far enough. *Damn it.* She floated upward towards the metal shutters of the observation deck's ceiling.

Below her, the IIS agent rebounded off the floor, somehow getting his feet beneath him, then pushed off along a trajectory that would take him towards the tablet.

Shit. Shit shit shit. But at least he couldn't fire again without risking knocking himself off his path. Addy still had time.

She bumped gently off the shutters, managing to find a handhold and stop her rotation. *Not enough time.* Getting to the tablet before the IIS agent would be almost impossible, and then she'd be a sitting duck for his slug-thrower.

But maybe there was another option. Lining herself up, she pushed off the ceiling with all her strength, aiming herself toward the body of Xi's unconscious security guard.

She and the IIS agent glided past each other like sharks in the night, eyeing one another, but unwilling to deviate from their courses. Addy craned her neck to watch him grab the tablet; a moment later she collided gently with the security guard.

As the IIS agent turned and fired off a shot, Addy wrestled the security guard's body in between them – she'd seen the armor he'd been wearing, and it deflected the slugs without significant injury to either of them, though the impact knocked them backwards toward the deck. The guard spasmed slightly and let out a piteous moan, but he was still alive and, well, if not kicking, then thrashing, as they bounced gently off the floor.

Addy fumbled around the man's belt, but couldn't find his gun – it must have floated away when the gravity went off. What he did have was a pair of plasticuffs and a concussion grenade.

Not that I'm complaining. Addy grabbed both, then risked a peek around the body. The shots had cost the IIS agent, who was floating backwards, propelled by the equal and opposite force the weapon had generated. But he still clung tightly to the tablet.

She couldn't let him have it. Kovalic had made that clear – the tablet couldn't fall into Illyrican hands. The cylinder of the concussion grenade was heavy, but it was all she had. Hefting it, she estimated the angles and the distances to the agent, who was still on the float, spinning towards the far bulkhead. But if he caught a handhold there, he could reorient himself and get to the exit. They might never catch up with him after that.

There wasn't time to agonize over it. Pulling the safety tab

Addy hurled the grenade at the IIS agent with an awkward two-handed throw. She spared a glance at al-Kitab, who had anchored himself with surprising adroitness, hooking his feet under a nearby table. *Sorry, doc.*

Her throw sent her flying back towards the deck; she bumped off it and started to float upwards again, spinning off her axis – this time, though, something caught her by the arm. She glanced over her shoulder to see Kovalic, hand wrapped around her forearm; he yanked her back down towards the deck, where he was somehow securely anchored.

What the…? Her eyes flicked down to his feet and noticed for the first time the gravboots Kovalic was wearing. *Where'd he get those?* But she didn't have time to say anything as the concussion grenade, having continued its tumble towards the agent, reached its mark.

The agent had rotated just in time to see the grenade a mere foot from him, and instinctively raised the tablet in front of his face just as the grenade exploded in a shockwave of light and sound.

A concussion grenade was generally designed to disable targets without causing significant destruction to objects, but something must have resonated with whatever material the tablet was made from. The artifact shattered, fragments flying in every direction. Addy couldn't tell who screamed louder: the Eyes operative taking a hail of shrapnel or the professor watching his life's pursuit disintegrate in front of his eyes.

"What the hell?" said Kovalic as he pulled her back down to the deck.

"Sorry about that. Just tell me you've got an exit plan, because we probably shouldn't stick around."

Kovalic looked up at the metal shutters overhead and

tapped his earbud with his free hand. "Aegis, we ready to do this?"

Besides them, Addy heard another groan and glanced over to see Xi's eyelids fluttering. "Uh, now would be good."

There was a flicker of motion from beside them as Taylor drifted to the floor with the impressive and somehow entirely unsurprising grace of a ballet dancer on pointe. "Updraft is in position. Hold tight everybody." Somewhere along the way she'd scooped up Xi's slug-thrower.

"Hold… ti…?"

Overhead came the loud sound of machinery as the metal shutters clanked open, revealing the transparent lattice of the observation portal and the void of space beyond.

"Going to borrow these," said Taylor, waving her sleeve at Addy's cuffed hands; the manacles popped open, and Taylor deftly used them to attach her belt to Kovalic's. Her arms circled Addy, who was watching the floating body of Xi stir. The gangster's dark eyes were wobbly as they focused on her, disorientation followed by a look of utter and complete contempt.

The shutters overhead ground to a halt, leaving only a small gap between them in which Addy could see the open starfield, shimmering through the latticework. *Why only partway open?*

Taylor tapped something on her sleeve. "Reactivating gravity in three… two… one…"

Reactivating gravity?!

And Addy suddenly felt all of her cells pulled back down at one g, watching as the floating objects and bodies drifting around the room fell to the deck with an assortment of thumps, clanks, and curses.

But she didn't have long as there was a high-pitched whine beneath them, and she looked down just in time to see Kovalic's gravboots still at full power. *Wait, you're not supposed to–*

And then the three of them shot upwards, hurtling towards the small gap in the shutters. As they rushed towards the viewport, she could see the individual hexagonal panels and the thin joins that formed the lattice.

Beside her, Taylor raised the slug-thrower and emptied the clip in a cluster that would have made any firearms instructor proud; the panel right above them spider-webbed with cracks.

She heard Kovalic reminding her to exhale and had just enough time to expel all the air from her lungs before the transparent aluminum was wrenched apart by the force of the vacuum and they were blown out into open space, the shutters immediately clapping shut behind them.

Black, harsh cold expanded around her, seeping into every inch of her being as she swore she could feel the blood starting to boil in her veins.

What the f–

Even as she felt the heat being leached from her body, her fingertips and toes going numb, something big and bright swooped overhead. And blearily, through the tears filling her eyes, she thought she saw a figure reaching out a hand, like that famous mural back on Earth. The one on the church ceiling... she could remember the name if only she could just stay awake...

CHAPTER 30

Tapper's voice crackled over the intercom of Ofeibia Xi's personal yacht, echoing in the cockpit. "Three for three aboard. Get us the hell out of here, kid."

"Roger that," said Eli, tapping the control to seal the ship's emergency airlock, then bringing the ship around. All they needed to do was outrun the *Queen Amina* – which hopefully had bigger things to worry about right now. "ETA to the Badr gate is thirty minutes." He slid the throttle up and felt the acceleration press him back into the pilot's seat.

Man, this thing really moves. Custom from stem to stern, just like Mal said. I wonder if Kovalic would let me upgrade the Cav *with some of the components.* Sure, they could just keep the whole ship, but something told Eli that the yacht might just be a little too recognizable for everyday usage.

But I'll enjoy it while I can.

The cockpit door slid open, nearly silent against the deep, throaty rumble of the ship's engine.

"Everything all right back there?"

"Yep," said Tapper. "We got 'em before their blood started to boil, so that's a real plus. Treating for exposure but they ought to be OK. Mal's keeping an eye out." Since humans had expanded into space, they'd gotten pretty good at treating these kinds of incidents. Accidents happened. *Probably fewer cases of people doing it intentionally, though.*

"Good," was all Eli said, focusing on the holoscreen overlay on the canopy. The HUD had isolated the gate, magnifying it so that Eli could see the blue-purple vortex of the wormhole glowing in its center.

A heavy hand descended on Eli's shoulder. "That was a damn risky move you pulled back there with the grenade, Brody," said Tapper, his voice even more gravelly than usual. "Could have gotten us all killed."

Eli pushed the hand away. "I did what I had to do." If his tone was a bit on the frosty side, it only mirrored how he felt. *I didn't get into this to barter human lives like so much commodity trading.* "We couldn't leave her behind."

Tapper collapsed into the co-pilot's seat as though all the energy had been siphoned out of him. "I get it. Look, you gotta understand, kid. Page..." The sergeant's voice turned uncharacteristically wistful, "he did some shit he shouldn't have. We – you, me, the major, the commander...and yes, even Sayers – we're a team. A family. And when somebody in that family betrays you, well, you take it hard."

Family, Eli thought, bitterness seeping in from around the edges. He knew a little something about being betrayed by the people you thought you could trust.

"If we're family, then I need to be *treated* like it, OK? You, Kovalic, Taylor – you can't keep this kind of stuff from me. I'm either on this team or I'm not."

For a moment, he thought Tapper would fight him, but the sergeant just let out a long sigh. "You're right, kid. I've been doing this a long time – probably longer than I should have. And that whole time, I've been looking out for people. My family. The soldiers in my squads. The major – even before he was my CO. You. Folks like Mal. That's what I do. Sometimes that means taking a bullet for 'em, sometimes it means not telling 'em the things that you think will hurt them."

"I'm not a kid! I'm out there facing death with you. Every time we go on one of these missions, we're putting our lives in each other's hands. You trust me enough to watch your back, you gotta trust me with everything."

"I know, I know," said Tapper, hands raised. "Like I said, you're right. I have to… recalibrate a bit. Not going to happen overnight, but I'll work on it. OK?"

Eli spared a glance from the controls to meet Tapper's eyes, and was surprised to see a warmth there that he'd never really noticed below the gruff exterior. He gave a grudging nod. "OK."

"OK," said Tapper. "So, what do you say we go home?"

Half an hour later, Xi's yacht was safely ensconced in the same wormhole they'd so recently exited, and Kovalic had assembled his team – minus the tech that Tapper had brought aboard and said he would explain when he had more time – in the ship's rather well-appointed and luxurious lounge.

Lowering himself gingerly into one of the couches, Kovalic heard from each and every bruise and pulled muscle in harmony with the aches from his – thankfully brief – trip in vacuum. Plus, his feet were still sore from the gravboots he'd pilfered from one of the other lifeboats. He'd gotten the idea from Brody's trip outdoors and was only slightly regretting the decision.

Nat and Sayers looked similarly worn out, but the good

news was that none of it was anything a cup of coffee and liberal application of pain relievers couldn't handle.

"Poor Dr al-Kitab," said Nat. "His whole life's work and now he'll never know the truth."

Sayers frowned from her couch, taking a sip of coffee to cover it, but Kovalic could read the tension in her pose.

"We didn't get *anything*?" Brody asked. "Didn't he make scans?"

"Preliminary only," said Nat. "There wasn't enough time for a full scan."

"Disappointing as that is," said Kovalic, taking each of them in turn, "the important thing is that the Illyricans don't have the tablet. This was a win, people."

Nobody in the room was exactly celebrating.

Brody was leaning against a bulkhead. "Seems like a lot of trouble for not a lot of reward."

"Some days that's the job," said Tapper.

"Tapper's right," said Kovalic. "This is about the big picture. And because of us, the Illyricans won't get their hands on new worlds to exploit."

"What about Xi?" said Sayers, and Kovalic could see the anger, hard and sharp, simmering in her eyes.

"Well, we did take her yacht," said Brody. "So, uh, she'll have to replace that."

"Oh, great," said Sayers, rolling her eyes. "That ought to take her about two days."

"We weren't there to take Xi down," said Nat. "Like it or not, she's part of the ecosystem. With her gone, we'd just end up with half a dozen fractured criminal organizations battling it out with probably a lot more bloodshed."

"I don't know about the rest of you, but I'm just bummed

that we're not any closer to knowing if aliens are real," said Brody. "Wait, if we destroyed the tablet, which could have proved the existence of extraterrestrials... are *we* part of the conspiracy?" He clapped a hand to his mouth.

"And on that note," said Kovalic, "I think we should all get some much-needed rest."

The others rose, Tapper nudging a still-thinking Brody towards the cockpit. Nat stretched and, at a look from Kovalic, headed aft, towards the ship's personal quarters.

That left him alone with Sayers, who was still sitting on one of the couches, massaging her hip while she stared off into the middle-distance.

"Something on your mind, specialist?"

She blinked, as if suddenly realizing they were alone, and hastily got to her feet, coming to a parade rest. Something flashed across her face – regret? – but it was quickly layered over with a stoic resolve. "I'd like to surrender myself, sir."

Kovalic leaned back, trying not to wince at the twinge down his spine. "Surrender yourself?"

Sayers's parade rest broke and she waved a hand in frustration. "I didn't follow orders, I compromised the mission by giving your identities to Xi, *and* I destroyed the mission objective. The only thing waiting for me on Nova is a court-martial."

She had a point. In a normal unit, Sayers would have been put on trial for any number of the choices she'd made during this operation, and would have been lucky to get a discharge over being thrown in the brig.

Good thing this wasn't a normal unit.

Kovalic let out a breath. "You're not going to be court-martialed, Sayers."

For the first time in their acquaintance, Kovalic saw

genuine shock on her face, a conviction that she could not have heard him correctly. "I... I... Sir?"

"Look, I'm not going to lie: I would prefer you not have given Xi our real identities, but I understand why you did." He waved a hand for her to fill in the blanks.

"I didn't know how much she knew," said Sayers. "If I'd used your cover identities and she already knew who you really were, I would have looked at best like a dupe, and at worst like I was still trying to play her. I had to sell it."

"Exactly. You picked what you thought was the best of a slew of bad options. Everybody else on this boat has done the same."

Sayers snorted. "Probably not Commander Taylor..."

"*Even* Commander Taylor. I'll vouch for that. Nobody's here because this job is easy. Sometimes you have to make the best bad decision you can. I'm not going to say your first outing was an *unqualified* success, but I still believe you have promise, specialist.

"Look, I offered you a job. I don't intend to rescind that now. If you want the gig, it's yours."

Blinking, Sayers opened her mouth, but no words came out.

"It's OK," said Kovalic. "Think it over if you need to. You know where to find me." He got to his feet.

"Wait! I mean, yes. Yes, I'll take the job."

"Good. I'm glad." He turned to go then paused. "And Sayers?"

"Yes, sir?"

"You did good. Boyland would have been proud."

Addy watched Kovalic go in a daze. *They want me...* She couldn't remember the last time someone had expressed that sentiment. Or anyone, besides Boyland, really. Even Schenk, back in their youth, hadn't seen beyond the utility of Addy's small frame being able to fit through a window or a crawlspace. When staying alive had consumed so much of her energy, friends had been a secondary concern at best.

Her head wasn't quite spinning, but it was close. She found herself wandering forward to the cockpit where Brody was staring out the viewport, feet up on the dashboard. He started at her appearance, his feet hitting the deck with a clump.

"Oh, hey. Sorry, not much to do right now," he said with a sheepish air. "Just watching the flashing lights go by – you all right?"

Addy had sat down into the flight engineer's station somewhat more heavily than she'd intended. Everything she'd been carrying over the last few days had caught up with her at once, like she'd just stepped onto a high-gravity planet. She felt wiped.

"Sayers?"

"Huh?"

"I asked if you were all right?"

"Oh. Yeah, just... tired."

A smile tugged at the corner of Brody's mouth. "Post-mission crash. Yeah, I've been there. After the first time, I think I slept for two days straight." He nodded to the seat. "I think there's a recline control there. On the side."

She flailed until she found the control panel and a smile crept across her face as she stretched out to her full length. "This is the best thing *ever*."

"Perks of a luxury ship, I guess," said Brody. "You don't get these on an Illyrican naval ship, let me tell you."

"Illyrican naval ship? How do you know about Illyrican ships?"

Brody froze, then laughed awkwardly. "Ah. Me and my big mouth. Well, it's a long story. And maybe one I'm not supposed to talk about?"

"S'OK," said Addy, feeling the warm waves of tiredness wash over her, like she was lying in the surf at a tropical beach. It was pleasant in the cockpit, the thrumming of the engines lulling her. "Kovalic says I'm on the team," she said sleepily.

"Hey, that's great! Welcome aboard. I guess that means you're cleared for all of this now."

"Guess so," murmured Addy, turning on her side to face the pilot. "So you can tell me your story."

"You sure?" said Brody, raising an eyebrow. "You look pretty comfy there. If you just want to go to sleep, that's fine. I'll keep an eye on things."

"Nah, I'm awake," said Addy. "Really. And I don't mind hearing you talk. It's, uh, kind of soothing, actually." Dimly, part of her brain registered that as the kind of thing that she once would have been caught dead before admitting, but she was too tired to care. It was just so cozy. "Go ahead."

"Oh, yeah, sure," said Brody, turning back to the console. Even with the blue-toned light illuminating his face, she thought she caught a hint of a blush. "Well, I grew up on Caledonia, and since I was a kid, I always wanted to be a pilot…"

Addy was asleep before the second sentence.

The door to the cabin slid aside for Kovalic, just in time for him to catch Nat exiting the bathroom, wrapped in a white bathrobe so fluffy that it might have been spun from clouds. She was toweling off her hair with an equally luxurious looking towel.

"Oh," said Kovalic, stopping short. "I didn't mean to interr... wait, did you just take a shower?"

There was a tinge of guilt in Nat's laugh. "You got me. But you have to see the refresher unit in this thing. It's *unreal*. Like eighteen different jets, instant hot water that doesn't smell like it's been recycled six million times over."

Kovalic grinned. "Don't worry, I can leave this all out of my after-action report."

Nat perched on the end of the bed, still drying her hair. "Speaking of which, how did we do, major?"

Kovalic waved a hand. "I know denying the Illyricans the tablet was the best outcome we had in front of us, but damn it if I didn't want to get the thing." He let out a breath. "Maybe it really could have ended the war."

Nat laughed quietly. "It's not that easy, Simon. You know that. No such thing as a magic bullet. Developing the information on the tablet would have taken years and required a huge investment from the Commonwealth. Who knows what would have happened in the meantime?"

"You sound like the general."

"I think we both just take the long view. Not all of our jobs are about shooting what's right in front of us."

Kovalic's eyebrows went up. "Is that all I am, Commander Taylor? A hired gun?"

"Oh no, you're a very smart hired gun, major."

"Well, I've got a good team behind me. Including an

executive officer that I rely on to tell me when *not* to shoot what's in front of me."

Nat finished toweling her hair. "An XO that you don't always listen to."

"Look, I might not always take the advice that's offered, but I always *listen*."

Nat's lips thinned. "You brought Sayers aboard."

"I did, but in my def–"

"I think it's the right call."

Kovalic blinked. "Sorry, I think I misheard you."

"Don't push your luck."

He put up his hands. "OK, OK. I thought you didn't like her?"

"She's... an acquired taste. Raw and rough around the edges for sure, but I'm starting to get what you see in her. I can't argue with her skills, and she's eager to prove herself. I think she just needs... someplace to belong. Someplace safe."

"Uh, I'm not sure I'd describe what we do as 'safe.'"

Nat gave him a look. "You know what I mean, Simon. Someplace where she won't feel judged, where she can be herself. And I... I didn't exactly help matters."

Kovalic shook his head. "It's not on you. I think I picked her in part because... well, because she wasn't Page. Maybe part of me expected her to fail and figured if she did, at least I wouldn't be disappointed. Again."

A chuckle escaped from Nat. "So I guess she let you down by *not* failing."

"Seems on brand for her."

Kovalic sat down next to Nat, feeling the damp heat radiating off of her. "I'm sorry I didn't consult you on Sayers. I'm used to making decisions on my own and dealing with the fallout myself. It's been an adjustment."

"I understand. I do." Any levity that had been on her face had vanished.

"But you still won't stay?"

Nat sighed. "I won't pretend I didn't miss being on the front lines, getting my hands dirty and feeling like what we do actually makes a difference. It's not sitting behind a desk analyzing reports, that's for sure. But I meant what I said before, Simon. I'm an intelligence officer, and as good as I am – and I'm fucking *good* – I can't do my job if you keep me in the dark." Her eyes met his. "This doesn't work any other way. Secrets already destroyed us once. I can't let that happen again."

Kovalic looked down, his hands worrying against each other. Twenty years of being a soldier, half of it in intelligence. Secrecy had been hammered into him, a part of his mind that he'd walled off from the rest in order to be able to do the job. And now he was supposed to open the gates from the inside? Inviting Nat in was one thing, but he was under no illusions: crack the door and other things would worm their way in as well. Second guesses. Doubts.

He stood, pacing to the other end of the compartment, aware of Nat's eyes on his back the whole way. The team had been chugging along just fine. Him, Tapper, Page. Now everything was different. First they'd dragooned Brody, then the general had brought in Nat, then Page had gone, and now they had Sayers. The only constant had been the cold comfort of the secrets he'd kept, trying to serve a higher purpose, that some days, to be honest, he had trouble wrapping his head around.

Nat was still watching him when he turned around, and if her blue eyes were unwavering, they were softened by an edge of sympathy.

He took a deep breath. And suddenly there was no decision at all.

"OK," he said. "I'll tell you everything."

Nat sat on the bed, listening silently, as he read her in on everything that had happened over the last year or so. It took a while, and he had a hell of a time gauging her reaction. When he finally reached the end, she took a deep breath.

"That is... a lot, Simon."

"I know."

One hand covered her mouth, and she shook her head slowly. "I'm going to be honest," she said between her fingers. "It's going to take some time to process all of this."

Kovalic nodded. "Understood." He'd done everything he could do: the decision of whether or not to stay was up to her. But he hoped she would. He couldn't fathom doing this job without her. Not anymore.

Nat rose, hesitated for a moment, then reached over to squeeze his shoulder. "But thank you. I'm glad you told me."

Looking up at her, Kovalic offered a crooked smile. "Yeah. So am I."

After she'd left, he let out a breath that he felt he'd been holding for months and then hit the shower.

Nat's assessment of the yacht's shower proved indisputable: it *was* pretty impressive. Every square centimeter of his body felt like it had been scrubbed thoroughly, sloughing off the weight of dirt, sweat, and grime that had accumulated over the past few days and turning him almost literally into a new man. He felt lighter, unburdened – though he supposed he couldn't attribute all of that to the shower.

By the time he was toweled off, the autofab unit had produced a simple shirt and pair of trousers in his size; after getting hosed down, putting on the grimy, torn clothes he'd been wearing on the *Queen Amina* sure seemed like a step backwards.

Making his way into the yacht's lounge, he found Tapper sitting at the table, drinking another cup of the ship's excellent coffee and skimming a tablet. "Boss."

Kovalic crossed to the coffeemaker and poured himself a cup. "Tap. Everything good?"

"Copacetic. Brody said we just exited the wormhole. Should be home in another few hours."

"Excellent." Kovalic peered over at the sergeant's tablet. "What're you up to?"

"Just writing a letter of recommendation for Maldonado. They helped us out of a couple of tough scrapes back there. Personally, I think we could use some technical support on the ground back home. What do you think?"

Kovalic smiled. "Still looking out for people, huh, Tap?"

"It's what I do."

"Something I've always admired about you."

Tapper laid down the slate, drumming his fingers on it. "So, you think this mission was a success?"

"Could have gone better," Kovalic admitted. "But our primary objective was accomplished. Plus, tough to argue that we didn't break in our new recruit."

The sergeant snorted at that. "Yeah, didn't exactly throw her a softball."

Kovalic frowned as the sergeant's fingers resumed their rhythm. Twenty years was more than long enough to recognize the man's tics. "Something bothering you?"

"Probably nothing."

"Oh, yes, your hunches are usually total garbage. Come on, spill it."

"I dunno," said Tapper. "I'm not some expert in alien artifacts, but it sure seemed like that tablet was pretty damn durable. Lasted *millennia* on that moon before people found it, in who knows what kind of environmental conditions. Plus being traded around the black market, changing hands probably dozens of times. And, from what you said, it seemed to be in pristine condition for all of that."

"What are you getting at?" said Kovalic, even as he could feel doubt worming its way into the back of his brain.

"Just surprised, that's all. Concussion grenades, well, the shockwave will knock you down, but it doesn't really have the explosive force to do much damage. That's why you can use 'em shipboard. Don't have to worry about pieces going everywhere, puncturing your hull..."

"But it managed to totally destroy what was, by all accounts, a pretty robust ancient artifact," said Kovalic, finishing the sergeant's thought.

"Like I said, I'm no expert. But yeah. Seems weird, doesn't it?"

"So, you think what? That it wasn't the real one after all?"

"Except you said that professor confirmed it was."

"Yeah," said Kovalic slowly, thinking back to al-Kitab's palpable excitement. If it had been feigned, the man was a hell of an actor. "He did, didn't he?"

"Ah, well," said Tapper. "Could be he was wrong. We all make mistakes sometimes. Even me. You want another cup of coffee, boss?"

"Huh?" Kovalic looked down at his cup, half empty. "Nah, I'm good. Thanks."

"Suit yourself." Tapper walked back over to the galley.

Kovalic stared into the coffee, as dark as the vacuum of space. Maybe al-Kitab had been wrong. But the man had spent his life studying every detail about the Aleph Tablet; if he was wrong, who the hell would have known any better?

And if he was *right*, well, then maybe it was Kovalic who wasn't quite as good at his job as he thought was. And maybe the real tablet was still out there, somewhere.

Kovalic shook his head to clear it. Go down that rabbit hole and pretty soon he'd be watching all of Brody's conspiracy theory videos. No, he dealt in the concrete, not the hypothetical. The tablet had been destroyed; he'd seen it himself. If he couldn't trust his own eyes, what could he trust?

But sometimes trust wasn't enough. He'd trusted al-Kitab, but he had no way of knowing what the professor had said was true. He'd trusted Page, and look where that had led him. And he'd trusted the general, ever since he'd put his life in the man's hands back in a house on Illyrica nearly seven years ago.

Talking to Nat, telling her everything, had given him some perspective – painted things in a different light. Trust was important, but it wasn't everything.

Sometimes you just had to see for yourself.

Rubbing his chin, Kovalic flipped open the lounge's terminal and initiated a secure connection to the nearest Commonwealth communications repeater, routing it through the most circuitous, convoluted path he could manage until it looked like it might have originated from anywhere in the galaxy.

He typed the request, then hesitated for a moment, fingers poised over the keyboard. There wouldn't be any turning back after this.

Yes, the doubt had wormed its way in to his mind, just as he'd predicted. But he was already starting to realize that what he'd feared would weaken his resolve had only strengthened it. The general had said he valued Kovalic's skepticism, and blind loyalty didn't do anyone any favors. Trust, as the old saying went, but verify.

He hit send, then sit back to wait as his request bounced through the labyrinthine connection, scouring every single database he had access to, legitimately or otherwise, and returning any mention of a project codenamed LOOKING GLASS.

EPILOGUE

The sun was just rising as the man stepped through the doors of the spaceport, shading his eyes against the orange glare. As promised, the black hovercar was waiting for him, a driver opening the door silently before loading his meager luggage into the trunk. Moments later they were speeding away from the hustle and bustle of arriving passengers and disappearing into the sprawling metropolis.

It wasn't a city he'd visited before, which was rare in and of itself, so he spent the ride staring out the window, taking in every detail. His hand draped across the smooth, cool leather of the case that sat on the seat beside him.

Forty-five minutes later, the car turned onto a side street, gliding up to a heavy metal gate set in a white stone wall. At some unseen signal, the gate rolled aside, allowing the car to pull through. The house at the end of the drive was not ostentatious, but it was elegant, with sharp cut corners of steel and glass. Clean, too, and situated among a well-tended garden of small trees and flowering shrubs, awash in color that contrasted the house's stark, monochromatic nature.

The car's door swung open and he stepped out, still keeping a tight grip on the case. The morning air was cool at this elevation, a slight chill rippling across his skin.

A woman emerged from the house. She was dressed in a smart, practical suit, the collar open at her throat to show a brown stretch of collarbone. The same touch of elegance in the house's design was visible in her bearing; she moved like one trained in poise and grace. A coif of glimmering chestnut hair was drawn up in a simple chignon.

"I trust your trip was uneventful."

He bowed his head. "Very pleasant, madam. It's not often I get to fly first class."

"I promised no expense spared, Mr Sadiq." It wasn't his real name, of course. "And I follow through on my promises." Her hazel eyes, which had been studiously avoiding looking at the case he held, now drifted to it. "I presume that is the item."

"Indeed. Shall we?"

The house's interior was no less chic than the outside, though it felt on the decidedly sterile side – there was no sign that it was occupied regularly, by his host or by anybody else. A safehouse, then; he'd seen more than his fair share.

Not that his employer's habits were of material concern to him. He was here because he was being paid, and paid well.

"This way," said the woman, her heels clicking against the marble floor as she led him into the house's central space, a large room with a glass-topped coffee table in the middle. A fire flickered in the grate and he felt himself gravitating toward it, reaching out a hand for warmth.

The woman sat on a snow white couch on one side of the coffee table and, after a moment of warming his hands, he took a seat in the matching armchair opposite.

Placing the case gently on the table, he pressed his thumbs against the dual biometric readers in the locks, then punched in a code on the keypad in the center. With a click, the case popped open; he spun it around to face the woman, and lifted the lid.

A succession of emotions paraded across her face, starting with eager anticipation and flickering through brief trepidation on the way to cold, dispassionate analysis. Her eyes came up to meet his. "You authenticated it?"

He'd spent the last few months of his life transforming himself into the man who was the foremost expert on this particular field – it had become more than a pretense, as with all his jobs, and he'd absorbed this knowledge down to the bones. Was there truly any difference in studying all this information to masquerade as an expert and actually being that expert? It was semantic, as far as he was concerned.

"Of course. I ran the scans against the details from your father's records. The mass spectrometer and half-life decay confirm it is the genuine article." A note of wonder crept into his voice, despite his best efforts to suppress it. "I'm not sure I believed in it myself."

"Belief is a funny thing, Mr Sadiq," said the woman, slowly closing the lid. "My father has been searching for this item for much of his life. And now, when it's finally within his grasp, he's in no position to enjoy it." She let out a sigh. "Life will have its little ironies."

He made a noncommittal grunt in response, too preoccupied with the sudden sense that they were no longer alone. Two of them, he thought. Both behind him, facing his host, who was showing no sense of alarm.

"Now," said the woman, smiling. "To the matter of the second half of your payment."

He tipped his head, resisting the urge to go for the blades in his sleeves. They'd know about them anyway. "Of course.

Might I say what a pleasure it is to work for a professional. A lesser person in your position might be tempted to, let us say, 'tie up loose ends.'" He smiled mirthlessly. "But someone of your caliber is smart enough to know that I would have taken precautions."

Her eyebrows went up. "Oh? What kind of precautions?"

"The usual. A secure dispatch on a deadman switch that would transmit all the details of my latest job to, let's say, a certain Commonwealth major that I've recently encountered."

For a moment, her smile went stiff, but she recovered gracefully. That training and poise again. "Of course," she said. Her eyes flicked behind him and then to one side, and he could tell the two people had withdrawn. He let himself relax, but only fractionally. "I don't usually work with freelancers, you see. But I had a suspicion that with my own people in place nobody would see you coming. I trust you have no reason to think your cover was compromised?"

"My false dossier was inserted in the *Queen Amina*'s local databases. Once they're off the ship, even a cursory look will show them that there is no Dr Seku al-Kitab at Rizkin University. But beyond that, they won't be able to locate me, much less trace me back to you." That was the guarantee he offered to his clients.

The hazel eyes glittered. "That had best be the case. I would hate for us to have to terminate what could prove to be such a productive working arrangement." But, he was sure, she would have no hesitation about it. She stood. "Thank you for your services."

He got to his feet as well. "Of course. If our business is concluded, I trust the remainder of my fee will be transferred to my account by the end of the day."

"You may count on it. Let me see you out."

They walked back to the front of the house, and though there was no sign of anybody else on the premises he was at least able this time to spot the concealed doors that kept armed personnel at her beck and call. He expected no less of someone of her station.

The driver was standing at attention outside and, as they stepped out the door, he moved to the rear of the vehicle, ready to open it for his passenger.

The woman turned to him. "A pleasure doing business with you, Mr Sadiq. I hope we'll have the opportunity to work together in the future. Perhaps I could interest you in a more permanent position in my organization?"

He smiled. The pitch often went as such. "That is very kind, and I will certainly keep it in mind for the future. But at the moment, I am already engaged upon my next job. So I'm afraid I must move on. Still, the offer is much appreciated."

"A pity. Very well then. Take care, Mr Sadiq."

"Your highness," he said, sketching a slight bow. Hopefully that wasn't over the top.

The woman smiled, though there was a tightness to it, as if she didn't like being reminded of how everybody else saw her. Then again, he saw it more as a signal that she had much more to lose than he did, should any information about this operation become public.

With that, he got back in the car, which pulled out the gate and headed back to the spaceport. As it turned onto the street, his sleeve chimed, letting him know that the rest of the money had been deposited in his account, and prompting him to authorize a twenty-four hour delay on the message that was in the queue. He tapped the "delay" button, and swiped the display off, then stared out the window, enjoying the feeling of the sun on his face.

Now that his business was concluded, he was starting to feel a bit hungry. Perhaps he should stop before the spaceport for a bite to eat. Everybody said that of all the places in the galaxy to have a real, honest-to-goodness taco, Mexico City was the one to beat. And why not celebrate? After all, it wasn't every day that one survived a meeting with the Director of the Imperial Intelligence Service.

ACKNOWLEDGMENTS

There's no "i" in "novel", any more than there is in "team", and a team is what it took to shepherd this book from start to finish. As always, I want to extend a heartfelt thanks to the many people who helped whip this novel into fighting shape.

My indefatigable and sartorially splendid agent, Joshua Bilmes, helped me develop this idea from a synopsis into a real story, deftly knowing when to push and prod, but always having my back. Thanks to him and the rest of the team at JABberwocky for being the very best at what they do.

Angry Robot's dynamic duo of Eleanor Teasdale and Gemma Creffield deserve boundless appreciation: they were always on hand to answer questions and make things happen. Simon Spanton's editorial guidance helped turn my rough musings into something that made a lick of sense, Paul Simpson smoothed out my gaffes, and Georgina Hewitt put together a stunning cover that I only hope the content inside measures up to. Thanks too to former Angry Robot staff Marc Gascoigne, Mike Underwood, Nick Tyler, and Penny Reeve for their enthusiasm for this book's predecessor.

As always, I entrusted early versions of this manuscript to some crack beta readers, including Jason Snell, Antony Johnson, Gene Gordon, and Anne-Marie Gordon. If even the slightest error remains in the text – whether factual, scientific, or grammatical – the blame is mine and mine alone.

Let us not forget the value of moral support in these trying times. Fellow authors and bahn-migos Adam Rakunas and Eric Scott Fischl definitely spent way more time hearing me bang my head against a wall than anybody should have to endure, and thanks as well to the rest of the Literarily the Worst crew, and all my friends at The Incomparable and Relay FM. Special thanks to Brian Lyngaas, Jason Tocci, Tony Sindelar, Jordan Atlas, Evan Ritt, Keith Bourgoin, and Phil Chu for always being there.

Harold Moren and Sally Beecher are, as ever, my most ardent supporters, and I could not have done this without their love and encouragement, even if they probably wonder whether or not I'll ever get a real job. To the rest of the Beecher/Kane/Moren clan, you're still the best family anybody could ask for.

Finally, to my best friend, partner, and now wife Kat, who, when I told her that I would be writing a book at the same time we were planning a wedding, still agreed to go through with it all, even though I had to turn in this manuscript about a week after the big day. You are my very favorite person: thank you for putting up with all my agonizing over a single word or comma, talking endless plot threads, and generally being a pain. Love you.

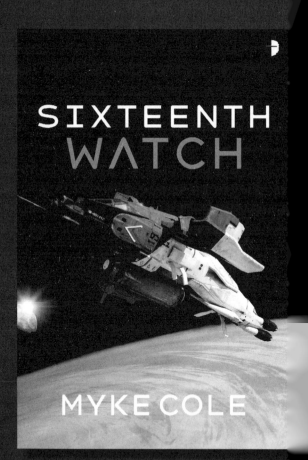

CHAPTER 1

"The top story tonight – military sports continue to dominate ratings for the twentieth straight week, with the Army's World's Best Ranger Competition capturing over 100 million viewers in the coveted prime time slot. Even bigger is this year's Boarding Action, which pits space-based crews in a simulated boarding of a hostile vessel in zero-gravity. The highest rated civilian sport is still the American NFL, but it doesn't even come close, with less than fifty percent of military sports' audience share in that coveted 18-39 demographic. It truly looks like the new age of military training competitions as a civilian spectator sport is here to stay."

JENNIFER SALVATORE, MEDIA MIX

"Now this," Captain Jane Oliver said, gesturing through the hatch of the Defiant Class response boat, "is a really bad place to put your shotgun."

The students in the boat maintenance class crowded closer, squinting through the fluorescent overhead lights at the weapons clasps. Then they stood back, looking at her with blank expressions, nobody wanting to question the wisdom of such a high-ranking officer. The instructor was used to Oliver pausing in her daily rounds to take over the class, and had patiently stood aside, but he spoke now. "Ma'am, that's the *proper* place for long guns. That's why the clasps are there."

"That's real nice," Oliver replied, "but you try getting it out of those rubber bands in four-foot swells when you need it in a hurry. In the clasps for inspection. In the seat-sleeve for ops. Trust me on this."

She smiled and the students smiled with her. To them, a captain was akin to a god, and she knew the reminder that their leaders rode the same rough seas they'd be tackling went a long way. She also knew there were precious few officers at her level that still did.

"That's gear adrift, captain," one of the students ventured. The rest glanced from his face to Oliver's in shock, and then with admiration once they realized that she wasn't annoyed by being challenged.

"New rule," she said, "unless there's water on the deck, gear isn't adrift. You can quote me on that. Now, are you insulting your coxs'un? Saying he can't keep water off the deck?"

She gestured to the two students with coxswain qualification badges, and the class laughed. "No, ma'am."

"Thought so!" She grinned. In the years since they'd assigned her here, she only ever smiled when she succumbed to the temptation to take over the classes and give them the real scoop on what life was like in the boat forces. And as the commanding officer of the training center, she could only do that once in a blue moon. The rest of the time was a video on repeat in her head – her shouting to Kariawasm to pour on the throttle, Tom's boat coming apart under a hail of autocannon fire.

The instructor exchanged a look with Commander Ho. Her XO only smiled. If Oliver was frustrated with being pulled off operational duty, then Ho was thrilled. The sterile halls and quiet contemplation of the schoolhouse suited him just fine. She felt a pang of jealousy at his obvious contentment and squashed it an instant later. She had promised herself that she wouldn't let Tom's death make her bitter. She would be happy for the happiness of others, and if she couldn't feel it, then she would damn well fake it.

She turned back the class and paused. Captain Sean Elias was walking through the maintenance bay doors. Behind him, the York River twinkled in the Virginia sun. He was wearing his "tropical" blue uniform, the hard shoulder boards and pressed shirt that he only wore for important business. That he'd come to find her in the boat maintenance facility instead of waiting in her office was troubling.

"OK, Chief," she said to the instructor, "I think I've stolen enough of the class's time, you have the conn. Thanks for indulging an old lady."

"It's our pleasure ma'am," the instructor said, but she saw his shoulders relax as he returned to the lesson.

Ho was at her side as she shook Elias' hand. "Hey Sean, you clean up nice."

Elias glanced down at his crisp uniform as if he were surprised to be wearing it. "Sorry to interrupt, you looked like you were on a tear there."

"Nah," Oliver said, "I was just wrapping up."

"That's a lie," Ho smiled.

Elias laughed. "Yeah, I don't believe that for a minute. Jane, do you mind if we do this in your office?"

Oliver cocked an eyebrow. "Depends on what we're doing. You look like you're about to summon me to a court martial."

"No, nothing like that. Just something best done in private."

Oliver's office was just plush enough to convey her

authority to subordinates, but not so well appointed that Oliver might start thinking she was an admiral. A long, glass-surfaced cherry-wood desk dominated the blue and gold rug, emblazoned with the crossed anchors of the Coast Guard. Behind the desk, a broad oil painting depicted the Coast Guard's sole Medal of Honor winner evacuating marines off Guadalcanal in a hail of machine gun fire. The same family picture she'd had on the *Aries* occupied the credenza beside her challenge coin display, Tom smiling out at the camera as if he would be waiting for her when she got off duty.

Ho's office was adjacent, but she motioned for him to stay, and he leaned against the credenza as Elias took his seat in the chair she reserved for students who were in her office for an ass chewing. She'd deliberately chosen chairs with short legs in order to make her charges smaller than her. She hadn't intended the effect for Elias, but she was glad of it anyway. If she didn't know what he was here to do, let him be intimidated while he did it.

"OK," she said, "what's this all about?"

"You want the good news or the great news?" Elias spread his hands.

"How about the cut-the-bullshit-news?"

Elias bit back his smile, "Well, there's a star for you, if you want it."

She saw Ho stir out of the corner of her eye. He was normally as still as a crocodile until he had to move. This was as much of a tell as a man like him gave. Oliver didn't move, but it was a long moment before she answered. Whatever she'd expected Elias to say, it wasn't this.

"I'm pushing thirty years in," Oliver said. "I can't take a star."

"Yeah, well. They're willing to make an exception in this

case. We can get you a waiver, and in this command, you'll… uh… well, you'll age more slowly."

"What the hell are you talking about?"

"The 16th Watch, Rear Admiral Select," Elias leaned forward, grinning, "the Moon."

Oliver felt her stomach turn over. The image of Tom's small boat ripped in two swamped her. She was there again, wrenching the frozen handle as she watched the wreckage of her husband's ship settle into the snow-like surface.

"I'm a blue water coastie." Oliver had to speak slowly to keep the tremor out of her voice. "I've been on the Moon exactly once. This has to be some kind of mistake."

Elias shook his head. "No mistake, Jane. They want you on SAR-1."

"You can't want an O6 kissing retirement to run search-and-rescue in a domain she isn't familiar with."

"SAR-1 is now part of the Tactical Law Enforcement Detachment on Mons Pico."

"SPACETACLET," Oliver said. "The lunar head shed. What's SAR-1 doing attached there?"

"SPACETACLET is the command element now. The Commandant wants a unified presence for all lunar ops. Law enforcement and SAR are one body. Putting SAR-1 front and center sends the right message."

"And what does the old man want me to do with SAR-1?"

Elias gestured at the silver eagles stitched to her collar. "You're a leader. He wants you to lead it."

Oliver stared at him so long that Elias began to talk to fill the silence. "Look, Jane. SPACETACLET was the main responding element at Lacus Doloris after you were knocked out of the fight. They lost people."

Before she knew what she was doing, Oliver had leaned forward, covering her face with her hands. She remembered the Quick Reaction Force prying the hatch open, dragging her out. She remembered them cracking the hardshells of Flecha and Kariawasm's suits, laying them out on silver blankets on the regolith despite the lack of atmosphere. It didn't matter, they didn't need air anymore. Somewhere less than a hundred yards away, she knew the Navy corpsmen were going through the same ritual with her husband's body.

When she looked up again, Elias' face was inscrutable. "Morale is low on Pico, Jane."

She stumbled over the next words, desperately searching for something to say. "Chief Elgin and Petty Officer McGrath... are they still attached?"

Elias nodded. "Both of them were due to rotate out last year. They requested extensions. Chief pulled in every card he had to stay put."

Elias looked uncomfortably at Ho. "Jane, maybe it would be best if..."

"Commander Ho has been with me for my entire career. Anything you can't say in front of him can't be said."

Elias shrugged. "Look, Jane. We both know you've been... adrift since Tom died. Are you sure you're ready to retire?"

"That's condescending as fuck. I've made it through worse."

Elias' position in the sunken chair didn't intimidate him at all. "We're all worried about you."

"Who is?"

"I am, everyone in the C-suite is. The boss is."

Oliver swallowed the anger that rose in the back of her throat. Tom's death was *hers*. Her loss. Her fault. It wasn't for Sean or any of the top brass or even the goddamn

Commandant himself to be deciding what that meant to her. She paused, steadying her breathing before she answered. "The Commandant doesn't know who I am."

Elias sighed. "You're the legendary 'Widow Jane.' Of course he knows who you are."

Oliver remembered an interrogation she'd done of the head of a metal theft ring, stealing copper wire out of offshore buoys. The man had an odd tic – whenever he was hiding something, he would lick his lower lip, darting just the tip of his tongue out to barely sweep it before reeling it back in. Elias did that now. Oliver's eyes narrowed. "Look, I appreciate the routine to make it seem like it's in my own best interests, but you're not here because you're worried I'll wilt in retirement. You want something. The Commandant wants something. I don't know a damn thing about space, Elias. I've been a blue-water coastie my whole career. The one tour I had out there was cut short after... what happened."

Elias ignored the reference to Lacus Doloris. He laced his fingers behind his head and leaned back in his chair, as if they were only talking about where to go for lunch. "Space-schmace. It's just another unforgiving environment, think of it like the dunk tank. You can't tell which way is up, only, it's all the time."

"You're not exactly selling it," Oliver stifled a smile.

"Yeah, well. The old man doesn't want you for space stuff. He wants you to teach." Elias leaned forward again.

"To teach what? I've been doing boarding actions all my life."

"That's what he wants you to teach."

"You want me to teach water-surface boardings to lunar SAR operators? What is wrong with you?"

Ho cleared his throat so softly it would have gone missed

had it been anyone else. "In all fairness, ma'am," he said, "you could teach fish to walk."

"Thank you, Commander Kiss-Ass." Oliver slapped her palms on the desk and turned to glare at him. Ho tugged his forelock, inclined his head and smiled.

"Here's the thing," Elias said. "Navy is making a big push to remove us from lunar operations. They want the Coast Guard earthbound, for space to be declared 'universal high seas.'"

Oliver sucked in her breath as she thought of the Navy small boats torquing into position over Lacus Doloris. She thought of their flat-gray, gun-studded hulls. She thought of the way the miners surged to the attack at the sight of them. "What? That's a terrible idea. We need less militarization of space, not more. The Navy's the wrong tool for the job."

"That's what they're saying about us, and the President is listening. Jane, I can't stress this enough, we're on the brink of war here. The Commandant has met with the Secretary of the Navy three times in the past month, and he can't convince him. You don't need me to tell you how bad this is. We're not going to bring peace to the Moon if the American and Chinese navies are skirmishing every time a quarantine-runner strays into the Chinese Exclusive Economic Zone."

"So what do you want me to do about it from Mons Pico? Shouldn't you make me Navy Liaison Officer or something?"

"That's not how the Commandant wants to handle it. Look, we've pretty much lost the argument that this is a law enforcement or customs issue. The government is sold that it's a military one. If the Coast Guard wants to take the helm here, we can't keep showing the President that we're the right SAR element to keep space safe, we have to show him we're the right *military* element to beat the Chinese."

Oliver felt the first touch of a headache behind her eyes. None of this made any sense. "Sean. We're the *Coast Guard*. We're not the right military element to beat anybody."

Elias laughed. "Well, you've got me there. Fortunately, politicians are easily impressed."

"What do you want me to teach these guys to do?"

"We need you to get them in shape for this year's Boarding Action. Commandant thinks if we win, it'll give us the hand we need. It's a major media event, watched by millions of Americans. If we win it, that'll give us the leverage we need to stay on, and if we stay on, we can keep the Navy from turning quarantine-runners into a pretext for war. SPACETACLET came close last year…"

Oliver blinked. "We're going to stop a war… by winning a game show?"

Elias smiled. "I know it sounds odd, Jane…"

"You're goddamn right it sounds odd!"

Elias passed over his phone. "Here, let me show you something."

"Look, I like baby pictures as much as the next gal, but if you're hoping to soften me up, you're going to have to…"

Elias laughed. "My daughter is a junior in high school and my son starts college this year. I've queued up two videos for you in my camera roll."

Oliver arched a skeptical eyebrow. "Should I be careful scrolling here? I don't want to accidentally run into…"

Elias waved a hand. "Jane, please. Humor me here."

Oliver thumbed through and played the first video. It was well familiar to anyone from hundreds of social media ads. Vice Admiral Augusta Donahugh, commanding officer of the Navy's 11th Fleet – in charge of the service's operations on the 16th

Watch. The vice admiral was a small woman, lean and healthy looking, her defiantly undyed hair and the wrinkles around her eyes the only hints that she was either north of sixty, or very close to it. She leaned into the camera, her eyes burning with passion for her mission, her solid gold shoulder boards bunching toward her neck. The video must have been shot in front of a green screen, washed out now and replaced with 11th Fleet's flagship – the USS *Obama*, its thousand-foot length stretching past the borders of the screen, toroidal chambers slowly rotating to bring spin-gravity to its sickbays and ops center. The film's producers had highlighted the ship's batteries, lightening them to make them stand out to the audience – ball turrets projecting autocannon barrels, missile pods with gleaming orange piezo-electric fuses. Navy small boats swarmed around it like a cloud of gnats, guns run out, a few flying American flags from their antennae mastheads.

"As a little girl, I dreamed of visiting the Moon," Donahugh said. "I never imagined the day would come when I'd stand at the helm of the one force that is making life there possible. The United States Navy has led the way to new frontiers for the entirety of our nation's history, projecting American power into the farthest reaches of our oceans, a truly global force for good. And now we're the tip of the spear, bringing justice and peace to that same Moon I dreamed of visiting when I was growing up. You don't need me to tell you how important this is. As the main source of Helium-3, the Moon is the future of clean energy for the entire world. It's imperative that the United States remain at the forefront of the fight to secure this critical resource."

Oliver had seen this video so many times that she knew the next bit by heart. The screen cut away from Donahugh to a scene of last year's winners of Boarding Action, the US Marine Forces Special Operations Command – 16th Watch team, moving and covering as they breached and cleared a large range tanker held by the second-place finishers, the State Department's Diplomatic Security team. The MARSOC16 team moved like they were flying, gliding through the micro-gravity like they were born in it, making the incredibly skilled DIPSEC operators look like kindergartners. The cameras cut to the studio audience for the show, cheering themselves hoarse as the show's announcers blinked in disbelief at the speed and skill with which MARSOC16 swept the opposition. "11th Fleet is proud of our marines, who've won Boarding Action for the third year running, a testament to the dedication and skill our people bring to the fight. The Navy is the right tool for this job, because we're the best there is. We train harder, work harder, and fight harder than anyone on Earth, or beyond it."

The camera cut back to Donahugh, standing now, surrounded by flint-eyed sailors and marines, all in their hardshells, helmets held under their arms. The American flag waved in the background, translucent, the surface of the Moon shining through it. "The 16th Watch is America's most important fight. And we can't win it without your help. Join us."

The video ended with the Navy's recruitment hotline number, email address, and chat handle, flashing yellow across the bottom of the screen.

Oliver looked up, met Elias' expectant gaze. "Sean, I've seen this a hundred times already. Everybody has. It's good."

"It's better than good," Elias said. "Navy is over 400 percent past their recruitment quota thanks to that, with the majority of the applicants pushing for contracts guaranteeing them tours on the 16th Watch."

"So? We're a smaller service. We don't run ads because we don't have to."

"Yeah, but nobody signing on with us wants to go to the Moon, and that's part of the why. Folks see it as a military matter. Well, that and they don't want to piss into a vacuum tube for a four-year stretch. Anyway, my point is that the Navy is winning the messaging war here. They are convincing the public that the Moon is a war zone already. This video is part of that."

"Don't you think you're being a little bit dramatic, Sean? It's just dick-measuring bullshit. Their target audience is boys about to graduate high school. Of course they're pumping the rah-rah it's a war stuff."

Elias shook his head. "It's worse than that. Watch the next video."

This video was wasn't familiar – a group of serious-faced men and women in sober suits sat around a horseshoe-shaped panel table of rich, golden wood. Oliver noted the regal, overblown red leather and green felt upholstery, the somber classical tones in the columns behind them. "Is… this the capitol?"

"Yup," Elias said. "That's the Armed Services Committee."

She'd have figured it out in another instant, anyway. The camera pulled back to show the service chiefs in their dress uniforms around a smaller table. Donahugh was standing beside Admiral Perea, the Chief of Naval Operations. Perea was seated, a look of performative concentration on his face as Donahugh gestured to the same recruiting video Oliver had just watched, finishing its last few seconds on a flat-screen monitor wheeled into the chamber.

Admiral Zhukov, the Coast Guard Commandant, was shaking

his head. "That is a recruiting video. Senators, I will caution you against making decisions based on marketing materials."

"Admiral Zhukov is absolutely right," Donahugh said, "and it is equally important that this committee keep in mind that these marketing materials are built on *facts*. Nothing I say in that video deviates from the strictest truth. The Navy is leading the fight on the Moon, and it's imperative we continue to do so."

Oliver tried to read the expressions of the senators, but they were studiously game-faced, wearing the same gravitas-laden performative looks.

"This presumes that this is a fight at all," Zhukov countered. "It currently isn't, and it doesn't have to be. This is a customs and border control matter, and the issue at hand is quarantine and evasion of vessel-inspections. That is something that the Coast Guard is uniquely equipped to do, and the reason this service was chartered."

"I'm not certain the families of those sailors killed at Lacus Doloris would agree with you, admiral," Donahugh countered.

"Jesus," Oliver whispered. "That fucking bitch."

"Yup," Elias agreed.

If Zhukov was rattled by the comment, he didn't show it. "The Chinese can tell the difference between a light-armed law enforcement vessel and a warship. They are well familiar with the difference between the Coast Guard and the Navy's authorities here. I grieve for the lives lost at Lacus Doloris as much as the rest of you, but that was *nothing* like a full-scale war. If we want to avoid the potential for that degree of conflict, we need to be showing good faith efforts to deescalate the situation. It has to be the Coast Guard."

"And if we were talking about the waters off Baja California or Miami, I'd agree," Donahugh said, "but China isn't Mexico or Haiti, and the stakes on the Moon are worlds higher. The national security implications of losing ground in our ability to exploit Helium-3 are several orders of magnitude more grave than our ability to keep recreational boaters from harming manatees."

"It's official," Oliver said, "I fucking hate this woman."

"So long as you respect her hustle," Elias said. "Because she's currently cleaning our clocks."

Now Zhukov appeared rattled. "That's a gross mischaracterization of the Coast Guard's mission. And it only distracts from the fact that I am not the one laying out the lanes in the road here. They are clearly expressed by the titles 10 and 14 of the United States Code. This is *our* job!"

"The US Code," Donahugh said, "has always been interpreted. US law is governed by precedent, admiral. And with the stakes so high, our interpretation here is critical. Let me ask you, do you agree with the position that noncooperative dockings, boardings, are the key to enforcement of customs controls on the 16th Watch?"

"Don't do it," Oliver said to the video. "Don't walk right into it." She looked up at Elias. "Tell me he doesn't walk right into it."

Elias sighed. "Watch."

"Of course they are," Zhukov said. "They're the main tool in our arsenal right now, at least until we can establish a culture of compliance. But that takes time."

"It does," Donahugh agreed. "It's impossible to say for sure, but the Naval Innovation Advisory Council is currently estimating at least a five-year horizon to turn the current culture of quarantine evasion around. Five years is a long time, admiral."

"We can do it much faster than that," Zhukov said. "We're

making headway every day, and I don't see what this has to do with…"

"Oh man," Oliver said. "This is bad."

"The worst," Elias agreed.

Donahugh had already turned to the monitor, clicked the remote, replaying the last section again – showing the MARSOC16 team's almost superhuman performance, the DIPSEC operators going down hard, the cheering crowd. "The Navy has proven, for *four* years running now, in the highest-pressure and most public forum available, that we are the best equipped, the best trained, the overall best at boarding actions on the 16th Watch."

Zhukov sputtered, his military bearing slipping. "You can't be serious. That's a game show!"

Donahugh looked at the senators now, still speaking to Zhukov. "If it's just a game show, admiral, why can't you win?"

Oliver stopped the video, unwittingly repeated the Commandant's words. "You can't be serious."

"As a heart attack," Elias said. "Ask me if that video has leaked to the public."

"I refuse."

"It's been trending on three social media platforms for a *week*, Jane. That's what we call a coup."

"Sean, this is reality TV! The SASC can't possibly…"

"This is the reality TV generation, Jane. The SASC is composed of senators, and senators care about getting reelected. This just became a platform issue. And the presidential election is right behind it. So, guess which way he's leaning?"

"Fuck."

"We have to win this thing, Jane. We have to prove the Navy wrong."

"And you think SAR-1 is how we win it?"

"With you pushing them, yes."

"Sean, they came in fifth last year. Behind the Mare Anguis Police Department."

"That's top ten. We need you to bump them up the other four slots."

Oliver's head spun with the inanity of the request. "Have you looked at my file? I don't know anything about non-cooperative dockings in space!"

Sean's face went serious. "I have, in fact, looked at your file. Hell, I've memorized it. You've done over two thousand contested boardings in your career."

"Those were on Earth! On the water!"

Elias was unfazed. "Every one of them is the equivalent of a non-cooperative docking in space, Rear Admiral Select."

"Stop calling me that!"

"Over 2,300, actually," Ho said.

Oliver turned to him slowly. She blinked, trying to make sense of his sudden interjection. "What?"

"Contested boardings, ma'am," her XO was smiling, "you've done over 2,300 in your career. I can double check the Personnel Records System if you want, but I'm pretty sure I've got the number right."

"Whose side are you on!?" Oliver slapped the desk again.

Ho shrugged.

"The issue isn't technical knowledge," Elias went on. "The acting commander out there says it's… morale holding them back."

Oliver's stomach turned over. "Morale how?" she asked, though she already knew the answer.

"They blame themselves for Tom," Elias said, "and for

Kariawasm and Flecha. They feel like they failed you."

It can't be their fault. Because it's mine. She cursed herself for what seemed like the thousandth time. If only she hadn't insisted on going on the boat personally. If only she'd… *No. That way lies madness.* She had replayed what happened on that day over and over again ceaselessly for years now. There was nothing to be gained from it. Her thoughts were poisonous loops. They held no answers, only whispers that all pointed to her as the culprit for everything that had gone wrong.

But she hadn't been able to spare the emotional energy to think that the same toxic lines would be repeating in Elgin and McGrath's minds. "Oh, come on, Sean," she tried to sound nonchalant, but her voice broke. "I don't blame them for what happened. I know they did the best they could. I wrote to Chief and told him as mu–"

"No, Jane," Elias said. "You know that's bullshit. It's one thing to hear that you forgive them. It's another to believe it."

The grief rose so suddenly and she only barely choked back the tears in time. "Sean, why are you doing this? Bench 'em. Get another team."

"You're not reading me, Jane," Elias' voice went hard. "They're the best we've got. There is no other team."

It took Oliver a full thirty seconds to gather herself. She sighed, cradled her head in her hands. "And you think that if I work with them…"

Elias finished for her, "That you might be able to help them figure it out, yes."

"Sean," and she let herself cry now, not caring if they saw. "I don't know that *I've* figured it out."

A hand squeezed her shoulder, but with her eyes closed, she couldn't tell if it was Ho's or Elias'.

But it was Elias who spoke, his voice soft now. "Well, of course you don't. The good ones never do. But, you have, Jane. Ask anyone in this school. Ask anyone who works with you."

Ho passed her a tissue and she nodded thanks, blotted her eyes, blew her nose. "You don't want a leader, you want a therapist."

"We want the whole package, Jane," Elias said. "That's why it has to be you."

She tried to answer, but the tears were back. She waved a weak hand at him. "Message received, captain. Just… just give me some time to think it over, OK?"

Elias stood, tucking his cover under his arm. The gold oak leaves on the brim reflected against the glass surface of the desk. "Take as long as you need, so long as that isn't more than three days. I look forward to making your transport arrangements, Jane. And I look forward to saluting you as a rear admiral."

She signaled Ho for another tissue as Elias left, closing the door behind him. She kept her eyes tightly shut, but she could hear him make his way to the credenza, take out a bottle of the bourbon she'd kept there ever since Tom had died. She finally opened her eyes and saw the label as Ho sloshed the brown liquid into two glasses. In a turn of gallows humor that surprised even her, the brand he'd chosen was Widow Jane.

He passed her a glass. "You OK?"

She stared into the liquor. "You know when they promoted me to captain and parked me out here, I figured it was because after what happened, they… didn't trust me to lead, but they felt bad about Tom, so they wanted me to retire on captain's pay."

Ho took a swallow and crossed his arms, swirling his drink and looking at her. "I'd say that's exactly what they did."

"So, why the fuck is this happening?"

Ho laughed. "You're good at stuff. They parked you here to grieve and wash out. And you went ahead and produced the best and brightest crop of boarding team members the guard has ever seen."

She finally took a sip, closing her eyes and relishing the burning as the liquid slid down her throat. "You are such a fucking suck-up that I can't stand it sometimes."

"You don't want compliments," Ho said, "stop being good at shit."

"It's just... I'm not just good at stuff. I'm good at taking care of people. I took care of the kids, and after Adam moved out I took care of Alice. Then I had to take care of her again when she left Matt. I guess I'm still taking care of her now, only it's over the phone. Then I was taking care of Tom."

"Tom didn't need taking care of."

"No, he didn't, and that was why I was so happy to do it. And now that he's gone, all I have to take care of," she waved a hand to the school outside her door, "are these people."

"Well, you're doing one hell of a job."

"Christ, Wen."

"It'll get you to Alice," Ho looked at her from under his eyebrows. "You said she still needs taking care of."

"Good luck getting her to admit that. She went to the Moon to get away from..."

"She went to the Moon to get away from the memory of Matt, and the embarrassment that she'd made a hash of her marriage, and for the illusion of a new start."

"She told you this?"

Ho shook his head. "You know I'm not wrong."

"No, you're not." She pounded the desk at the memory of Alice handing her the phone with the email announcing her selection for the space elevator's next open running. "I still can't believe she won that fucking lottery. I still can't believe she left."

"Well, you do this thing, boss, you'll get to be up there with her. That's not nothing."

"No," Oliver admitted. "It's not."

They drank in companionable silence for a while, and when Ho was done, he turned to put the bottle back, but Oliver held out her glass for a refill. "Think this one's a two-banger."

Ho cocked an eyebrow. The Widow Jane was not known for having more than just one. "Wow," was all he said.

She waved her glass, sloshing a little over the side. "Man, I was really looking forward to retirement."

Ho laughed out loud. "Like hell you were. I've never seen anyone more frightened of anything in my entire life."

She downed the second drink in a single swallow, set the glass down with a click, met her XO's eyes. "So, what do I do?"

Ho leaned forward, and the intensity in his gaze reminded her so much of her husband that it frightened her. "Your job."